FE.... NOTHING BUT GOD

GARY KEARLEY

APE OR EDEN

Published in 2022 by Ape or Eden Books, Bruton, England.

ISBN: 9798848202021

DEDICATION

This book is dedicated to the ordinary people of the West Country who simply wished to protect their religion and their right to worship in freedom, only to be sacrificed to the ambitions of powerful men.

ACKNOWLEDGMENTS

I would like to thank my wife Susan for her patience, encouragement and proof-reading skills. Her diligence has saved me from many embarrassing mistakes and any that remain are entirely of my own making.

Battlefields Trust walks organised by Julian Humphrys (Norton St Philip), Christopher Scott (Bridport) and Revd. Chris Keys (Sedgemoor) have been invaluable to my understanding of the terrain over which the various engagements were fought.

Special thanks go to my stepdaughter Rebecca Barry for the cover art and Andrew Pickering who has been instrumental in getting this work published.

The pictures that appear at the head of many of the chapters are taken from sets of playing cards that were produced shortly after the end of the rebellion.

PRINCIPAL CHARACTERS

Royalists

King Charles II. King of England (reigned 1660-1685).

King James II. King of England (reigned 1685-1688). Brother of Charles II.

Earl of Feversham. Louis de Duras, Lieutenant General. Commander of the royal army.

Lord John Churchill. Major General. Second in Command.
Later 1st Duke of Marlborough.

Judge Jeffreys. Baron George Jeffreys of Wem, the Lord Chief Justice.

Rebels (Historical)

James, Duke of Monmouth. Eldest son of Charles II.

Lord Ford Grey. 3rd Baron of Wark. Commander of Monmouth's cavalry.

Robert Ferguson. Scottish Presbyterian minister. Monmouth's speech writer.

Samuel Venner. Political agitator and former soldier. Lt Col Red Regiment.

John Foulkes. Professional soldier. Lt Col White Regiment.

Abraham Holmes. Baptist minister. Lt Col Green Regiment.

Richard Bovett. Former Somersetshire militia colonel.

Lt Col Blue Regiment.

Nathaniel Wade. Bristol lawyer. Major in the Red Regiment.

Daniel Foe. Hosiery salesman from London. Gentleman scout in the rebel army.

Rebels (Fictional)

Nathaniel Carver. Blacksmith from Lyme Regis.

John Carver. Blacksmith from Lyme Regis. Nathaniel's father.

Thomas Edgecott. Shoemaker from Lyme Regis.

Hezekiah Sprake. Baptist minister from Lyme Regis.

Samuel White. Gamekeeper and former Cromwellian soldier.

William Pearce. Weaver from Taunton.

Henry Outwell. Dyer from Colyton.

Thomas Cleeve. Carpenter from Stoford.

Amos Thorne. Carter from Chideock.

Stephen Dabinett. Joiner from Chardstock.

Non-Combatants (Fictional)

Eliza Sprake. Seamstress from Lyme Regis. Daughter of Hezekiah. Fiancée of Nathaniel Carver.

Daniel Carver. Blacksmith from Lyme Regis. Son of John and brother of Nathaniel.

Nancy. Maid to the Carver family.

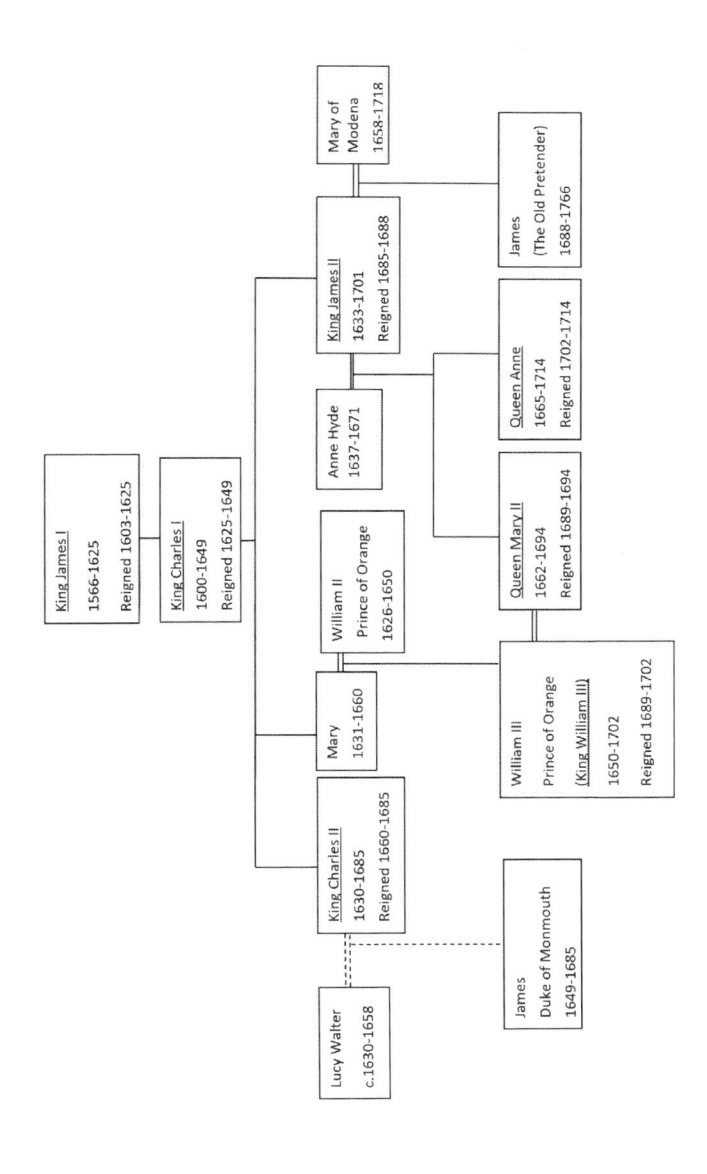

SIMPLIFIED FAMILY TREE FOR THE STUART KINGS AND QUEENS OF ENGLAND

Map of the West Country of England 1685

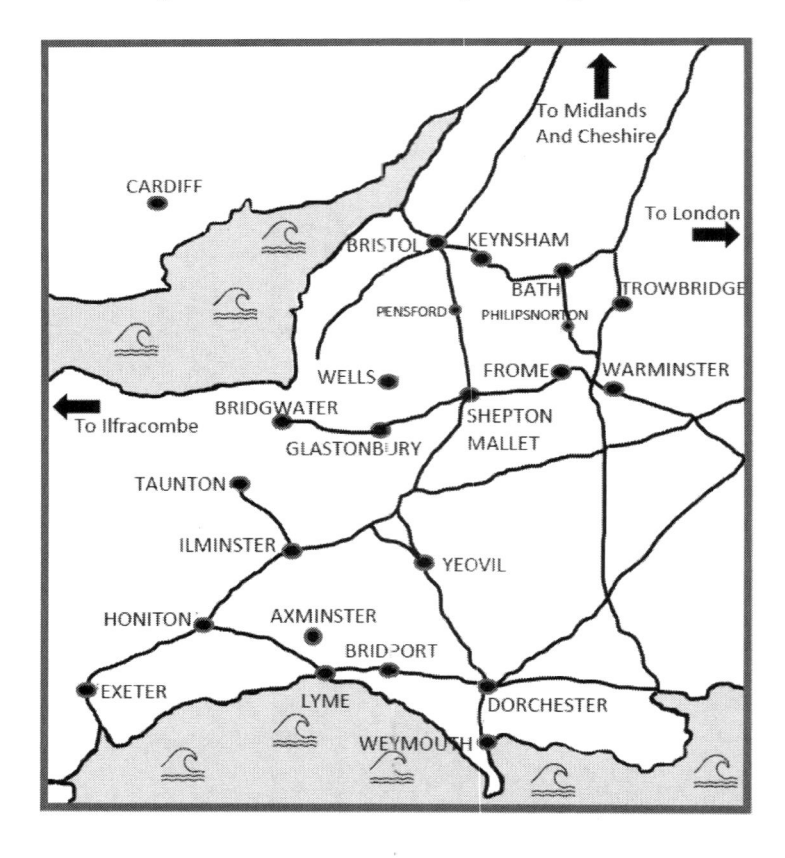

1 INVASION

Thursday 11th June 1685

The small rowing boat crunched onto the shingle beach where the River Winniford ran down into the English Channel just south of the Dorset village of Chideock and three men leapt ashore. As the oarsmen rested, awaiting the signal to return to the small flotilla of ships that were mere black silhouettes against the star-studded sky, Thomas Dare, Hugh Chamberlain and Samuel Venner raced for the scant cover afforded by the headland. It was the early hours of Thursday June 11th 1685 and the rebellion had begun.

2 UNITED PROVINCES OF THE NETHERLANDS

(12 days earlier)
Saturday 30th May 1685

A soft warm wind blew across the docks as Lt Col John Foulkes stood on the deck of the *Helderenberg* which was tied to a wharf on the Isle of Texel at the mouth of the River Zee. Wrinkling his nose at the smell of fish guts and tar he watched the loading of the final supplies with increasing impatience. He knew that time was of the essence if this most daring, some had said foolhardy mission was to succeed. The port authorities seemed ambivalent to the preparations but the longer they delayed their departure from Holland, the greater the chance that one of the many agents acting for the English court would discover that the ship now being provisioned was not really bound for either Königsberg or Danzig in the Baltic Sea as was commonly believed. King James was well aware that his nephew James, Duke of Monmouth and Archibald Campbell, 9th Earl of Argyll had met to discuss their respective invasion plans. Argyll had left Holland for Scotland aboard the *Anna* on 2nd May and it was possible that the two men had sailed together. They hadn't but the longer that misconception held, the greater the chance that Monmouth's own small flotilla could reach the south coast of England undetected.

Foulkes was not alone in wondering why the late King Charles II had chosen his brother James to succeed him, rather than his own first-born son. Foulkes had met the dashing young Duke of Monmouth some months earlier at a reception in the Binnenhof Palace in The Hague, given by the duke's cousin Mary and her husband the Stadtholder of Holland, Prince William of Orange. At the time Foulkes had been an officer in the Earl of Bellasis' regiment, a British unit in the service of Prince William, but he had grown weary of the inactivity that followed the Peace of Nijmegen which had brought an end to years of war between Holland and France. The promise of action and an immediate promotion to Lieutenant Colonel with his own Regiment had convinced him to join the small band of officers who would accompany Monmouth to England in an attempt to wrest the crown from his uncle.

Right from the start it was clear to Foulkes that Monmouth had taken some persuading to launch his rebellion. Having lived abroad in exile for so long the duke was somewhat out of touch with the reality of the situation in England and had to rely on the advice of others regarding the prospects for an invasion and the support he would receive. Foulkes had the uneasy feeling that the impressionable young duke had fallen too far under the influence of agitators and dissidents who may have been using him to further their own political and personal ambitions. There was no denying Monmouth's religious convictions but Foulkes wondered if the promises of men such as Ferguson, Danvers and Dare would prove true.

The *Helderenberg* was a powerful ship mounting thirty-two guns, necessary Foulkes reasoned in case they ran into the Royal Navy or pirates in the English Channel. The downside of hiring such a large vessel was that it had taken a huge chunk of the limited funds which Monmouth had begged or borrowed to finance his expedition, money that could otherwise have been spent on extra muskets, powder and shot.

At last the tiny convoy consisting of the *Helderenberg* and her two small support ships was ready to start the four-hundred-mile journey to England. They waited impatiently for the last of the ebbing tide before slipping quietly out of the harbour, knowing that the imminent change in the tide would hamper any pursuit. Foulkes noticed that his knuckles had turned white from gripping the side rail as he watched the gangplanks being withdrawn, but there was no attempt to stop them when the Dutch sailors finally cast off. He breathed a deep sigh of relief as the Dutch coast slowly fell astern. He was not a natural sailor and the long low swell made him feel slightly queasy as he made his way to the cramped cabin that he was obliged to share with two other army officers. He took a large draught of brandy which he hoped would help him to sleep despite the unaccustomed motion of the ship.

He awoke in the early hours and quickly made his way up the companion ladder, anxious to reach the open air before he was sick. As he emerged onto the deck he was assailed by a strong wind that whistled through the ship's tarred rigging. The deck was pitching wildly and he had great difficulty in reaching the rail before emptying his stomach over the side. He was not the only man suffering.

'You know the best thing for sea sickness?' said a fellow officer as he dabbed his mouth with a handkerchief.

'Prey tell me.' Foulkes was willing to try any remedy.

'A spoonful of honey.'

'How the hell does that stop you being sick?'

'Oh it doesn't stop you being sick, it just tastes so much better when it comes back up!' He slapped Foulkes on the back and made his way back down below. Foulkes couldn't believe the turn that the weather had taken in such a short time. The strong wind threatened to blow them all the way back to Holland and the small flotilla was forced to tack constantly to make any headway at all.

Not long after dawn there was a sharp cry from the lookout perched perilously at the top of the main mast.

'Dek daar, zeil ahoi!'

The ship's captain, Cornelius van Brakell and those senior army officers who were clustered near him at the wheel turned to stare in the direction that the man indicated with his outstretched arm. A small ship was closing rapidly from astern, its sail configuration allowing it to sail much closer to the wind than the *Helderenberg*. As the pursuer came alongside the frigate a strong voice hailed them through a speaking trumpet. He spoke in heavily accented English.

'My name is van der Block of the Dutch Admiralty. I am acting on orders from Bevil Skelton, the English ambassador to the Hague. Heave to and prepare to be boarded, you are all under arrest.'

Van der Block had arrived at the dock some hours after Monmouth's small flotilla had sailed having been tipped off by a docker in the pay of one of King James' spies but had been prevented from giving immediate chase by the turn of the tide and the need to commandeer a suitable ship.

'Your orders your grace?' asked Captain van Brakell.

'Ignore the fellow,' said Monmouth who had rushed from the spacious stern cabin that the captain had graciously made available to him as soon as he heard the hail from the masthead. The wind was so strong that he had been obliged to leave his elaborate wig in the cabin. 'There is nothing he can do to actually stop us and by the time he returns to report to that weasel Skelton in Holland we will be long gone. He will have no idea where we are headed, especially in this weather.'

Van der Block knew that he was seriously outgunned by the powerful frigate and when his quarry showed no signs of surrendering he had no option but to bear away to return to the Texel where he would at least be able to send confirmation to London that Monmouth had not sailed with Argyll and that he was in fact at large in the English Channel.

The rest of the voyage down the Channel was largely uneventful although the adverse winds meant that the journey took far longer than was expected. As the wind at last turned in their favour Foulkes was joined at the ship's rail by the duke.

'A fine morning at last Foulkes. I do believe that the delay caused by the poor weather will have aided us in our endeavour.'

'How so your grace?'

'If my uncle had guessed that we were headed for the south coast of England he will have expected us to have landed some days ago. Now he will be even more uncertain as to our true destination, he may even have stood the militia down. Van der Block will be able to confirm that we are not sailing for the Baltic Sea but that aside he will have no idea where we are headed.

The Late D. of M. entring Lime with 2500 Men.

3 A SAFE LANDING

Thursday 11th June 1685

Nathaniel Carver was unaware of the events that had taken place in Holland 12 days ago or indeed those just down the coast at Chideock only hours before as he went about his labours in his father's smithy in Lyme Regis, close to the old town mill on Coombe Street. He had been working since first light, having risen early to stir yesterday's hot coals into life to fire the forge. The bad weather of a week ago had been replaced with days of unbroken sunshine and once the early morning chill passed it promised to be another hot day as the temperatures rose rapidly in the workshop.

'Morning Nat,' called his father John as he entered the smithy from the door that led into the small cottage next door.

'Good morning father. Another warm day ahead I fear.'

The business had been passed down to John by his father, John senior and would no doubt pass to Nat and thence to Nat's children, should he have any. Nat was a man now, having turned twenty-one at the end of last month, but there was still time a-plenty to think about marriage, for although by law he could legally wed at fourteen, most men in Lyme left it until they were in their late twenties. That seemed like a lifetime away to Nat, besides he had little time to ponder on such things today. There was plenty of work on hand, including fabricating all the metalwork for the refit of the mill which had stood on its present site for longer than anyone could recall but had been idle since being badly damaged in the late civil war. In the heat, the noise and the smoke of the smithy it seemed that it would be just another long tiring day at work; little did he know that his life and the lives of all those he cared for was about to change forever.

Nat was so engrossed in his work that he failed to notice that his friend and neighbour Thomas Edgecott had entered the smithy, red faced and breathing heavily.

'Nat come quick, the town's all-a quiver, there be three strange ships approaching the Cobb!'

'Can I go and have a look father? You know how Thomas will keep pestering me until I do.'

John Carver nodded and Nat quickly dropped the billhook that he had been crafting into the dunking barrel and headed for the street, wiping his hands on his dirty apron as he went. Lyme was a busy trading port and it was not unusual for strange sails to be sighted, so there must be something different about these latest arrivals to arouse such a commotion.

'Why so much fuss about a couple of ships Thomas? Strange vessels dock here every day of the week.'

'Well, the lead ship's said to be a warship, not a trading vessel. A gert big frigate with a heavy broadside. It don't carry no flags or pennants and they b'aint fired the customary salute.'

'Strange indeed,' agreed Nat as they reached the junction with Church Street, where a great press of townsfolk was heading down the hill towards the coast, alive with speculation about the identity of the strange vessels.

'Now that's even stranger,' said Nat as the pair rounded a corner from where they could see down the length of the beach to the Cobb, the sturdy breakwater that protected the small but well sheltered harbour. 'It looks like they've sailed right past the Cobb and anchored off the beach on the far side. What's going on?'

It seemed to Nat that all of the town's three thousand inhabitants were making their way down to the seafront. As they walked Nat and Thomas caught snatches of conversations, some folk thought that the ships must be French and up to no good, whilst others dared to hope that the ships heralded the much-anticipated arrival of James, Duke of Monmouth. There had been rumours for months that the 'Protestant Prince' would return from exile in Holland to oust the Catholic usurper King James and claim what most people in the west country thought was his rightful place as King of England. That Monmouth would choose to land at Lyme, so far from London made this an unlikely scenario but people argued that he had to land somewhere, so why not here. Most townsfolk had spent their whole lives in Lyme, hardly venturing out of the town, let alone over the county border into Somerset and had no real idea where London actually was. Nat had travelled further afield than most of the people in Lyme, often borrowing old Paul's cart to deliver finished ironwork to outlying farms and the large houses owned by the gentry, but even he couldn't begin to guess how long it would take to reach the capital. Word had reached the south coast some days previously that a rebellion had been raised in Scotland by the Earl of Argyll and it was generally supposed that Monmouth would follow shortly, unless of course he had accompanied Argyll north of the border as many thought he might. Just to be on the safe side King James had ordered that the county militias should be mustered, and they were now stationed all along the south coast as a precaution against a landing, although by good fortune none were currently occupying Lyme.

'Do you really think it could be Monmouth?' asked Thomas.

'Could be. You weren't at prayers on Sunday when Pastor Sprake told the congregation that several prominent local Protestants had been rounded up and taken to London. That shows that the authorities are taking the threat of an invasion seriously.'

Lyme was a staunchly Protestant town. Forty years ago, when the civil war had torn the country apart the town had declared for parliament and had held out for eight weeks against the royalist siege forces led by King Charles I's nephew Prince Maurice. Nat's grandparents, John senior and Martha had both been killed during the siege, John whilst manning Gaitch's fort and Martha as she helped the women of the town to dig the ditches and ramparts that formed the Town Line, defences that had played a significant part in keeping Maurice's army out. John and Martha had left a new-born infant, Nat's father John, who had thus inherited the family business before he could walk or talk. John senior's brother Silas had run the smithy until John was old enough to take over the reins himself. John had no recollection of his parents, but Uncle Silas had told him all about them, and the desire to avenge their deaths burned strongly in him. He had been an implacable enemy of the Stuart monarchy ever since it was restored in 1660.

As Nat and Thomas neared the town hall they met Pastor Hezekiah Sprake and his daughter Eliza.

'Well met Nathaniel,' smiled the pastor, pointedly ignoring Thomas.

'Pastor Sprake,' nodded Nat, 'Mistress Sprake.' Eliza Sprake was a real beauty. Twenty years old, of middling height, some eight inches shorter than Nat, with a fresh open face dappled with tiny freckles, a comely figure and hair the colour of ripening corn, full of rings and curls that hung almost to her waist when let down. She was full of life, being one of those people who found the good in everybody and everything. Hezekiah by contrast was a stern looking man in his mid-fifties. He didn't have an ounce of fat on him and with his thinning black hair, tinged with grey at the temples and dark bushy eyebrows above a large, hooked nose he made a somewhat mournful figure, although the first thing that most people noticed about him were his bright piercing eyes that seemed to look straight into a man's soul. People meeting him for the first time would swear that he was a man who had never laughed in his life, but to those who knew him well he was a kindly man with a wickedly dry sense of humour. It was a source of wonder to all in the town that such a man could have fathered the beautiful Eliza, who in truth took after her mother Charity, a farmer's daughter from the village of Symondsbury, who had died of the pox when Eliza was just ten years old. Hezekiah and Eliza had come down from the Goodman's house on Silver Street which served as a meeting place for the town's many Baptists, one of many unofficial chapels that had sprung up in towns right across the west country to serve their strong non-conformist communities.

Some twenty years previously the recently deceased King Charles II had banned so-called conventicles, religious meetings of more than five people outside the control of the Church of England, so the meetings in Silver Street were supposed to be secret affairs but everyone knew of them and they were generally tolerated. From time to time though the local militia, bullyboys for the most part, would appear under the command of the Deputy Lord Lieutenant and demonstrate their martial prowess by breaking up the Baptist services and laying into any among the unarmed worshippers who dared to offer any resistance. Luckily for the people of Lyme these attacks had recently stopped after the Dean of Salisbury had declared that the area was free of such illegal meetings, but it was during the last raid by the militia that Nat had been forced to intervene when one of the nastier militiamen appeared keen to show Eliza the error of her ways. Years of working in the blacksmith's shop had given Nat a strong physique and the militiaman soon backed down. With Pastor Sprake's consent Eliza and Nat had started to walk out, had quickly grown very close and now they planned to marry, but they wanted to do so in front of the whole town, not in secret as if their union was something to be ashamed of. Surely when the crown was in the hands of a true Protestant king the Baptists would again be free to worship openly in peace and then they would wed.

Nat regularly attended prayers led by Pastor Sprake at the Goodman's house, even though the parish church of St. Michaels, which had stood since Norman times on the site of an earlier wooden Saxon church was only yards from the end of Coombe Street where he lived. Like many in the town he had become disillusioned by the orthodox church which many believed had veered from its true mission, becoming remote and decadent. Thomas who lived just a few doors down from the forge in Coombe Street had no interest in religion and so never attended the services in Silver Street, hence the distain that the pastor had shown him. Thomas had prayed long and hard for his mother and father when both had been struck down with consumption, but when his prayers went unanswered and both parents had died he blamed God for their loss and swore that he would never set foot inside any sort of church or chapel again. He was fortunate that the shoemaker for whom his father had worked had agreed to take Thomas on as an apprentice, giving him both a job and a home. Nat and Thomas had played together since before either of them could remember although like all friends they had fallen out from time to time. Whenever their disagreements had come to blows it was always Nat who came out on top as he was taller and stronger than Thomas, even before the long hours in the smithy had added hard muscles to his big frame. Where Nat was tall and broad shouldered with dark broody eyes and closely cropped black hair, Thomas was short and wiry with a brown curly mop. He was quick to laugh but easy to anger and had a malevolent streak that Nat sometimes found hard to ignore. If anyone was to be found tormenting a stray cat or pulling the legs off a daddy-long-legs it was Thomas. Before Eliza and Nat had become so close the two friends had often talked of her as young men are wont to do and Thomas would tell Nat that he would marry her one day. Even after her father had given his blessing to Nat walking out with his daughter Nat had often caught Thomas watching her and noticed that he became distant and sullen whenever Eliza and Nat were together. It was clear to Nat that Thomas had not completely given up on his dream. Thomas eventually sought solace through alcohol, maybe hoping that Eliza's disapproval of strong drink would serve to drive a wedge between them, making it easier for him to accept her choice of Nat. In the event he found consolation not in strong ale or cider but in the arms of Sarah, the landlord's daughter at the Mariners' Inn. She was a year or so younger than Thomas, a little shorter and plumper than Eliza, but beggars can't be choosers he thought. She had round rosy cheeks, was a real giggler when she'd had a drop to drink and he told himself that she would make a fine wife as he tried without success to convince himself that his feelings for Eliza were a thing of the past.

Nat, Thomas and the Sprakes fell in alongside Solomon Jackson, an old rogue who was known to undertake the odd bit of smuggling to supplement the money that he made fishing the fruitful waters of Lyme Bay.

'Now that there frigate looks to be Dutch, though whether it be in Dutch, French or English service I can't say,' he stated somewhat unhelpfully. 'Such ships are always being captured by one side or t'other. The two smaller vessels are called a *pink* and a *dogger*, you can tell that from their masts and rigging and they're definitely Dutch.'

They were carried by the crowd to the Cobb Gate, the entry port to the town where goods were assessed for duty, then west down the old Cart Road that ran along the edge of the beach. Arriving at the Cobb itself they were relieved to see that the newcomers appeared to have made no attempt to land.

'That's good,' said Thomas enthusiastically, 'it means we've missed none of the fun.'

Just as they found a place among the onlookers a small boat pushed off from the Cobb and pulled slowly towards the frigate. Mayor Gregory Alford who was watching the scene unfold from the cliffs high above the beach had made no move to contact the strange ships nor had the Collector of Customs Anthony Thorold, but clearly someone in authority had decided to find out just what was going on.

'That's Thomas Tye the Surveyor of the Port in the stern of the small boat,' Hezekiah said as he shielded his eyes against the bright glare of the water. 'I pray to the Almighty that he is not fired upon.'

To the obvious disappointment of many of the crowd the small craft reached the frigate safely and Tye climbed aboard using a rope ladder that was dropped over the side.

'Now we'll find out what's going on,' said Thomas, but hopes that Tye would return quickly so that the crowd could learn the identities and intentions of the new arrivals were dashed as the afternoon dragged on with little happening. After an hour or so Samuel Robbins, a fisherman from nearby Charmouth tied up alongside the frigate and was seen to be trying to negotiate a sale of his wares.

'Typical of old Sam,' grumbled Jackson, 'niver one to miss the chance of making some money that one.'

Robbins concluded his business and rowed away but there was still no sign of Tye.

'Somethings a-miss,' said Pastor Sprake. 'It's Thursday and Tye would not pass up on the weekly bowling club dinner unless he was being held captive.'

'Unless of course the newcomers have even better fare on offer,' remarked Jackson.

Mention of the bowls club caused Thomas to look again to the cliff top where members of the bowling club, including Mayor Alford, would normally be enjoying a post meal game by this time of the day. Alford who owed his position to his strong support for the crown was a hugely unpopular man with the townsfolk, especially after he had forced Protestant preacher James Short out of his living and seen him fined the huge sum of £40. Alford could be seen putting his spyglass to his eye time and time again as he tried to determine what the small armada intended. As mayor it was his job to investigate but he had made no move to do so. It was a warm afternoon and some enterprising lads set up a small stall to provide refreshments for the crowd who were reluctant to leave the sunny shore and return to their homes and businesses. They were prepared to await developments with a strange mix of excitement and disquiet.

Unbeknown to the onlookers, the excitement on board the *Helderenberg* had reached fever pitch. Foulkes and many of the others had harboured a secret fear that the flotilla would be fired upon as soon as it came within range of the guns on the Cobb but Tye had reassured them that there were no government troops in the immediate area and that Monmouth would receive a friendly welcome. A council of war was called by the duke to agree the final details for the landing including the need to secure the heights above the town; news of their arrival would spread quickly and the approaches to the town would have to be guarded as rapidly as possible. At about half past five shouts went up from those at the back of the crowd announcing that the mayor was at last coming down to the beach to assert his authority. Some wondered if he had been stirred to action by news from London, as the daily mail coach generally reached the town about five in the afternoon. Word had indeed come from London that Monmouth had sailed from Holland some twelve days earlier with three ships including the 32-gun frigate *Helderenberg* and there was no longer any doubt who the strangers were. As soon as he reached the Cobb, Alford started to issue orders.

'Sound the drums to summon the town guard!'

Most of the assembled crowd ignored Alford but one man, no doubt hoping to win favour with the mayor, ran back along the beach towards the main town to call out the watch.

'And get the guns on the Cobb trained on the traitors.'

'I regret that there is no powder for the guns Gregory,' said Thorold who had just emerged from the small building occupied by the customs officers.

'How can that be man?'

'It was all expended during the celebrations for your appointment and for the granting of the town's new charter.'

'And why was the powder not replaced?'

'There has not been time. However, there is a ship tied up half-way down the Cobb that has recently arrived from the Indies and I understand they have a quantity of powder aboard.'

'Then have it confiscated immediately!'

'I shall see to it at once.' Calling to three of his customs men Thorold ran down the Cobb where he was soon involved in a heated exchange with the ship's skipper who insisted on retaining half of the powder for his return trip to the Indies and demanded to know who would pay for any powder that he was willing to give up.

As all this was happening a number of small boats were lowered from the frigate and began pulling for the beach. The crowd surged forward to get a better look at the tall, beautifully dressed young man wearing a purple and red coat who waded ashore from the lead boat then fell to his knees in prayer. Above him fluttered a huge green and gold banner bearing the legend FEAR NOTHING BUT GOD. Rising to his feet the young man drew his sword and led the small party, which Nat reckoned numbered no more than sixty, up the old stile path towards the top end of town, no doubt anxious to gain the high ground as soon as possible.

'The duke is come, blessed be God!' cried a voice from the crowd.

Alford and Thorold realised that there was little they could do other than get out of town quickly and raise the alarm.

4 THE PROTESTANT PRINCE

Thursday 11th June 1685

Nat found it hard to draw his eyes away from the handsome young man as he started to climb the steep path away from the beach. Five years ago Nat had travelled to Forde Abbey near the town of Chard to see James, the Duke of Monmouth when the young duke had toured the west country and he had rejoiced that such a brave soldier would be the next king. The Protestant Prince they all called him. The fact that King Charles had constantly refused to acknowledge that he had secretly married the boy's mother Lucy Walter made no difference to the majority of the huge crowds that flocked to see him that day. Everybody believed the old wives' tale that if a man looked like his father it proved that he had been born within wedlock, and Monmouth's remarkable likeness to his father confirmed his legitimacy beyond doubt. It was strongly rumoured that the old king was a closet Catholic hence his decision to name his papist brother James as his successor rather than his first-born son.

The crowd on the Cobb split, some following the procession up the steep path, others rushing back along the shore in the expectation that the duke would head for the market cross as soon as he had secured the heights. It was total chaos in the town when Nat and the others arrived back at the market square. The crowd were chanting 'A Monmouth, A Monmouth' as the duke's small army began its march down Broad Street towards the town hall. The press of people wanting to touch their prince was intense and the duke's sergeants had to force a way through, holding the enthusiastic crowd back with their long halberds. Halfway down the hill the duke paused to talk to and then kiss Agatha Blythe, a young woman who had shouted that she had once been in the service of his sister, Mary Fanshawe in St James's. This small act of kindness drew renewed cheers from the crowd, here was a man worth following they thought, a man of the people despite his privileged upbringing. When the duke's party reached the market cross, close to where the River Lim cut through the centre of the town in its deep channel, the call went out for silence and in a clear strong voice one of the duke's supporters, Joseph Tiley read a prepared message.

'The declaration of James, Duke of Monmouth and the noblemen, gentlemen and others now in arms for the defence and vindication of the Protestant religion and the laws, rights and privileges of England,' he began.

Claims followed that King Charles II had been murdered by his brother James, as part of a secret plan to return the country to Rome's authority.

'He hath poisoned the late king and fomented the Popish plot.'

These accusations were met with a mixture of boos and whistles from the crowd. In truth King Charles had not been greatly liked due to his persecution of the Baptists and other non-conformists, but James was far worse, he was a Catholic. The proclamation seemed to ramble on for ever and Eliza noticed that some at the back of the crowd had begun to drift away, but the main message that Monmouth was here to protect the Protestant faith and would pass power back to a recalled Parliament, accepting whatever role they chose to give him was all that most wanted to hear. Those townsfolk that the crowd identified as royalists were quickly rounded up and thrown into the cockmoil, the town lock-up, whilst a desk was set up in the marketplace to enable men to enlist in the duke's army. There was never really much doubt that Nat would join the rebels, but when Eliza pushed through the crowd to squeeze his hand and remind him that Monmouth's victory would speed their wedding day the cast was set. He queued up to give his name to a Master Ferguson who had arrived with the duke and was now acting as recruiting officer. Many others followed including Thomas and as soon as their names had been taken they were dispatched to the town hall to collect their new weapons. John Carver was already at the town hall having been called upon to use his largest blacksmith's sledgehammer to break down the locked doors. To Nat's surprise his father presented himself for enlistment but when Ferguson asked his name and trade he put down his quill and looked up at the old man.

'Your ardour and enthusiasm to fight for our noble cause is to be applauded sir,' he said kindly, 'but I think your fighting days are over. As a blacksmith you would better serve the duke by preparing new weapons for the recruits that will flock to his holy banner once word of our arrival spreads.' Nat had foreseen just such an eventuality and had chosen to give his occupation as 'tobacco cutter' rather than blacksmith. The next man waiting to sign up was already in uniform, the red coat of the Dorsetshire militia. Silas Brown had been the only militiaman to show up when Alford had called out the town guard and he had immediately defected to the rebels. Thomas and Nat were posted to the newly formed Red Regiment under the command of Lt Col Samuel Venner who had travelled to Lyme in Monmouth's party.

'Have you heard anything about our commander Nat?' asked Thomas as they waited to be issued with their new weapons.

'I were told that Colonel Venner 'as been living in exile in Holland ever since his father were executed for leading a rebellion against King Charles back in 1661. He's said to have fought alongside Oliver Cromwell so he should have something about 'im.'

'Yet now he's fighting for the grandson of the man that Cromwell beheaded! Strange bedfellows!'

'Indeed, and I hear that his deputy, Major Wade is a barrister from Bristol.'

'A lawyer appointed to a military post. Makes no sense to I.'

'Me neither but I'm sure the duke knows what he's up to.'

Their chat was interrupted by Amos Thorne, a carter from nearby Chideock.

'Heard you two talking 'bout Colonel Venner. I saw him come ashore early yesterday. I were down on the beach helping old George with his nets, when his worship lands in a rowing boat. I took him for a smuggler at first given the hour of the day but it were soon clear from the cut of his clothes and his tone of voice that he were no villain.'

Encouraged by the pals' obvious interest and that of several other new recruits who had gathered around anxious for any gossip, Thorne continued his tale.

'He asked me if I'd seen any militia about and whether I thought the county be ready to rise in support of the duke. Well, imagine him asking the opinion of an honest but humble man like me, and what's more believing me at my word.'

Nat had trouble suppressing a smile at the word honest, but Thorne didn't notice and continued.

'He asked the route to Hawkchurch and as soon as I told him he signalled for the boat to be readied to leave. He told one of the gentlemen with him, I think he called him Mister Dare, to ride for Taunton via Hawkchurch to raise the countryside and bring what men he could to Lyme. He were a proper gentleman, even gave me and George some canary wine and neats' tongue for our troubles. I said to George, if that's the fare on offer I'm all for more of it.'

His reminiscences were cut short as orders were given for the men to form a line ready for the issue of their new muskets which had been off-loaded from one of the two small transport vessels. Monmouth himself now appeared and much to everyone's surprise spoke to each man in turn.

'Sir,' he said to Nat, 'thou art an honest looking fellow, and I'll take care and provide for thee; Thou deserves encouragement, I have arms enough for thee and many more.'

The duke appeared to be everything that the London pamphlets had said him to be and when he left to attend to other duties the new recruits cheered until they were hoarse. From the way that the men talked it was clear that whilst most were fired with religious fervour, others saw the rebellion as an opportunity to improve their personal position, with the cloth trade going through one of its frequent lulls. As he looked around Nat was surprised that he and Thomas were two of the younger recruits, most being older family men.

Monmouth rested that night at the Old George Inn on Coombe Street and Nat and Thomas had to fight their way through the crowds to get back to their homes which lay at the far end of the street. When they arrived back at the smithy John Carver was waiting for them.

'Thought I should tell 'e Nat that I'll be going down to try to enlist again as soon as my work at the smithy will allow.'

Nat tried to remonstrate with him, but he said that his mind was made up.

'My dear parents were both killed helping Colonel Blake defend this town against the damned royalists in '44 when I myself were just a babe. There's a debt to be paid by the Stuarts.'

'I understand that father, but the Duke of Monmouth's a Stuart himself.

'Don't judge the man by his father, the bible says. He's promised to restore parliament and I'm ready to give him the benefit of the doubt till I see otherwise.'

'But what about the smithy? Your father and your Uncle Silas both worked their fingers to the bone to establish this business, to be able to pass it to you, and you would now risk it all on this venture, however righteous the cause?'

'Tis true that they worked harder than many a man and I have tried to do the same. I intend to make sure that the business is fit to be passed to you and God willing to your own children in their turn, but if a thing is worth having it's worth fighting for. It's not just the smithy Nat, tis our whole way of life that be at stake here and I for one will not lie easy in my bed with the threat of Popery hanging over us.' He could see that Nat was concerned and tried to lighten the mood. 'You know of course that the smithy is worth more than fifty pounds a year, meaning that by law I 'as to pay for the equipping and training of one militiaman. Be just my blerry luck if it's the one that I pays for as shoots me dead before this thing has played out.'

Their discussion was interrupted by a sharp knock at the door summoning Nat for guard duty. If this was army life he thought it was already proving to be very exhausting. Some of the men in his regiment had been ordered to guard the military supplies that had already been brought ashore and were now housed in the town hall whilst others were unloading the stores that were still on the transports. Nat hoped that he would get this duty so as to get to his bed before too long, but he was to be disappointed. He was destined to spend the night under the bright June stars on the eastern outskirts of the town, guarding the road to Chideock. He was told to keep watch for the militia, direct any new recruits to the town hall and prevent anyone from leaving Lyme. Rumour had it that Mayor Alford had been seen riding out of town in the direction of Honiton, presumably to warn the government forces stationed there and whilst his treachery could not now be stopped it was hoped that the pickets could prevent others from doing the same. Their presence on the road was more symbolic than practical.

'Not sure what we're s'posed to do if someone tries to leave,' complained one of Nat's fellow guards, 'We ain't been showed 'ow to use these new muskets yet and we've not been given no powder or shot even if us did know how to load and fire the things.'

When Nat eventually returned home in the early hours his father told him that he had heard that customs officer Samuel Dassel and his friend Thorold had also managed to leave the town that evening by a different route, using their knowledge of the area to avoid the outposts, and were thought to be heading for London to raise the alarm.

5 WORD REACHES TAUNTON

Thursday 11th June 1685

Taunton, in common with much of the west country relied heavily upon wool, but the trade was in recession and times were hard. William Pearce, who described himself as 'a weaver by trade and a Baptist by the grace of God,' lived with his wife Rebecca and their four girls in a small cottage belonging to Lambrook Mill on the banks of the River Tone, some two miles from the town centre. He was a slight man with a pronounced paunch caused by too much ale and his lank light-coloured hair was fast receding to leave a prominent brow. He would have loved to have had a son but he worshiped his daughters and believed that they needed a proper education if they were to better themselves. As a consequence his eldest girl Ginny attended Mary Blake's Taunton Academy for Young Ladies in the town. The school fees meant that the family often went hungry but both William and Rebecca felt that it was a hardship worth suffering. That Thursday evening Ginny arrived home from school with momentous news. It took Rebecca some minutes before she could get the girl to calm down enough to tell her tale.

'The whole town is alive with rumours that the Duke of Monmouth has come to claim his father's crown. The Good Lord has given him a safe landing at a place called Lyme Regis in Dorsetshire.' she squealed.

'Calm yourself child,' said her father gently. 'Now I believes what you say but I must go into town to see for myself if this be true,' and without a further word he grabbed his hat and coat and made for the door.

'Now don't you go and do anything stupid William Pearce,' Rebecca called after him.

William arrived back later that night full of religious fervor and strong ale in equal measures.

'The whole of Taunton was rejoicing when I got there and I took myself off to the Red Lion when I heard that William Savage the landlord was offering free beer to any man who would march to join the duke's army at Lyme. Not that I needed the promise of ale to decide that I must away to Lyme this very night. The threat of the papists must be opposed by all true God-fearing Englishmen.'

Rebecca was about to protest but stopped herself. She knew that once her husband had set his mind on a course of action there was no changing it. God's work must be done and the family would get by somehow until William returned home. Taking his stout stick from beside the fire and snatching up a half-loaf to eat on the journey he bade farewell to his family, tenderly kissing the heads of the two youngest children who had fallen asleep long before he had returned from the town. Ginny, now fourteen and her sister Alice, two years her junior burst into tears and it would be left to Rebecca to explain to them just why their father was leaving.

The authorities in Taunton were well aware of what had happened in Lyme and had called out the militia to stop anyone who was foolish enough to try to leave the town to join the rebel army. Fortunately for William his home was well to the north-east of the town and thus outside the cordon that was being hastily set up. Taking the back lanes to Haydon he was able to make his way south without interference until he got to within two miles of Lyme when he was stopped by three armed men who appeared suddenly from behind a thick hedge.

'Halt, who goes there?' came the challenge in a thick Dorset accent. 'Step forward and be identified. State your business being abroad this night.'

'That depends on who's asking,' Pearce replied somewhat truculently.

'Quickly now unless you want a ball in your guts for your insolence.'

'I've come to see for myself if the rumours of a rebellion be true.'

'And if they are?'

It was a dark night and Pearce was certain he could easily disappear back into the inky blackness if these men were loyal to King James, so he told them his purpose.

'If it be true then I wish to offer my help to return the country to proper Protestant rule, so help me God.'

He was pleased to note that the men visibly relaxed and had lowered their weapons. He took a step towards them.

'Not so fast,' said the man who was clearly in charge of the picket. 'You've yet to tell us your name and place of dwelling.'

'William Pearce, weaver from Taunton.' He sensed a stiffening in the men's postures.

'Taunton you say? Then come no closer friend. We've heard that there be smallpox in Taunton and we won't have anyone bring that distemper to our town. The last outbreak here saw nigh on half our children carried away to God's mercy.'

'Fear not, fear not,' William replied cheerfully, 'the pox is only afflicting those who live or work near the old castle in the middle of the town. Me and my family lives a fair way outside of the town and thank God the pestilence has not touched me nor any of my neighbours.'

And so it was that William Pearce was allowed into the town and following the instructions of the picket made his way down to the town hall to enlist. His enthusiasm to fight for the Protestant cause was to be sorely tested over the following weeks.

6 FORDE ABBEY NEAR CHARD

Friday 12th June 1685

Another man heading to join the rebels at Lyme was fifty-seven-year-old former soldier Samuel White. He had been born in a small cottage alongside the packhorse bridge in the tiny hamlet of Dowlish Wake in Somerset and was the third son of a fervent puritan minister. At the age of sixteen with the blessing of his father, but against his mother's wishes, he had enlisted in the parliamentarian army that had been at war with King Charles I for the past two years.

He first saw action at Marston Moor where he played a very minor part in parliament's victory, acting as a drummer boy in one of Lord Fairfax's infantry brigades. A year later he had grown sufficiently strong to be placed in the fourth rank of a pike block at the battle of Naseby where a spent musket ball had hit him in the shoulder. The wound was not life threatening but the muscle damage he suffered meant that he could no longer manage the heavy pike and he was issued with a musket instead, thankful that it came with a rest to take some of the weight.

At what turned out to be the final set piece battle of the war at Stow-on-the-Wold he was part of a musketeer unit that was guarding the right flank of one of Colonel Thomas Morgan's pike blocks. Despite the noise and smoke his attention was drawn to a young parliamentarian officer who had been thrown from his horse directly in the path of a royalist cavalry charge. Oblivious to his own safety White had dropped his musket, run to the fallen rider and in a self-sacrificing act had thrown himself down on top of the man as the first of the enemy horsemen thundered past. Miraculously neither man was touched by the flying hooves and White was able to drag the stunned man into the cover of an abandoned artillery wagon before a second wave of horsemen churned up the ground where the two had been laying. The cavalry charge was the last forlorn attempt by the royalists to save the day and the battle was soon over.

The young man whose life Samuel White had saved was a close relation to the lawyer Edmund Prideaux who owned the former Cistercian monastery of Forde Abbey, some six miles from Samuel's home. The injury he had picked up at Naseby had been exacerbated by his brave action at Stow, preventing him from finding work when the war finished. Hearing of the heroism that had saved his kinsman, Prideaux found a place for him as a gamekeeper on his estate where Samuel slowly rebuilt his strength. Prideaux was awarded a baronetcy by Oliver Cromwell in 1658, only to die the following year when he was succeeded by his son, also called Edmund. It was a condition of the old man's will that White be kept on after his death. The restoration of Charles II had seen a fall in the family's fortunes with the baronetcy cancelled and Samuel could only wonder what other sanctions would have been handed down if the old baron had been a signatory to the document that ordered the execution of the new king's father. It was an open secret that the new owner of Ford Abbey longed for a return of parliamentary rule and the restoration of the family title, so when rumours began to circulate of a possible invasion by the Duke of Monmouth, Prideaux had started to make plans. Samuel White had been summoned to the big house, entering the east wing by the garden door and making his way up to the first floor where a footman told him to wait on the small bench outside the library. Prideaux soon appeared, striding down the corridor from his saloon.

'Ah White, thank you for coming, please come through.' He opened the door into the library and ushered the gamekeeper inside. It was the first time White had seen any of the private rooms at the abbey and he was struck by the magnificence of the high wooden ceiling and huge fireplace.

'Used to be the upper refectory when the monks had the place,' said Prideaux. 'I spend much of my time in here, it catches the sun at each end of the day. Anyway, down to business. I have it on good authority that the Duke of Monmouth is considering a challenge to his uncle's throne and I wish to be ready should that day arrive. I want you to provide some rudimentary military training to the estate workers and lead them to support the duke if it comes to a fight.'

White had readily accepted the task and could be found putting the shepherds, gardeners and others through their paces on the lawns that fronted the house at the end of each working day, with Prideaux watching from the window of his saloon. As soon as word of the actual landing at Lyme reached Forde Abbey White was again brought to the house where Prideaux imparted some astonishing news.

'You have done a good job with the men and I am thankful to you. Now I want you to march them to Lyme where you are to enlist them in the duke's army. I would go myself but my friends in London have advised me that my donation of five hundred pounds to the duke's war chest has come to the attention of the authorities. I expect to be subject to arrest and imprisonment at any moment.'

Samuel was amazed at the sum involved; it would take him a lifetime to earn that amount. Not that he begrudged the rich their wealth. He knew that there was a natural order to society and he knew his place within it. As long as the Prideaux family continued to treat him as well as they had in the past then he was content.

The next morning White led twenty armed men to join the rebellion. They had a much more straightforward journey than William Pearce and arrived on the heights above Lyme about mid-morning. They were stopped by a picket of ten rebels who stood behind a large farm wagon that had been drawn across the road. The guards looked nervous at the approach of a force that clearly outnumbered them so White told his men to wait a short distance away and approached the picket alone.

'Stop there old man and identify yourself,' demanded the sergeant in charge of the picket.

'Any more of the old and I'll have the skin from your back you villain! The name's Samuel White and I'm bringing these gentlemen from my master's estate to join the duke's cause.'

'Your men look fit enough but are you sure that you're up to the task yourself. It strikes I that you've seen a few too many summers.' The other men in the picket laughed at their sergeant's jest.

The colour rose in White's cheeks and he balled his fists ready to launch himself at the man when a young lieutenant rode up from the town and reined in beside the makeshift barrier.

'Thank you, Master Smudge, I'll take it from here.'

When the young officer heard that White had come from Forde Abbey he broke into a broad smile. 'I know the place well; I was present five years ago when his grace the duke stopped there on his tour of the West Country.'

'Indeed he did,' replied White. 'My master Edmund Prideaux the younger entertained him, why I almost met the duke myself that day. I still carries Richard Janeway's pamphlet as a memory of the occasion.'

He reached into his waistcoat pocket and withdrew a carefully folded copy of *A True Narrative of the Duke of Monmouth's Late Journey into the West* which he handed to the officer.

'A fine keepsake to have Master White. Do you have any experience of warfare?'

White told him of his time in Cromwell's army.

'Then you are most welcome here. Even if your ...er...maturity... prevents you from fighting, your experience will be invaluable to the duke as he looks to train the raw recruits that are flooding in.' He turned to the sergeant. 'Pull the wagon aside if you will.'

White led his men into the town following the officer's directions. Ferguson was acutely aware of the need for skilled men to mould the new recruits into an effective army in as short a time as possible and allocated White to the Red Regiment as a sergeant in charge of training.

White's chest swelled with pride and whilst he tried hard to maintain a proper martial bearing, his untidy shock of bright white hair and stooped stance made him look anything but the archetypal sergeant.

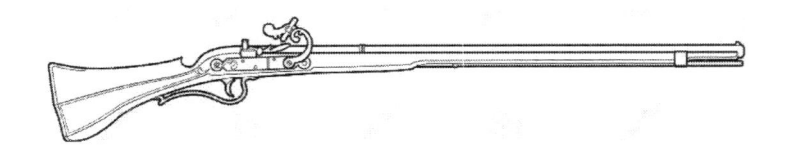

7 BASIC TRAINING

Friday 12th June 1685

Nat had managed to snatch a few hours' sleep after finishing his night's watch and gulped down a meagre breakfast before being called out again to assemble on Church Hill for basic training. He was lucky that he had been able to grab a bite to eat as it appeared that no arrangements had yet been made to feed the many men that had come to the town to join the fledgling army. Thomas had also snatched a quick breakfast and he soon picked up on the grumbles of the men who had arrived during the night.

'I thought the duke would have sorted out provisions for the men,' moaned Thomas.

'I'm sure that deficiency will be rectified soon enough,' responded Nat. 'I imagine that his grace thought it more important to spend his money on guns and powder,'

'He's Charles' heir! He's been living the life of luxury abroad, don't try to tell me that he ain't got no money to spare to feed us!'

'If the newssheets are to be believed 'is Uncle James held sway in court before the old king's death so I doubt that much money found its way to Monmouth.'

'Aw me 'art bleeds for the poor sod. I 'ear that he's just announced that today the army'll observe a solemn fast to ensure that his venture attracts divine blessing. Most of the God-fearing simpletons here believes that, but it don't fool me none. Just an excuse not to feed us!'

'I wonder why you signed up in the first place Thomas if you don't believe that this here rebellion is for the glory of God and the protection of the Protestant church.'

'I signed up 'cos I was bored and I wanted the chance to fight, to prove to myself and others that I'm a man.'

It was another warm day in a summer that was already among the hottest that any could remember and showed no signs of breaking. As soon as the training started it was apparent that the majority of the recruits had no clue about military matters and those few that had fired a foaling piece, either as gamekeeper or poacher were confused by the strange looking muskets that they now held. The training was being conducted by Samuel White who was proudly wearing his old red army jerkin that he had carefully packed away in a trunk some forty years earlier.

'His grace the duke has spared no expense in providing for you boys,' he shouted, 'by purchasing these 'ere muskets in 'olland. Now the first thing you needs to remember is that the powder is ignited by a burning match, which you will need to keep lit. Get the match wet and it won't light and then you can't fire, so when you're not using them, keep 'em under your hat to protect them from the rain.'

'If we ever gets any rain,' came a voice from the ranks.

'That's enough of your chatter,' shouted White. 'You're in the army now and will only speak when you're spoken to. Right, now listen and pay attention well. I needs to get some basic drill into you country boys if you're to stand up to the king's men. I notice that some of you 'ave brought your own pieces with you, doglocks and snaphances for the most part by the looks of it. For the benefit of you others, they are somewhat better than the matchlocks which you've got as they'll work even in the rain 'cos they use a flint to spark the powder rather than a burning match. As such they 'ave a different sequence to prepare 'em to fire but as musket fire is most effective when delivered in a volley, that's everybody firing at the same time, you gintl'mun with your posh pieces will just 'ave to play along with the others as we goes through the motions.'

Everyone was aware that the recruits had to learn fast. There was no doubt that by now news of the landing would have reached the king in London and that regular troops would soon be dispatched from Blackheath to bolster the local militias, so they practised hard.

'Carry your arms well! .... Rest your muskets! .... Cock your muskets! .... Guard your muskets! .... Present! .... Fire!'

The order to fire was met with a series of loud clicks as hammers fell onto empty pans. There was no point wasting what little powder the duke had brought with him from Holland until they had mastered the complex series of evolutions and the men were encouraged to shout 'bang' as they pulled their triggers.

'Recover your arms! .... Half cock your muskets! .....Clean your pans!'

And so it went on all day with twenty-nine different operations to complete just to fire one volley and prepare the musket for the next. As they became more accustomed to the complicated drill the gap between the volleys slowly came down but each was still taking more than two minutes to complete.

'Not bad for a bunch of washerwomen. Now with a bit more practice I'm sure that, in time, even you lot will be able to get that down to a little above a minute.'

'Time may be zummut we don't 'ave too much of,' Nat whispered to Thomas. 'I'm surprised that the militia 'ave left us alone for as long as they 'ave. They must know that the sooner they move against Lyme, before we're properly ready, the greater their chance of success.'

'Don't knock it young'un,' said Thorne, the carter from Chideock. 'The longer they delay the more hope we 'as.'

'Not as far as I'm concerned,' put in Thomas. 'The sooner I can get stuck into 'em the better.'

Mid-way through the afternoon there was a moment of panic when a body of horsemen was seen approaching, especially as none of the recruits had received any training in how to protect themselves against cavalry and they hadn't yet tried firing their muskets with powder and ball.

'Don't 'e worry lads,' called Amos Thorne, 'they be friendlies. I recognises the man leading them, tis the same gintl'mun I met on the beach a few days back, Master Dare who I sent on 'is way to Hawkchurch.'

Thomas Dare had ridden to raise rebellion in Taunton but had been prevented from entering the town by men of the Somersetshire militia. He had not returned empty handed though as he had 'liberated' a number of horses in the duke's name, a much-needed boost to the rebels' mounted arm. The training started up again and Thomas and Nat joined the other recruits in shouting the drill to try to commit it to memory.

'Handle your primers! .... Prime! ... Shut your pans! ... '

In the next field another group of men were being put through pike drill. Their training sounded very much like Thomas and Nat's.

'Advances your pikes! ... To the front charge! ... As you were! ... To the right charge! ... '

The two friends were glad that they had been allocated to a unit of musketeers and had not been issued with one of the clumsy sixteen-foot long, steel tipped ash poles that looked incredibly heavy and unwieldy. As well as carrying their pike the men had to contend with the weight of the metal breastplates that Monmouth had brought with him.

'They must be hell to wear in this bloody hot weather,' mused Thomas.

The pikes themselves were being made locally by a couple of willing carpenters and John Carver was hard pressed to keep up with them as he forged the steel tips. All other work at the forge had stopped but John never once complained about having to do the work for free. Nat feared that his father would ask for him to be recalled from the duke's army to assist but with Nat's younger brother Daniel helping out in the forge John was just about able to keep up with the demand. In normal times John, Nat and Daniel shared the labouring tasks at the smithy whilst a young maid named Nancy looked after the household. Nat's mother Sarah had died giving birth to Daniel some fifteen summers ago.

Daniel had pleaded to join the army as well but his father had said that one son was enough of a risk until the Lord showed which way the wind was blowing. Most other families in the town had adopted a similar stance.

When White eventually called a halt for the day Nat hurried down the hill towards Coombe Street anxious for his evening meal. He was quickly learning that in the army a man took every opportunity to eat and sleep, not knowing when the next call to duty might come. Stopping briefly beside a horse trough to wash the worst of the day's grime from his hands and face, he was greeted by a young man watering his horse.

'Thirsty work,' said the stranger, 'Master...?'

'Carver, Nathaniel Carver, at your service.'

'Daniel Foe, well met sir. Has the weather been this hot for long in Dorsertshire?'

'For about a week now and showing no sign o' changing.'

'Same as in London from where I have ridden this very day. The weather is so fickle of late, why it wasn't that long ago that the River Thames completely froze over in the capital and the ice was so thick that markets and fairs were held on the river.'

'I remembers that winter well Master Foe, we even had ice in the sea here at Lyme, well in the shallows anyway.'

'Strange times indeed. Now Master Carver, do you know where an honest man might find victuals in this town, it seems to me that there is no bread or wine to be had anywhere?'

'Tis true friend that the influx of so many has put a strain on the inns.'

Nat had taken an instant liking to Foe. He had an honest open face and was a man of some substance judging by the way both he and his mount were turned out. He wore a long dark woollen overcoat, which he called a Brandenburg, with a rich dress coat beneath, open to show off an elaborate waistcoat. His stockings were made of fine silk and his boots sported large highly polished buckles. Apart from the quality of his clothing two other things made him stand out, his long curly wig and the fur muffs which were attached to his belt. He noticed Nat staring at the strange hand-warmers.

'All the fashion in London at the moment.'

'A trifle unnecessary in this weather surely?'

'Not at all, one has to maintain appearances.'

'Not zummat we worries too much about down 'ere. Now if I may be so bold Master Foe may I invite you back to my father's house, tis but a short walk from here. I'm certain that he would be happy to share what little food we have in exchange for news from London.'

'Thank you, Master Carver, I would deem it an honour.'

'Please call me Nat.'

'Then thank you Nat, that is a most generous and Christian act. Pray lead the way.'

After seeing his horse safely into the small stable beside the smithy Foe introduced himself to John, Daniel and Nancy and explained that he was a hosier from London. Upon hearing news of the landing he had managed to evade the guards on the road west out of the capital to ride and join the duke's army, leaving both business and new wife behind. Nat could not doubt Foe's willingness or sincerity but was left to wonder what sort of a soldier a clothing merchant would make. No better or worse than a blacksmith or a shoemaker he supposed. His manners and clothing made him stand out as the sort of person that folk were beginning to call a 'middling sort', meaning that whilst he was in trade, he was doing well enough to be comfortable. Nat imagined him living in a large London townhouse with cooks and servants, a gardener and maybe even a groom. The smithy had customers from all walks of life and all parts of society and it always struck Nat as odd that even the most prosperous tradesman, like his father or a merchant like Master Foe here would struggle to join the gentry no matter how much wealth they accumulated, yet an impoverished gentleman with no ready funds to pay for even a simple blacksmithing job was given almost unlimited credit as long as he had the right family name and connections. It was assumed that a gentleman would be good for his liabilities no matter how long it took him to pay and it would be unquestionably rude to even mention the debt in the meantime. Friendships across the different strata of society were not common but Nat's simple act of charity had already forged a firm bond between him and Daniel Foe.

After Nancy had cleared away the remnants of the meal the men took out their long clay pipes and shared an amiable smoke, discussing the events of the last few days and what might still be in store.

'God be praised that the duke saw fit to bring the armour for the pikemen with him otherwise we would be out of metal within the day,' John exclaimed. For young Daniel Carver the constant comings and goings of so many men in arms was more excitement than he could remember and he was full of questions.

'What do they need the pikemen for father? Surely the musketmen would shoot the enemy soldiers down long before they could come to grips,' he asked.

'The pikes are there to protect the musketeers from enemy cavalry,' John explained carefully. 'It takes so long to load them pieces that the horse would be on them afore they could fire off one shot. One pike to every two muskets was the accepted way during the late war and I can see no reason why the duke would need to change that.'

It was deep into the night that the first blood of the rebellion was spilt. A small rebel cavalry detachment under Major Manley had been sent out following a rumour that the militia were stopping men from Chideock and Bridport from joining the duke at Lyme. Manley had surprised a troop of militia horse, killing two of them before retiring on Lyme. Everyone was heartened by news of this early success, but Hezekiah Sprake still thought it proper to offer a prayer for the souls of those killed even though they were now his enemies.

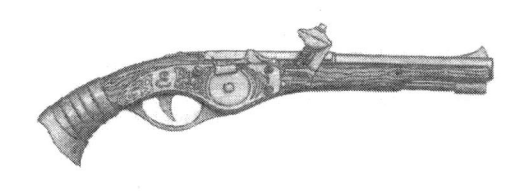

8 BLOOD ON THE STREETS

Saturday 13th June 1685

Nat awoke to the sound of drums calling the troops to their duties. He was cold and stiff having slept on the hard flagstones in front of the fireplace after giving his bed to Daniel Foe. Foe had been reluctant to accept but Nat had insisted and in the end the effects of his long ride from London had caught up with him and he gratefully accepted the kind offer. It was still not fully light when Thomas called at the door and the two friends made their way slowly back up onto Church Hill for what promised to be another long hot day of training. With more men continuing to arrive in Lyme from across Somerset, Devon and Dorset a second regiment, the Greens was formed under the command of a Baptist minister named Abraham Holmes.

Repetition was beginning to instil the complex process of loading and firing the muskets into men's minds and the orders were now shortened so as to speed the procedure, 'poise...! Shoulder...! Order...' White was pleased to note that his charges were going through the evolutions considerably faster than the men in the new regiment but he knew that there was still a long way to go before his Reds would be battle ready. About mid-morning he called a halt and the men were permitted to sit on the warm grass and smoke, eat or drink as they fancied. Nat lay back and listened to the gentle hum of the summer insects and the distant lapping of the waves far below.

'Right my lucky boys, time to get back to it, look lively!' called White. The men groaned as they rose to their feet. 'Now, I want all those pipes put away safely because I think the time has come for you to put what you've learnt into practice. He beckoned to a group of boys who had been stood to one side beside a wagon piled high with boxes and barrels. The new recruits burst into excited chatter as the boys began to distribute powder and shot. White called them to order.

'Now some of you will be acquainted with the sound of guns being fired, especially the poachers among you.' A number of the men giggled and nudged each other. 'But I doubt none of you have experienced the noise and sheer percussive force of a full volley. When I give the order to fire, I want you to pull your triggers and open your mouths as wide as you can!'

'Why open our mouths Sergeant?' asked Thomas.

'Cos the noise'll go in your ears and just bounce around inside your empty head Edgecott unless your mouth is open, which it often is I must add, to let the noise out again. It might just save your hearing.'

He had their full attention now as they went through the now familiar routines.

'Present! ... Fire!'

A ragged volley tore the air, startling birds from the nearby hedgerows. Some of the men were so shocked by the noise that they actually dropped their muskets, others were so excited that they began to reload before the order was given, so keen were they to fire again.

'Stop, stop!' yelled White. 'Pick those muskets up this instant! His grace didn't go to the expense of bringing them all the way from bloody 'olland just for you to throw them around. Take good care of them, the chances are that in the days to come they may just save your miserable lives. Now we do this all together, at the same time. Remember your drill.... Recover your arms! ... Return your match! ...'

It was another stifling hot day. Whenever there was a break in the musketry practice a strong offshore breeze whipped the powder smoke away to reveal the majestic sweep of Lyme Bay, the sun sparkling off the wave tops in a bewildering display. During one such break in the arduous training coloured sashes were issued to the men, either red or green as appropriate to denote which unit they belonged to. The men took an inordinate pleasure in the simple rags which constituted a uniform of sorts and a friendly rivalry immediately sprung up between the two regiments with insults shouted across the open field. The officers did nothing to interfere, knowing that a sense of belonging and comradery were vital elements in creating an effective fighting unit. As Nat tied his sash around his waist he turned to the man beside him.

'I've not seen you before friend.'

'What?'

'I said I've not seen you before,' shouted Nat.

'Sorry, couldn't 'ear a word, bloody ears ringing like church bells!'

'Nat Carver...'

'What is?'

'Me, Nat Carver!'

'Ah right. Sorry. Henry Outwell. Came in yesterday from Colyton where I works as a dyer.'

'Well met Master Atwill.'

'Outwell...O .. U .. T .. W ....'

Their conversation, such as it was, was interrupted by White, calling them back to their training and soon the shouts of 'Draw forth your sowers! .... Charge with bullet! ....' rendered any further conversation impossible.

After a hard day's training, Nat and Thomas were hopeful of a restful night but they were to be disappointed. At around ten in the evening some four hundred men drawn from the Red Regiment and another new regiment, the Whites were ordered to assemble at the market cross. As Thomas and Nat walked past the George towards the assembly point a number of officers spilled out onto the street obviously slightly the worse for wear. Two of the finely dressed gentlemen were engaged in a heated debate, evidently over a fine-looking horse that was tied to a post outside the inn. Nat had seen Thomas Dare the previous day when he had ridden into Lyme with a troupe of horsemen but he did not recognise the taller man. The street was crowded and the pals had no option but to stand and watch as the matter played out. Lt Col Foulkes of the White Regiment tried to interpose himself between the two protagonists but to no avail.

'As commander of his grace's cavalry, it is only right and proper that I have the best mount!' shouted the tall man in a broad Scottish accent.

'My dear Lord Fletcher,' responded the man angrily, 'I found this fine mount so tis mine and that's the end of the matter, now if you don't mind!' With that Dare mounted the horse, clearly intent on putting some distance between him and the Scottish laird but Fletcher was not prepared to yield the beast so easily and tried to wrestle the reins from Dare's hands. In desperation Dare lashed out with his riding crop, catching Fletcher across the shoulder. The enraged Fletcher drew a pistol from his belt and shot Dare stone dead. A stunned silence followed as the onlookers held their breath waiting to see what would happen next. Nat and Thomas had been practising with their muskets for two days and were under no illusion that in due course they would be expected to use them against fellow human beings, but this was different. This was cold blooded murder, death close-up and nasty. A young man pushed his way through the huddle at the inn's door.

'You devil, you have killed my father, I demand satisfaction!'

The officers began shouting, some supporting the dead man's son others claiming that Dare had brought it on himself by his disrespectful actions. The situation was threatening to get out of hand and Monmouth himself was obliged to step in, physically restraining the dead man's son and sending Fletcher back to the *Helderenberg* under escort. Ferguson, concerned that the episode would be detrimental to morale leapt onto an empty barrel and delivered a stirring speech; it would not be the last time that the men were to hear him and be inspired by his words. He told the men why they had been assembled.

'Word has reached his grace that the Dorsetshire and Somersetshire militias are gathering at Bridport and are determined to march on us. His grace has decided that we should strike first, before the enemy has gathered all his strength. Deserters tell us that there are already some twelve hundred foot and a hundred horse stationed in Bridport, but they are not proper soldiers, they are poorly trained militia, the majority of whom wish to play no part in opposing our crusade, for that is what it is my friends, a crusade, smiled upon by the Lord God Almighty to rid this country of James and the rest of the papist puppets who dance to the tune of Rome.'

Many of those assembling for the six-mile night march to Bridport knew members of the Dorsetshire militia. They were just ordinary men, no different to the rebels themselves, some even worshipped with them and they were convinced that Ferguson spoke the truth when predicting mass desertions. Besides, God was on their side, who would be able to stand against them.

'They have no love for the tyrant James,' he continued, 'and they will welcome the chance to join us in our just fight!' As a parting comment Ferguson shouted, 'we fight for England and England will fight for us!'

The men cheered even though many were still somewhat shaken by the incident outside the inn, but Thomas summed up their feelings well.

'Bloody gentry. They lives by their own rules. Tis not for us to question or even try to understand their ways.'

Lord Grey had been given the honour of leading the force against Bridport. He had forty men of his own troop of horse and the four hundred soldiers drawn from the two foot regiments. It seemed a small number to throw against so many but few of the rebels expected there to be a fight, the militia would surely throw down their weapons just as Ferguson had said. None of the officers had had the time to fully scout the lay of the land and so it was agreed that Amos Thorne should guide them at least as far as his home village of Chideock. Many of the men marching that night were born and bred in Lyme and knew the way well enough and couldn't understand the need for a guide. Their route would be easy enough even in the dark, they only had to follow the sound of the church bells ringing the hours in each village along the route, but they supposed that using a scout was the proper military way of doing things. To avoid any militia patrols that might be watching the main road to Bridport, Thorne suggested that they use Long Entry, the old shoreline path towards Charmouth which started just below the church. The locals all agreed that this was a wise decision as they set off.

Ferguson and the captains had stressed the need for a quiet approach but Bridport was still miles away and the sound of the sea echoing off the sheer cliff face to the men's left would mask any noise that they might make. Even so the horses' hooves had been wrapped in cloth to deaden any sound and their tack had been similarly muffled. It was a lovely clear night with the near-full moon providing sufficient light to travel by and the men's spirits rose as they encouraged each other with talk of an easy victory. Spread out on the narrow path the small force seemed to stretch for miles and they felt invincible. The militia were poorly trained they told each other, they didn't even practice with live ammunition. Some men said that they had heard tell that the militia's muskets were so badly maintained that they could never be made to fire and others said that they had it on good authority that lack of use and care meant that their swords were often rusted into their scabbards. Those that didn't desert as soon as they spotted the rebels approaching would have nothing to fight with they claimed. They were no more than bullies others crowed, only good for breaking up illegal conventicles, but like all bullies liable to take flight when opposed and hadn't Manley shown the militia's real worth by routing their cavalry so easily the previous night. Spirits were high but Henry Outwell who marched beside Nat saw through the false bravado.

'It's important for them to burn off their nervous energy in such speculation, but you wait and see Nat, men who crave for action and excitement when there is no danger near will be praying to their God or calling for their mothers when battle is joined.'

Outwell had fought briefly as a lad in the civil war and was fully aware that these men, so confident as they marched off to war had yet to be tested under fire. The chattering stopped as they approached the River Char and they shuffled into single file to cross the old wooden bridge over the fast-flowing water. The bridge was set in the middle of a wide plain and old soldier Samuel White felt terribly exposed as he crossed, especially with the moon giving so much light, but no alarm was raised, no shots were fired out of the night and once safely across the river the march was resumed, keeping close to the shore as before. They continued along the coast until they arrived on the little beach where Thorne had first encountered Dare and the others of the advanced party. Here the small force turned inland away from the sights and sounds of the sea and were almost immediately enclosed by the tall hedges on either side of Mill Lane. To bypass the village of Chideock they crossed the River Winniford well below the first farm and climbed slowly towards the top of Eype Moor where they would join the main road that led into Bridport. Chideock was known to hold strong Catholic sympathies and it would only take one dog picking up a strange scent or a farmer appearing at his backdoor to relieve himself to destroy any hope of surprising the enemy.

Once on the old Roman road that ran from Exeter through Bridport to Dorchester, the going became easier. The sound of the sea which had returned when they topped Eype moor had disappeared again as the column marched behind the bulk of Frogmore Hill. Although Chideock had been safely avoided caution was still needed, the openness of Eype Moor being replaced by thick hedgerows where every bush or tree could hide a militia musketeer. A number of prisoners were taken along the route, some wanting to join the rebellion, others deserting from the militia rather than face the determined men of Lyme, each one helping to re-enforce the belief that the militia would not stand when push came to shove. As the hedgerows, thick with whitethorn and dogwood gave way to more open country again, the word was passed for silence. In the early hours of the morning the mist began to rise, at first lying in the hollows between the hillocks, then slowly creeping up the sides of the hills towards the clumps of trees at their summits, making the hilltops appear to be so many islands scattered across a grey sea. The mist served to deaden the sounds of the marching men but could just as easily conceal the approach of enemy cavalry who could burst from cover at any minute and turn the march into bloody ruin. Thomas was not alone in being afraid of the thought of big men on big horses using their long swords to crush skulls as easily as a cook breaks eggs and this fear did more to quieten the men than any rebuke from the officers.

As second in command for the night's operation Lt Col Venner rode ahead with Lord Grey, so control of the Red Regiment had fallen to Major Wade. Wade was well aware from the London newssheets and from the talk of fellow officers over dinner of the circumstances surrounding the duke's battle with the Scots at Bothwell Bridge back in 1679. It had been the young duke's first independent command under the old king and he had won a famous victory. The major factor in that celebrated triumph had been the success of Monmouth's regular cavalry against poorly trained irregular foot soldiers, hence the need for caution on these seemingly deserted Dorset lanes where history could easily be repeated if enemy cavalry fell upon the untried men of the rebel army. In the half-light the column crossed the River Simene between the villages of Symondsbury and Allington. The river was little more than a stream at this point but the soft tinkle of the water over the small stones in the riverbed was enough to let the locals in the force pinpoint their exact location. The Simene ran into the River Brit just below the stone bridge that marked the western edge of Bridport and that bridge was to be the first objective in the fight to come. The men now moved in complete silence and the normal night sounds returned, the hoot of an owl hunting in a nearby pasture and the plaintive cry of a mating vixen, sounding just like a child bawling. The joking and false bravado from earlier in the march was gone as each man prepared himself for the test that awaited them.

9 BRIDPORT

Sunday 14th June 1685

Any doubts that the old soldiers had harboured over the wisdom of taking raw recruits on a night march lessened as the outlines of Bridport's buildings came into view through the thickening mist with no shouted challenge or deadly volley. It was now close to dawn and a halt was called to put the men into proper order, check equipment and issue final instructions for the assault. In hushed nervous voices men prepared themselves for what for most of them would be their first taste of action. Nat wondered how he would react in combat, how would he feel when another man, maybe even someone in the militia that he knew tried to take his life and whether to save his own life he would have to take another's. Despite his belief in the eternal afterlife, Nat realised that he feared death. He dreaded not seeing his family or his dear Eliza again. Would he be able to put that fear aside or would he let his new comrades down at a crucial moment? Another fear pushed its way into his head, what if he were to survive the night but be wounded. A cripple, unable to work again, a burden to his family with nothing to look forward to but a short and painful life. Would Eliza be able to live with that? He feared death, injury, failure, shame and, if he should end a cripple, the well-intentioned but misplaced sympathy of his neighbours and friends. Thomas was clearly thinking along similar lines.

'Are you ready for what awaits us?' he asked the drill master Samuel White, hoping to draw comfort from the old soldier's calm demeanour.

'One is never ready for what awaits us,' came the terse reply.

Bridport was built on a small hill with roads from all four compass points meeting in the middle of the town at its highest point. There was a stout stone bridge at either end of the town where the main road dropped down to cross the River Brit to the West and the Mangerton River to the East. Nat was selected to be part of the initial assault, to be led by Captain Thompson and Lieutenant Mitchell whilst Thomas was kept back in the main body of the rebel force. The advanced guard approached the bridge over the Brit cautiously, encouraged by the fact that they could not discern the tell-tale lights from the slow matches which the bridge guards would need to keep burning to fire their pieces. If he had been commanding well-trained veterans Thompson would have considered sending men forward to quietly overpower the guards, but with so many raw recruits in the force he knew that this was not an option. He knew that men lost some of their fear when shouting, transferring that fear onto the enemy and Nat and his fellows were happy to do anything that made the upcoming ordeal easier. At a signal from Mitchell the rebels let out a huge roar and rushed the bridge. The dozen or so guards at the bridge were taken completely by surprise and fell back without firing a shot, although one man slipped and fell onto the cobbles and was soon taken prisoner. In the dim light he recognised Nat.

'Nat! It's me, Richard, Richard Wills.'

'Bloody hell Dick! I wondered if you might be here tonight, God you could have shot me!'

'No chance of that Nat. Couldn't 'ave shot you even if I'd wanted to. We wuz ordered to extinguish our slow matches cos it would cost too much to replace 'em if we kept them burning all night!'

The bridge guard could be seen running up the wide main street towards the high point of the town where a larger body of their comrades waited at the crossroads. Nat could see no more than fifty men facing them and felt a wave of relief flood through him, having been told by Ferguson that the militia greatly outnumbered the duke's force. As the assault group regained their breath Lt Col Venner brought the main body of rebels up to the bridge and Thomas was one of a dozen who were ordered to hold the crossing under the command of Lieutenant Ascue. Venner knew that it was imperative to keep the initiative, to keep his men moving forward and the enemy going backwards.

'Onwards my brave lads, don't let them dither!'

'Can't I go with 'em?' Thomas pleaded with Ascue, 'I wants to get stuck in!'

'You will do as you are ordered soldier!' snapped Ascue.

As the rebels ran up the steep slope towards the crossroads a number of dismounted militia cavalrymen appeared from one of the stout stone cottages that lined both sides of the street, come to see what had caused the sudden commotion. Their officer quickly took in the situation and began to form his men into a rough line, but seeing the way that the rebels came on, they too fell back without firing a shot. At a shout from the officer commanding at the crossroads the running cavalrymen threw themselves to the ground as the line of militiamen brought their muskets up to their shoulders. Nat froze and it seemed to him that every single barrel was pointing directly at him. His thoughts flew to Eliza and he began to offer up a prayer that he would be spared but got further than 'Dear God...' before the enemy line disappeared behind a bank of dirty smoke, shot through with bright fingers of flame. The thunder of the volley was followed instantly by the whistle of lead bullets as they passed over Nat's head, close enough to make the air quiver. He realised that he had been holding his breath waiting for the pain to come, but none of the rebels appeared to have been hit and he recalled the words of Sergeant White during the long hot hours of practice... 'remember lads, always aim low, because the recoil will always send your shot higher than you anticipated.'

'Onto them now lads, before they have a chance to reload!' screamed Lieutenant Thompson, but the militia weren't going to hang around long enough to fire again. They could see that none of the rebels had been dropped and they turned tail and disappeared over the crest of the hill towards the eastern end of the town, several dropping their muskets in their haste to get away.

'Keep after them boys!' shouted Mitchell.

Nat was breathing heavily when he reached the road junction and the lack of sleep over the past 48 hours was starting to tell. Realising that there was no catching the fleeing militia before they could reach the safety of the formidable barricade that had been thrown up across the far bridge Thompson reluctantly called a halt. To avoid the chance of a musket being discharged accidently on the approach to Bridport the rebels had marched with unloaded muskets and Thompson now gave orders for weapons to be loaded. First the firing pan was primed the with a pinch of fine powder from the men's' powder horns. Then they bit the end off of a paper cartridge and keeping the lead ball in their mouths they poured the loose powder into the barrel, spitting the ball in after it. The remains of the paper cartridge were stuffed into the barrel to act as wadding before packing the whole lot down tight with their ramrods. The lit matches which could have given away their approach were passed forward by the supporting troops and snapped into place. Lieutenants Lillingstoke and Brinscombe were given twenty men each and sent to watch the roads to the north and south as the main body set off again. A hundred yards beyond the crossroads stood an old coaching house, the Bull Inn outside which a number of frightened horses were tied to rails. They would make fine prizes for the duke thought Nat but as the rebels moved forward to take them gunfire erupted from the Inn's windows.

'With me!' shouted Venner without hesitation.

The big double doors to the inn stood open and a dozen men followed Venner through to find themselves in a large courtyard, under fire from all sides. Nat dived for cover behind a sturdy looking barrel, just as a shot fired from an upper window tore a thick splinter from the barrel's rim. He was breathing heavily as he psyched himself up to join the battle. With a final deep intake of acrid air he swung his musket out and prepared to fire, but the gun-smoke was so dense that he could find no target. He ducked back behind the barrel again as lead balls left dirty grey smears on the cobbles or flattened themselves against the wall behind his head. The shouts and screams of the combatants, the bark of the muskets and the whinnying of frightened horses produced a cacophony of sound that struck him like a physical blow. Men started to go down and for the second time that day that Nat feared that he would not live to see his family again. Through the dense dirty smoke Nat watched as Venner and two or three others attempted to break down one of the doors that led into the inn's interior. With a loud crash the door splintered and the men disappeared inside. Nat's saw the open doorway as his salvation and rushed to join them, trusting that the terrible visibility would save him from anything other than a lucky, or rather an unlucky shot. He ducked under the low lintel in time to see Venner take a pistol shot to the body. As he fell Venner managed to discharge his own pistol and his assailant was thrown sideways, a bloody stain spreading across his gaudy waistcoat. Nat expected further gunfire but the violent exchange seemed to have frozen the combatants on both sides and the men just stared at each other as the smoke in the room slowly cleared. The spell was only broken when several more rebels burst in through another door. The militia officers realised that they were hopelessly outnumbered and lowered their weapons. Nat realised that once again he had been holding his breath and exhaled loudly only to start coughing as he took in a lungful of the bitter tasting smoke. Lieutenant

Goodenough approached the man who was clearly the militia's leader.

'Gentlemen, I believe that you are my prisoners, your names please.'

'Strangeways,' replied the man, 'Deputy Lord Lieutenant of Dorsetshire, and no damned rebel shall take me hostage, go to hell you traitor!' He raised his pistol aiming straight at Goodenough's head but Nat reacted quicker. Almost without realising what he was doing he raised his musket and fired from the hip. The noise of the discharge was horrendous and Strangeways was flung back against the wall, before slowly sliding to the floor, leaving a lurid red smear on the dirty plasterwork. Nat looked down at his musket as if seeing it for the first time, saw the devastation that it had caused and dropped the weapon to the floor. He would have fled the building had he not collided with Major Wade who had pushed his way into the room and quickly took control. He looked Nat in the eye and saw the shock and horror there.

'Go and find my Lord Grey and tell him that as Lieutenant Colonel Venner is incapacitated I shall lead the Red Regiment until the duke makes other arrangements.' He had to shout, as the discharge of so many firearms in the confined space had near deafened Nat. 'And pick up that bloody musket!'

Nat bent to retrieve his weapon and staggered out into the yard where he promptly vomited. Luckily the fight in the courtyard had stopped, the smoke slowly dissipating and the neighing of terrified horses and the crying of injured men cut through the ringing in his ears. He vaguely heard Wade giving orders for men to find a bed in the inn for the colonel until a surgeon could be found, although Nat feared that Venner's wound would prove fatal. Wiping his mouth on his sleeve he staggered towards the road to look for Lord Grey. The street was in chaos as the horsemen who were to have supported the foot were now in full retreat back towards Lyme. Nat spotted Grey and hailed him.

'My lord, my lord, I have a message for you from Major Wade!'

'Out of my way you devil, the battle is lost and every man must now look to his own safety!' He dug his spurs viciously into his horse's flanks and clattered away.

Nat starred after him. He understood that many of the horses were unused to the sounds of battle, having until recently been draught animals or coach ponies but he expected better horsemanship and leadership from Lord Grey. He returned to the inn and reported to Major Wade, who took the news without a flicker of emotion.

'If Lord Grey has seen fit to retire the horse and with Lieutenant Colonel Venner badly injured then I now command here.'

Leaving two of the rebels to take charge of the prisoners he led the remaining men back into the street. The cavalry had gone and those foot soldiers that hadn't fled with them were milling about unsure what to do next.

'We must take the far bridge if this day is not to end in ignominious defeat and the rebellion finished before it has properly begun,' Wade said.

With the help of the sergeants and corporals, the men were pushed into tight lines that stretched from one side of the wide road to the other. As they marched down the hill towards the bridge that crossed the Mangerton it soon became clear why the rebels had encountered so few militiamen in the town. The enemy had set up camp in the water meadows on the far side of the river and had thrown up a barricade across the bridge, which now bristled with muskets. The further the rebels advanced towards the bridge, the narrower the road became and they found themselves becoming more and more tightly bunched together, so much so that they were obliged to carry their muskets before them in a position that White had told them was called high port. Suddenly fire erupted from the upper stories of the houses on each side of the road in a perfectly timed ambuscade. There was a soft wet thud as a lead bullet struck the man next to Nat in the neck, his blood pumping brightly into the early morning air. At the same instant Amos Thorne was hit in the shoulder but such was the crush of bodies that both men remained upright, for the simple reason that there was no space for their bodies to fall. The rebels were unable to return fire, such was the crush that they had no room to raise their muskets to their shoulders. Those at the back of the group hesitated in the face of such destructive firepower and held back, relieving the pressure somewhat. More and more rebels were hit and without the press from behind their bodies dropped to the road.

At last the rebels could fire back although the militiamen firing from the small windows made poor targets compared to the thick crush of rebels in the open street below. Still in shock from the death of Strangeways Nat realised that had omitted to reload his musket and he could only stand and watch as his fellow rebels delivered a ragged volley. Despite their training several men had forgotten how to prepare their pieces properly under such withering fire from front and sides. Some omitted to prime their pans so that the match had nothing to ignite. Others had forgotten to withdraw their ramrods after tamping down the cartridge and lead ball, so that when they fired the thin wooden rods were shot from the end of their barrels. This was the first time that most of the rebels had been on the receiving end of fire and it proved too much. They were unable to stand. They ran.

Nat grabbed Thorne by his stout leather belt and dragged him away back up the slope towards the crossroads. He stopped at the Bull to see whether Colonel Venner needed any help but was told that he was already on his way back to the chirurgeons in Lyme. It was something of a hollow gesture by Nat as he was already supporting the badly wounded Thorne, but his part in the drama that had played out in the inn made him feel some responsibility for the colonel. The main bulk of the rebel force had yet to be engaged and although they advanced on the bridge and exchanged volleys it was clear that the militia were not to be moved. The battle was over and Wade gave the order to retire towards the western bridge which they had taken so easily just an hour or so before.

Weapons that had been discarded following the rout of the first wave or dropped by the militiamen were calmly collected and Nat used an old wooden pallet that he found in the inn's stables to lay the unfortunate Thorne on. The Chideock man was bleeding heavily and his arm seemed to be held to his shoulder by little more than skin and muscle. Nat was certain that the joint had been smashed and he could see no way that Thorne would keep the arm, in fact he doubted that the man would live till nightfall. The outposts were recalled as the rebels withdrew and Nat was reunited with Thomas, who had heard the gunfire and watched the horsemen retreat but seen no action himself. He helped Nat pull Thorne's improvised sled as the friends headed for home, taking the direct route through Chideock as there was no longer any need for caution.

Every door and window was shut against them and they had to hammer long and hard and threaten to break their way in until at last Mistress Thorne opened her door. She cried aloud when she saw her husband lying on the doorstep. Thomas and Nat wanted to stay to see that Amos was put safely into his bed and to do what they could to ease his suffering but the sergeants hurried them out. Mistress Thorne was also keen for them to go.

'I do thank'e for bringing my Amos back, but now get away with you both. Don't you think there's been enough harm done here already without you two hanging around to draw attention to this house. With luck my neighbours'll be keeping away from their windows and won't have seen Amos brung back like this. Many in this village are for the king, and God alone knows what'll happen to us if it be seen that Amos has turned traitor.'

Nat and Thomas hurried on their way, thankful that they had survived their first action, but their joy was cut short when Major Wade ordered that an ambush be set to discourage the militia from following. Stopping at Thorne's house had put the two friends at the back of the rebels' group and they were told to take up position behind some thick hedges just outside Morcombelake where the road passed between steep hills which would prevent the enemy from outflanking them.

'Well my friend it seems that our day is not yet done and we may still get to meet our maker on this sabbath day,' said Nat as they waited.

'Your maker, not mine,' said Thomas as he checked that his musket was ready. 'I dearly hope that I'll get the chance to see some action today.'

'Be careful what you wish for, it might just come true,' cautioned Nat. 'I do recall that you yourself had thoughts of joining the militia once.'

'That I did, once. But it's not proper sol'juring, them's only playing at it like overgrown boys. I were told that they don't even practice with powder and shot for lack of funds. A couple of weeks each year in a training camp where their colonels can show 'em off and play with 'em like toys, the rest of the year putting down conventicles or chasing runaways. That's not the sort of sol'juring I want.'

'Well I'm glad that you didn't join the militia Thomas, otherwise it might have been you that I was fighting back there in Bridport.'

They fell silent, each lost in their own thoughts, the only sounds being the screeching of a far-away barn owl in some woods to their right and the whispered conversations of the other rebels that waited in ambush. The militia eventually came into view but they were wary of an ambuscade and seeing that the road ahead of them was empty their lieutenant called off the pursuit. They turned around and went back to towards Bridport, boasting loudly to each other about the part that they had played in their victory and happy that they would not be called upon to expose themselves to further risk of harm. Once they were out of sight, the signal was given for the ambush to be abandoned and the two friends climbed slowly from their positions behind the hedgerow and set out back towards Lyme. Thomas wanted to talk but Nat had no mind to.

'Why so morose Nat, we have both survived our first action, if indeed it is now over. A stroll back to hot food and a comfy bed awaits us both.'

Nat said nothing, he just stared at the instrument of death that he carried in his shaking hands. As they approached the outskirts of Lyme a familiar figure came hurrying towards them.

'Thank the Lord you are both safe!' cried John Carver. 'I was afeared that you were dead.'

'Why so?' enquired Thomas.

'Lord Grey rode back into the town exclaiming that all was lost and that the army had been cut to pieces. The duke set out immediately to assess the situation for himself and to cover any retreat only to find the army retiring in good order but when I couldn't see you two among the men my heart sank. It was only when old Aaron Smith, who took a light wound in his leg told me that he thought you might have been left behind in ambush that I dared to hope.'

Nat looked into his father's eyes, his own wet with tears. 'Father, did you ever knowingly kill a man? The Good Book instructs that we should not kill and yet I have this day ended a man's life.'

John sat down at the side of the road and bade Nat to join him. Thomas had the good sense to leave father and son alone.

'I know the teachings in Exodus,' said John softly. 'During the siege of '44 I fired my piece numerous times at the king's men that threatened our town but I cannot truly say if I ever hit one of them, even though I intended to. If your soul is troubled then speak with Parson Sprake when you get home.'

This seemed like good advice and Nat sought out Hezekiah immediately upon his return despite the early hour. Eliza, her eyes still full of sleep and her hair untidy was overjoyed to see Nat in one piece and wanted to hear the whole story but Nat told her that he needed to speak to her father first. Parson Sprake listened to him without interruption.

'My soul is in torment; I killed a man in Bridport. I can't get the image of him out of my mind, I can see him slithering down the wall leaving a thick smear of blood every time I close my eyes.'

'I am pleased that you find the act so troubling my son as nothing stains a man's soul as horribly as killing. Too many men rejoice in such things, young Thomas among them I fear. Truly God commanded that thou shalt not kill, but sometimes the taking of another's life is justified. Does Matthew not warn that they who take the sword shall perish with the sword and Leviticus confirms that their blood will be on their own heads?'

Nat nodded his agreement but still looked troubled.

'War is evil Nathaniel, a necessary evil sometimes, but an evil all the same. Just do your duty to your religion and your family and only kill if you have no alternative.'

Sprake's wise words helped but Nat was in no mood to spend time with Eliza, knowing that he would be poor company and he returned home to his bed in Coombe Street. Young Daniel wanted to hear the story of the night's action just as Eliza had, but John cuffed his ear and told him that Nat needed to rest.

'There be plenty of time for stories once your brother's rested a while.'

As Nat curled up under his thin sheets he knew that it would probably not be the last time he would be called upon to kill a man and he prayed to God that it would never get easier.

Thomas called into the smithy the next morning and as they breakfasted John told the pair what he had been able to piece together from the various rumours and tales about the action at Bridport.

'It would seem that we lost one man in every ten last night.'

'As many as that?' questioned Thomas.

'So I'm told, although about half that number are missing rather than listed as dead or wounded. I've little doubt that some of those will come creeping back home in the next day or so.'

'Can't really blame them for keeping their heads down when the action started,' Nat said. 'The reality of warfare is a long way removed from the romantic notion that some folks have of it. And what of the enemy losses?'

'About the same as ours its reckoned by our sergeant.'

'Would have been a lot more than that if I'd been able to get at them instead of being stuck back at the bridge,' complained Thomas.

'Don't you be so keen to get killing young Thomas,' cautioned John. 'Anyways it seems that the enemy losses were all killed or wounded, they had none go missing as far as we can tell.'

'What none? What about all those that deserted the militia and came over to us as was promised?'

'None, not a single man 'parently.'

'But we knows that there were some cos we saw them on the way to Bridport, didn't us Nat? We took several prisoners and any number of deserters.'

'They always say that the first casualty in war is the truth,' nodded John sagely. 'I know t'was expected that more would change sides once the fighting started, what with so many of the militia being good Protestant boys at heart, but the thinking is that with them being in the houses and behind the barricade, their officers were able to keep a close eye on them. It'll be a different story if we take them on in the open where men can slip away easier, you mark my words.'

Nat had been listening to the conversation as he used a thick slice of bread to mop the last of the egg from his plate. 'Wasn't a total disaster though,' he said as he stuffed the last morsel into his mouth. 'We took upwards of thirty horses and we've made them think twice about marching on Lyme. Gives us more time to recruit and train.'

'True enough son,' said his father 'and you boys was facing overwhelming odds from what I can tell and still came out evens.'

'And if the bloody horse under Grey had shown any metal we would've carried the day easily,' added Thomas.

Rebells Marching out of Lime

10 THE RACE TO AXMINSTER

Monday 15th June 1685

The army was allowed to rest after returning from Bridport and most took the opportunity to attend Sunday services, either at the various meeting houses or the parish church. With so many men come to join the duke the town was crowded and Pastor Sprake was obliged to hold his prayer meeting in the street outside the Silver Street property, such were the numbers wishing to attend. After the services, the rest of the day was given over to repairing equipment and making fresh cartridges. Nat was sat at the big table that dominated the kitchen in the small cottage attached to the smithy showing Nancy how to produce the cartridges, following the instructions he himself had been given only the previous day.

'First you need to measure out the correct amount of powder, like so. Place the powder onto the paper, pop in a ball then roll the paper into a tube being careful not to spill any!'

'Right done it, what next?'

'Twist both ends of the paper tube and you're done.' Nat had only fired that one fateful shot on the previous day but still felt the need to make extra cartridges for the battles that surely lay ahead, as the king in London was unlikely to give up his throne without a fight. Some of the men had been issued with bandoliers that held twelve measured charges in stoppered wooden tubes, the so called twelve apostles, carrying the balls separately in a pouch, whilst others had a cartridge box which they attached to their belts. Nat had neither and had to make do with his coat pockets, prepared cartridges in one and a flask of fine powder for priming his pan in the other.

'I think that's enough Nancy, thank you. We're making an early start in the morning so I will wish you a good night.' He opened the door that stood to the right of the hearth and took the steep stairs that led to his room.

The drums sounded at 3am, calling men from their beds. It would be nearly another hour before the false dawn lightened the eastern sky and another hour beyond that before the sun appeared over the horizon. Word was that they were to leave the town and strike out for Taunton, a hotbed of non-conformity that many said was the most rebellious town in the whole of England. William Pearce confirmed that the town was full of men ready to join the cause and they knew from old Amos

Thorne that agents had been sent to raise the town even before the duke had landed at Lyme. When they had marched to Bridport the previous night they had carried only enough food for one day but now the order was for each man to have provisions for four days, easy enough for those who lived in the town but all but impossible to source for those who had come in from the surrounding country. Nat's two shoulder bags were stuffed with dried fish, fresh baked bread and hard cheese. He had two boiled eggs carefully wrapped in cloth, a large potato that had been cooked in the embers of the fire and a large meat pasty, baked for him by Nancy. In addition, he had a couple of pints of rough cider in a stoneware flagon and two apples that had been picked the previous autumn and carefully stored. There would not be much to take from the hedgerows at this time of year and he hoped that the contents of his bags would suffice, but he doubted it. It was simply not possible to carry enough food for four days with his pockets already full of cartridges and powder.

Opening the cottage door Nat was assailed by the noise of an army preparing to march. Horses snorted, orders were being barked and farewells were being exchanged. The men marching away wondered when they would next see their homes and loved ones, those remaining feared that they may be waving goodbye for the last time. Nat thanked Nancy for the pasty and said a tearful goodbye to his brother Daniel, but when he came to take his leave of his father, John told him that he would be going with him.

'The army will need a good blacksmith to march with it,' he said. He was wearing a green sash across his greatcoat, denoting that he was part of Lt-Col Abraham Holmes' regiment.

'You just look out for yourself father!'

'Don't you worry about me son. That fine young man who came to dine with us, Master Foe, 'as been attached to my regiment as a gintl'mun scout so he can watch out for I.'

Nat spotted Eliza in the throng and excusing himself to his father pushed through the crowd to talk to her. He had avoided her all day Sunday but she seemed to understand why and Nat supposed that her father must have told her of their earlier conversation.

'Hurry home safely, we have a wedding to arrange,' she cried. 'Remember though we be miles apart it'll be the same moon shining down on us both, so promise me that you'll say goodnight to me each night by the light of that moon.'

And thus they parted. Little did Nat know that apart from in his dreams he would not see that sweet face again for many long months.

It was nigh on thirty miles from Lyme to Taunton and whilst a fit man could do that distance in a day, the new recruits were soon to learn that an army on the march is ponderously slow, hence the need for them to carry so much food. They knew they'd receive a friendly welcome in Axminster, which lay on the road to Taunton, as Hezekiah Sprake had received such assurances from the minister of the large congregational church there and Nat hoped they would be able to top up their supplies there. More men had arrived since the night attack on Bridport and the army numbered near three thousand when they started up Silver Street, heading for the village of Uplyme which stood astride the road to Axminster. The troops were cheered all the way to the top of the town and beyond and Nat felt ten feet tall as he climbed the steep hill. The Red Regiment, now commanded by Major Wade following Venner's incapacitation, had been given pride of place in the column, the vanguard. Confidence was high due to the number of new men that had come in and the prevailing opinion among the rank and file was that blame for the debacle at Bridport could be laid firmly at the door of the badly mounted, inadequately trained and poorly led cavalry. It would be a different story next time they told themselves.

Not every man carried a musket or pike, there were simply not enough to go around although all had some type of weapon even if it were only a logging axe or pitchfork.

'I thought the duke had promised us that he had more than enough arms for us all,' Thomas complained to Nat.

'I've heard that he expected more men to bring their own weapons, muskets taken down from their hangings above fireplaces or squirrelled away since the civil war.'

Even so the army made a fine sight as they marched, the men singing psalms and the crowd cheering. As they followed a tributary of the River Lim into the hills to the north of Lyme they left behind the familiar smells of seaweed and salt, the plaintive calls of the gulls and the sound of the breaking waves, and many of the men wondered when they would experience these smells and sounds again. Little were they to know that many in the column would never see Dorset again. It was hot work toiling up the hill and the pikemen were glad that they had been ordered to discard their heavy body armour.

'Waste of good metal if you asks I,' complained John, 'although I'm sure that young Daniel'll be able to pick some up for use in the smithy. One man's rubbish is another man's treasure as the saying is.'

'Shouldn't of brung 'em in the first place,' said his marching companion who was armed with only a stout wooden cudgel, 'then there might have been money to get me a musket like yours.'

The lead elements soon crossed the border into Devon passing through the villages of Uplyme and Yawl where the stream had cut a deep valley through the soft limestone of Yawl bottom. The old soldiers in the army feared that the steep wooded hills would make for a good ambuscade, but Monmouth had posted his few precious horsemen on either flank and the column was able to proceed in relative safety. Most of the infantry had little faith in the cavalry after Bridport and many openly questioned why Lord Grey had retained his command as he strutted about in all his finery.

'Like a bloody peacock on heat,' moaned Thomas. Nat nodded his agreement and was about to comment when Pastor Sprake rode up. Because he owned his own horse the pastor had been given a post in the duke's cavalry.

'Good day Nathaniel.' The pastor always used Nat's full name. Once again he refused to acknowledge Thomas. 'A fine day. Can't stop to chat I'm afraid, picket duty calls.' As he made to ride off Nat quickly asked him about Lord Grey.

Sprake leant down from the saddle and spoke quietly, 'the duke is reliant on men of quality and position joining him if this noble venture is to succeed so he cannot be seen to dismiss my Lord Grey, the only titled gentleman who has so far answered the call to arms. Truly it does not sit easy with me either, but that is how it has to be at least until further members of the gentry come in. If history has taught us anything it is that even with the help of God, popular rebellions need the support of the nobility if they are to succeed.'

As the stream they were following petered out and the valley sides fell away the vanguard came to a crossroads where the track to Axminster was crossed by the main road from Bridport to Honiton. There was a fine sturdy tavern at the junction, ironically called the King's Head and the men were all for stopping to slake their thirst, but the corporals and sergeants prevented them from doing so.

'Keep moving, keep moving! The militias of Somersetshire and Dorsetshire b'aint far off and the duke needs to reach Axminster afore them.'

Harsh words were exchanged as a few headstrong characters, new to military discipline and unused to obeying orders decided to stop anyway to sample the inn's wares. Samuel White noticed that the landlord had decided he could make good money from what must have seemed to him to be an endless supply of customers and was charging a groat a quart, well above the normal asking price. Thomas and Nat marched past the inn, but not without a wistful glance back as those that had broken ranks were dragged out and reminded of the solemn covenant that they had signed, or at least put their mark to, when they had joined the duke's army.

They had been on the road for some two hours when riders on lathered horses approached the front of the column and the rumours regarding the nearness of the militia forces were confirmed. Those from Devon had left Exeter the previous morning and had already passed through Honiton, whilst the Somersetshire militia had left their camps in Chard and Crewkerne and were advancing along the line of the river Axe. The race was on to reach Axminster and the rebels needed to gain the town before the two converging enemy forces could unite. The Red Regiment being at the front of the column were sent to cover the most immediate threat, the Devonshire men who were approaching from the west. Whilst the bulk of the army made straight for Axminster, Wade's men were directed to the south of the town to cross the river Axe near the ruins of Newenham Abbey. With their officers chivvying them along they began to climb out of the wide river valley towards the village of Kilmington where the tower of St Giles church could be seen poking its head through the trees on the hillside. All semblance of order was lost as the men hurried to take the high ground of Shute Hill. It was near three miles from the crossroads with its welcoming inn and it seemed to Nat that they had run the whole way. Having reached the summit, the men started down the far side when Major Wade called on them to stop. He had spotted what he believed to be a strong defensive position overlooking the Umborne Valley through which the road from Honiton ran and the men sank to the ground in thankful exhaustion.

'On your feet men!' came the cry just as they had started to remove their boots and massage their aching feet. 'These guns have to be sited afore the enemy arrive.'

Two cannons had been dispatched from the main army and as they were dragged past him by commandeered plough horses Nat noticed that the barrels were different sizes. The sweating gunners called on the infantrymen to help move the heavy guns and being interested in anything made of metal Nat took the opportunity to question them about the pieces.

'This bigger one's called a saker which fires a five-pound ball. The small one's a Falcon, that fires a much lighter ball at just under three pounds, but still enough to make a mess of anything that gets in its way.'

'And how far will they throw a ball?'

'Both of them are effective up to a mile or more, but the closer the better.'

'Surely having different sizes means that you need two lots of ammunition. Doesn't that cause problems?'

'Of course it do, but the duke had to buy what was available. King James' agents made sure that most of the usual sources were closed to us.'

The guns were soon in position and the men were told that they could rest again. It was just past midday and the sun was at its hottest as the soldiers sat and sipped at their quickly diminishing supply of cider or stuffed down food from their bags, knowing that they could replenish their supply when they reached Axminster. Thomas noted that old Sergeant White ate sparingly.

'Not hungry old man?'

'Enough of the *old*, Edgecott. It's Sergeant White to you! When you've been in the army as long as I have you learn to eat only what you need to and save the rest in case you can't find no more.'

Nat had just closed his eyes and laid back on the soft turf when they were ordered to their feet again and sent across the road and take position behind a thick hedge. Many of the hedges they could see from their elevated position were thin and straight, planted within the last twenty years or so by the gentry to enclose what had once been common land. Being denied access to the land which had been used by their forefathers for generations, many ordinary country folk had found their circumstances much reduced and White reckoned that this was a factor in many joining the rebel ranks. The hedge that Nat now crouched behind was much older and was thick with ash and blackthorn, so dense in fact that Sergeant Stuckley had called for loopholes to be cut through it so that they might get a better view of the approaches to the hilltop. The valley of the Umborne was stretched out before them, a patchwork of fields with the odd yellow patch showing where the grass had already been cut and set aside to provide winter fodder. The brook itself glittered in the early afternoon sun while the hearth fires in the tiny hamlet of Wilmington sent up thin columns of smoke that hung lazily in the clear blue sky. A darker smudge on the horizon indicated the position of Honiton. Most of the colourful spring flowers had gone over and the bright whites of the last of the cow parsley and hogweed were starting to dull. In a few days the dog roses and elders would come into flower to transform the hedgerows where now the only splash of colour was provided by the profusion of red campions. Some of the younger lads with energy to spare despite the long march began throwing the dart-like ears of false barley at each other, scoring points whenever one of the projectiles caught in hair or beard. The bees hummed busily and Nat had just closed his eyes again when the bucolic tranquillity was shattered by a cavalry scout who arrived from the west and slid to a halt beside Sergeant Stuckley. After a brief exchange he was on his way again, to report to the duke in Axminster.

'Stand to!' shouted Stuckley. 'The Dorsetshire militia have reached Wilmington and will be upon us within the half-hour.' Men rose to their feet somewhat reluctantly and checked their weapons. There were no pikemen with the picket, so to protect themselves against any enemy cavalry the men would have to rely on the shelter of the hedge and the short swords or bayonets they had been issued with. The bayonet had to be inserted into the end of the musket barrel meaning that once attached, the musket could not be fired, so it was only to be used as a last resort. William Pearce, the Taunton weaver, hoped that he would not need to use his bayonet as this would mean that the enemy horsemen had survived the hail of musket balls that the rebels would fling down the slopes and would soon be among them dealing death with their long swords. Old soldiers had frightened the new recruits by telling how a cavalryman could cleave a man from the top of his head to his breastbone with one powerful stroke. Nat watched the valley nervously and at length the enemy came into view, keeping to the north bank of the Umborne Brook. It was the hint of movement on the otherwise still plain and the cloud of fine dust that they kicked up that caught Nat's attention, as unlike the militia they had fought at Bridport these men wore coats of green that merged with the surrounding fields and hedgerows. Despite the different coloured coats their appearance was enough to bring back horrific memories for Nat of the charnel house of the Bull Inn. The militia reached the foot of Shute Hill and started to climb the long slope, their colours hanging limply in the still air and the rebels made ready. The guns had been well sited and when the enemy vanguard came within half a mile the gun masters touched their glowing slow-matches to the quills that had been filled with fine loose powder and inserted into a venthole in the top of the barrels. There were two deafening bangs as jets of flame erupted from the end of the barrels together with a huge cloud of dirty black/grey smoke. It was the first time that the raw recruits had heard the cannons fired and those closest to the guns found that their ears were ringing.

'Sorry about that!' grinned the nearest gunner. 'I should've warned you!' The effect of the cannon fire could not be discerned at such a distance, apart from the fact that the enemy lines had stopped dead. It seems that they were as unused to artillery as the rebels and had not expected to be welcomed into Axminster in such a manner. Thomas expected another discharge from the guns and covered his ears but nothing happened. In response to his pleas to fire again the master gunner, a dutchman named Anton Buyse who had arrived on the *Helderenberg* with the duke replied in his broken English that they would be happy to oblige, but that it took five minutes to prepare their pieces for another shot. Encouraged by their officers the enemy took advantage of this delay to continue their advance. White had told them that a musket had a maximum range of some 300 yards, although they were not accurate above twenty, but Sergeant Stuckley ordered the men to fire as soon as the militia had covered half of the distance towards the hedge. They were well out of effective range but Stuckley didn't really expect to actually bring any of the enemy down, instead he was hoping that the musket fire added to the threat of the cannon would be enough to persuade the enemy to reconsider their position. It worked, the frightened militia deciding that discretion was the better part of valour and realising that they would not be able to clear the hill they turned back the way they had come.

'At them boys!' shouted the sergeant. 'Don't let them rest, chase they buggers all the way back to Honiton.'

The rebels gave a great shout and left the cover of the hedgerow, Thomas to the fore hoping to make up for his inaction at Bridport. Struggling to fix their bayonets as they went, they started down the slope hooting and hollering, only to be halted by the duke himself who had ridden from the town to assess the situation.

'Let them go! It is not my business to fight this day. Our need is to press on to Taunton before my uncle can send his regular troops.'

Nat received these orders with mixed feelings. He was happy that he would not be exposed to further danger and that he would not be faced with the prospect of taking another life, but it did seem that they were passing up an ideal opportunity to gain some degree of revenge for the setback at Bridport.

Thomas was more obviously frustrated. 'Just when will I get my chance to fight?' he snarled.

Nat was struggling to remove his bayonet from the end of his musket's barrel. 'God help us if we ever need to rely on these things.' He had managed to cut his hand quite badly trying to ram it into the barrel in the first place and several of the men were complaining that the stupid things had fallen out of the barrels for want of pushing them in hard enough. Leaving a picket guard of horse to keep watch on the militia, the foot soldiers trudged back through Kilmington to Axminster and were directed to a field high above the River Axe which wound its lazy way northwards towards Chard, and told to make camp.

11 FIRST NIGHT AWAY FROM HOME

Monday 15th June 1685

Whilst Nat and Thomas had been helping to put the Devonshire militia to flight on Shute Hill, the rest of the army had reached Axminster, brushing aside small detachments of enemy militiamen on the way. As the balance of Wade's Red Regiment and Foulkes' Whites secured the town itself, John's Green Regiment were sent to guard the approaches from the east where the Somersetshire militia could be seen regrouping in preparation for an attack. Having not been involved at Bridport this would be the first action for Lt Col Holmes' men and they were suitably apprehensive. Holmes picked up on their fears and strode up and down the line of rebels manning the hasty barricade that they had thrown across the road.

'Remember men, they are more frightened of you than you are of them.'

'Blerry doubt that,' came the reply. Holmes pretended that he was out of earshot.

'But just to make things a little more uncomfortable for the enemy I intend to deploy a small deception that I have seen used once before.' As he said this a number of draught horses approached from the direction of the town dragging sawn off tree trunks behind them.'

'Us've already got a big enough barricade I reckons,' said one of the men.

'Indeed we have,' replied Holmes, 'but if you look you will see that I have ordered that the ends of the trunks be covered in black tar. Placed end on towards the enemy they will look like cannon barrels. I believe that will be sufficient deterrent to stop them approaching any closer.'

The militia under their inexperienced commanders saw what Holmes wanted them to see and kept their distance and in time the majority of the rebels were allowed to leave the barricade in search of food and shelter.

It had been another scorching hot day and Thomas realised that he had not eaten since midday. He and Nat collected firewood from a copse that stood in the corner of the field where the army had made their camp and they soon had a good fire going to enable them to make a thin stew, each man around the blaze contributing what he could from the supplies that they carried in their bags. Although told to bring four day's rations with them this had proved all but impossible as Nat had feared and many were already beginning to run low.

Some of the men had brought their wives with them rather than leave them at home even though this was not officially permitted, but there was no stopping the poor wretches from simply following the army as it advanced. It was just as well for the rest of the men that the women were present for they had had the foresight to bring pots and kettles with them, very few of the men having thought to do the same.

After they had finished their meal the men discussed the day's events, each one looking to talk up his own part, even though in truth most had done very little.

'I'm sure I saw the bugger I was aiming at fall!' boasted Thomas.

'I doubt it at that distance,' replied Nat.

'Well I'm counting it anyway,' said Thomas as he carved a small notch into the stock of his musket. 'One to me!'

Nat shook his head sadly. 'I do worry for your soul Thomas.'

'My soul be damned! Ain't no such thing. I'm here to kill the enemy. Ain't no point being in the army if you ain't going to kill anybody!'

At that point John came to sit with them and scraped some stew from the pot, leaving a small quantity in the bottom. After listening to the exaggerated tales of the brush with the Devonshire militia he told those still around the fire how things had gone on the other side of town.

'As soon as we came within sight of the town it were clear that the Somersetshire boys had beaten us to it. Even so we advanced bravely and before a shot could be fired they dropped their weapons and fled, throwing off whatever they could to lighten their load. Major Perrott had us chase them but there were no catching 'em so we contented ourselves with collecting their off-casts. Now half of Colonel Holmes' regiment be sporting nice government issued red coats and every man who wants a musket can have one.'

'Why did they run? Are the Somersetshire men so much worse than the Dorsetshire boys who wuz so resolute at Bridport?' Nat asked his father.

'They had no fight in 'em son. Unlike at Bridport where the officers were able to keep a firm hand on 'em, out here in open country so to speak they were able to slip away more easily. I shouldn't be s'prised to see some of 'em that scarpered make their way over to us once it gets full dark. Oh their officers did manage to round up enough to threaten us but Colonel Holmes' ruse put paid to that.' He described the trick with the tree trunks to everyone's amusement.

John's prophecy about deserters proved right as a number of former militiamen presented themselves to the rebel's pickets throughout the night. One such was Ralph Cleeve who after being briefly questioned by Lieutenant Ascue was allowed to join the rebels clustered around the dying embers of their campfires. John and Nat shuffled apart to let the newcomer sit between them.

'Welcome master.....?'

'Cleeve, Thomas Cleeve of Stoford.'

'Another Thomas!' cried Nat, 'just what we need!' The other men laughed, even Thomas Edgecott seemed to enjoy the jest, although he stopped smiling as soon as the attention moved away from him.

'Well met Master Cleeve, please ignore my son,' said John, before introducing Cleeve to the others who were sat around the fire. 'Would you care to share what's left of our poor supper?'

'Thank you kindly, I've not eaten since this morning.' Cleeve helped himself to the remains of the stew that nestled in the bottom of the blackened pot.

'I see you wears the colours of the militia, how do you come to be sat by our fire?'

In between mouthfuls Cleeve told his tale.

'As I said, the name's Thomas Cleeve. I have work as a carpenter in Stoford. It's a small village just to the south of Yeovil,' he added seeing the blank looks on their faces. 'I've been in the militia for a couple of years now. The girls seemed to like the uniform and it was a bit of an adventure when we went off training. Three or four times a year, just for a couple of days at a time with a longer gathering once a year when we'd meet at Ilchester with other militias and get a chance to fire our muskets and march about a bit. We were given a good set of clothes and a bit or pay, it was all a bit of fun really, until they started to use us to break up the conventicles that is.'

'We had plenty of experience of that ourselves in Lyme,' said Nat, 'nasty bullies the lot of 'em.'

'Don't be so quick to judge them so harshly Master Carver, most of us disliked that job and made up any number of reasons to be excused from the duty. Most of the militia around here are just like you, honest Protestants who want to be left alone to practice their religion in peace. Tis true that some relished the chance to throw their weight around and rough up those who can't defend themselves, but not the majority. Besides, our colonel is the local squire and would see to it that any man refusing an order would soon find himself with no home and no work in the parish.'

'But now you're here with us. How so?'

'This war, if it can be called a war when one is facing one's own countrymen, brings out the worst in people.'

Nat glanced at his friend Thomas as Cleeve continued.

'I always used to enjoy the company of my fellows as I may have said, but recently some elements have taken to heavy drinking and blasphemy. What had been good natured tomfoolery turned to the making of hellish oaths and ribaldry and I realised that I was on the wrong side of the fence so to speak, so when I saw how close your fires were I decided that it was time to change sides. It wasn't easy to avoid the pickets and I had to wade chest deep through the River Axe to reach the duke's camp, but I must admit that I already find the company here more agreeable!'

'Thank you!' smiled John. 'Were you part of the action on the east of the town? We wuz expecting a stiff fight there, but the militia simply turned around and marched away.'

'I was there. We were all ready to attack, most of us against our better conscience when we saw them cannons pointing straight down the road at us. You must remember that we are little more than part-time soldiers so the sight of them dirty great big gun barrels was more than enough to dissuade us.'

To Cleeve's bewilderment the others chuckled. John explained the ruse.

'Well they looked real enough to us,' laughed Cleeve, 'although I doubt if regular troops would've been fooled.'

The more Cleeve talked, the more the others realised that the men of the militia were very much the same whichever county they came from. Decent men for the most part, men who had no great desire to fight against fellow Englishmen, most of whom shared their own religious beliefs and were as keen to see the end of the popish threat as the rebels were.

Morale was still high. The campaign was just four days old but was going as well as most could have hoped. John was missing his home and family as much as any other man in the army but he still had some food in his bag, the local populace were supportive and even allowing for Bridport it was clear that most of the militia had little stomach for a fight.

'One bit of bad news I did hear though,' he said, 'is that the pastor of the Congregational Church in Axminster has declared that the bible forbids any of his flock from bearing arms, no matter how just our cause.'

'But Pastor Sprake was convinced that the bigger part of the town's non-conformist community would join the army. He told me he had received assurances to the fact. Perhaps he'll be able to talk them round.'

'Well whatever happens I must be off back to the Greens,' said John sleepily. 'Wouldn't do to wake up in the wrong regiment.' The men around the fire said their goodnights then fell silent, each lost in his own thoughts.

As so often happens after a cloudless day, the night was clear and chilly and Nat was glad that he had thought to stuff his nightcap and a warm linen full-shirt into his bag, his daytime half-shirt would not have been anywhere near warm enough on its own. None of the new recruits from Lyme and the surrounding countryside were used to campaigning as the old hands called it and so had not foreseen the necessity of bringing blankets, thinking that they would be moving from one friendly town or village to the next with accommodation provided. It had not occurred to them that the army was so large that even the biggest borough in the west country would be hard pressed to find so many beds. Nat gazed up at the bright moon and said goodnight to Eliza as he had promised. It took him a fair while to get to sleep as he lay on the grass, now wet with the evening dew and he resolved to barter or beg for some form of bed clothing when he reached the next village. He wasn't the only one thinking of the fair Eliza that night. Hard though he tried to conjure up an image of Sarah at the Mariner's Inn, it was the face of Pastor Sprake's lovely daughter that Thomas saw when he closed his eyes.

12 THE MARCH CONTINUES

Tuesday 16th June 1685

It seemed to Nat that no sooner had he dropped off than the drums were sounding and orders were being given to break camp. He was used to rising with the sun to set the smithy up for the day's work but quite why the army felt it necessary to rise so early he did not yet understand. So much of this military life was still strange and new to him. The men shuffled into column without the chance to break their fasts and made ready to march. Thomas Cleeve marched with Nat and Thomas and was not surprised by the large number of men he saw wearing the uniform of the Somersetshire militia.

'Added to the number of men I knows for certain did a runner after seeing they cannons pointed at us yesterday, I'd say that the Duke of Somerset must have lost near half of the thousand militiamen he started the day with.'

As the column prepared to leave the town, Pastor Lane of the Congregational Church presented himself to the duke.

'Your grace, although my conscience prevents me from taking up arms, I wish to accompany the army to provide spiritual guidance and support to those of my community who have decided to join you.'

Despite Lane's opposition upwards of a hundred men from the town had made their way to the campsite during the course of the previous day to swear their allegiance to the duke.

'I thank you for your offer and would be pleased to accommodate you in this,' Monmouth replied. He knew the value of reminding the men that they marched to do God's will but in truth he already had more than enough preachers in the army and Lane would be just another mouth to feed.

Axminster to Taunton is about twenty miles and Thomas Edgecott's experience of the march from Lyme told him that they would be unlikely to reach that great town on the River Tone by nightfall. A man walking on his own could make the distance easily if he put his mind to it but not an army with its long lines of men, wagons and horse drawn cannon. And so it proved. It was a scorching hot day again with the weather showing no signs of breaking. As they marched Thomas and Nat fell into conversation with John Harries, a weaver from Lyme and a couple of others who had joined the army at Axminster. The Axminster men were complaining about the early start.

'Well I for one likes these early starts,' said Harries. 'A brand new day, fresh as a daisy with all the promise of new adventures, new sights and maybe a pretty girl or two along the way!'

'We could all do with a pretty girl or two,' quipped one of the Axminster men drawing a round of laughter. Thomas noticed that Nat had not joined in.

'Not our Nat! He's strictly a one-woman man, he can think of none other than the lovely Eliza.'

'What's she like then Nat? Does she plough well?' one of the Axminster men asked to more laughter.

Nat rounded on the man, balling his hands into fists. 'That's enough of such ungodly talk. I'll ask you to keep your filthy tongue to yourself! There will be time enough for intimacy once Eliza and I are wed.'

'Once we are wed,' Thomas mimicked under his breath. 'Fuck that, I'd show her what a real man could do long before any wedding.'

The army took The Fosse Way, the old Roman road that followed the course of the River Axe. The road clung to the sides of the valley some little way above the river which lay to their right, whilst to their left the land rose gently towards the bulk of the Blackdown Hills. By the time they reached the tiny village of Tytherleigh they were ready for a rest and with the militias seemingly dispersed there was far less urgency than on the previous day's march, so the captains allowed the men time to sit and prepare a quick meal. Being an old soldier White knew that in the army one had to take every opportunity to eat, sleep or obtain clean water, so he slipped down to the Axe and replaced the tepid water in his earthenware bottle. He paused in his climb back up from the river to admire the spectacle of the rebel army spread across the fields outside the village. It was an impressive sight even for a man who had marched with Cromwell's Army, although he was saddened to think that once again so large a force had been assembled to fight against fellow Englishmen.

After Tytherleigh the army left the Fosse Way, turning away from the river which swung sharply to the east, and without anyone being aware they crossed the unmarked border into Somerset. Stephen Dabinett, a joiner who had walked from the nearby hamlet of Chardstock with twenty of his neighbours had been allocated to the Red Regiment to replace its losses from Bridport and he said that the road they were following led to Chard, some three to four miles further on. Tatworth, Winsham and Thorncombe all provided recruits as the army marched through the area and the fresh food and cider that they brought with them was most welcome. Whilst some like Dabinett were used to fill gaps others were being formed into new regiments. Samuel White, Thomas and Nat had been in the Red Regiment from the start, and John was in the Greens, but there was now a White Regiment under two of the professional soldiers who had landed with the duke at Lyme, Lt Col Foulkes and Ensign Fox. A Yellow Regiment had also been formed under Lt Col Edward Matthews, an ex-guards officer, whose second in command was a London brewer called Major Perrott, famous for having once tried to steal the crown jewels from the Tower of London. All the regiments, new and old, were commanded by Lieutenant Colonels so as to leave the colonelcies open for the nobles that were expected to join the rebellion but such niceties were lost on the men who simply referred to their leaders as 'colonel'. The men marched as if in a daze, plodding along the dry stony track. Thomas was chatting to the man next to him.

'I can't wait to see some action. Can't be long before we meets the enemy. What'ya think?'

The other man didn't answer, he was staring over Thomas' shoulder. Thomas turned to follow his gaze and saw a dust cloud that seemed to be getting nearer by the second.

'Horsemen!' he cried, 'the bloody militia must've reformed!'

'Unless they be reg'lers.'

'Prepare to receive cavalry!' shouted the sergeants, although in truth there was no time to deploy properly. The cavalry were too near and the rebels insufficiently trained or practiced to undertake the necessary manoeuvres. Nat was in two minds whether he should attempt to prepare his musket to fire or fix his bayonet and it therefore came as a great relief to all when the horsemen reigned in and waved in greeting.

'Thank fuck for that!' muttered Thomas having lost some of his bravado in the face of a mounted attack.

The duke was advised of their arrival and rode over to meet them as their lathered horses munched contentedly on the luscious grass that grew beside the track. Thomas was too far away to catch what passed between the horsemen and the duke but word soon made its way through to the waiting soldiers that the horsemen had ridden across from Ilminster under their captain John Speke. The thirty or so men were a welcome addition to an army already brimming with confidence but still lacking in cavalry. After that first inconclusive fight at Bridport the enemy had shown their reluctance to come to terms and the rebels were now within half a day of Taunton where they were promised a great welcome.

'I can't wait for they buggers in the militia to try and take us on again. We'll soon put 'em to flight,' boasted Thomas to Samuel White after he had regained his composure. The weavers, tradesmen and artisans who had rushed to join the rebellion may have been confident, but White who had seen plenty of action before added a note of caution.

'Enthusiasm be a good thing, but the duke'll have to guard against over-confidence. I likes your faith in the boys young Edgecott but have a mind we've only faced up to they militia so far, it'll be a different matter when us comes face to face with the reg'lers. That's when over-confidence can be dangerous; it's far too easy to get carried away and make mistakes and in war a mistake is usually fatal.'

'Silly old fool, what's he know about anything?' Thomas muttered once White had moved away.

The extra horsemen that Speke had brought with him were put to immediate use guarding the flanks of the column as it tramped on towards Taunton before being turned off the track into a large field just outside the town of Chard. As the men clustered around their campfires the conversation turned to James' succession and it was clear that not all in the rebel army were fighting purely to protect the Protestant church.

'I tell'e, in our village there weren't much fuss made about James becoming king,' said one of the men.

'Because...?'

'Because, after all the turmoil with the first King Charles being killed, Cromwell's commonwealth ending as it did, then Monmouth's father coming back it was nice for power to pass peacefully....and he did swear to protect the Church of England.'

'Oh, and you trusts him to keep his word do you?'

'Why not?'

'Why not? Cos he's a bloody Catholic that's why and he's so far up the pope's arse that he'll come out his holiness' mouth if that papist bastard burps. If that weren't bad enough he's married to a bloody for'in Catholic so even if he'd a mind to keep 'is promises you can bet she'll persuade him otherwise. We all know how much power wives really have over their husbands!'

'Keep her legs closed and he'll do or say anything to open them again!' They all laughed at that.

'I'm just saying that kings rule by divine right,' persisted the first speaker, 'it's not man's place to question that.'

'And by divine right the new king should be Charles' eldest son, in other words the Duke of Monmouth!'

'Unless he be base born.'

'Don't start that argument again! If you're not bothered about seeing a proper Protestant on the throne why are you in this army then?'

'I'm here cos I've no work what with the downturn in the wool trade and the duke's army seemed to offer .... opportunities.'

'Some bloody opportunities!' snapped another man. 'No food, no pay...'

'There'll be plenty to go round when we wins. They'll be made to pay!'

'And who do you think *they* are? If you haven't noticed we're fighting our own people, there's no winners in a civil war.'

'I'm just here to fight!' chipped in Thomas.

'So you've said, many times,' sighed Nat.

'I do wonder if we wouldn't be better off just waiting for King James to die,' said the man who had tried to defend James' succession. 'He must be well into his fifties by now, he can't have long left.'

'Oy! I heard that!' protested John to more laughter.

'And when he dies?' asked another man.

'Well he's got no male heir that he admits to and he's not going to get one at his age, especially after all those years of marriage.'

'I reckon that Italian bitch of his must be barren, I mean he had two daughters with his first wife, God bless her soul.'

'Exactly my point. Mary'll become queen when James goes and she's been brought up as a decent Protestant.'

'And if James does manage to sire a son before he goes to his maker?'

'He won't, not now surely!'

'At least if Monmouth seizes power we knows where we all stands.'

'Do we? The problem with power is that it attracts the worst of people and corrupts the best.'

Nat found it hard to get to sleep again, thinking of Eliza and young Daniel but they were pleasant thoughts as they were both safe in Lyme, far from any fighting. In the days that followed Nat would have occasion to be deeply worried for their safety.

Wednesday 17th June 1685

A quiet night was followed by an early rise, marked by the beating of drums. Nat was still struggling to understand why he had to get up so early each day, only to stroll from town to town with no apparent urgency and then make camp long before the day was done. He decided to ask Sergeant White.

'Tis normal enough practice in every army that I've ever known. Firstly, we need to be ready should the enemy attack. Tis a common tactic to attack just before dawn when men are at their most vulnerable, so we have to be up and ready, just in case. I don't imagine that the militia will be up for such a thing, but we 'ave no idea when the reg'ler troops'll get here from London so we 'as to be on our guard.'

This seemed sensible up to a point, except that no enemy had been seen at all since the militia had put up such a poor showing at Axminster.

'Secondly, the duke will 'ave planned where he wants to be at the end of the day's march. He will 'ave picked a place large enough to take the whole army, with a good source of fresh water and safe from attack. It's no good us aiming to get there at dusk only to find that a delay on the road leaves us short of our destination in the middle of nowhere when night falls.'

Nat nodded his head slowly, he supposed that it all made sense. The column started up and continued their slow progress northwards towards Taunton although what lay beyond that was anybody's guess. By this point most of the rebels were on unfamiliar territory but they still had enough faith in their leaders and their guides to believe that they knew what they were doing. That faith was soon to be sorely tested.

As they traipsed through another poor village an old woman dressed in rags approached Lieutenant Mitchell who was leading Nat's unit.

'Be off with you mother,' snarled Mitchell. 'There's nothing for you here.' The old hag spat and cursed vehemently and Nat broke from the ranks to hand her a piece of stale bread from his bag. The lieutenant demanded to know what he was doing.

'Beggin' your pardon sir but tis dangerous to get on the wrong side of old women, lest they put a witch's curse on you.'

'Don't be daft man, witches indeed. You country boys with your old-fashioned superstitions. I thought you were a God-fearing man.'

'I am and that's why I knows that the Devil has put witches on this earth to torment us.'

'Ha! Talk of witches in a London coffee house and they will laugh in your face before throwing you from the building.'

'Well, with respect, down here folk knows that witches are still about, even if London society has decided to ignore the fact. Three were hung down in Exeter so not long back.'

'Times are changing. The gentlemen of the Royal Society who study and understand matters of natural philosophy have long decided that witches don't exist. As for killing those accused of witchcraft, I'm certain that will soon be outlawed, just as it is no longer lawful to burn heretics.'

Nat was not convinced. He had never heard of the Royal Society or natural philosophy and he prayed that honest men would never drop their guard against the works of the Devil.

As the men plodded through the village a small scruffy dog chased after them, yapping and snapping at their heels. Some of the men picked up sticks and stones from the road to chase the scrawny beast away but the poor mongrel reminded Dabinett of his own dog Molly and he stooped to offer her a piece of cheese. He was lucky not to lose a finger as the hungry animal snatched at the proffered food. After slinking off to a dark corner to eat the cheese the dog reappeared and trotted alongside the column long after it had passed the last cottage.

'Looks like you've got yerself a new friend Stephen.'

'Only friend he's got!' laughed one of his neighbours from Chardstock.

The day grew hotter and with no wind the air hung heavy as if a thick blanket had been thrown across the countryside. Before long the passage of so many marching feet caused clouds of choking dust to rise from the tracks, adding to the discomfort of the men until a halt was called in mid-afternoon.

'Another half day! You can tell that the army is led by nobs, probably not done a full day's work in their lives,' said Thomas. 'Not that I'm complaining mind. I likes a bit of sunshine as much as any man but I prefers to be laid on my back in the grass rather than tramping along a dusty road. I just wish we could have a fight!'

The army were directed to a large field outside Ilminster where a fast-flowing stream provided fresh water for those willing to risk it and a chance to bathe for those so inclined. Working in the heat and dirt of the smithy every day Nat was used to washing the grime and sweat off in a tin tub, so he had no hesitation in plunging into the cool waters, but other were more reluctant. Nat knew that most people seldom bathed believing that there were harmful things in water, which is why most folk preferred to drink cider or ale if they could get it. Of course, from time to time it was necessary to remove the lice that lived in their rough clothing but the common practice was to wash the clothing using soap, rather than wash the body. Unfortunately, very few of the soldiers had thought to bring any soap with them, after all laundering was a woman's work. Seeing the opportunity to earn a few coins a number of women had come out from the small village that ran down to the stream and were soon hard at work at the waters' edge scrubbing the men's clothes before beating them out on the large, rounded stones that had clearly been used for that purpose for generations. Thomas watched the women closely, wondering if they might be prepared to offer other, more personal, services for a few of the battered tin or lead farthings in his purse. A quick hump whilst thinking about Eliza would be nice but in the end he decided to hold on to his money, reckoning that there would be opportunity aplenty for such things before long without the need to pay for it. After his dip in the river Nat lay on the riverbank drying under the hot sun. Something seemed odd and at first he couldn't put his finger on it. Then it came to him, he could hear birdsong, clear and sweet, so different from Lyme where the forlorn cries of the seagulls tended to drown out all other sounds apart from the crash of the waves. It all served to remind him of just how far he was from all that he knew and loved.

As night began to draw in the men huddled around their campfires and the dog who Dabinett had unsurprisingly named Molly laid by his side and shared his meagre rations. Nat and Thomas were continued their discussion from the previous evening.

'What I still can't understand,' said Nat, 'is why the old king didn't name the duke to succeed him before he died. He always admitted that he was his eldest son and he was clearly his favourite what with all those titles he gave him. Don't make no sense to me.'

'It's blerry obvious Nat. The old king knew that the duke were a bastard,' sneered Thomas.

'That's a scurrilous suggestion! I'm certain that the old king married the boy's mother. Are you sure that you're fighting for the right side Thomas?'

'I'm just saying, that's all. I mean why wouldn't he name Monmouth as his heir if he was legitimate?'

'The problem King Charles II had,' interjected Foe who had joined the pals and was busy warming his hands by the fire, 'is that a king or a prince is rarely free to choose his own wife. When he was living in exile in Holland with no prospect of taking the throne he was free to do as he wished but when parliament invited him to return in 1660 having had a wife who'd produced a son would have been a problem. If he confirmed that he had married Lucy Walter then that boy, the Duke of Monmouth, would be heir to the throne. Although Lucy died before Charles was crowned, finding a suitable new bride would be difficult.'

'Suitable in what way?'

'When a king is to be married he is meant to choose a bride, or have one chosen for him, that will either bring new territories or cement a foreign alliance.'

'And why would that be difficult?'

'Well, Charles would be less of an attraction to a foreign royal family as any children of the new marriage would rank behind the Duke of Monmouth.'

'Down at the Three Swans,' said another man, 'it's said that Charles was a secret papist and that his brother James found out and threatened to expose him if he didn't name him as heir.'

'Oh and I suppose the king's household often drops into the Swans to discuss their affairs,' said Nat with a laugh.

'Just saying what I've heard.'

'There could well be something in that actually,' said Foe, 'but I don't suppose we will ever find out for certain. I do however have it on good authority that Charles converted to Catholicism on his deathbed, but whether he practiced that foul religion before then I know not.'

'Well that's all very interesting,' said Nat, 'but I'm for my bed, I have picket duty after midnight.' As he wandered away from the fire to find a quiet spot to sleep he glanced up to the bright moon and whispered a goodnight to Eliza.

Thursday 18th June 1685

Nat found that he enjoyed being on picket duty as it offered the chance for a rare period of peace and tranquillity away from the hustle and bustle of the army and it gave him time and space to think of his future with Eliza. He especially liked to have the last watch of the night as then he could listen to the dawn chorus as the birds greeted the coming day and grab a bite to eat before starting the day's march. This particular morning he was nibbling the last of his rock-hard cheese as he sat watching the eastern sky brighten before the sun burst over the horizon, replacing the grey hues of the night with the colour and light of a new day. He was shaken from his reverie by the banging of the drums and couldn't help the selfish smile that spread across his face as he watched the other soldiers getting slowly to their feet, grumbling about another early morning start with no chance of breakfast and he immediately chastised himself for such un-Christian thoughts. Not that most of the men had much left to eat anyway. It was clear that no thought had been given to providing victuals for the army and that each man was expected to fend for himself. Food bags were getting lighter by the day and at this time of the year there was little to be had by foraging in the hedgerows and woods as they went but hopefully Taunton would provide them with the chance to re-supply.

As he marched along the dry rutted road that took the army through Hatch Green, John gazed at the flat land that stretched to the horizon, so unlike the hills and valleys that he was used to. The hamlet was a miserable place that was so small that he was surprised that it even had a name, there being only a scattering of hovels and a few poorly tended fields. West Hatch was even smaller but it did at least have a church, although the Lord alone knew where its congregation came from. All these villages looked much the same and smelt much the same. He was used to seeing the itinerant rakers who visited Lyme periodically, ringing their bells to let folks know they were in town, ready to empty any cesspit that needed it, but out here in the countryside everything was simply dumped on the midden heap that lay behind each cottage and left to rot. Most of the hovels he saw were built on the one level and thatched with old, discoloured straw although a few had a second storey where the villagers would have their rooms, keeping their animals on the floor below. Small pigs and chickens nosed around the middens looking for scraps but they were quickly gathered up by the villagers as the army approached lest any found their way into the soldiers' pots. Some villagers were prepared to sell their livestock and with so many hungry men they were able to charge monstrous prices. The army commissaries had been charged with buying food, but the villagers preferred the men's coins to the paper promises that the army issued believing the old proverb that a bird in the hand was worth two in the bush. Coin was coin whereas the commissaries' pledges would only be honoured if the duke was victorious.

The long column struggled up a steep slope and came to another small settlement where an old man sat beside the track on an upturned barrel. His long straggly hair hung down his scarred face, partially obscuring the dirty rag that covered his empty right eye socket. Only one leg protruded from his threadbare coat and his footwear was in an even worse state than that of the marching men.

'Alms for an old sol'jur...'

'What's this place called grandfather?' asked one of the men as he stooped to drop a farthing into the man's outstretched hand.

'This be Stoke St Mary sir, named for yonder church.'

'How came you by your injuries?'

'Fighting for parliament and the commonwealth under my Lord Fairfax,' he replied proudly.

'Then God go with you,' said the rebel, adding another coin.

The sturdy church he referred to was sat high on the western side of the hill upon which the village was built and as they passed the churchyard the men were rewarded with their first sight of the wide Tone valley in the middle of which sat Taunton, the largest settlement most of them had ever seen. By the time the tail of the column had left the village the old soldier was happily examining the small pile of coins and scraps of food that the rebels had given him, their generosity fuelled by the thought that they too might one day be left in such reduced circumstances. Nat reflected that the villages they had passed through had been uniformly miserable and desperately poor but that at every place they had been met with smiling faces and kindly folk pressing bread or cider bottles into their hands. He felt humbled that people who had so little were prepared to share what they had to show their support for the duke's cause. Each village and hamlet also added numbers to the army, fifty from Thorncombe, thirty more from Combe St. Nicholas and fifteen from tiny Winsham. Nat hoped that the campaign would end before the harvest was due to be collected as the army seemed to be sucking all the able-bodied men out of each place.

On the road down into the Tone valley a man had presented himself to Lieutenant Mitchell, begging to be allowed to join the army. He wore no shirt and when he turned his back it was clear that he had been ill-treated. It transpired that the man was a vagrant and in accordance with the law he had been whipped out of the village by the local constable. Nat knew that only those born in a parish could receive cash payments from the parish overseers to support them; a widow with children to provide for could expect to receive up to twelve pence a week but such sums had to be raised from those in the parish that could afford it. If the man had no work and was not born locally the law said that he should be physically driven from the parish. It was a harsh law but everyone accepted it as there was only so much money to go around. It made good sense that people should look after their own first even though the bible urged Christians to follow the example of the good Samaritan and help any that was in need, neighbours or not. Lieutenant Mitchell allowed the man to march with the column and told him that he would probably be allocated to the new regiment that the duke intended to raise from the men of Taunton.

Thomas was excited at the prospect of marching into the town although he reflected that marching was a strange way to describe their progress to date. He thought that amble would be a much better term as they never seemed to cover more than a dozen miles a day. He had heard the campfire gossip that suggested that with the extra men the duke expected to pick up in Taunton the army would be strong enough to march on London and force the usurper James to stand down. Others had cautioned that there would not be enough weapons for these new men so that they would be forced to turn south and make for the massive arsenal of arms held at Exeter.

Even with his rudimentary knowledge of geography Thomas thought that this seemed unlikely as it was in the opposite direction to London. Politics and the affairs of state were not for the likes of him to ponder but most of his fellows knew enough to realise that at some point they must move on London and face the king's regular army. A third option seemed to be to take Bristol, a city of some twenty thousand souls. That was Major Wade's hometown and he had assured the men on many occasions that the city, the most important in the West Country was ready to open its gates to the duke. That would be a real feather in the rebels' caps and would show those who were still undecided that his grace meant business. There would be food, arms and recruits a-plenty, not to mention women. All well and good but after that? The pamphlets from London had told how the duke had been most royally received in Cheshire, wherever that was, so maybe they would go there. One thing was certain, no one apart from the senior officers and other such gentlemen of rank had the first idea of what exactly was going on.

As they neared Taunton the roads became busier. The verges were lined with well-wishers and a great crowd hurried ahead of the vanguard, anxious to join the celebrations that would be held to mark the duke's arrival. All the soldiers wanted was a proper bed for the night and some good hot food, but they were to be disappointed as a little after midday with the town in sight they were turned off the road into a large field and told to prepare camp. Despite the generosity shown by ordinary people in places like Stoke St Mary food was beginning to run low again. Bread, cheese and dried fish are fine for a few days but most of the men had had no decent cooked meal for some days. Scavenging in the hedgerows had produced some leaves for the pot, and whilst the broth that resulted was tasty it lacked any real body. Nat yearned for a bit of fresh meat to thicken the pottage but orders had been issued forbidding the use of firearms to bring down a bird or a rabbit and there had been no time on the march to fashion and set traps. It was still illegal for anyone with an income of under a hundred pounds a year to hunt or set traps for wild animals, being a privilege reserved for the gentry, but Nat reckoned that if the opportunity had arisen a blind eye would have been turned, given that they were on a God given quest to install the rightful monarch. As if the Devil himself was tempting them, William Pearce spotted a leash of deer on the far side on the next field.

'What I wouldn't give now for a nice haunch of venison,' he lamented as he watched the miserable fare bubbling in the pot. 'I couldn't help but notice that there's no sheep or cattle in any of the fields, even though there's plenty of droppings to show that they were here not too long back.'

'Aye, the people might welcome the army,' agreed John Harries, the Lyme weaver, but no one's gunna risk their treasured livestock with several thousand hungry men looking for a bite to eat!'

As they sat waiting for the pottage to come to the boil a troop of horsemen trotted past, each man well mounted and armed.

'Captain Hucker,' said Pearce in response to the unasked question. 'I think he 'as a house in Taunton. Looks like he's picked the best of our cavalry to ride with him, must be looking to impress someone.'

'Bloody horsemen,' muttered Thomas. 'They do sod all until they sees the chance to grab the best accommodation, food and women then they gallop off and leave us poor bloody foot sol'jurs to fend for ourselves. Can't see the nobs roughing it in the fields with us!'

'That's a bit unfair,' said Pearce, 'I s'pect they've gone to make arrangements for our entry into town tomorrow.'

'In that case why hasn't the duke gone with them?' wondered Nat as he watched the duke's servants erecting his tent in the centre of the field.

Sergeant White had wandered over to the fire, hopeful of being invited to share the hot meal that Nat, Thomas, William Pearce and John Harries were taking it in turns to stir. Nat shuffled to his right to make a space for the grizzled veteran. 'You're welcome to a portion sergeant, but b'aint nothing but a thin gruel again. Still, we should be able to get zummat better tomorrow. Any idea why his grace hasn't gone into town with ... what d'you say is name were William?'

'Hucker.'

'...With Captain Hucker,' finished Nat.

White pulled a long clay pipe from his bag and spoke with it clamped between his teeth as he bent to take a light from the fire. 'The duke is too important to risk.

He's the figurehead around which the rebellion is built, he's our only hope for protecting the Protestant church. Hucker has taken men to ensure that Taunton is as safe as we have been led to believe. A delay of one day is a small price to pay to ensure the duke's safety.'

Hucker returned before nightfall and word of his findings soon spread throughout the encampment.

'The whole town's in uproar and has been since four this morning!' beamed Pearce, proud of the support being shown by his neighbours. 'Everyone's out on the streets dancing and singing, with the duke's badge of green boughs hung from every door and balcony!'

'Well if that's the case let's get in there now I says,' said Thomas. 'Be a shame to let all that goodwill go to waste!'

'I'm with Thomas on this,' chipped in Pearce, 'I can't wait to see Rebecca and the girls again.'

'Not our decision to make,' cautioned White, 'so I suggests you all tucks down for the night 'cos you can bet there'll be an early start tomorrow.' For once the prospect of an early start was greeted with universal approval. The sun dipping below the low hills to the west set the sky on fire, reflecting red and purple off the thin clouds, promising that another fine day was on the way.

'Red sky at night, sailors' delight,' said Nat.

'Red sky at night, shepherd's delight, surely,' answered Pearce.

'Each to their own,' replied Nat as he said a silent goodnight to Eliza.

13 A WARM WELCOME

Friday 19th June 1685

The whole camp was awake even before the eastern horizon turned a pearly grey heralding the coming dawn. There was a palpable sense of excitement as the men formed up in the long dew-wet grass, most deciding to forgo eating their remaining rations so sure were they that Taunton was full of provisions and people willing to share them. They were made to wait until it was full light as the duke wished to make as grand an entrance as possible. During the night scouts had ridden in to report that the Duke of Albemarle had regrouped the Devonshire militia and had occupied the town of Wellington, no more than a couple of hours march to the west, so men had to be detached from the rebel army to watch that road. More men had arrived in the dark from the surrounding villages to swell the rebel force, bringing further intelligence of the enemy's movements. Most told how they had had to evade militia checkpoints to reach the duke's army. The militia had shown that they could not be relied upon to stand up to the rebels in battle but they could do plenty of damage to the rebellion by choking off the flow of new recruits.

'D'you get the feeling that we're being slowly squeezed?' Nat asked Thomas as they waited to march into Taunton.

'I do rightly enough. Hemmed in on all sides as far as I can tell, just waiting for the reg'ler sol'jurs to arrive. I heard that some have already reached Bridport and Axminster.'

'That means they're between us and Lyme. I pray that they follow us north rather than looking for vengeance in Dorset. The militia being there is one thing, many of them have relatives in the area but the regulars will be strangers. God alone knows what mischief they might get up to.'

Nat watched as the men detailed to watch the Wellington road trouped off, obviously disappointed that they would miss out on the welcome that awaited the rest of the army in Taunton. He was thankful that he was not one of those sent to watch for the militia; hours spent watching an empty road would give him too much time to worry about those he had left behind in Lyme. The army was now over four thousand strong and in high spirits, anticipating the welcome that awaited them despite their concerns that the royal forces were closing in, surrounding them, forcing them to go where they wanted them to go. Tightening the noose.

Finally the order was given to march and the men put aside their fears and followed the duke down the shallow hill towards the town. As the leading regiments reached the outermost cottages they were assailed by a wall of sound causing the horses to snort and whinny with fear. Just as Hucker had reported the whole town was out to cheer the duke and every step of the way men were pressing through the crowds to join the ranks. Every door was hung with boughs, herbs and flowers and the townsfolk all had green ribbons tied around their hats or in their hair, reminding John of the May Day celebrations that had so recently taken place in Lyme. As a good churchgoing Christian, he knew that he should have been celebrating the feast day of St Philip and St James on 1st May but country traditions die hard and the old pagan festival still took pride of places in most towns and villages. The violence, theft and rape that had accompanied both armies during the late civil war had naturally made folk wary of soldiers and their ungodly ways, but here there was no disguising the people's joy. The duke made sure to put their minds at rest over the behaviour of his army by having Lieutenant Goodenough read a declaration against such deprivations. John could not hear all that was said but he caught the phrase, 'it being our full resolution to do justice to all persons whatsoever,' and he smiled, sure that his decision to follow this particular Stuart was the right one. The troops were treated like conquering heroes and showered with gifts of food, drink and clothing. The only thing lacking was weapons to arm the new men and with this in mind the Red Regiment was sent off under its sergeants to scour the town for hidden weapons. Samuel White was leading Thomas and Nat down one of the side streets that led off the main town square when a jolly looking man with big bushy eyebrows and wearing a blood-stained apron over his large belly stepped out from his butcher's shop.

'If you be looking for the bloody militia they fled the town just after midnight, having seen your campfires.'

'We're not looking for them friend but we are looking for any weapons that they may have left behind.'

'Now there I might be able to 'elp you. One of my delivery boys used to be in the town guard and he always said that they kept all their equipment safely locked up in St. Mary's Church.'

The church tower was clearly visible above the thatched houses and White thanked the man profusely before leading his men off. The church door was unlocked and the men's footsteps echoed loudly as they split up to comb the large cold empty building. While some checked the nave and the apse and others were sent to locate and search the catacombs, Nat and Thomas were directed towards a stout wooden door, behind which stairs spiralled upwards. The two pals climbed to the top of the tower and emerged through a small doorway onto a leaded roof which gave views over the whole town and the wider valley of the river Tone. Nat had heard travellers describe this vale as a land of milk and honey, claiming that it was the most fertile valley on God's good earth and he could see why. He found it hard to drag himself away from such a wonderful vista to resume the search. It was clear that there was nowhere to hide anything on the roof or on the spiralling stone staircase but as he stepped out into the ringing chamber, where the thick ropes that were used to toll the bells hung limply from the ceiling he felt one of the floorboards move under his foot. A closer examination showed that the boards had been lifted and refitted. Excitedly he prised the loose boards free with his bayonet.

'Hallelujah! God be praised!' he shouted. 'Muskets, swords, powder and all manner of clothing!'

He called down to Sergeant White who soon formed a chain of men to move the cache to a commandeered wagon which would convey the haul to the rebels' armourer.

'Well done Nat!' beamed the sergeant, 'I can't believe they just left this lot behind. You should grab yourself one of these red coats, better than that tatty thing you're wearing.'

'Perhaps they thought to return to it once we'd left,' replied Nat as he searched for a coat big enough to cover his muscular frame.

'Maybe, but it all belongs to the duke now! I can't think that there'll be more to find here so you and Thomas are free to explore the town, see if you can't get yourselves some food and maybe a girl each. With their permission of course!'

'Not our Nat,' smirked Thomas, 'he's saving himself.'

With nothing specific to do they made their way slowly back into the centre of the town where they heard that some sort of ceremony was shortly to take place. Seeing a small number of men from their own regiment standing together they pushed their way through the crowd.

'New coat Nat? Mind you don't get taken for a militiaman!' grinned John Harries.

'There's plenty with the army wearing them already so I should be safe, but I thank 'e for your concern John!'

'I see you two lucky buggers didn't get sent on sentry duty then.'

'Not us,' replied Thomas, 'Besides Nat here's the new armourer-in-chief to his grace, found a huge pile of guns and powder hidden in the church!' The other men laughed at the jest.

'Soft beds and hot food from now on then Nat if you've become an officer!' They were in a good mood knowing there was a good chance that most of them would be able to find shelter in the town, rather than spend another night under the stars. William Pearce was at the front of the crowd beaming with pride.

'The girls from Mistress Blake's school are to parade and present flags that they've made to the duke,' he explained, 'and my Ginny is to be one of them!'

Drums sounded and the procession came into view, each schoolgirl attended by a fully armoured trooper.

'There she is! There's my little girl!' shouted William waving madly.

As each girl presented her flag to the duke they were rewarded with a kiss and a few words. The last in line was an older girl who William identified as Mary Meads the head-girl. She carried a beautiful flag embroidered with the royal crown and the letters 'JR'. Nat had been given some book learning by Pastor Sprake and knew that this meant 'Jacobus Rex', King James.

'Not likely,' he whispered to Thomas as he explained the Latin motto. Finally came the two teachers, Mistresses Blake and Musgrave, who presented the duke with a sword and a bible. Thomas and Nat were close enough to hear the duke accept the gifts saying,

'I promise to uphold the truths contained in this book.'

One small group that stood somewhat apart from the general crush had caught Nat's eye. An elegantly dressed gentleman and what Nat assumed was his wife, a frail looking woman who had covered her entire face with an ornate mask were attended by a young black boy dressed in blue and gold livery.

'Who are they?' Nat asked William.

'That be his worship Sir William Portman, the local member of parliament,' Pearce replied with evident distaste. 'A nasty piece of work. The woman would be his second or is it third wife, Mary I think her name be. Tis said that she wears the mask to protect her complexion! The boy is their servant, Righteous they call him, brought over from one of their plantations in the western colonies. I've seen him about the town sometimes, running an errand or whatever. Poor little bugger always has to wear that silver collar with his master's name and coat of arms on it. I don't hold with slavery, it's ungodly even though the blackamoors themselves ain't Christian. It's still wrong in my eyes.'

Nat had seen black men before, they sometimes served on the ships that used the sheltered harbour in Lyme but they were all free men. Righteous was the first slave he had ever encountered. 'Sir William doesn't look too pleased.'

'I expect he's here to see who else is here if you get my drift. He's a king's man through and through and is prob'ly taking note of which aldermen are paying homage to our duke. I don't like him one bit, I voted for t'other candidate.'

Nat gasped. 'You voted? In the election? Voting's only for the wealthy.'

'Not in Taunton it ain't. I'm what folks call a potwalloper.'

'A what?'

'A potwalloper. Any man in the borough with a hearth large enough to boil a cauldron gets to vote and our little cottage out at the mill was built with a huge fireplace, so I gets to vote!'

Their conversation was interrupted by Sergeant Stuckley, who addressed the small group of men from the Red Regiment.

'Major Wade is away with the rest of the regiment guarding the approaches, so you men are free to find lodgings in the town if you can. If any of you are from Taunton then you have leave to return to your own homes until tomorrow morning, when you must re-assemble at the Market Cross.'

'That's very crafty of the duke,' remarked John who had joined his son. 'Let the men go to their own homes so that the army don't have to feed 'em.'

Nat turned to ask William where he would suggest they look for a bed. Taunton was home to some six thousand souls, living perhaps five to a dwelling, so finding space for an extra four thousand tired soldiers would mean each family finding room for three or four men. Clearly finding a place was going to be harder than they had at first imagined.

'You'll be lucky to find anywhere in the town this night,' said William as he confirmed Nat's reckoning. 'Best thing you can do is come back to Lambrook with me. You too Thomas and you John, come and meet my wife and children.'

Rebecca and the girls had set off for their cottage as soon as the parade had finished but Nat, John and Thomas first had to return to the regiment's tents to collect their meagre belongings which they had left there when they went searching with Sergeant White. They were in a friendly town but there would always be someone ready to make off with another man's goods.

Nat was glad to be out of the town, if anything the smell there was worse than the villages they had passed through, though whether this was because the rakers weren't as efficient as those in Lyme or because of the profusion of slaughterhouses, fulling mills and tanneries he wasn't sure. Whatever the reason, he longed for the fresh sea breeze that kept Lyme so wholesome by comparison. William was eager to be reunited with his wife and children and the others had to hurry to keep up with him as he strode along. Keeping to the south of the river the group left the town on what William called Priory Walk. They skirted a large house with well-tended gardens, which William said was built on the site of a long-demolished Augustine priory, hence the name of the track. As they approached the small hamlet of Lambrook, the River Tone that had been on the far side of the grand house now turned to run alongside the track and several areas alongside the river had been fenced off to make sheep washes, although none appeared to be currently in use. Ahead of them stood a large mill beside a very generous mill pond and Nat could see several other smaller buildings huddled around it. Nat was thinking how peaceful everything looked when William stopped suddenly and held out his arm.

'Something's amiss!' he whispered, 'tis too quiet.' He was right, there was no sign of his family or anyone else for that matter.

'Quick, in here!' he said and pushed the others into a broken-down woodshed that stood at the side of the track. No sooner had they cleared the road than they heard a horse whinny.

'That's why there's no one to be seen,' whispered John.

'Aye. People have long been wary of horsemen in these parts.'

'But surely this close to Taunton they must be the duke's men,' reasoned Thomas.

'Let caution be our guide,' said William, peeping through a gap in the woodshed door. 'Damn! They're the king's men, at least a dozen of 'em', he spat.

'How can you be so sure?' queried Thomas.

'They are too uniform in their appearance. Every man has the same blue coat and buff waistcoat. Our horsemen are much more of a mixed bag and look see, one of them is carrying a flag.'

Nat had no idea what unit the standard represented but it looked like nothing he had seen the rebel horse using. The infantry had only received their flags that day and as far as he knew the cavalry had nothing similar. This flag was far more lavish than those handed out by the schoolgirls, being crimson with a fringe of crimson and gold and a crown with what looked like the seal that Nat had seen on legal documents in the centre. He thought that he should commit the design to memory so that he could report back to his officers, should they get out of this alive. The horsemen showed no signs of leaving, three of them were watering their mounts in the millpond and two others had dismounted and were headed towards the nearest cottage.

'We need to get rid of them, now!' said William, 'There's no way of telling what they may do to my wife and daughters.'

'But there are only four of us, armed though we are,' Thomas pointed out somewhat unnecessarily. Again his thirst for action had dimmed with the prospect of actually fighting.

'Aye but we do have surprise on our side,' Nat said. 'If a couple of us can cross the track to that pigsty we can fire on them from two different directions, make them think there are more than just the four of us. Hopefully that will be enough of a shock to scare them away.'

It was a risky plan but they had little choice as three more troopers had dismounted and were making for the cottage that William had identified as his. Thomas and Nat took their chance and dashed to the pigsty. They loaded their pieces quicker than they had ever done in training, aimed at the nearest enemy trooper and fired, deliberately discharging their muskets one after the other to try to give the impression of greater numbers. One of the troopers fell although whether it was to Nat's shot or Thomas' they knew not, but Nat noticed that Thomas made another small nick in his musket stock. The other cavalrymen looked about them to see where the shots had come from, not a difficult task given the huge amounts of smoke that the muskets made, but before they could move towards the pigsty, John and William opened fire from the woodstore on the opposite side of the track. None of the enemy appeared to have been hit this time but coming under fire from two different directions was enough for the king's men and they hurriedly mounted and disappeared along the track that skirted the millpond, leaving their fallen comrade behind.

'Well, that went better than I could have hoped,' Nat said.

'Shame they buggered off,' complained Thomas, his confidence and blood lust returning, 'I fancied plugging another couple.'

'How can you rejoice in the death of another human being? And what's with the notch on your musket?'

'Just keeping a tally, that's all.'

The rebels cautiously left cover and moved into the centre of the hamlet, reloading as they walked. Nat went to look at the man that they had brought down. He was dead. There was a neat red hole in the breast of his jerkin, but when Nat rolled him over there was a hole the size of a small plate in his back where the lead had exited his body. His examination of the body was interrupted by a scream from one of the cottages and as William ran to check on his family the others took up positions near the outer-most cottages in case the enemy returned. They thought it unlikely as the enemy horsemen were probably only there to scout the approaches to Taunton and they now knew what they had been sent to discover, that the hamlet was garrisoned and guarded! Similar rebel patrols had been coming and going all day as the duke tried to find out exactly where the enemy were and now they had first-hand evidence that the enemy were doing the same thing. After waiting for fifteen minutes or so and with no sign of the enemy coming back, Nat, Thomas and John trotted over to Pearce's cottage. Rebecca was clearly still very shaken and the youngest daughter would not let go of her mother's skirts. As introductions were being made John happened to look out of the small dirty window.

'More horsemen!' he shouted. They were coming from the direction of Taunton but William was taking no chances. The girls were taken into the back room by Rebecca whilst the men checked their weapons. There were about thirty horsemen, far too many for four musket armed men to frighten away with the same trick as before, but they would do what they could to protect William's family. The horsemen looked to be well armed although no two appeared to be dressed alike and they carried no flag or banner.

'They're ours!' Nat shouted with relief.

'How can you be so certain?' asked William, still worried for his young family.

'Look who's leading them!' he called to Thomas, ''tis Pastor Sprake.' He threw open the door to greet his prospective father-in-law, forgetting that he was wearing his red greatcoat and as such could easily be taken for a Somerset militiaman by the nervous horsemen. It was only when three of the horsemen opened fire that he realised his mistake. Luckily the mounted men were firing from the saddle and the shots went well wide.

Nat dived back through the doorway before shouting through the open window, 'Hezekiah! It's me, Nat Carver! Don't shoot!'

'Is that you young Nathaniel? What in the Good Lord's name are you doing here? Trying to get yourself killed if I'm any judge of the matter.' He turned his horse to face his men and told them to lower their weapons. 'The Devil take any man who puts a shot through my future son-in-law!' Turning back to Nat he called, 'what are you doing here Nathaniel?'

Nat opened the door and stepped outside. 'I could ask you the same thing sir,' he replied. 'We were visiting with Master Pearce's family, accepting his kind offer of shelter for the night. We've just seen off a squadron of the king's men and were afeared that you were more of the same.'

'Then I thank you for your service. We had reports of gunfire and were sent to investigate. We have been in the saddle for hours and I cannot deny that I am well pleased to see that there is no more fighting to be done here today.' He dismounted slowly and walked to greet Nat, stretching his aching muscles as he did so.

'Have you seen action too then?' asked Nat as he shook the old man's skeletal hand.

'More than I should like. We ran into a strong patrol of the usurpers' men near the village of Ashill as we rode up towards the windmill there, hoping to get a better idea of the lie of the land. It shames me to admit that they got the better of us. Poor Cornet Legg was killed in the fighting, a fine young man, gone to meet his maker way too early. Mark me though, these were regular troops and are a cut above the militia that we have had to contend with to date. They chased us right back to the fringes of Taunton.'

This news troubled Nat greatly. The pastor and his men were well mounted and armed. Each man carried a brace of pistols, a sword and a double-barrelled long piece. That they should have been so easy bested was a concern. The army had passed through Ashill shortly after leaving Ilminster, so the enemy were clearly following closely. Once again Nat couldn't help but feel like a hunted animal, with the trap slowly closing in on him the whole while.

Pastor Sprake said that his men would spend the night in Lambrook in case the enemy should return and seek revenge against those who had fired upon them. Pearce welcomed their presence but decided that his family should travel back to Taunton with him first thing in the morning. They would be safer in the town and he knew people there who would shelter them. Fortunately there had been no more cases of smallpox in the town in the week since he had taken leave of his family.

Mistress Pearce and her daughters scurried to put a meal together, boiling a pot in the huge fireplace that William had described to them earlier. Nat and the others added what they could, the most welcome contribution being a brace of coneys that the pastor donated.

the Late D. of M: writing
a letter to y'D of Albermæl

14 GOD SAVE THE KING

Saturday 20th June 1685

The next morning dawned clear and bright and as soon as it was light a large group set out from Lambrook towards Taunton. Several other families from the cottages near the mill had taken the opportunity to seek safety in the town and together with the pastor's horsemen there were close on sixty people taking to the road. Nat realised in horror that for the first time since leaving Lyme he had not looked to the moon to wish Eliza a goodnight. How he could have forgotten with her father's presence under the same roof to remind him he had no idea, but he promised himself that it would not happen again.

As they neared Taunton they were challenged by a picket of musketmen that popped up from behind a thick hedge. Nat thought that they would have recognised the pastor and his men who must have ridden through on this same track the previous evening, but maybe the pickets had been changed during the night. They seemed edgy and were mightily pleased when finally convinced that the column was friendly.

'Is that you Martin Hoddee?' Nat asked suddenly, spotting one of his neighbours in the picket. Martin had been allocated to the Green Regiment, so their paths had not crossed until this point although John had mentioned seeing him. Like many of the men who had joined in Lyme Martin was a man of middling age, with long straggly hair and more gaps than teeth when he smiled.

'Aye young Nat, tis I. Sorry didn't see you there! And John and Thomas too I see now. Quite the reunion!' He smiled and shook their hands in turn before adding in a more sober tone, 'I don't suspect you've heard, but word has reached us that royal troops under a Colonel Churchill have arrived in Lyme.'

Nat, Thomas and John stared in shock. They knew that royal troops had been to Axminster and Bridport but this was the first report of them actually being in Lyme. Their friends and families were still there and they had no way of knowing how the king's men would treat them.

'There be talk that some of the men are of a mind to return home to protect their loved ones, but unless the whole army goes there together, there would be little they could do, so that's not going to happen. Besides, men have joined the duke from all over Somerset, Dorset and Devon so most have no particular ties to Lyme. Why would they want to go to protect the people of Lyme when their own communities might also be at risk?'

'Can't see the duke wishing to retrace his steps anyway,' said Nat, 'especially as the ships which brought him to our shores will surely 'ave been captured.'

Having seen the families from Lambrook safely into Taunton the pastor's men turned about to return to watch the Bridgwater road. Nat knew that he must report the events of the previous day to his superiors and he soon spotted Sergeant Stuckley who said he would take him to the regiment's headquarters to report in person.

'I'm quite happy to tell you sergeant and you can pass it on.'

'No lad, tis better that you report direct, lest anything be lost in the retelling.'

Regimental headquarters turned out to be a small collection of tents erected in the outer grounds of Taunton Castle. Each cluster of tents flew a flag of their regimental colour, the same banners that had been presented by the schoolgirls. In addition to the regimental tents there were those of the commissary, the armourer and the small artillery train. There were large enclosures for draught animals and lesser ones for the small number of hens, sheep and pigs that accompanied the army to supply the duke's table. The comings and goings of so many men, the shouting of orders, the noise of the animals and the constant hammering from the various temporary workshops combined to make a chaotic scene. The smell coming from the animal pens, the horse lines and the hastily dug latrines left a foul taste in the back of Nat's throat. The duke had established himself in the great hall of the castle and Nat and Stuckley had to be constantly alert as horsemen charged to and fro through the encampment, delivering scouting reports or taking his grace's orders to outlaying pickets. The main castle buildings appeared to be in fine repair although no other fortifications were to be seen and it was clear from the unevenness of the ground that stout walls and defensive ditches or moats, such as John had described at Lyme had once surrounded the open green on which Nat now stood. They were ushered into the largest of the Red Regiment's tents where Major Wade and Lieutenant Thompson, both of whom Nat recognised from Bridport were hunched over a makeshift table, covered in maps and papers. Stuckley waited patiently at attention until Major Wade indicated that he could make his report.

'Sir! Young Carver here has news concerning the presence of enemy horsemen, to the east of the town.' Nat quickly told what had happened at the mill.

'Sounds like members of the Oxford Horse from the colours and uniform you describe,' said the major. 'Thompson see that this information is passed to his grace. Well done Carver, I like a man who shows such initiative.'

Nat was shown out of the tent and he and Stuckley made their way down to the fields on the edge of town where those members of the regiment who had not been lucky enough to find lodgings within the town were camped. From time to time small groups of men arrived without uniform or weapons to replace those who had dropped out due to injury, sickness or desertion. Being so far away from home and loved ones, with no idea when or if they might see them again was starting to take its toll on the rebel army. For now the majority seemed prepared to see the adventure through but the men of the Red Regiment had been recruited in Lyme and news that the town was now in the hands of the enemy was too much for some. A dozen or more had slipped away into the night whilst Nat was at Lambrook, and guards had now been posted to stop any more leaving. The morning passed very slowly as men checked their equipment and tried to make repairs to clothes and especially shoes which were already beginning to wear out. The army had been in Taunton for more than two days and the men were wondering what the next move would be. The scouts were reporting direct to the duke, but word spreads quickly in an army and it was clear that the king's forces were converging.

'What do you think will happen next Nat?' asked Thomas. 'Think you we be headed to Bristol or do us strike out for London before the enemy gathers more men to oppose us?'

'I'm as much in the dark as you are Thomas. I'm sure that the duke and his advisers 'ave a plan but it's not the way of things for them to indulge the ordinary soldiers like us.'

'Even his grace's armourer-in-chief?' grinned Thomas.

'Even him,' replied Nat with a smile. He had become increasingly concerned with Thomas' jibes about Eliza and his desire to kill so it was nice to see traces of the old cheeky friend that he knew so well.

About midday Nat was called away to help repair some horse furniture in a small smithy that had been commandeered in the town. Although he had claimed to be a tobacco cutter when he signed on word had somehow got out that he was in fact a blacksmith. It felt strange to be back in such familiar surroundings but without Daniel or John.

'Wondered if I might find you here,' called a voice from the street.

'Come to help father?'

'No, though there have been many times this past week or so when I have wished that I was back in our own smithy on Coombe Street. I've come to tell you to get down to the high cross. It's said that the duke will be making an appearance and that all are required to attend.'

By the time Nat arrived in the marketplace there was already a large crowd gathered around the cross, all clamouring to see the great man. Nat spotted Thomas and he and John pushed through the crowd to stand next to him.

'Seems like not everyone's pleased to be here,' said Thomas indicating a party of prosperous looking men who were being shepherded into the marketplace at sword point. 'I wonder who they are.'

'My guess is that it's the local magistrates being persuaded to attend, somewhat against their will.'

Their musings were interrupted by a huge cheer as the duke appeared to cries of 'A Monmouth' and 'God save the Protestant prince.'

Once the crowd had calmed down Master Tiley, who had read the proclamation in Lyme climbed to the top step of the cross, ready to deliver another prepared speech. The hushed anticipation was broken by a man dressed in dirty rags who forced his way onto the bottom of the steps.

'Know that your sins will find you out! Prepare for the day of atonement! Repent, repent before it's too late!'

Eager hands pulled the man down and he was pushed roughly towards the back of the crowd.

'Damned fanatics,' muttered Thomas.

Once order was restored Tiley began to read. The proclamation delivered at Lyme had been met with huge popular acclaim, but not so this one.

'......do recognise, publish and proclaim the said high and mighty prince, James, Duke of Monmouth, our lawful and rightful sovereign and king...' read Tiley.

'Did I hear that right?' asked Thomas with a bemused look. 'Did he just say that the duke is declaring himself king?'

'I think so...' said Nat shaking his head.

'But when he landed at Lyme, I thought he'd vowed not to take the crown but to accept whatever position parliament might give him.'

'Well something's happened to change his mind and it don't seem to be going down too well with the crowd.'

There were a few shouts of protest but in the main the announcement was met with stunned silence. When the friends returned to their camp there was only one topic of conversation as men prepared their meals; why had the duke gone back on his word? Many of the men, especially those that people called 'old Cromwellians' saw the rebellion as a means to re-establish a commonwealth and they were now showing signs of open mutiny. John in particular was unhappy at the prospect of another Stuart monarch having lost both his parents fighting them. Tempers were rising and the army was in danger of tearing itself apart. In the nick of time Ferguson arrived in the camp and the sergeants called for quiet.

'Gentlemen. I know that many of you are confused by the recent declaration and I am speaking to each regiment in turn to explain the situation. It was King Monmouth's wish to see this country returned to parliamentary control, alongside a constitutional monarch and a strong Protestant church. That is still the case.'

It was the first time Nat had heard the term King Monmouth. He assumed the name was chosen to distinguish the duke (as Nat still saw him) from the king in London, what with both of them being named James. The men assumed that there was a 'but' coming and remained quiet as Ferguson continued in his soft Scottish accent.

'The king prayed long and hard before deciding to take the title, but in reality he was left with no choice. We have to attract the gentry to our cause, many of whom were waiting for our holy crusade to be legitimised in this way before committing themselves. We will shortly see the fruits of his majesty's declaration and the whole country will rise and unite behind us to support our most noble cause. The papists will never again threaten our Protestant religion.'

Ferguson went to explain the legal protection that the declaration offered against charges of treason, but most of the men listening intently to his speech had no idea what this meant. For them Ferguson's general assurances about the new king's intentions once the old king was removed reassured them and they cheered loudly when he finished talking and moved off to address the next group. The army would fight on for its new king, for now.

About seven in the evening Daniel Foe was summoned to Monmouth's rooms where he was greeted by the king's personal chaplain Nathaniel Hook.

'Master Foe, good of you to come. I am told that you are familiar with the country here abouts.'

'Indeed I am sir. I have travelled this way many times in my business.'

'Then you are just the man for the job.' He took Foe by the elbow and led him to a quiet corner. 'The king would like you to deliver two letters for him.'

He held out two envelopes but retained a tight grip on them when Foe tried to take them from him. He looked Foe in the eyes and said in a whisper, 'you should be aware that the contents are somewhat .... delicate. It would not do for the letters to fall into the enemy's hands or even be seen by many on our side. If there is any chance of that happening you must destroy them. You have a tinder box I imagine?'

'Of course. The envelopes are unaddressed, who are they intended for?'

Hook glanced around to ensure that their conversation could not be overheard. 'This first one is for The Duke of Albemarle.'

'The commander of the Devonshire militia?' Foe asked in surprise.

'Quietly man! Yes the very same, hence the need for discretion. His majesty wishes to secure the defection of Albemarle and his militia.'

'Is that a real possibility?'

'His majesty believes so. The two men are very old friends and comrades in arms and the rank and file of the militia will need very little encouragement to join our cause. They are all west country Protestants, like the majority of our own army and it is only their loyalty to Albemarle that prevents wide scale desertion. Persuade Albemarle to defect and his men will follow. His majesty has instructed that you should read the letters now before sealing them, so that should you be compelled to destroy them, you will be able to deliver the messages verbally in person.'

Foe read through the letter carefully. Rather than a mere request, the letter took the form of a royal summons for Albemarle to present himself and his force at the king's camp where he would 'not fail of a kind reception.' Foe refolded the note before replacing it in the envelope.

'Where should I look to find his grace the duke?'

'We believe that he is currently encamped near Wellington.'

Foe nodded then extracted and started to read the second letter which began 'my dear John.'

'John?'

'Churchill. He currently commands James' army who are presently at Chard.'

Foe looked up in shock before reading the rest of the letter, which followed in a similar vein to the one for Albemarle. It stressed the legitimacy of Monmouth's claim to the throne and called on Churchill to join the rebellion 'out of duty and friendship.'

'Be sure to hand the right message to the right man. God's speed and good fortune go with you.'

Back in Lyme things had turned grim. Churchill's troops were busy taking whatever accommodation they wanted and were systematically stripping the town of everything of value. It was a rebel town after all so the royal commanders decided that the normal rules against looting did not apply. Mayor Alford had returned and was happily identifying those townsfolk who had been most vociferous in their welcome for the traitorous Monmouth and those that had not marched off with the duke or fled into the surrounding hills were rounded up and imprisoned in the cockmoil, the royal soldiers happily confiscating their property. Daniel was trying to keep up a pretence of business as usual at the smithy with occasional help from Nancy. They put the story around that John had taken sick and been confined to bed whilst Nat was said to have left some days ago, borrowing old Paul's cart to deliver some new gates to an estate near Chard and that they supposed he had been prevented from returning to the town by militia pickets. Those that knew the truth stayed loyal to the family and so far the authorities had believed their story, but for how much longer they didn't know. Thankfully Alford had not been present when John had smashed open the doors of the town hall. Without the protection of Nat or her father, Eliza felt very vulnerable, a pretty young girl in a town full of unruly soldiers, drunk on stolen ale and looking for a bit of fun. She took refuge in the Goodman's house, hidden in their spacious attic and the old ladies of the town brought work and food to her whenever they could do so safely. Eliza's anxiety was compounded by the fact that no news of the progress of the rebellion had reached the town. When Daniel had been out and about making deliveries, he was constantly running into militia checkpoints and on each occasion his reasons for being on the road were closely questioned. It was no surprise therefore that no news had made its way down to the coast.

15 MAPS AND TOBACCO

Sunday 21st June 1685

The men had been told that they would leave Taunton the next morning but with it being a Sunday many hoped that the departure would be delayed long enough for them to attend a religious service, especially as they had heard that Ferguson would be giving a sermon in St Mary's wearing vestments that he had borrowed from the vicar.

They were to be disappointed as the drums roused them very early and they grumbled as they shuffled into column, having had no opportunity to satisfy either their spiritual or nutritional needs. The little food that had been provided by the commissaries or the sympathetic townsfolk of Taunton was consumed as the men marched but there was never going to be enough to go round especially after Monmouth formed another new regiment, the Blues from the men of Taunton under the command of Richard Bovett a former Somersetshire militia colonel. Nat had noticed that a number of heavy wagons had followed the army from Lyme and he hoped that these contained much needed food and drink, but as he looked on their contents were revealed. Case after case of muskets were unpacked together with a large number of fine red coats with purple lining. The new king arrived to watch the unloading accompanied by Bovett.

'I brought these guns and coats with me from Holland to reward the men of the most loyal town in England. Your regiment should look perfectly splendid my dear Lieutenant Colonel.'

'Indeed your majesty. I thank ye most humbly. I have no doubt that the stout men of Taunton will do you proud when we bring the enemy to battle.'

Turning to his aides the king issued instructions for the commanders of each regiment to attend him at their earliest convenience. Major Wade who was still covering Venner's absence hurried to obey the summons and was soon back to announce that the king wished to convert a number of men from each of the regiments to grenadiers. The chosen men were issued with six grenades each and seeing the blank looks on most faces Samuel White explained how they were to be used.

'As you can see, these 'ere grenades are similar in design to the shot fired by the smaller calibre cannons, being simple hollow metal shells filled with powder. All you needs to do is light this 'ere fuse which penetrates the outer casing and then throw the bloody thing at the enemy before the fuse burns down to ignite the powder and it goes off in your 'and. As you can imagine, timing is somewhat important.'

'How long have us got to throw it before it goes off then sergeant?'

'Depends.'

'On what?'

'On what, *sergeant*, I think you mean.'

'Sorry sergeant. So how long 'ave we got?'

'It depends on how well they've been built, whether the fuse 'as been cut properly and how much powder is inside. You should be alright if you count to three after lighting the fuse. I assume all you country boys can count as far as three.'

There was a ripple of nervous laughter before White continued.

'Just be sure that you don't panic and throw them before counting to three, else the enemy might just be able to pick them up and throw them back at you before they goes bang!'

White could see that some of the men had started to try to stuff the projectiles into their coat pockets.

'Now his majesty the king don't expect you to carry all these 'ere grenades like some juggler at the county fair so he's provided you each with a bag to carry them. It goes across your body like this,' he said slipping one of the bags over his left shoulder so that it hung on his right hip.

'But some of us wears our cartridge bandoliers on that shoulder sergeant. Can't see how we can wear both at the same time. Are we to give up our muskets and just 'ave the grenades then?'

'No my son. You will keep your muskets but the bandolier will be replaced with this 'ere cartridge box which attaches to your belt like so.'

Thomas nudged Nat and pointed to the new cartridge boxes. 'I hopes that there's some of those new boxes left over. I'd like to be able to transfer the cartridges from my coat pocket to make room for some food, if any can be found that is!'

Thomas didn't get a cartridge box but he was handed one of the bandoliers given up by the grenadiers which was the next best thing. Nat was not so lucky and was obliged to continue to carry his cartridges in his coat pockets.

The officers told them that they were to march to Bridgwater, another town well known for its republican, Protestant sympathies and all hoped that the authorities there would be better placed to supply them. The distance was only ten or eleven miles and whilst the army had walked twice that distance to reach Taunton from Axminster, that march had taken a sorry toll on their footwear and Thomas who was suffering worse than many due to his shoes being well worn even before he left Lyme complained that he would be barefoot by the time he reached Bridgwater.

'Not much of an advertisement for a shoemaker to be going around in such poor footwear,' teased Nat.

'Give I some decent materials and my tools and I could soon knock up a decent pair of boots,' retorted Thomas.

Samuel White said that he had heard a rumour that huge quantities of food and clothing had been procured by King Monmouth from South Wales and would arrive in Bridgwater via the River Parrett. Nat placed his trust in the Good Lord to provide for his needs and prayed that the people of Bridgwater would be His instrument.

William was hoping that when the army left Taunton it

would take the track past the old priory so that he could say his goodbyes to those of his neighbours who had chosen to stay in their cottages near the mill, but after the men were assembled in the market square they were marched north past the castle grounds where Nat had delivered his report on the previous day. The long column crossed the River Tone then headed east along its northern bank. With each regiment proudly bearing its newly acquired flag and with the drummers and fifers playing lustily the men felt that they were now part of a proper army, albeit a hungry one. Whilst the marches of a week ago had seemed little more than a gentle Sunday stroll in the countryside, there was now a real sense of purpose and urgency. The enemy were closing in, and mounted patrols came and went all day, both to check that the way ahead was clear and to dissuade the royal troopers from nibbling at the flanks of the army. It wasn't long before the surface of the dry track broke up and those at the rear of the column found themselves marching through clouds of choking dust that found its way into their noses and mouths and stung their eyes. To their left as they marched the land was broken by a series of forested hills, the start of the Quantocks, whilst to their right the terrain was completely flat for as far as the eye could see. The land there was shrouded by a mist that the local men in the regiment said rose from the marshy moorland every day before being burnt off by the strengthening sun. This flat land was so alien to the men of Lyme, used as they were to the sea and the wooded hills and deep valleys of home.

Their route north took them through a number of small hamlets where a few people turned out to watch them, but more and more frequently the marching men found only locked doors and shuttered windows.

Leaving one such village their guide took them off the narrow track and across a series of meadows which were carpeted with wild flowers, the sight and smell reminding Nat of the long walks he had enjoyed with Eliza after Sunday services in what seemed like a different life. It didn't take long before the delicate blooms had been crushed beneath the boots of so many marching feet and the more superstitious among the men hoped that the sight wasn't an omen for their hopes. Swifts, swallows and martins darted above the heads of the men, feasting on the miasma of insects that the soldiers had stirred up and as Nat watched them he caught sight of a lone kestrel hovering high above the meadow, its head held perfectly still by the small adjustments that it made to its tail and wings. Without warning the kestrel dropped into a steep dive and disappeared into the long grass off to the side of the track.

'Lucky bugger's found 'imself zummut to eat,' commented the man marching beside Nat.

Around mid-morning the column halted at a village called North Petherton. Sergeant Samuel White had no idea whether or not there was a South Petherton or an East or West for that matter and in all honesty he didn't care, all he wanted to do was rest his tired feet, preferably in the shade of one of the small cottages that were clustered around the large church. He was in a foul mood having received the sad news that his master Edmund Prideaux had been arrested as he had predicted and taken to London for questioning.

Nat had taken advantage of being near the front of the column to rush for the shade of St Mary's tall tower, moving to one side to make room for Thomas when his friend finally trudged into the village. Nat had just closed his eyes when he heard someone calling his name.

'Master Carver, Thomas. How do I find you both this fine day?' Nat squinted into the sun to see Daniel Foe looking down from the back of his horse. He looked hot and his fine clothing was travel stained. He slid from the saddle and dropped wearily to the ground beside Nat before offering him his water bottle.

'I warrant that I find myself in a better circumstance than you appear to be,' Nat replied as he unstopped the bottle and took a long drag. The water was warm but welcome none the less.

'True, my friend. I have scarce been out of the saddle these past two days.'

'Is it true that our enemies surround us?'

'Not quite,' Foe answered quietly, 'and I would caution you against spreading such stories which can only be harmful to our king's cause. Tis true that they press us close and I expend all my time trying to keep them from harrying the army further. What I do know is that the way to the north is still clear and the route to Bridgwater, and beyond that Bristol is open.'

'That be our destination after Bridgwater then? Bristol?'

'I believe so from what little I have picked up at table. All of Bristol is said to be waiting for us to arrive. Capturing that fine city will send a powerful message to the gentry who still vacillate and they will flock to our banner. After Bristol has fallen the new king will have the option of making for Cheshire where he is said to have substantial support or move directly for London.'

Nat was still wondering what vacillate meant as Foe unfolded a piece of vellum, pointing to a cluster of small black rectangles, which the tiny writing identified as North Petherton. He could see the look of confusion on

Nat's face.

'This is a road map Nat, produced by a Master John Ogilby in 1675, which I purchased from Nathaniel Crouch at the Bell in London. As you can imagine maps such as these are invaluable.'

He traced his finger along a black line which Nat assumed was the road they were following. Lyme was clearly marked as were Axminster, Taunton and Bridgwater. Nat followed the line as it wound its way north before stopping in Bristol. He had no idea such documents existed and could not think how anyone would even start to compile such a document as there were generally no signs at road junctions telling travellers which route to take and local guides often only tended to know the way to the next village.

'I studied geography under Master Charles at Newington Green,' Foe continued, 'and with the help of maps such as this I can generally find my way around. Of course, it only shows the main routes and not what lies far to either side, for that information we need to send out patrols and question the locals.'

'It's not for me, all this book learning,' said Thomas who had wandered over to see what all the fuss was about. 'I can learn all I needs without books!'

'I beg to differ Thomas. It is books that lift us above the level of the animals, it's only greed and ambition that drag us back down. Take Shakespeare for example.'

'Niver heard of him!' said Thomas.

'Really? The man is a master of words, even though he wrote neigh on a hundred years ago. Once you tune your ear to his language it is almost magical.'

'I'll 'ave to take your word for that.'

'I will lend you Romeo and Juliet, I have a copy in my belongings, wherever the baggage wagon is!'

'What's it about?'

'It's a tragic love story....'

'Don't bother yerself,' interrupted Thomas, 'but I'm sure that Nat'll be interested,' he added with a sneer.

'Indeed I would. Have you ever written a book yourself Master Foe?' asked Nat as he drew a long clay pipe from his bag and lit it from his tinder box.

'I have not but I hope one day to have the time and, God willing the skill to do so.' He wrinkled his nose, 'are you still smoking that foul Virginian tobacco Nat? Here try some of this Spanish weed, it's more expensive but tastes so much smoother.'

Foe passed him a ready filled pipe, which Nat accepted gratefully, snuffing out his own pipe and returning it to his bag. 'You too Master Edgecott?'

'Nah not for me. I've things to do,' said Thomas and without elaborating further he wandered off.

'A troubled soul I think,' said Foe between puffs.

'I fear you are right. I worry that this war is bringing out the worst parts of his character.'

'It does none of us any good, but it is necessary I think.'

'Tell me Master Foe, do you have any idea why the people in the villages we pass through seemed suddenly reluctant to show their support?'

'Tis easy enough to understand really Nat. The enemy are pressing us close as you know and as soon as we have passed through a village, King James' men are there within the hour. People are frightened, they have heard that reprisals are being taken against all who have shown us any favour. The people may support our cause, but once we have left their village they are at James' mercy and those few misguided fools who are loyal to that papist puppet are only too quick to ingratiate themselves and point fingers at their neighbours.'

Foe's words gave Nat further cause to worry about his loved ones in Lyme, even though he knew that he could do nothing about that now. His only option was to carry on, to see this thing through, see King Monmouth crowned, parliament recalled, the true faith protected and then return to Lyme and marry Eliza. He prayed that day would come sooner rather than later.

16 A CHANGE IN THE WEATHER

Sunday 21ˢᵗ – Monday 22ⁿᵈ June 1685

It took the rebel army all day to cover the eleven miles to Bridgwater.

'If I weren't marching with this bloody army, I'd niver 'ave believed 'ow long it takes to get anywhere,' complained Thomas.

Men were getting tired in the heat and dust and were constantly dropping out of the line of march for a rest or to relieve themselves, while others slipped away among the trees in search of prey for the pot. The officers tried to keep the men moving but every time someone disappeared the whole unit slowed, so that their friends could re-join them rather than reappearing in the middle of the next unit back and incurring the wrath of their sergeants. Being a Sunday, ministers moved up and down the line and impromptu services were held, again slowing progress. Invariably spokes or axles on wagons broke on the rough road surface, blocking the track until they could be pushed to one side or repaired. Cavalry patrols thundered back and forth forcing the foot soldiers off the track time and time again and when any wagons were obliged to leave the track further delays were incurred as infantrymen were pulled out of line to help manhandle them back into position. William Pearce was looking over his shoulder at the thick plumes of black smoke that rose into the still air behind them.

'There's another cottage or barn gone up in smoke. I s'pect it belonged to some poor bugger who did nothing other than upset one of his neighbours who was only too happy to tell the enemy that they had aided us.'

He felt that he should really be at home himself to protect his family against such barbarity. When he left Taunton to join Monmouth's army in Lyme he thought that Rebecca and the girls would be safe in Lambrook, but the war had followed him back to the Tone valley and now he feared for their safety.

The enemy cavalry kept on the rebels' heels all day. Mostly they were content to watch from a safe distance but from time to time they would charge in to nip at the column's flanks, before withdrawing again, like so many dogs baiting a chained bear.

As the army approached Bridgwater orders were given for them to camp on a large pasture outside the town.

'Why aren't we going straight into the town then, I thought we was welcomed there. I was looking forward to a hot meal and a warm bed, maybe a jug of cider as well,' complained Thomas as he slumped to the ground beside Nat. He couldn't stop the image of Eliza popping into his head when he had mentioned a warm bed.

'You and six thousand others I expect,' replied Nat, chewing on a stalk of grass. 'Can you imagine the chaos of so many men all arriving in the town at the same time, all looking for food and drink and a place to sleep?'

'Looks like the nobs will get the best of it as usual,' said Thomas as he watched the king's party trot off in the direction of the town.'

'That's as maybe, but least it shows that the king believes the townsfolk are kindly disposed, so we should be well received when we do get there.'

As on previous days, the men were subjected to two hours of drill before they were allowed to fall out and start to prepare their evening meals and Samuel White was happy to note that the musketmen were slowly learning their trade. Firing with live ammunition had ceased again with the need to conserve their limited supplies of powder but they could still go through the complicated evolutions. The slow and ragged volleys of the raw recruits at Lyme had been replaced with the regular bang of hammers snapping down on the un-primed pans in unison, as good as any militia unit could produce, although still some way short of the performance of James' regulars. Most of the training was now concentrated on improving co-operation between the various arms and in changing from one formation to another as battlefield circumstances demanded. The tired cavalrymen were called upon to play the part of the enemy so that the infantry could practice the manoeuvres required to deal with a mounted attack whether they were caught in a firing line or surprised on the march. The continual training was beginning to pay off though as the men were responding quicker to commands and Samuel began to have hope that they would be able to stand firm if and when horsemen attacked them for real.

Once drill practice was over the men were dismissed to their campfires and were able to spend a quiet evening at rest. Nat lay on his back starring up at the stars and was again filled with wonder at the magnificence of God's creation. He had been told at Sunday school that each star was an angel looking down protectively on mankind and he had no doubt that this was true. He imagined that the occasional shooting star was an angel rushing to where their celestial help was most needed and he prayed that at least one of the angels was looking out for him and Eliza.

The next morning the army entered the town to cheering crowds. The mayor and other local dignitaries turned out in their finest clothes and regalia and promises were given of free lodgings, food and drink for all. It appeared to Nat that the people living in the towns felt more secure in showing their support for the new king than those living in the outlying villages. Spirits that had been dampened by the less than enthusiastic welcome they had received on the march were revived and as at Taunton men could be seen pushing their way through the crowds that lined the streets so that they could join the army. After the proclamation declaring Monmouth to be the legal king was read in the market square to the cheers of the populace the men began to disperse to seek the promised victuals. Nat and John were just about to leave the square when Sergeant Stuckley caught up with them and told Nat that he should report to Lieutenant Ascue. Nat wondered if he was to receive a reward for finding the arms in St Mary's church and Stuckley went so far as to suggest that he might be made up to Sergeant. Neither thing came to pass.

'So, it's Sergeant Carver now is it?' asked his father with a grin when Nat emerged from the tent.

'Afraid not.'

'Oh. I'm sorry son.'

'I'm not. You know that I'm not really cut out to be a soldier.'

'What did they want to see 'e for then?'

'I'm to become a blacksmith again, for a while at least and you and Thomas are to join me.' As the three of them followed the directions Nat had been given to the smithy in Broad Street, Nat explained what was required of them.

'It seems that despite the arms that we found in Taunton there's still not enough weapons to equip the whole army. Lieutenant Ascue told me that the duke was praying for divine inspiration in a small chapel when he looked up and noticed the scenes painted on the walls.'

'You mean the king, not the duke! I thought that the puritans 'ad destroyed all the old paintings in the churches.'

'I can't get used to calling him that! Anyway, it seems that the local lord had his servants cover the pictures with a thin coat of plaster to hide them, which they were then able to clean off again once the Stuart line was restored.'

'And just what did these pictures show?'

'The grim reaper, taking souls with his scythe. The *king* has already issued a warrant for the seizure of all scythes in the area and we are to help the local smith turn them into weapons.'

When they arrived in the Broad Street blacksmiths workshop it was obvious that the locals had been anxious to show their support for their new king. There were hundreds of the scythes, normally used for cutting the harvest, already stacked in the smithy with more arriving all the time.

'I don't understand,' said Thomas, 'I knows that scythes can be wickedly sharp but the cutting edge is on the inside of the blade and it's fixed to the shaft at such an angle that you'd be as likely to hit your mate stood beside you as harm the enemy.'

'Which is why we are needed,' replied the smith picking one of the scythes from the pile. 'You're still thinking of using this as a harvesting tool. No, what we are to do is take the chine, the blade as you calls it off and reattach it so that it sticks straight out from the end of the snaith, the shaft, rather than sideways.'

'So it'll look a bit like a pike?'

'Exactly, but with a shorter shaft and a much longer blade. With a pike you can do little other than stab it at somebody stood in front of you and it they dodge to one side and get inside the point the pikeman is in mortal danger. The weapons we are to make can be stabbed forward but can also be swung in an arc. It's a brave man who'll face one of these in the hands of a strong man.'

Many of the collected scythes had already been sharpened ready for the forthcoming harvest but a number were found to be blunt.

'Us'll have to re-peen these afore they can be used but we'll soon put a paper-thin edge on 'em, then God help anyone who stands in their way,' said John, quickly warming to being back in a smithy again.

Re-configuring the scythes was a simple job but the work took them well into the afternoon such were the number to be converted. Nat had just finished one scythe and was about to start on another when two soldiers appeared at the open entrance to the smithy.

One had linen wrapped tightly about his jaw and was clearly in pain.

'Little job for you master smith. My friend 'ere 'as a grievous tooth ache and needs the bast'ud thing sorted afore it forms an impostume. I've some cider brandy here to dull the pain of the pulling and a little extra for you if you've a mind to 'elp.'

This wasn't an unusual occurrence in those villages that didn't boast the services of a chirurgeon. As the unfortunate man was given a liberal dose of the sweet alcohol, the smith selected the most suitable pair of tongs for the task. When all was ready the patient was sat on the floor with his back against the anvil and the smith gripped the troublesome tooth with the tongs, placing one knee against the man's shoulder for added purchase. As it was, the tooth came free easily and the grateful man washed the blood and pus from his mouth with another swig of the brandy.

No sooner had the grateful man left than Sergeant White appeared with a detail of a dozen men, sent to collect the finished weapons.

'We've a goodly number for 'e sergeant but we 'ave plenty more still to do,' said John.

'Well keep to it Master Carver. We'll take what you've finished for now and come back for more later. The king intends to arm a hundred men in each regiment with these.'

Other blacksmiths were busy converting scythes in smithies throughout the town but it was dusk before Nat, Thomas and John were done. White had called again to collect the last few weapons and he advised Nat that due to his size and strength he had been selected to be one of the new scythemen in the Red Regiment. Secretly Nat was happy to give up his heavy musket, knowing that it had taken the life of a fellow Christian at Bridport, and his coat pockets could now be used for the bountiful food which had been promised rather than having to carry cartridges. He had been so busy working on the scythes that he hadn't stopped to consider what damage they could do to a man, but now as he weighed one of the fearsome new weapons in his big hands he could imagine it cutting deep into another man's flesh, heavy enough to break bones and sharp enough to take off an arm or a head. He shuddered to think that he would be the one to inflict that sort of harm on another, especially as he would be close enough to smell his enemy's breath and see the fear in his eyes.

'I wouldn't mind using one of these against the enemy,' said Thomas longingly, snatching one of the scythes from the pile and causing Nat to jump aside as he swung it in the tight confines of the smithy, but his slight physique was unsuited to the new weapon and he was to remain a musketeer.

The people of Bridgwater were kind and generally supportive, being prepared to share what little food they had and whilst the army were thankful they longed for the arrival of the promised supplies from Wales. John thought that Bridgwater and Taunton were very much alike. They were of a similar size with strong independent churches, both had suffered equally badly during the late civil war and he sensed that there was a degree of competition between the two which extended to a desire to be seen to offer the greater support to the new king. Whether this was out of a genuine desire to see the rebellion succeed or in the hope of a more tangible reward once Monmouth was on the throne he could not tell. Either way it was most welcome after the increasing indifference that they had noticed in the villages and hamlets.

After their work in the smithy was finished John,

Thomas and Nat found a quiet spot beside the river and settled down to a lazy evening, sharing what little bread and beer they had. Nat kept glancing at his new scythe, wondering if keeping the musket would have been the lesser of two evils, at least with that you couldn't be certain that a fallen enemy had been felled by your action, with the scythe there would be no doubt. Would he be able to look an enemy in the eyes and then take his life he wondered?

They had only been on the road for a week since leaving Lyme and although the pace was leisurely, the work in the smithy, the poor victuals and the state of their footwear meant that they were exhausted, mentally and physically. Despite this and the fact that there was no news of the ships said to be bringing the supplies from Wales, confidence and morale remained high. The militia had been seen off at Axminister and even James' regular troops appeared to be reluctant to attack, whilst the set back at Bridport was still being blamed on the poor performance of the mounted arm, which many of the foot soldiers did not feel was a proper part of the army anyway.

'Seems to I that the air's been getting heavier all day,' remarked John looking to the skies.

'I think you're right father. I noticed that many of the pinecones that had fallen from the tree beside the smithy were tightly closed. There's definitely rain on the way.'

'Thank the fuck for that!' swore Thomas. 'I don't fancy marching another day under this damned sun.'

'You be careful what you wish for young Thomas,' warned John. 'And watch your language too.'

'Whatever you say you stupid old fool,' Thomas muttered under his breath.

By evening thick clouds had rolled in from the west and a bright halo around the moon was further proof that there would be a change in the weather before too long.

The advance resumed the next morning under leaden skies, the dull rumble of distant thunder promising rain before the day was out. Following Nat's conversion to a scytheman he now marched at the very front of the Red Regiment as Major Wade had decided to use the newly created unit as his personal bodyguard under Lieutenant Ascue, with Samuel White as sergeant. Nat knew that he would miss marching with many of his former comrades but was relieved to find that Henry Outwell had also been made into a scytheman. Thomas, being a musketeer, continued to march in the main body of the regiment with William Pearce and Sergeant Stuckley. Nat was happy that he would be separated from Thomas for although they had been friends for a long time, army life seemed to have brought the worst aspects of Thomas' character to the fore. Nat feared going into action because of his strong religious beliefs about the sanctity of life, whereas Thomas seemed to relish the chance to kill.

'What happened to the promise of fresh supplies?' complained Thomas as he tramped through the streets of Bridgwater. 'We were told there would be plenty for all but I'm still hungry and in desperate need of some new boots, especially with another long march ahead of us.'

'They're probably on the way,' replied William Pearce, 'it's just that we're leaving the town too soon.'

'Or maybe it was all just so much bloody talk,' moaned Thomas, before cursing as a sharp stone in the rough road made itself felt through the wafer-thin soles of his boots.

'God will provide,' answered Pearce. The long

column marched down Fore Street past the near ruins of the castle just as the king emerged, surrounded by his officers and advisors.

Thomas grimaced at the sight. 'Have you noticed sergeant that the king's party seems to have grown no larger. I thought that the proclamation in Taunton was s'posed to attract more gintl'mun of position and standing to the army, but I don't see none.'

'I think you're right,' Stuckley replied sadly, 'but keep your voice down lest others overhear and think such talk treasonous. Much though I would prefer to see this venture end peacefully, I fear that we need a victory on the battlefield to convince those same gentlemen that we can win this war, for war is what it is. No doubt they're waiting to see which way it'll go before they declare their allegiance.'

As soon as the last of the rebels left the town Royalist cavalry appeared on either side of the column, always taking care to remain outside of musket range. Once again William Pearce felt like a sheep being driven helplessly towards a pen. At the front of the column men wondered aloud why King Monmouth didn't turn and fight them, but from his conversations with Daniel Foe, Nat knew that the king did not have enough mounted men to challenge the 'shepherds' and when on the odd occasion that units of rebel foot threatened to advance on the horsemen, they simply moved away only to resume their vigil once the soldiers had re-joined the march.

As they slogged along the dusty road Nat spotted Foe watering his horse in a small stream and hailed him. 'Why do you think the enemy aren't attacking us?'

'Are you that desperate for a fight then Master Carver?' he laughed. 'They do not fight because they do not need to, not yet anyway. Their job is to keep an eye on us and prevent more men from joining us and as they watch us they are gathering their own forces, waiting for Churchill to come up from the south and other royal troops who are no doubt heading down the London road towards us as we speak.' He lowered his voice further so that only Nat could hear. 'Ensure this advice goes no further but we are slowly but surely being bottled in, like eels in a trap. There will be a fight and soon.'

'When do you think Churchill will make his move?'

'Well it's probably not up to Churchill anymore. Word has it that he's been replaced as commander in chief by the Earl of Feversham.'

'How do you hear of such things Daniel?'

'Monmouth still has friends in London Nat, some of them inside James' court.'

'So who is this Feversham character then?'

'Feversham, the Marquis de Blanquefort to be exact is a Frenchman although he has lived in London for the past twenty years.'

'And how does a Frenchy get to command the royal army?'

'He was given his first command by our new king's father, Charles the Second, then promoted by James when he succeeded to the throne.'

'Stole the crown you mean!'

'Indeed. Strange thing about Feversham is that he's a Protestant.'

'I can't imagine King Monmouth's too happy about things, being faced by a man who owes his status to his late father.'

'No! Nor Churchill of course. I'm certain that he saw this campaign as his chance to make a name for himself. I believe the king hopes that Churchill's nose will be so put out of joint that he may be persuaded to switch sides.'

'Could that really happen?'

'I can't say too much more and you must keep this to yourself but I understand that an approach has already been made to Churchill and the king awaits his reply.'

It had been getting steadily darker as the men marched, rain was coming and many looked forward to it after such a long spell of hot dry weather which had turned every track to powder, throwing up clouds of choking dust. A spot of rain would come as a relief to the tired men who struggled along under the burden of their weapons and other equipment. As they passed through the village of Westonzoyland, the heavens opened and they were all were soaked through within minutes. Some of the men muttered that the change in the weather was a bad omen and although Nat did not believe in such nonsense he knew there was many a countryman in the army who clung to such ungodly superstitions.

He hoped that the rain would extinguish the many fires that could be seen blazing all along the horizon marking the progress of the royal troops as they followed the rebels, taking their vengeance against those who had helped Monmouth's army. He thought of villages like Thurloxton where he had seen individuals loyal to King James in the stocks on the green being pelted with rotten vegetables by fellow villagers. They would surely now be enjoying their revenge and he lamented the enmity that was being caused between Christian neighbours. Thomas on the other hand had no time to spare for the villagers, he thought only of himself, and the lovely Eliza. Out here on the Somerset levels he felt much more at ease, the landscape being so flat that there was very little chance of the column being surprised by enemy cavalry and there were precious few buildings that could conceal royal musketmen waiting to launch an ambuscade as the rebels tramped past. The cooking fires in the few hovels which they did see were giving off thick dark foul-smelling smoke as the absence of trees forced the householders to use peat as a fuel. Each cottage had large piles of cut peat left outside to dry in the sun whilst many of the walls of the rough shacks were smeared in cow dung, to be removed and used as winter fuel once it had been thoroughly dried over the summer months. The recent change in the weather would not be welcomed in those homesteads.

'Never mind the rain lads,' called William Pearce. 'Not far to go today, look there be Glastonbury already, that great hillock with the remains of the old church atop it.'

It soon became clear that William was wrong though as the column turned sharply to follow a track that led away from the hill. To add to his frustration they were moving at a snail's pace as usual, despite the easy going on the flat moorland. The column could only move as fast as its slowest element. Sometimes that was the guns with their teams of horses and bullocks, other times it was the herds of animals that were being driven along by the small boys and women who accompanied the army to provide fresh meat for the officers, but most commonly it was the heavy baggage wagons that meant the army moved so painfully slowly.

'You've got the wrong hill young'un,' said Humphrey Wilmott who had joined the army at

Bridgwater. 'That there be Tuttyate, though some calls it King Alfred's Fort and others Burrow Mump. It has any number of names but Glastonbury bain't one of 'em. You'll know Glastonbury Tor proper when you sees it. Like a huge great tittie with a gert big nipple on top it be. Tuttyate be more like a pimple alongside it'.

Some of the men laughed at the crude comparison, but many didn't. Thomas knew that the majority of men had joined the ranks to fight for the Protestant church but that others were there for different reasons and from his vulgar language he guessed that Wilmott was one of the latter. Thomas knew which faction his own aspirations matched and he glared at the men who had so openly displayed their disgust at Wilmott's comments.

'Bloody God-botherers,' he muttered.

As they crossed the low-lying moorland, criss-crossed with drainage ditches and small canals their destination became clear despite the heavy rain as the imposing mass of Glastonbury Tor with the forlorn tower of St. Michaels church on its summit could be seen rising almost impossibly out of the flat landscape, dwarfing Tuttyate hill as Wilmott had said. Nat was reminded of the story that Pastor Sprake had once told him about Joseph of Arimathea, the man who had buried the Lord Jesus after his crucifixion. Joseph had apparently travelled to Glastonbury from Jerusalem and a thorn tree had miraculously grown when he stuck his walking staff in the ground and was still to be seen to this day. Another tale told how the monks who resided in the abbey before its dissolution had found the grave of King Arthur and his bride Guinevere, and Nat wondered whether he would get the opportunity to see either the tree or the grave.

Entering the town, the troops were directed to the abbey and while the high sturdy walls that enclosed the extensive grounds still stood, the abbey itself was in ruins.

'Not much shelter,' complained Samuel White as they tramped under the ornate gatehouse.

'I can see zummat over yonder,' answered Nat pointing towards the old kitchen building that stood alone in the vast enclosure, 'but as usual the cavalry 'ave got there afore us and nabbed all the best accommodation.'

'Bloody horsemen, do nothing useful all day then grabs the best cover for themselves.'

'I think you're being a bit unkind to them sergeant, the last time I spoke to Master Foe he looked all in.'

'Yeh, all in the dry that is! And you can bet they've got their horses in there with them even though we're stuck out in the wet!'

A few of the internal abbey walls had survived the dissolution and the ravages of time, standing sentinel over the weed strewn remains. They reminded Nat of the sea stacks that he had once seen off the coast of Dorset when Solomon Jackson had taken him and his father fishing. He ran for the nearest section of wall knowing that the lea side would at least provide some respite from the bitter wind and driving rain. All such shelter was soon taken and the men arriving later would find no respite from the weather at all. Nat watched silently as the musketeers and pikemen of the Red Regiment filed slowly into the abbey grounds, wet, hungry and with rags on their feet instead of boots.

The much-anticipated rain had only served to dampen the mood of the army and although the townsfolk had taken pity on their miserable condition and brought food and drink from their homes, spirits were low. Fortunately, there was a large stock of well dried wood to hand and the men were able to light huge bonfires in an attempt to dry themselves out. Nat had saved enough space for Thomas to be able to join him. He had been pleased at first when his conversion to a scytheman meant that he marched at the head of the column, away from Thomas and his increasingly ungodly attitudes but they had been friends for a long time and he was happy to see him again. They sat together shivering as they eked out the last of their meagre food.

'I've heard it said that the hill on which the old church stands was once an island, surrounded by a huge lake and stinking marshes until the monks of the abbey drained the land,' Nat said.

'If it keeps on raining like this us'll be stranded on an island again,' came the terse reply.

Perhaps sensing that the men needed encouragement, Ferguson was touring the campsite. He told them that Bristol was not far off and would fall without a fight, after which King Monmouth would march on London and throw the Godless usurper and murderer James off his ill-gotten throne. They would, with God's help and guidance be in London by Saturday.

'By God,' said Nat after Ferguson had moved on to the next group of wet men, 'the man's a good talker.'

'I feel sorry for that God of yours,' answered Thomas. 'Once Ferguson gets going 'e niver stops! The almighty must get fed up with 'is voice!'

Ferguson's stirring speech, the food provided by the good folk of Glastonbury and the warmth provided by the fires had restored some of the army's battered morale. As the fires started to burn down the men tried to settle for the night but their clothes were still damp and most found sleep hard to come by. Nat looked to the dark skies to wish Eliza a good night by the moon as he had promised, but it was obscured by the storm clouds and he chided himself for thinking however fleetingly that this was a bad sign.

Others were also thinking of home and worrying about how their loved ones were doing. John prayed that Daniel and Nancy had managed to keep the smithy going and that they were safe from the deprivations of the king's men who were said to occupy the town. William Pearce fretted about Rebecca and the girls back in Taunton, frightened that the pox might return and Samuel White was concerned that reprisals may have been taken against the estate at Forde Abbey now that Master Prideaux had been arrested.

17 BRISTOL BECKONS

Tuesday morning dawned cold and wet. The rain had continued uninterrupted all night and Nat ached all over but wisely held his tongue knowing that most in the army had endured a far more uncomfortable night than he had. After a miserably poor breakfast the army were on their way again. The sky ahead of them was noticeably lighter than elsewhere indicating that they must be marching eastwards although the rising sun remained hidden by the heavy clouds.

'I thought we wuz 'eaded for Bristol,' Nat said to Sergeant White, 'and I understood that were north of here.'

'And so it is Nat, but we needs to get over the River Avon afore we get to Bris'ol, so we're going east first to find a crossing. We're headed for a place called Shepton Mallet, from where we turns north for the bridge at

Keynsham. Shepton's some eleven miles off, so pick your feet up!'

Nat was becoming concerned with the falling morale of the men in his regiment. The increasing indifference of the general population, the absence of the gentry, the hunger, the poor weather and the seeming lack of any direction all contributing to a rising malaise. No one wanted to fight a battle, except Thomas perhaps, but there was a growing acceptance that one was coming, and Nat felt that it would be better to get it over and done with before the condition of the army deteriorated further and before more royal troops arrived.

They left Glastonbury with the towering bulk of the tor on their left and a wide shallow valley to their right, the land dropping down gently to the River Brue before stretching away again to a range of low hills. Thankfully the rain had lessened and when the sun did manage to peak through the clouds it sparkled off the myriad streams and drainage ditches that criss-crossed the valley floor. Once past the tor the land to the left also flattened out, running for miles before meeting the Mendip hills in the far distance. The route to Shepton Mallet was generally level and they made slow but steady progress in a light drizzle. After a few miles the road they were following took a sharp turn to the left to avoid a heavily wooded spur of the Pennard Hills, affording the men one last look at the tor over their left shoulders. The wooded spur had masked a long ridge that could now be seen to lay across their route, a church tower half-way up the slope indicating the presence of a village and the men groaned as they realised that they would need to drag themselves up the steep road ahead. The rain intensified adding to their misery. The men were permitted to march with whom they wanted as long as they stayed within their units and Thomas was usually to be found in the company of John Harries, the weaver from Lyme, the Chardstock joiner Stephen Dabinett, Thomas Cleeve the Stoford carpenter and William Pearce. They made sure that they stayed close to Sergeant Joshua Stuckley who they looked to for advice and guidance.

'If it ain't too hot it's too bloody wet,' moaned Thomas. 'What I wouldn't give for just one day when we didn't have to contend with so *much* weather.'

'Or worry about my poor feet,' replied Harries.

'Or my empty belly,' said Dabinett.

They were told they could rest for twenty minutes when they reached the top of the ridge having passed through the tiny village of Pilton, even though most of them wanted to press on to Shepton Mallet where they hoped to find some refuge from the rain. In the event shelter was hard to come by when they eventually entered the small market town and while the new king went off to lunch with some local worthy at nearby Downside, the men were left to find whatever cover they could. Being at the front of the column Nat, Henry Outwell and Samuel White reached the town first and laid claim to broken-down cattle shed where they were able to light a poor fire, putting a small pot of water on to boil. They were just about to drop some elderflower leaves and nettles in to make an infusion when Daniel Foe popped his head into the shed.

'I thought it was you Nat. What have you got there then, some good strong tea I hope?'

'No tea here I'm afraid,' replied Sergeant White sadly, 'just some leaves that we've been able to pick along the way.'

'Then put those back into your bag and save them for another day, I have tea leaves a plenty to share.' With that he unwrapped some bluish-green leaves from a fold of linen and dropped them into the boiling water.

'Singlo tea leaves from China. Expensive but strong enough to do for three or four infusions. Please feel free to keep the leaves once we've drunk and you can use them again.'

Neither Nat nor Samuel had ever had proper tea before and it was far stronger than the hot drinks that they were used to.

'Is there no end to the wonders that you've brought with 'e? It seems odd to I that folk in London eat, smoke and drink so differently to uz here in Dorset.'

The fact that they had crossed the unmarked border into Somerset some days ago had not registered with Nat.

'No disrespect Nat but journeying down here is like stepping back in time. London is so buoyant, with new ideas coming across from the continent daily.'

'I don't much hold with these new for'in things,' grumbled Samuel. 'I've spent too many years and lost too many friends fighting the Frogs, the Dutchies and the Dagos to start taking on their devilish ways. Right I needs a piss.'

As soon as he had gone Nat turned to Foe. 'Any more news about that matter we discussed recently?' he asked quietly.

Foe looked around to make sure that no one was listening before indicating that Nat should move closer.

'Not good news I'm afraid. It was I who delivered King Monmouth's letter to Churchill. The man said he would not countenance such treachery and I was only permitted to leave his camp as I had entered under a flag of truce. I had hoped to have better fortune with the Duke of Albemarle with whom I was able to broker a meeting.'

'The king met up with Albemarle? The commander of the Devonshire militia?'

'The very same. They drank and talked together, in strict secrecy of course. The two of them are well acquainted from their time in London.'

'You said that you hoped to have better fortune. I assume that this failed also?'

'Sadly yes. The duke's actual words were that Monmouth, he refused to call him king, had better have left this rebellion alone. We can expect no help from either source I'm afraid.' The two friends fell into contemplative silence as they sipped their tea.

After Foe had left to attend to other duties Nat and Samuel were summoned to the ornate hexagonal market cross in Town Street where it was rumoured that the new king would address the army. The space was nowhere big enough to accommodate everyone and Nat who had met up with Thomas on the way to the meeting was towards the back of the crush of bodies and was forced to rely on those nearer the front to relay the speeches.

'The king has just thanked Edward Strode for his hospitality at Downside and for his generous cash gift towards the cause,' said a man in front of them. He turned back towards the market cross and listened as the man in front of him passed on the next part of the king's message.

'Hospitality! Cash Gift! No chance of the poor ordinary men seeing any of that,' grumbled Thomas. Those stood next to him shushed him as they strained to hear the news. There was a cheer that started near the front and made its way back as the news was passed from man to man.

'It's confirmed that we are marching on Bristol,' said Nat and Thomas' informant.

'No more than Ferguson told us last night,' moaned Thomas.

'The king says that he has received word that the gates to Major Wade's birthplace stand open to us and that there will be all the food, drink and arms that anyone could wish for.'

'At least now we as a definite destination, although what happens after Bristol is still anyone's guess,' whispered Nat to Thomas.

'More aimless wandering about the bloody countryside I expects,' came the reply.

The man to their front continued his commentary, 'right, the king's stood back and Ferguson has moved up to take his place.'

There followed a prayer and a blessing before Ferguson said in a voice that carried clearly to the back of the vast crowd.

'...God has entrusted us with this holy crusade and we will not be found wanting. Never again will England endure to be ridden like a hackney of Rome,' he concluded. The men cheered again before dispersing in search of shelter from the heavy rain. Sergeant White had shrewdly ordered one of the men under his command to stay and guard the byre, rather than attend the meeting at the market cross so that they had somewhere dry to return to.

Wednesday 24th June 1685

The men were roused early, ready for the eighteen-mile march to Bristol, although most doubted that they would reach that fine city within a day given the rate the army normally moved. Morale had recovered somewhat now that the men had some certainty over where they were going, food and drink provided by the villagers helped as did the news brought by a rider from the nearby market town of Frome that the proclamation declaring Monmouth to be king had been read in the marketplace, had been well received and that upwards of two hundred men were already on their way to join the army.

The steep climb out of Shepton led to a series of villages all set astride a wide stony road that rose and fell as it made its way through the Mendip Hills. More than six thousand men plus carriages, wagons, guns and animals stretched for nearly five miles along the once quiet country lanes like a giant snake. It would take two hours for the entire army to pass any one point and it wasn't unusual for the head of the column to enter one village before the tail had cleared the last one. The joined hamlets of Binegar and Gurney Slade, then Ston Easton, Farrington Gurney, Temple Cloud and Clutton all came and went with hardly a single man joining the army, so unlike the response they had witnessed in Dorset. Doors were closed and windows shuttered in a pattern that was becoming all too apparent. The larger villages and towns felt confident in their numbers to be able to show support for the rebels, whereas the isolated hamlets were far more vulnerable to royal reprisals.

The bad weather had abated somewhat but it was another tiring day on poor roads with inadequate footwear, so the news that passed down the long line of troops that they would rest for the day when they reached Pensford was most welcome. Most had no idea how far off Pensford was but the very fact that thought had been given to stopping short of Bristol was enough. Before long the army dropped into the valley of the River Chew and the afore mentioned village. It was only early afternoon but presumably the army commanders wanted the army to be well rested before pushing on the final few miles to Bristol the following morning. With food again running low a detachment that included Thomas and William Pearce were ordered to scour the surrounding hills and woods for supplies.

'Not sure what they expects us to find at this time o' year,' complained Thomas. 'There'll be no fruit or berries this early, maybe a few leaves and roots, some ransoms, but not much else.'

The men paired off and dispersed with a warning to be wary of enemy horsemen who were bound to be hanging around the edges of the rebel army looking for easy targets.

'Great,' said Thomas. 'So now we're sending the sheep out to look for the wolves!'

The bare fields held no promise so the pair headed for a thick copse that grew higher up the valley side and would provide some shelter from the rain that had returned with a vengeance. The deeper they pushed into the woods the safer they felt. Enemy soldiers could be hiding anywhere in the dense undergrowth ready to spring an ambush but they had seen no royal foot soldiers since Axminster and no cavalryman in his right mind would try to penetrate this far under the low hanging branches. They gathered what herbs and leaves they could but found nothing substantial to add to the pot. William spotted a tree which boasted some very small wild apples but they were still some months off being properly ripe and tasted extremely tart. Nevertheless, he started to gather this poor fare when Thomas hissed at him to stop and stand quiet.

'I can smell smoke.'

'Maybe there's a dwelling where we can beg or buy some food.'

'Or steal it if necessary.'

'I'll have no part in thievery Thomas.'

'Knowing our luck it'll be an enemy patrol sat around a campfire just waiting for us to blunder into them!'

They pushed on cautiously, being careful not to give their position away by snapping any of the twigs that littered the ground.

'I can hear voices,' whispered Thomas. 'Although it's hard to judge distances in these woods, I reckon they can't be more than a hundred paces ahead.'

'I wonders, be they friendly or not,' William whispered to Thomas.

'Only one way to find out. You wait here, I'll try to get closer. Make sure you keeps an eye out, watch my back,' said Thomas as he slipped off his heavy topcoat, dropped his ammunition bag and propped his musket against the bole of an old oak. Taking only his bayonet he slipped into a nearby thicket of brambles and wild roses and disappeared from sight. William could hardly detect his friend's progress and was impressed as Thomas made his way slowly towards the voices. He had done a fair bit of poaching in his time and the soft wet leaf mould underfoot meant that Thomas was able to move almost without a sound. He jumped nimbly over a deep watercourse with a trickle of water in the bottom and pushed his way through some young beech and oak saplings. He could see that the trees ahead of him were beginning to thin so he dropped to his hands and knees and crept cautiously forward. There was a clearing ahead in the middle of which he could see smoke rising lazily from a number of smouldering heaps. Thomas watched as two old men slowly collected wood which they then piled up before covering them in soil, turf and straw, leaving a small opening at the base into which they fed live coals.

'Charcoal burners,' Thomas said to himself. Deciding that the old men posed no threat to him he stood and stepped into the clearing. The men were shocked by his sudden appearance and snatched up stout poles as if to defend themselves. If Thomas felt shabby in his dirty clothes, he was dressed like a lord compared to these two. They were so caked in grime that it was impossible to tell where one item of clothing stopped and another started. Thomas walked slowly towards them with his arms out wide, level with his shoulders to show that he meant no harm but he could see that they were both watching the hand holding the long bayonet. He dare not drop the weapon until he was sure that they would not attack him but seeing the distrust on their blackened faces he slid it carefully into his belt, thinking he would have time to retrieve it should they turn on him. He spread his arms wide again.

'A good day to you neighbours. I have come from the king's army in search of victuals. Know you where I might buy food and drink?'

'Be you a sol'jur then? You don't look like one in that there torn waistcoat and with no proper boots on y'ur feet. We don't hold with sol'jurs round these parts. Nothing but trouble be sol'jurs.'

'Be assured friend, we are all good God-fearing Christians,' he grimaced at being obliged to use such language, 'we are not here to steal from you. King Monmouth will pay well for wholesome supplies.'

'King who? I thought that the late king's brother, James be sat on the throne.'

'Then you have not heard that the Duke of Monmouth, first born and favourite son of Charles, God rest his soul, has come to recover his father's crown from the usurper James, promising to protect the Protestant church and recall the parliament.' He hoped that his false piety would play well with the two old men.

'If that all be true then you be welcome here young'un, but we've no food to spare, we scarce have enough for our own families.' Looking at them Thomas had no doubt that they were telling the truth so he thanked them and had just turned to make his way back to William when he heard the sound of hooves. Spinning around he was alarmed to see a horseman bearing down on him with drawn sword. He turned and ran for the cover of the trees as the rider, ignoring the charcoal burners who had dived for cover behind one of their clamps, used his knees to turn his big horse to give chase. The horseman grinned then let out a shout as if he were chasing down a fox.

'William, William, where are you?' Thomas panted as he ran. William had been too far away to hear the conversation with the charcoal burners but the urgency in Thomas' voice was enough to tell him that there was trouble. Due to the heavy rain the men had been instructed to remove the powder from the pans of their muskets and wrap the locks in cloth to keep out the water and knowing that he wouldn't have time to load his weapon William fumbled to attach his bayonet, looking up just as Thomas ran past him. He realised there was no time to fit the bayonet as the horseman crashed through the undergrowth in pursuit so he grabbed his musket by the barrel and swung it towards the horse's head. There was a sickening noise as the heavy stock of the musket caught the horse in the mouth, the poor beast shied sideways and in doing so caught its leg between the heavy branches of a fallen tree, a sharp crack telling William that the horse had broken its leg. The crippled animal fell pining its rider beneath it. Thomas heard the commotion and ran back, bayonet ready. The trapped rider, resplendent in a fine red coat and cloak, both with blue lining with large blue turnbacks was struggling to reach the pistols that were still in their holsters attached to the front of the saddle but Thomas reached him first. He stamped on the man's wrist to prevent him drawing his pistol then sat on his chest, using his knees to keep the rider's arms pinned to the ground. His lips drew back into a sneer as he rested the point of his bayonet in the shallow dip below the man's Adam's apple.

'Chase I, would'e? Well you won't be chasing anyone else,' he said as he leant on the handle of the bayonet slowly pushing the point down into the man's gullet. The rider gasped, his eyes widening as the blood bubbled in his mouth, then his arms went limp and he lay still. William was sickened by the evil grin that spread across Thomas's face as he drove the blade in even deeper, twisting it as it went, long after it was clear that the man was dead. Thomas finally withdrew the blade before wiping it clean on the dead man's cloak. He began to pull off the rider's tall stiff black boots.

'He won't be needing these anymore and they looks about my size.'

'They won't do you any good,' said William recovering from his horror, 'they be meant for riding, not for walking in. You'd be better off going bare foot than trying to march in they boots.'

'I'll know that once I've tried 'em won't I,' snapped Thomas, 'Now let's see if this pretty boy 'as anything else useful on 'im.' A search of the man's pockets and coat seams produced several silver coins and the canvas bags attached to either side of the saddle contained fresh bread, cheese, ham and a small bottle of fine French brandy. All these went into Thomas' bag which he had recovered from beside the oak tree.

'Better fed than we are, perhaps I am on the wrong side as Nat suggested,' moaned Thomas as he slid the two silver handled pistols from their holsters and thrust them into his belt. 'A fine collection for a couple of minute's work, if I says so m'self, and I'll have that fine new cotton undershirt too, mine's crawling with lice.'

After Thomas had finished looting the body, William removed the dead man's coat and the black felt hat with its yellow ribbons and looked for anything else that might help to identify the rider's unit, thinking that such information might be useful. He decided that the heavy blackened-metal back and breast plates that protected the rider's body were too non-descript to be of any help and instead took the man's carbine belt and one of the pistol holsters.

'Now to put this poor animal out of his misery. His leg's broken, it'll be a mercy to end things.'

'Don't bother wasting your time,' sneered Thomas. 'Let's get back to the village. I do quite fancy a bit o' horse meat but we ain't got time to butcher this 'un, there might be more horsemen about.'

William thought he had come to understand Thomas on their long marches together, but this was a side of him he had not seen before and he didn't like it. The pleasure he had taken in killing the defenceless trooper and his lack of compassion for the horse was disquieting. He had heard that such changes could come across soldiers, but usually only after long exposure to battle had worn down their humanity, but as far as he knew this was the first time that Thomas had seen action and he was disturbed by the ease with which Thomas had killed. He snatched one of the trooper's pistols from Thomas's belt and shot the horse between the eyes before thrusting the pistol back into Thomas' hand and stomping away.

While Thomas and William were away foraging, Nat and Samuel had left their gear with John and had gone to have a look at the old church, dedicated to St. Thomas á Becket, which sat on a spur of land with water on two sides, running in deep channels. Two further streams joined the main river here with a network of bridges and a mill above, producing a maze of waterways and arches. They were sitting quietly on the parapet of one of the sturdy stone bridges watching the damsel flies that danced above the rushing waters and the bright butterflies that flitted from one campion plant to another.

'A penny for your thoughts Nat.'

'I was just thinking how this little river reminds me of home.'

'How so?

'Back in Lyme the river Lim cuts right through the centre of the town, making for the sea. Most of the time 'tis little more than a gurgling stream running in a very deep channel between the houses, but when the winter snows melt it becomes a raging torrent. I wonder if these little streams do likewise.'

'Aye it looks quiet enough now but the rain waters bain't come down off the hills yet.'

They turned to see a man in his late sixties, with a scruffy beard and a lopsided smile that revealed that most of his teeth had long since rotted away. For a community of perhaps two hundred souls, having in the region of six thousand armed men descending on it would be something to tell their grandchildren about and several of the villagers had ventured out of their homes to see the sight.

'The recent 'ot weather 'as baked the ground hard,' he continued, 'so all the rain we've had this last few days won't soak in, it'll all come down here and in a day or two the level will rise by a good ten foot.' Nat and Samuel had difficulty understanding the man, what with his unfamiliar accent and the lack of teeth which meant that he whistled slightly as he spoke. They assumed that they had misheard him.

'Did you say ten feet?' exclaimed Nat.

'True enough, as God's my witness. The whole town were flooded just this last winter. If you'da been stood on this bridge here then, the water would've been over your head young'un.' With that he pointed to a line drawn high on the wall of the cottage that stood at the end of the bridge. 'That there mark shows 'e just how far the waters rose.'

As Nat stared in wonder at the high watermark scratched into the rough stonework John ran up, clearly struggling for breath. 'Nat! Bad tidings from home,' he panted. 'Word has come that even more royal troops have entered Lyme and have captured King Monmouth's ships.'

'We wuz told when we wuz in Taunton that the royal troops had been seen in Lyme,' replied Nat.

'True, but tis said that the latest arrivals includes Irish, even though the law don't allow it. If that doesn't condemn James nothing will. God knows what those Papist bastards will get up to.'

Nat was not so concerned about the loss of the ships even though it meant that the king had lost his lifeline back to the continent. He was more worried about what would become of Daniel, Nancy and most of all Eliza. Everyone knew about the atrocities that the Irish Catholics had committed against Protestants during the so-called Irish Rebellion of 1641 and Nat had no reason to doubt that such hatred still ran deep. His head was filled with questions. Would the royal commanders be able to control their men? Would the townsfolk be treated with Christian respect? Would the town be fired for supporting the new king and would anyone tell James' men that it was John who had broken down the doors of the town hall?

Father and son fell silent each lost in their own dark thoughts until John pointed along the river and shouted, 'soldiers!' Nat and Samuel sprang to their feet and followed John's gaze.

'Where? I can't see them.'

'Over on the far bank, up the hill a little ways, just comin' out'a the woods there.'

Still Nat could not see them. He looked to Samuel who shook his head.

'Look son, there! Can't you see? Some be in yellow coats, others in white. Not the red we normally see the Somersetshire or Dorset militia in, so it must be the reg'lers come down from Bris'ol or some other county militia. Raise the alarm!'

Finally Nat realised what his father had seen, large banks of yellow wild mustard and white hogweed swaying gently in the evening breeze.

'I didn't realise your eyesight had got so bad father. When we do get back to Lyme us'll go see Master Symes the apothecary and see if we can get 'e a pair of they eyeglasses that the gintl'mun do wear.'

'No need for that young'un,' said John embarrassed by his mistake, 'Symes'll see me right in the old-fashioned way.'

'You mean by mixing the ground up ashes of the head of a dead black cat into your cider?' Nat scoffed.

'Aye, the old ways are the best and I knows he 'as some o' they ashes put by in a box for just such a treatment.'

The light-hearted moment was soon forgotten as thoughts turned back to John's news about Lyme. John wandered off grumbling about the aches and pains of old age and failing eyesight while Nat returned to the cooking fires of the Red Regiment in low spirits, reflecting on the many things that had happened since he had signed his name to join the rebel army. He'd gone hungry, he'd seen a lot of death and suffering, he had actually killed a man himself, but this news from the coast hit him hardest of all. He lapsed into a state of melancholy, knowing there was nothing he could do about any of it.

Food was again running short, with nothing but leaves, roots and a few mushrooms gathered from the hedgerows to add to the thin broth that steamed away over a myriad of small campfires. The biggest fire by far was being tended by a small thin woman who gave the impression of being little more than a collection of rags as she stirred the contents of a huge iron cauldron that was merrily bubbling away. Nat remembered when the woman had first joined the march at Axminster with her weaver husband. The men had laughed at the sight of the miserable woman with her hair pulled back in a severe bun, her dirty apron and lack of footwear, dragging the massive pot behind her on a rough hand cart. The cart also carried several stoppered earthenware pots one of which had now been unsealed and the contents, salted hare, dropped into the boiling water along with nets of prepared vegetables which she had likewise brought with her. Juices from the cooking meat seeped into the water to make a broth. Nat had to admire her foresight as the men that had laughed at her were now more than happy to hand over their last few pennies for a portion of the thin pottage that she served up, paying twice as much if they wanted some of the meat as well. Drawn by the smell of the food Thomas and William approached the group gathered around the large fire. Thomas was wearing the shirt that he had stripped from the dead trooper and he dropped his old, soiled undershirt into the flames and was rewarded by a series of small pops as the fire reached the lice that had been living in the seams and causing him such torment. William looked on enviously, scratching the itchy bites that dotted his paunch and wishing that he had taken the trooper's undershirt instead of Thomas. He was an honest man at heart and would not have dreamt of stealing, even from the dead but he was coming to realise that he may have to re-evaluate his conscience if he was to survive.

William had reported the incident in the woods to his lieutenant, showing him the various items he had taken from the dead horseman.

'You've done well but it's ill news you bring,' said the officer. 'I will need to speak to the major to confirm my thinking but I believe this to be the dress of the Life-Guards, meaning that James has sent his best troops against us.'

The afternoon dragged by as men ate what little they had, mended clothing as best they could and checked their weapons. One of the lads from Colyton had found a large flat field with a gate at either end down in the water meadows and quickly arranged a football match against men from the neighbouring village of Colyford. A few of the soldiers wandered over to watch as the young men ran around chasing their makeshift ball, happy to have some distraction but most were content to simply sit down and rest their weary feet, knowing that in the morning they would march on Bristol. Nat laid back in the soft grass and gazed up at the clear sky, he could hear skylarks but try as he might he could not see them. He thought of home, the warm comfort of the smithy, his cosy bed in the adjoining cottage, Sunday services in Silver Street and the lovely Eliza who would one day soon become Mrs Carver. All seemed so far away in time and place even though he had only left Lyme a little over a week ago.

As darkness fell the pickets on the hills above the village reported that the skies were aflame in the direction of Bristol and the men rushed to witness the spectacle. Word had come that the city garrison of nine hundred militiamen had been reinforced by thousands of troops from South Wales and that their commander Henry Somerset, Duke of Beaufort had threatened to set fire to the city if it was endangered. There was speculation that Beaufort was merely burning the hovels that lay outside the city walls to deny the rebels cover, some insisted that the fire was a pre-arranged signal from Monmouth's supporters within the city that the inhabitants were ready to rise in support, whilst others feared that the city had indeed been fired as threatened. As Nat stood watching the glow on the horizon trying to determine what it meant, a body of horsemen thundered past, heading for the city.

'Now I wonder where they be off to in such an 'urry?' he asked no one in particular. The answer was provided by Daniel Foe, who had wandered up to stand beside Nat to look at the fiery sky. Foe seemed to be well aware of everything that happened in the new king's army.

'Captain Tiley and his men,' he said nodding at the horsemen. 'He's been sent to Keynsham to check on reports that the bridge over the Avon has been destroyed. On the advice of Major Wade, the king intends to cross the river to attack Bristol from the north side where the defences are weaker. Tis said that the river is docile enough to be waded by men and horses but the wagons and more importantly the guns will need a bridge. Tiley used to be a clothier in Bristol so he'll know his way about in Keynsham, even in the dark.'

As the fires in Bristol died down men slowly returned to their own campfires to reflect on what the next few days would bring. Many looked forward to a fight, to resolve matters one way or another after so much seemingly aimless marching but they had no idea where they would be sent after Bristol. Rumours still circulated about moving on to the midlands or to Cheshire although most men had no clue what or where the midlands were, nor Cheshire for that matter. The names meant nothing to them other than that they promised to take them further from their homes and loved ones. Nat, Thomas and John sat under the meagre shelter provided by the dead trooper's cloak which they had stretched over a framework of sticks.

'I can't help thinking of home,' said Thomas 'I wonder how everyone is. Eliza is forever in my dreams.'

'Eliza? Surely you mean Sarah,' interjected John, before Nat could challenge him.

'Did I say Eliza? Course I meant Sarah,' stammered Thomas, 'I only said Eliza as I were just thinking about 'ow joyous y'ur wedding'll be when we do get 'ome Nat.'

They fell into an awkward silence, till at last John bade them all a good night and rose to return to his own unit. In the incessant rain none of them slept comfortably, Nat taking longer than most to find sleep, musing over Thomas' slip. His old doubts about his friend had resurfaced.

18 RAIN AND BLOOD

Thursday 25th June 1685

The rain had abated somewhat by morning as the men made ready for the march to Bristol. There was some confusion as the column left Pensford, as they did not take the steep hill that they knew from the previous night's fires led to the city, instead they stayed in the deep valley and followed the River Chew towards the east.

'I thought we wuz headed for Bris'ol,' commented the scytheman marching beside Nat.

'I understands we needs to go to Keynsham first to cross the river.'

'But we're already on the Bris'ol side of the blerry river!'

'Not this river, this is the Chew. We needs to get across the Avon which lies between us'n Bristol.'

'How d'you know all this stuff Nat? Anyone would think thee was an officer or zummut.'

'Friends in high places!' chipped in another man.

'Tis true that my friend Daniel Foe does keep me well advised.'

'Well per'aps the king should let the rest of us know a bit more, then there wouldn't be s'much bloody grumbling.'

'If they tells you what's going on Zach with that big mouth o' yours, James' men 'ud know all our plans within minutes.'

'You mean we've actually got some plans?'

Their route towards Keynsham led them through the small quiet hamlets of Publoy, Woolland and Compton Dundo, the latter place remarkable only for the steeply sided hill that rose high above the valley floor. Nat could make out horsemen on the fringes of the trees that crowned the summit of the hill, an ideal lookout post he thought, though whether they were friend or foe he could not discern. There were no cheering crowds or well-wishers pressing cider bottles into eager hands as they tramped through the empty villages. News of royalist retribution was obviously moving ahead of the rebels as they advanced.

'Not much cheer here Nat,' said Samuel.

'No, but we'll be alright once we reach Bristol. Folk say that it's the largest port in England after London and there should be food and drink aplenty awaiting us, as well as cloth to repair clothing and shoes. *If* the citizens open the gates to us as promised....'

'I'm certain they will,' Samuel replied without much conviction.

The long column of troops marched into the narrow streets of Keynsham about mid-morning to news that the bridge had indeed been destroyed as reported, but that Captain Tiley had seen off the royalists that had been left to guard the remains of the crossing and had already affected repairs. Only one of the central arches had been broken down but the gap had been easily patched up with baulks of timber liberated from a nearby sawmill. The route across the Avon was open and the army crossed to the northern bank only to be ordered to halt.

'What's going on now?' complained Thomas. 'I thought we was going to attack Bris'ol. We should push on.'

'Quiet there!' shouted his lieutenant. 'It's not up to the likes of you or me Master Edgecott to decide what the army does or doesn't do.'

'More's the bloody pity!'

'Enough! We wait 'ere till we're told otherwise.'

A rider soon detached himself from the king's party and rode over to speak to Major Wade, who still led the Red Regiment in the continued absence of Lt Col Venner who was said to be recovering slowly from his near fatal shooting at Bridport. Stood as he was at the front of the regiment with the colours Nat heard the conversation clearly. The king had decided to hold a parade of the whole army, it being felt that a show of strength was required to win over the locals. The men were marched onto Sydenham Mead where the meandering River Avon ran around three sides of a flat piece of land to form a natural parade ground and despite the intermittent rain a large proportion of the town's population turned out to watch. Many of the rebel soldiers were still in their dull everyday clothing with no more than a coloured sash to denote their regiment but the red and purple coats of Bovett's Blue Regiment and the large number of red coats of former militiamen made a splash of colour. In addition, each regiment now carried a pair of flags, one predominantly white, the other in the regimental colours and with the senior officers resplendent in their finery, all lace and feathers despite the strong puritan influences within the ranks, the rebel army made an impressive sight.

The bold display was cut short however as the heavy rain of the previous day returned, sending the spectators scurrying back across the repaired bridge, with more than one losing their footing on the now slippery timbers only being saved from a dunking in the cold water by the attentions of their fellows. With no shelter to be found on the northern bank of the Avon, the army was ordered to re-cross the river and find what refuge they could in Keynsham village. While Sergeant White went off to look for accommodation for the bulk of his scythemen, Sergeant Amos Gough established a picket in the White Hart Inn at the top end of the High street. Gough was another old soldier with experience from the civil wars and had come in from the town of Chard where he worked as a weaver. Like many of his ilk he was keen to see a restored commonwealth. His small command comprised a number of scythemen, including Nat and a detachment of musketeers amongst them Stephen Dabinett, who Nat had first met at Tytherleigh, with the ever-present Molly at his side. The inn was warm and dry and the men were happy to get such a posting, given that covered accommodation could not be guaranteed for everyone in such a large army.

'Right lads, with the weather as it is it looks like we're here for the rest of the day at least, so we might as well make ourselves comfortable. We'll have two men at a time to watch the road, two hours to a duty and the rest of us can get some sleep. And no drinking, well not to excess anyway.'

Gough quickly paired the men off and arranged the order in which each pair would take turn to stand guard. Then he found himself a pile of old sacks in a corner of the room and, as is the way with old soldiers was soon fast asleep.

Dabinett was snoring gently when he was shaken awake. 'Your turn on duty Stephen,' whispered Ben Smith, before moving on to wake Aaron Tucker.

Ten minutes into their stint Dabinett and Tucker were chatting softly when Dabinett suddenly held up a hand to quieten his friend.

'Did you hear that Aaron?' Molly tipped her head to one side and growled quietly.

'Hear what? All I can 'ear is the rain and the thunder.'

'I'm sure that I 'erd an 'orse and Molly seems to have picked something up. Do you think I should wake the sergeant?'

'Rather you than me, the old boy looks very comfortable. You'll be in deep shit if you wakes him for no good purpose.'

'I'll be in even deeper if there is zummut going on out there and I don't wake 'im!'

He moved away from the window and gave Gough a gentle shake. The sergeant was awake in an instant and Dabinett made his report, stressing that he couldn't be certain given the thickness of the walls and the noise of the rain.

'You did well to wake me son. If there are horsemen out there they could be ours returning from a patrol but I'm taking no chances.'

He woke the rest of his detail and told Dabinett to open the inn door and step outside to check that all was well. Dabinett stepped into the heavy rain and was instantly knocked to the ground by a large horse as a unit of cavalrymen thundered down the High Street. As Dabinett struggled to sit up a flailing hoof caught him on the temple and he went down in an untidy heap. The deep blue coats of the mounted men showed them to be regular cavalry from James' army and while the natural inclination of the other rebels in the inn was to slam the door shut and hope that their presence would not be noticed, Gough knew his duty.

'On your feet! The Devil and his horsemen are amongst us! Musketeers to the windows, scythemen into the road but keep close together, horses will not willingly ride into your blades. They have sharper eyesight than you or I and even if they can't see you in this foul weather, they'll certainly smell you.'

Being so rudely roused the men were groggy but responded well enough to Gough whose calm authority demanded obedience. No sooner had Nat and his fellow scythemen edged into the road than more ghostly shapes appeared out of the sheets of rain that blew down the road. A sudden flash of lightning illuminated the scene and for a split-second time seemed to stop, the horses frozen in mid stride, individual raindrops suspended in their fall. Then as the brilliant light died everything suddenly burst back into life and the riders were past the rebel picket before anyone could stop them. Soon the sound of musket and pistol fire filled the air from the centre of the town, mixed with the screams of injured men and frightened horses.

Gough grabbed Aaron Tucker. 'Get you out the back door Aaron and see if you can find a way to get to Major Wade. Tell 'im what's happening.'

Tucker was certain that with all the shooting the major would be well aware of the situation but he did as he was ordered, slipping quickly into a fetid back alley that ran parallel to the High Street. As Tucker headed for the middle of the village the noise of battle to his right intensified as more and more rebels were roused to form a defence. He was breathless by the time he came to the newly built Ship Inn where the regiment's senior officers were quartered. As he was delivering his message to Major Wade a runner arrived from the southern end of the village to advise that they too were under attack by horsemen.

'Damn their eyes!' exclaimed Wade. 'I have no idea how they could have co-ordinated their attacks so well in this dirty weather.'

In the confusion there was too little reliable information on which to plan a response, but the noise was such that all the rebels were now fully awake and for now they would have to fend for themselves. With most of the rebels sheltering indoors from the heavy rain the royal cavalry could find few targets and milled about in the streets as rebel musketeers took shots at them from the upper stories of the shops and houses that they had occupied.

Just when it looked like they would achieve little from their surprise attack, the leading troop of royal cavalry rounded a corner and barrelled straight into a unit of rebel horse that had just returned from a patrol across the river. The momentum of the royal cavalry took them clean through the rebels, many of whom were caught in the act of dismounting and were knocked to the ground. Those few that were still in the saddle turned to face the royal horsemen who were reforming at the far end of the street. The royal horse discharged their pistols, wheellocks that didn't rely on a slow match and could therefore be used in the rain, before charging into the unorganised mass of rebels and a confused melee took place as the men struggled to tell friend from foe in the gathering gloom and the heavy rain.

Elsewhere the fighting went on for a little more than half an hour, flaring up and dying back down at various points throughout the village until a trumpet blared, clearly a pre-arranged signal and the royal horsemen broke off and galloped back to the northern and southern ends of the village from whence they had come so unexpectedly.

Most of Gough's picket were content to let the horsemen go but Benjamin Smith was determined to avenge his friend Dabinett. Stepping into the middle of the road he swung his reversed musket at one of the mounted raiders as they thundered past. The horseman sensed rather than saw him coming and with a touch of his heel turned his horse to bowl him over. As Smith started to get to his feet another rider bore down on him, leaning from the saddle ready to take the rebel in the chest with his sword. Without stopping to think Nat stepped out to protect his fallen comrade swinging his scythe as he came, the finely honed blade connecting with something solid sending a shockwave down his powerful arms. The horse, caught squarely across the muzzle cried in pain and reared up throwing the rider from the saddle. The downed rider must have been one of the last to try to leave the village as no others followed on behind him and suddenly the street was empty and all was quiet, save for the feeble scrabbling of hooves as the mortally wounded horse bled its life out onto the rain-washed cobbles. Dabinett showed no sign of movement and Smith who had emerged unscathed from the encounter crawled across to his friend and gently lifted his limp body into his lap. Molly lay whimpering beside the pair.

'I think his skull's broken,' Smith sobbed.

Nat grabbed the fallen horseman by the collar and dragged him to his feet. He was dressed in a long blue coat with red turnbacks and gold-coloured buttons. It was the first time that Nat had seen one of the royal horsemen up close and he was impressed by how well equipped he was. An iron helmet with three vertical bars, what White would have called a lobster pot encased his head and blackened metal breast and back plates covered most of his body. Thick buff leather gauntlets and tall black boots completed the protection.

'Sergeant Gough! I've caught on o' the beggars, what shall I do wi' 'im?'

'Kill the bastard Nat!' screamed Smith. 'He's the one what did for my mate.'

'Let's see what the sergeant has to say,' replied Nat.

'Sergeant's dead Nat,' came a voice from the door of the inn, 'took a pistol ball to the head.'

'Right. One of you look after Ben, while I takes this one to the major,' called Nat over his shoulder as he marched the shaken cavalryman down the middle of the street which was now strewn with wounded men, horses and discarded equipment.

As they walked the horseman found his voice, 'I must thank'e for not killing me.'

'I'll not kill a man unless I have to. I once heard tell that it's not just the man that you kill that suffers, you do yourself harm as well. What's inside you is damaged too, so by not killing you I'm doing myself a favour.'

'Well thanks anyway.'

As they neared the Ship Inn the prisoner stopped and turned to Nat.

'You seem like a sensible man, for a traitorous rebel that is. You do realise that this mad rebellion is over don't you? The king, the real king not your upstart Monmouth, has four thousand regulars, that's proper fighting men, not militia, coming up from Somerton and they'll be here this very day. More are expected daily on the road from London and Bristol is held against you, my Lord Beaumont 'aving installed five thousand loyal Welshmen to secure the city. You'll be trapped against the city walls and then you'll surely hang as a traitor if you're not killed in the fighting first. Why not do the sensible thing and take the offer of the king's pardon.'

Nat had not heard tell of a pardon being offered but thought it a villainous idea. Coming to the regiment's temporary headquarters Nat pushed the prisoner into the gloomy interior.

'And who is this?' demanded Major Wade.

'Nat Carver sir, from the picket in the White Hart. Got a prisoner for you.'

'Have you now? And who are you?' he asked the cavalryman. 'Speak man!'

'Hatton Wolrich, your honour, Oxford's Royal Regiment of Horse.'

Having delivered Wolrich Nat was at a loss what to do, so he stepped back into the shadows as Wade questioned the prisoner. Nat listened carefully but didn't hear much more than Wolrich had already told him on their way from the White Hart.

'So, the regulars are at Somerton are they? This news must be passed on to the king at once. See to it will you Lieutenant Thompson?'

Having dispatched Thompson and seen the prisoner taken away, Wade turned to Nat.

'Get yourself back to your picket soldier and tell the sergeant in charge to keep a sharp watch in case they try something else.'

'Begging your pardon sir but Sergeant Gough's dead, along with Stephen Dabinett.'

'Ah, a pity that. Gough was a good solid man. Afraid I didn't know Dabinett. It seems then that we need a new sergeant Master Carver. You were at the Bull in Bridport if I remember right.'

Nat nodded sadly as he recalled the sight of Strangeways sliding down the wall amid the blood and smoke.

'Well go back to your picket and take command, Sergeant Carver. Oh, and keep quiet about this supposed pardon.'

He glanced at his clerk, 'Wallis, make a note of Sergeant Carver's promotion in the regiment's records if you'd be so kind.'

Nat wandered back to the inn through the pouring rain wondering how a man like him, a pacifist at heart and so unsuited to military life as he was, could suddenly be a sergeant. Arriving back at his new command he soon re-organised the picket and saw that Smith, who was bleeding profusely from a head wound was taken to the chirurgeon before sinking down in a corner to get what rest he could.

There were a number of scares throughout the rest of the day with every small noise in the street causing alarm, but no more attacks came. Then just after darkness had fallen and the men were looking forward to a quiet night, Nat was woken by a sentry.

'Sergeant White's approaching Nat.'

Nat stepped out into the rain to meet him.

'Well Sergeant Carver is it now? Now I know that there's no-one with any sense running this army! Get your lads together Nat, we're on the move.'

'To Bristol? In this weather?'

'Nope, not Bristol. This afternoon's attack must've put the wind up the king. Tis said we are marching to Bath instead.'

'When do we leave?'

'Immediately.'

'That's a shame, we've a couple of men in the unit who worked in the slaughterhouse. They wuz 'oping to butcher the dead horses for meat. You knows we could all do with a decent hot meal.'

'You'll 'ave to wait 'til us gets to Bath for that Nat.'

Nat wondered how much of Wolrich's story had been believed and whether his news of the nearness of the regular army had had any bearing on the move away from Bristol. He couldn't help wondering if the story of royal reinforcements might be a falsehood, fed to the horsemen to pass on in the event that any were captured. He voiced his thoughts to White.

'Possible', nodded White, 'although Wallis, the major's clerk, told me that the king has received reports that there are four thousand horsemen waiting to join us in Wiltshire. It seems it was a toss-up between heading to Wiltshire to meet up with them or marching north towards Cheshire to collect men said to be waiting for us there under a Lord Macclesfield.'

'And Bristol?'

'Reinforced, as I believe you already know and we don't 'ave enough guns to break down the walls.'

'Let's hope then that these Wiltshire horse are no mere phantoms, like all the others we've heard about.

We seem to do nothing but run around the countryside looking for non-existent men.'

'Now that's enough of that talk Nat. You're a sergeant now and you need to keep those sort of thoughts to yourself. Men will be looking to you for reassurance.'

'I've no doubt about the righteousness of our cause Sam, it's just the way we're going about things. Any idea what the butcher's bill was for this afternoon's little entertainment?'

'About fifteen killed and twice as many more wounded I've heard. The dead will be left in the care of the church and the wounded are being loaded onto carts as we speak. Now let's be off.'

The rebel army mustered and left the Bristol area marching east through the short, wet June night. Molly could not be persuaded to leave Stephen Dabinett's body and had to be left behind in Keynsham.

19 BATH AND PHILIPSNORTON

Friday 26ᵗʰ June 1685

Keynsham to Bath is only eight miles but the disconsolate army moved so slowly along the southern bank of the River Avon that the wan glow of dawn was already creeping over the land when the high walls of Bath came into view. Hopes were high that they would receive a warm welcome from the city as King Monmouth had been regally entertained there during his last visit. The men sat and waited under lowering skies as a trumpeter was sent forward to parley.

'Open the gates in the name of the king!'

A single shot rang out and the herald fell dead from his horse. A collective groan went around the rebel ranks.

'Shit!' swore Thomas. 'Is the whole bloody country against us? We've already 'ad to fight the militias from Devonshire, Dorsetshire and Somersetshire. Bris'ol was full of Welshmen and I 'erd tell that the bridge at Cainshum was 'eld by the men of Gloucestershire. Every door in every village is suddenly shut against us and now Bath turns its back. So much for that bloody idiot Ferguson and his promises of the whole country coming to our aid!'

'Well at least we 'as the promise of the Earl of Macclesfield waiting with an army in Cheshire,' said William Pearce. 'A friend of mine said he heard one of the officers' servants say that the king nearly took us north after Cainshum but decided to head first into Wiltshire where a large body of horse are waiting for us. Maybe we'll strike out for London after that, the capital is said to be ready to rise.'

'I've 'erd about enough stories of who might or might not be waiting to join us or to rise in our support. I means Cheshire, wherever that is may as well be on the moon. If the men of Cheshire are so keen to fight why don't they just march down here and join us then? And if there really be troops in Wiltshire an army of this size can't be hard to find, why do we have to go a looking for them?'

'Aye that's a fair point young Thomas,' said Pearce as the pair struggled to their feet. 'Keep it quiet like, but I reckons this whole thing is starting to unravel. That servant I was telling 'e about reckons that the king was afeared of attacking Bristol lest it be put to the torch. 'God forbid that I shall be accessory to the ruin of my friends,' he was heard to say.'

'I don't think Monmouth 'as the faintest clue what he's doing to be honest with 'e. We just keeps traipsing from one place to another, with no shoes on our feet and no food in our bellies. Let's come to grips with them and show 'em how West Country men can fight. That episode in the forest has given me a taste for action and I can't wait for more o' the same. Bring 'em on I say.'

Once again William was struck by the vehemence of Thomas' words and his desire to inflict violence.

The clatter of hooves heralded the arrival of another of the rebels' cavalry patrols and the waiting infantrymen were forced to the side of the track as the horsemen made their way past. It was clear that they had been riding hard, the horses were flecked with spittle and their flanks were heaving. Thomas caught sight of Pastor Sprake.

'Enjoying a nice quiet ride in the countryside while we have to slog along on foot?' sneered Thomas.

With barely concealed contempt Sprake leaned from the saddle.

'Master Edgecott. I'll have you know that we have been in the saddle for two days solid, the king needs information.'

'What sort of information?'

'About the enemy of course! The most important thing in any war is determining where your enemy are and what they intend.'

'Well if that's the case then I'd say that our king has pulled off a master stroke, cos it seems to me that we don't have a damned clue what we're doing or where we're going, and if we don't have any clear plans how could the enemy possibly guess them?'

There was little point waiting under the walls of Bath, especially with the main enemy force said to be so near, so once again the men were pushed into column and the long exhausting march resumed. From the position of the sun they could tell that they were headed south, away from Bristol and away from London as they began the long hard slog out of the valley of the River Avon. When they eventually reached the high ground that overlooked Bath they found that the ridge was a false summit as the land fell away sharply again to a hamlet called Midford at the confluence of three streams, the Midford Brook, the Cam Brook and the Wellow Brook, all of which had carved out their own little valleys in the soft rock. The road that led south out of Midford was in an awful state after the heavy rains and was so treacherously steep that the local guides recommended following the course of the Wellow Brook instead.

The sun was beginning to peek from behind the clouds but it would be some hours before it would have any effect on the state of the ground. The water meadows made for easy going at first but the soft grass was soon churned to a thick glutinous mud which sucked at the men's feet as they marched and Nat dreaded to think what state the fields would be in by the time that those at the back of the long column tried to traverse them. After two miles or so they reached an old stone bridge that carried a track across the brook. The track climbed the steep slope to their left leading back to the main road but this route appeared even less promising than the earlier route, with water cascading down the steep roughly cobbled surface.

'An arduous journey Nat,' said Henry Outwell.

'Indeed, but is anything truly worthwhile not likely to be difficult?' he replied. 'I can see that we'll have to climb this hill at some point but there's no chance of us dragging the cannons up there.'

As if echoing his thoughts orders were given to continue following the brook. A short distance further on a small stream ran down from the heights to join the brook and, directed by the guides the column turned and started to climb its shallow valley. The army was becoming increasingly disorganised. Every time the column came to a stream or a bridge or a piece of particularly swampy land, they would bunch up as the lead unit struggled to cross the obstacle. Once clear the unit would hurry on its way opening a gap back to the next unit in line as they too laboured to negotiate the hurdle. The column was being split into a number of distinct parts and looking back down the valley Nat thought that the army resembled nothing so much as a string of sausages hanging in a butcher's window. He smiled at the analogy until realising that if the enemy chose this moment to attack they would have little trouble annihilating the whole rebel force piece by piece.

From his position at the head of the valley King Monmouth seemed to have spotted the danger and he ordered the Red Regiment to halt and wait for the others to catch up. Whilst grateful for the chance to rest, the men were unnerved by the sight of enemy horsemen above them on the high ground which surely heralded the imminent arrival of the main royal force. They were soon on their feet again and after following the stream uphill through a small wood, they emerged onto another track which although steep looked more practicable than the last one and they were directed to follow it up to the ridge above. Nat was beginning to appreciate the value of local guides.

'I do miss those levels that us crossed after Bridgwater,' mused Nat as he struggled uphill. 'Nice easy going that.'

'True,' replied Henry, 'though that marshy land ain't any too healthy. I've known many a man fall prey to sickness down among they reeds. But, as you say, at least it were flat.'

Nat and Henry were glad that they marched towards the front of the column, as those further back were constantly being detailed to help drag the guns and baggage wagons up the steep road when the horses and oxen couldn't cope.

One of those labouring to move the wagons was Thomas and he wasn't impressed.

'Does anyone actually have any idea where we're going now or is the bloody king making new decisions every time he comes to a road junction?'

The senior officers had clearly picked up on the growing dissent in the ranks and although they felt no need to inform the ordinary soldier what was going on, they did confide in their junior officers, and they in turn spoke to their sergeants so that eventually the information would make its way down to the common recruit, but as is the nature of such things the news became more unreliable with each retelling.

Nat was still new to army life and even newer to holding some responsibility but he was beginning to understand a little of manoeuvre and tactics, based mainly on the advice of the older men in his regiment, many of whom had seen action in the civil war, but it was still all very confusing. He too thought that the army was wandering about the countryside without any clear plan, despite the reassurance of his lieutenant, but he felt that given his new status he should not voice such views openly. Instead he turned his thoughts to home as he tramped up the steep track. He hoped that Eliza was safe and that Daniel and their maid Nancy were well. He was worried by stories that James had brought Irish officers into the royal army even though the law forbade it; further proof, if such was needed that King James intended to take the country back into the arms of Rome. Thinking of home brought him no comfort and his dark mood was not helped by the weather.

Further back down the column Thomas was engaged in a heated discussion with his sergeant, Joshua Stuckley.

'If you still 'as any doubts about our new king's legitimacy then perhaps you ought to read this,' Stuckley said unwrapping a tattered pamphlet from its protective square of waxed cloth.

'Like I can read proper!' sneered Thomas. 'What's it say?'

'It's titled *His Grace the Duke of Monmouth honoured in his Progress.......*'

'What's it say, not what's it called!'

'What's it say *sergeant*! Well I ain't gunna read all of it if you can't be arsed to, but it tells of how Monmouth cured poor Elizabeth Parcet of Crookham of the King's Evil just by touching her. What more proof do you need?'

'Proves nothing to me apart from how gullible some people can be!'

Stuckley carefully refolded the pamphlet and returned it to his pocket. He really couldn't be bothered trying to convince Thomas but he was concerned that his increasingly belligerent attitude might rub off on some of the other men. He would have to watch him closely and report it to his lieutenant if it got any worse.

By late afternoon the head of the weary column arrived in the hilltop village of Philipsnorton. It had started to rain heavily again and with little chance of such a small village being able to provide adequate covered accommodation for such a large host, the men were forced to fashion whatever cover they could in the surrounding fields. Nat and Samuel White were luckier than most as they found an old dovecote which was dry, albeit that the floor was covered in years of bird droppings. By the end of the night some thirty scythemen were crowded into the tall round building, their weapons stacked outside in the rain for lack of space. Thomas wasn't so lucky, his only protection against the elements as he sat on the wet grass was the cavalry cloak that he had taken at Pensford. He and two other musketeers had used their muskets to fashion a frame over which they draped the cloak. It wasn't ideal but it was far better than many of the men had.

'Why the hell didn't the king think to bring tents with him from Holland?' he asked his companions.

'Couldn't afford them I reckons.'

'Bloody half-arsed effort this rebellion if you asks me. No money for food, no pay, no money for tents and nowhere near enough weapons neither.'

'So what would you have done diff'rent then Thomas?' asked his companion.

'Well first off I would have left the bloody officers' baggage wagons behind. We've dragged them all over the country just so the nobs can have nicely decorated dinner tables and dry stockings. I'd kill the oxen and let the men have some decent meat for once.'

The men spread across the sloping fields outside Philipsnorton tried to light fires in a futile attempt to dry clothing or get something warm inside them and every so often there would be a loud bang as one of the soldiers used a little too much gunpowder when trying to get his fire going.

The men were becoming increasingly disconsolate, and as they huddled together for warmth their muted conversations betrayed their concerns. There were complaints about the paucity of food, the constant marching, the apparent lack of any plan and the fact that once again the officers had ensured that they were warm and dry inside the large inn that stood at the high point of the village, whilst the men had to suffer in the rain and the mud. There was much talk of slipping away in the night and finding their way home. Thomas, desperate though he was for a fight, was definitely thinking of leaving and returning to Lyme and he let his imagination run free, using it as a shield against the miserable conditions in which he now found himself. Not that there was much for him in Lyme he reflected. He wasn't sure that he wanted to spend the rest of his life with Sarah from the Mariners' Inn. She was fine as a distraction after losing out on Eliza but little more than that. Suddenly a thought popped into his head, uninvited but not wholly unpleasant, what would Eliza do if Nat failed to return?

Nat wasn't sure what was holding the army together. The ideals on which the rebellion was founded hadn't changed but the practicalities of campaigning were having a detrimental effect on the men. They were hungry, tired and in need of boots. They had no idea when they would get to see their homes again and all the while the enemy seemed to be gathering their strength. He reckoned that the only thing stopping many of the men from leaving was the contempt of their fellows and the difficulty of piercing the ring of enemy cavalrymen that surrounded the army. Even amid the scythemen who considered themselves the cream of the infantry, thoughts of deserting were now being discussed openly around their campfires as Nat discovered when his duties took him out from the shelter of the dovecote to make a tour of the pickets. Despite the tight security around Bristol a number of men had made it out of the city to join the rebels and several were now sharing the scythemen's watch-fires.

'What I can't understand is why you didn't attack the city when you 'ad the chance,' said one of the new arrivals.

'We 'erd that the place was crawling with militia from Wales,' replied one of Nat's men. In the faint loom cast by the guttering fire Nat could not identify the speaker.

'So there was, but there be plenty in the city who would 'ave welcomed the duke.'

'You mean the king.'

'The king then....'

'Enough support to 'ave overwhelmed the militia though?'

'Possibly. We did what we could to help by setting fire to the *Abraham and Mary* what was tied up in the 'arbour. That drew a lot of the defenders away from the walls. That was the moment to attack.'

'We saw the flames but were afeared that the Welsh had started to carry through their threat to fire the city if it were attacked. The king couldn't risk the lives of so many people.'

'A missed opportunity I reckon,' said the Bristol man.

'Let's 'ope it don't prove a fatal one!'

Nat thought that the news of this missed opportunity would further damage the already fragile morale of the men and wondered if it was his place to stop such talk. His musings were interrupted by Lieutenant Ascue who strode across to tell him that it was time for him to relieve Sergeant Stuckley in charge of the picket who were guarding the road south towards Frome. Nat nodded and walked the short distance up Bell Hill towards the crossroads which stood at the centre of the village. He relieved Stuckley who hurried for the warmth of the dovecote and Nat huddled down beside the fire. He had not been there for more than five minutes when the quiet was shattered by a shot, followed by a lot of shouting and the sound of running feet.

'Stop that man, he's just shot the king!'

Nat took up the chase as the culprit ran past him in the direction of the Bath road but before he could catch him the man blundered into a picket on the far edge of the village and was being roughly manhandled back to the George Inn, the main hostelry in the middle of the village where the king was staying. The inn was in uproar as officers ran this way and that in confusion.

'Is it true? Is the king harmed?' demanded Ferguson, grabbing Monmouth's servant William Williams by the arm.

'No, God be praised, the king is unharmed. This villain fired a shot from the roadway at his majesty while he was stood at the window shaving. The ball, or rather the metal button, for that is what the projectile was, is lodged in a table in the king's chamber.'

The would-be assassin was locked into an empty wine cellar to await his fate. Everyone knew that King

James had offered a reward of five thousand pounds for the man who killed Monmouth, an almost unimaginable sum for an ordinary man. This wasn't the first attempt on the king's life and it probably wouldn't be the last. Nat returned to his picket's fire and spent the rest of his duty watching the preparations that were being made for the army to move the eight miles south to Frome, where huge quantities of supplies and hundreds of new recruits were promised. There would be more covered accommodation for the men in the market town and it was hoped that the horsemen from Wiltshire would also join them there. Teams of oxen were hitched to the four guns, the wagons carrying the wounded from Keynsham and the officers' baggage and the men pushed into a rough column of march.

All of this took several hours and it was morning before they moved off, the sound of ungreased axles and iron shoed hooves echoing off the walls of the solid stone-built houses that lined both sides of the road to Frome. At the end of the village the cobbled road gave way to a narrow track made muddy by the constant rain as the king led his bedraggled army away from Philipsnorton.

20 BATTLE IS JOINED

Saturday 27th June 1685

The rear of the long slow-moving column had barely left the narrow streets of Philipsnorton when trumpets sounded from the village, followed by the rattle of musket fire. The column halted and a mounted messenger pushed his way through the thick gaggle of men and equipment to report to Monmouth.

'Your majesty, Captain Vincent begs to advise you that the enemy has attacked his rear guard.'

Vincent had been left behind in the village with fifty men to guard the barricade that had been erected across the end of North Street, the main road that led from the village back in the direction of Bath.

'In what strength pray?'

'At least five hundred musketeers, supported by cavalry with more arriving all the time. Captain Vincent says that it is unlikely that they can be held for long enough to allow the column to escape.'

Nat and Samuel White were marching in their normal place with the colours of the Red Regiment at the front of the column and were perfectly placed to witness what followed. The king who until a few moments ago had been riding slumped in his saddle, seemingly with the weight of the world on his young shoulders suddenly became animated. His face came alive as he began to issue orders that saw the whole column turn-about to retrace its steps towards the village.

'Long enough for the column to escape! If that damned French rascal Feversham wants a fight then by God I shall give him one!'

There was utter confusion as the tired men tried to manoeuvre in the confined space between the hedgerows that lined the lane to Frome. Sergeants shouted, horses whinnied and oxen bellowed. The cumbersome wagons had no chance of turning and remained where they were, all but blocking the narrow track. Monmouth and his officers forced their way through the mayhem, the men in the column pushing through the hedgerows and spilling into the adjacent fields to allow them passage and, as the senior unit, the Red Regiment under Wade followed their king into the temporary void.

Vincent's men were under severe pressure but the cover provided by the barricade meant that they were just about holding their own as the first few sections of the Red Regiment ran down North Street to reinforce them, their equipment banging and slapping against their sides as they ran. Some tried to load their muskets as they ran, but this inevitably slowed them down and the sergeants bellowed at them to keep moving. The important thing now was to bolster the numbers manning the overturned carts that formed the barricade in the hope that the sudden appearance of a large body of rebels might be enough in itself to deter the attackers. Nat and the other scythemen were held back. In the tight confines of the narrow street this was a job for the musketeers and pikemen. The king had stopped at the market cross, near the entrance to North Street and was giving orders to the other regiments as they came up. Command of the defence of the barricade fell to Major Wade. He sent men into the houses and paddocks that lined the street to protect his flanks and as Nat watched on waiting for orders, one of those men returned.

'Major Wade, Lieutenant Mitchel sent me to tell 'e that 'e believes there's a way to outflank the enemy what are attacking the barricade.'

He turned and pointed to a stout wooden door that was built into a high stone wall to the right of the road.

'That there gate leads into the gardens of a large house. The grounds extend all along behind these cottages and the Lieutenant says we can ... enfilade? ... the enemy.'

Wade smiled briefly at the clumsy way in which the soldier had pronounced the unfamiliar French word, but it confirmed that the message had indeed come from one of his well-educated officers. Wade seized upon the opportunity immediately and began feeding men through the gate as they arrived at the barricade.

'Through you go my brave lads, show them how a west country man can fight,' shouted Wade in his strong Bristolian accent.

Nat was still awaiting orders and had to steel himself not to duck as musket balls directed against the barricade whistled overhead or flattened themselves against the stone walls of the cottages that lined the street. He was a sergeant now whether he liked it or not and was expected to set an example to the other men. There was a yelp of alarm and pain as a ball struck the man behind him. Nat turned expecting to see the man writhing on the ground but he found him still standing, staring down in disbelief at the dirty smear of lead on his broad belt buckle.

'Two inches lower and your Mabel wouldn't 'ave welcomed you home Jake,' laughed the man next to him, before he was knocked back in a spray of blood, as a musket ball carried away his lower jaw. Nat stared at the fallen man in horror until Wade grabbed him by the sleeve.

'Carver, take your scythemen through the gardens as well, I can see enemy horsemen on the hills opposite, we must discourage them from joining in.'

Thomas had just arrived with his section of musketeers and joined Nat in running to the door. 'Now we've got the bastards,' he screamed, as he pushed past Nat, anxious to join the fight.

The rebels who had made their way through the gardens were soon pouring fire into the flank of the royal troops who could make no headway against the resolutely defended barricade. The royal musketeers and grenadiers began to edge toward their right, away from the murderous counterattack from their left but by this time the Green Regiment had arrived and had been thrown into an orchard on the left-hand side of the road, coming up on the other flank of the men assaulting the barricade. The royal troops were being assailed from three sides.

Having seen to the deployment of his army, the king rode down North Street to see the situation at the barricade for himself. Wade was alarmed to see him there.

'Your majesty, I beseech thee to have a care. You cannot put yourself in such danger, if you were to fall all would be lost.'

'My men need to see that I am prepared to risk all for this venture.'

Their conversation was cut short as a cheer went up from the men defending the barricade. One of the enemy officers had been unhorsed and was struggling to regain his feet.

'By God exclaimed the king as he stood in his stirrups to look over the barricade, that's Henry Fitzroy, the Duke of Grafton, my half-brother by the Duchess of Cleveland.

'Another royal bastard then,' sneered one of the men stood close by.

The king rounded on the man and was about to strike him with his riding crop when Wade laid a gentle hand on his arm and shook his head. The king was so surprised at Wade's action that he did not reprimand him for having the temerity to touch his royal personage. He quickly regained his composure but was unwilling to let the insult go unanswered.

'I hope sir, that your comment was not directed against me also?'

The soldier quailed under the king's stare. 'Of course not your grace, yer 'onour, your majesty I mean,' he stammered before rushing to the barricade in the hope of demonstrating his loyalty.

'Thank you Major,' the king said quietly. 'It would have been wrong of me to strike a man whose only crime was to have fallen for the lies and falsehoods spread about me by my uncle.'

'Indeed sire. All England knows that your late mother and father were properly married, making you the rightful heir.'

Monmouth nodded before looking back to the barricade.

'I did entertain the hope that Grafton and other officers of the Guards would have joined my banner by now. It seems like the whole world is against me.'

Trumpets blared announcing that Feversham, the royal commander, had seen the perilous position of the grenadiers and foot guards that made up his forlorn hope and had sent his cavalry forward to extricate them. Due to the confined nature of the battlefield with its numerous hedgerows, behind which the rebel musketeers were all but immune to enemy cavalry, the royal horse could do little other than to provide a distraction whilst their foot soldiers attempted to withdraw. Thomas was laughing aloud as he fired at point blank range into the confused mass of infantry and cavalry. He grinned as he saw an enemy officer topple from his saddle.

'There'll be some rich pickings there as soon as we've forced them back lads. There's another three notches to go on my musket butt once I get a minute.'

Nat and the other scythemen were lining a hedgerow that stretched along one edge of a shallow valley, on the other side of which the bulk of the royal troops were drawn up. He turned in alarm at the sound of jingling bridles, then smiled with relief when he saw that they were rebel horsemen being led by King Monmouth in person. Through the thick gun smoke that choked the battlefield Nat could see that more horsemen had been sent around the other flank and that the royal troops were now in full retreat, infantry and cavalry alike. A great cheer went up from the rebel ranks; they had finally come face to face with James' regulars and had soundly beaten them. The enemy fell back until they reached a thick hedge which they lined with musketeers, their horsemen racing past them, heading for the safety of the far slope.

'Now's the time to flush the fox from his lair!' shouted Monmouth and with a roar the whole rebel army advanced. James' men paused long enough to fire a ragged volley before withdrawing to another hedgerow and the rebels followed. Nat was about to advance towards the new enemy position when Lieutenant Ascue stopped him.

'Nat! Samuel! Take your men back to the village. The king has ordered that the cannon be brought up and sited near the village cross and he wants scythemen there to protect them from enemy cavalry.'

The two sergeants quickly gathered as many of their unit as they could find in the confusion and trotted back towards the village where they could see two guns being emplaced. Thomas had started forward with the rest of his unit but had stopped to go through the pockets of the officer that he had seen fall from his horse. He looked up and realised that he was on his own, half hidden by the dense clouds of musket smoke. He spotted the scythemen running back past him, Nat among them and saw his chance. Before all this madness had begun he would never have thought of harming his best friend but the past few weeks had turned the world on its head. All the early promise of an easy victory had gone and now there was the future to think of, a future with the lovely Eliza. Raising his musket, he aimed at his old friend, torn between his love for Nat and his lust for Eliza, then he closed his eyes and pulled the trigger. His actions went unnoticed in the noise and confusion of the battle.

Nat felt a fleeting pain, light exploding in his head before everything went black. Samuel White noticed Nat go down and dropped to the wet grass beside him. He saw that he was bleeding profusely from a wound to the head and was not moving. Samuel knew there was little he could do for him, besides which he understood where his duty lay and he slowly climbed back to his feet and led the rest of his men towards the guns. Thomas ran in the opposite direction to catch up with the rest of his regiment, not daring to look back at his fallen friend. He could not believe what he had done and briefly wondered whether or not he should add another notch to his musket stock. There would be time for doubts and self-recrimination later, for now there was more killing and more looting to be done. He licked his lips in anticipation, but when he caught up with his unit he found that the rebels' attack had stalled. The enemy cavalry had retired to the top of the slope on the far side of the shallow valley and although no guns had yet made it up the steep paths from Bath, the enemy infantry were safe behind their hedge some 500 yards away across a ploughed field.

'Major Wade!' shouted the king. 'Get your men to start tearing down the hedges to their front. We shall take the battle to our enemy before he has the chance to regroup. This will be our day, God willing.'

Under the direction of their sergeants the men set to their task with a will, as the rain which had held off during the fighting returned with a vengeance. Thomas and William Pearce had quickly hacked a hole in the hedge to their front and now crouched to peer through the gap at the wide expanse of open ground that lay between them and the next hedge-line where the enemy's colours hung limply in the rain.

'Can't say I fancy charging 'cross that there bloody field straight into they guns,' said William.

The rebels had acquitted themselves well so far but there was a big difference between defending a barricade or a thick hedge and attacking regular soldiers across open land. Monmouth had started back towards the village to organise the other regiments that had not yet been engaged when Wade caught up with him.

'Well done Major. Your men performed commendably well.' He looked to the skies which were already starting to clear. 'It looks like the storm is abating.'

'I fear your majesty that the real storm has yet to hit. The enemy has managed to drag his cannons up the road from Bath.'

'Very well, let us see what Feversham is about.' He turned his mount and spurred back towards the front line.

'It seems that he intends to use the guns to cover a withdrawal,' said Wade as he used his spyglass to examine the enemy positions. 'His infantry and cavalry are already pulling back into the trees on the high ground. We shall be unable to catch them now,'

'Damn him!' said Monmouth snapping his own glass shut. 'He knows that I have insufficient horse to be able to follow. Very well, get our other two guns placed and let us see what damage our gun captain, the Brandenburger, can do.'

The men of the Red Regiment waited behind their hedges, applying bandages to light wounds and checking their supplies of cartridges whilst they awaited orders. The rain had already ruined many of the prepared charges although it was unlikely that any of the muskets could be made to fire if the downpour continued. An aide rode over and spoke briefly to Sergeant Stuckley before hurrying back to the king's party.

'Right,' said Stuckley. 'It looks like our job is done for now, take a break lads.'

Thomas and William sank to the ground with their backs to the hedgerow as the two sets of artillerymen fired at each other above their heads. Biting into the paper cartridges to separate the ball from the powder had left their mouths dry and they drank thirstily from their canteens. Looking back towards the village they could see several indistinct humps where men of both sides had fallen and it was clear from the different coloured coats of the dead that the rebels had had by far the better of the day. Thomas wondered which body was that of his old friend Nat but his feelings of guilt disappeared almost as soon as they came to him as he thought of the reward that awaited him in Lyme.

'They guns are making a deal of noise but I can't see that they're doing much damage to either side,' observed William.

'After all the effort it took to get them here too! I reckon they're no good for anything other than frightening the horses,' replied Thomas.

The rest of his sentence was lost in the noise of a cannonball as it rent the air within feet of where they were sitting.

'Fuck me that were close! You reckon they was aiming at us sergeant?'

Stuckley did not reply, his body lay spreadeagled in the wet grass, blood gushing from the top of his neck. His head was nowhere to be seen.

A desultory artillery duel continued for some hours as

the tired troops on both sides withdrew, the rebels back into the village, the royal troops into the trees on the far side of the valley. Where they went after that Thomas could not guess and didn't much care. The rain continued unabated and the gathering dusk persuaded the gunners to give up the largely ineffectual contest and the guns fell silent.

'Do we collect our dead?' Samuel White asked Major Wade.

'No. We shall leave them to the tender mercy of God and the local clergy. The king has spoken to the vicar and the man has promised the dead of both sides a proper Christian burial. Let their remains stay in the place where they gave their lives for our holy cause. We will be pulling out of the village this night but I want your men to build large fires. The enemy will see them and assume that we are still camped here, allowing us to slip away without fear of being followed. By the time they realise their error we will be in Frome where food and men are promised.'

Fires were lit using tables, chairs and any other dry timber that they could find in the villagers homes and once more the exhausted men were cajoled into forming a rough column as they made ready to leave Philipsnorton for the second time. Sensing that the army's mood was poor, Ferguson moved up and down the column offering words of encouragement.

'Lift your hearts, be glad! God has given us a great victory.'

The soldiers were too tired or too wary of Ferguson's standing with the king to answer back, save one man who had stumbled upon a quantity of spirits in a house on West Street and had drunk enough to loosen his tongue but dull his wits. He turned to face the preacher.

'Victory? I can't see no signs of a fucking victory.

Strikes I that we're slinking off with us tails 'tween our legs, again.'

'Enough of such talk! We have achieved a glorious victory against the ungodly forces of the usurper. The enemy has retreated to leave us in possession of the field.'

'So after marching and suffering for two weeks now what 'ave we achieved? We've won a fucking field! And having won that field we're now marching away from it!'

Ferguson was furious. He had the man arrested for being drunk and he was hauled away before he could sow any more discontent but the incident had done nothing for the morale of those men who had witnessed it.

Despite not having been actively involved in the fighting John Carver had been hit by a spent musket ball. It had lost most of its momentum by the time that it smacked into his shoulder but for a man of his age it was enough to put him on his back and most probably out of the campaign. His injury would be properly assessed in Frome and he was loaded onto a large cart already overflowing with injured men. He lay there exposed to the rain until about eleven o'clock at night, when with a crack of a whip and a jolt the cart creaked its way on its un-sprung axles down the rutted track out of the village. Each time the solid wheels hit a pothole, hidden beneath several inches of thick mud, the injured men cried out in pain. Placing them in a cart was meant to be an act of kindness but in reality it made many of their wounds worse and John wondered how many would still be alive by the time they reached Frome.

21 A FEAST FOR THE CROWS

Sunday 28ᵗʰ June 1685

The following morning the villagers crept from their homes to gawp at the aftermath of the battle and to loot the bodies. The wounded of both sides had been carried off by their comrades but the dead still lay where they had fallen. Some lay in grotesque poses, horribly maimed with missing limbs, the flies already laying their eggs in the open wounds. Others looked totally peaceful as if they had simply fallen asleep oblivious to the carnage all around them.

'A proper feast for the crows,' said one villager as he plucked a wedding ring from a dead man's finger.

The cold morning rain woke Nat. He had been drifting in and out of consciousness all night having lost a lot of blood. He opened one eye and immediately wished that he hadn't done so, he had the worst headache he could remember. It was daylight yet there was no one to be seen and it was eerily quiet after the noise of yesterday's battle. The fight was clearly over, but he had no idea who had won or why the victors weren't still there. As he tried to make sense of it all he heard voices, quiet at first but coming closer. He closed his eyes and tried to still his breathing in the hope that they might pass him by, at least until he had more idea about what was happening.

'Look 'e 'ere Amos. I thinks this 'uns still breathing. Shall I stick 'im? It'll be easier to search 'im if e's dead. Looks like an ordin'ry sol'jur but 'e might 'ave a few coins sewn into his seams.'

Nat knew that he had nothing of any value on him, his last few coins having been spent days ago, but even if he could summon the strength to speak he was certain that the looters would pay little attention to him.

'Might as well 'Enry, he looks half dead already, I'm surprised he lasted the night. Put the poor bugger out'a 'is misery.'

'Wait! Hold your hand Henry!' cried an authoritative voice. 'Leave that poor soul alone, God knows there's been enough killing here already.'

Nat opened his eyes and the pain seared through his brain again. He could vaguely make out the shape of a tall, heavyset man wearing dark clothes and a wide brimmed hat before he passed out.

When he came to, Nat realised that he was in a darkened room and was laying on a soft bed. There was a dressing of some sort wrapped around his head and as he took in his new surroundings he saw the man he had seen earlier on the battlefield approaching the bed. He had removed his hat and the light of a nearby candle shone on his bald pate. Nat's aching head was full of questions.

'Who are you? What's happened? Where am I?'

'Easy now, you are in no danger young man. My name is Edward Piggott. I am the vicar at St. Philip and St. James here in Norton and you are in my house. You've taken a nasty wound to your head but I think that it looks worse than it is, praise be to God. My rudimental examination shows that a ball has creased your skull but thankfully has not broken the bone. Such wounds produce a lot of blood, it's no wonder that you were left for dead.'

'What happened after the fight? Where is everyone?'

'Gone. The king's army left once it fell dark. Old Jake who lives over towards Midford on the Bath road said that they went away in the direction of Bradford. The rebels, who I believe had the better of the day, left last night as well though they left fires burning to convince the Earl of Feversham that they were still in the village. They've gone to Frome.'

It was clear from the way that the vicar differentiated between the king's men and the rebels that he still considered James to be the legitimate ruler. It was a view shared by many in the established church who believed that kings ruled by divine right and that mere mortals had no place challenging the issue. He saw that Nat caught the meaning of his words and he placed a kindly hand on his shoulder by way of reassurance.

'Have no fear my son, I am a man of God. We are all his children, whichever side one takes in this affair. Tis ungodly that good Christians should kill other Christians and I pray that this devilish war comes to an end sooner rather than later, but I for one will not criticise a man for following his beliefs, however misguided they may be.'

'I thank you for your help,' said Nat struggling to get to his feet, 'but I must be on my way. As soon as the sentries notice that King Monmouth has left they will surely come into the town and you will be put in mortal peril if I am found in your house.'

Piggott raised his bushy eyebrows and sighed at Nat's usage of the name King Monmouth.

'They would not dare enter my house without leave to do so, but you are right, there could be some ... misunderstanding if you were found here. I think you are well enough to travel; I will get my man Smithers to show you the backways to Frome. Go in peace my son.'

The vicar crept quietly from the room closing the door behind him and Nat heard him calling for his servant. Much though Nat wanted to lie for as long as he could in the soft bed after so many nights sleeping on the cold hard ground, he knew that both his life and that of the kindly vicar would be in peril the longer he delayed his departure. Swinging his legs out of bed he was surprised and delighted to see that his old worn-out boots had been replaced. The 'new' pair had clearly seen a lot of use but had recently been re-soled and he gave thanks to God that in this crazy world of war and killing there were still people willing to show Christian charity to strangers. There was a gentle knock at the door.

'Ah I see that you have found the boots, I hope that they fit. I'm Walter Smithers, the vicar's man servant. We should leave as soon as you are able, the king's horsemen are already on their way into the village.'

They slipped out of the vicarage's back door and struck out across the fields to the south. The eight-mile journey to Frome was largely uneventful as Smithers led the way, bypassing the villages of Beckington and Lullington. On three separate occasions they saw or heard horsemen, patrols sent out by Feversham to gather information or hunt down stragglers, but each time Smithers was able to find cover or an alternative route. Nat's head was pounding and he had to stop and sit down more than once as his dizziness returned but after three or four hours of painstakingly slow progress the pair arrived on a slight rise that overlooked the market town of Frome.

'I think you should be alright to make it on your own from here. I must get back in case any of the king's officers pay my master a visit demanding food and ale.'

Nat thanked him profusely and lamented that he had no small token to give him to show his gratitude. As Smithers slipped quietly into the trees and headed back towards Philipsnorton, Nat made his way down into Frome, crossing the broad stone bridge that spanned the fast-flowing river that gave the town its name and on into the lower of the two marketplaces. He had to find his father and Thomas, both of whom would surely have missed him by now and maybe even considered him lost. He also needed to find a chirurgeon as his wound had started to bleed again.

He reported to the first officer he saw, who happened to be from his father's Green Regiment. He was directed to nearby Cheap Street where a number of the houses that lined both sides of the steep narrow road had been commandeered by the army and where the injured were being treated by a combination of army and local chirurgeons. He asked the officer if he could get word to his father that he was safe.

'What did you say your name was again?' the officer enquired, but Nat had passed out again through loss of blood.

While Nat was starting out on his painful journey from Philipsnorton, the wagon carrying John jerked to a halt in the upper marketplace in Frome after a slow and agonising journey. Two of the men in the wagon had died of their wounds on the way and a couple of the others looked as if they would not last much longer. From his elevated position on the wagon he watched the usual chaos when an army on the march arrives in a small market town. He needed to find where the Red Regiment was camped so that he could let his son know that he was alive, but the main column had arrived some hours earlier and the men had dispersed in search of food, drink and shelter. Each injured man was quickly assessed as they climbed or were lifted off the wagon and at last it was John's turn.

'Ball's still in the shoulder, but not too deep. We'll soon dig that out of you old timer, but you won't be able to use the arm for some months. See the regimental chirurgeon first then report to your officer for discharge, the king will have to finish this business without your help.'

John was treated by a local apothecary who had offered his services to the new king. The man wished to become a chirurgeon in time and saw the steady stream of wounded men as an ideal opportunity to get some practical experience whilst for their part the rebels were happy to receive whatever help they could get. As the apothecary worked, John questioned him about the town and the supplies and reinforcements that everyone had been told to expect.

'We're solidly behind the new king, well the townsfolk are leastways, although the nobs who live on their big estates at Marston, Orchardleigh and such still cling to their old papist views and support James. I fear though that you will be disappointed if you hope for any material support from the town. There were a goodly number of men here waiting to join and a fair supply of food and arms, but alas no longer.'

'Why what happened?' John asked before winching in pain as the apothecary probed his wound for the musket ball.

'Four days ago, the Earl of Pembroke rode in from Warminster with a force of horse from the Wiltshire militia. Ah got the bugger!' He held up his blood-stained tweezers to show the ball to John, before dropping it to the floor. 'Anyway, they carried off as much as they could and burnt the rest. The men were dispersed and the earl took away the Constable, Robert Smith who had read King Monmouth's proclamation from the market cross just two days earlier. God knows what will become of him!'

He fell silent as he finished dressing John's wound.

'Right, that's you sorted, try to take things easy. It will be very sore for a few days but you should get most of your movement back in time although at your age I can't make promises.'

John thanked him then walked out into the drizzling rain and made his way back to the marketplace where he hoped to find news of where both his own Green Regiment and Nat's Reds were camped. He did not want to leave the army but the pain in his shoulder told him that he would be of no further use to the king and with any luck he could be back in Lyme within the week where he would be able to look out for Daniel and Nancy.

He was told to look for the Red Regiment at the end of Pilly Vale, a narrow track which ran between a newly cut mill stream and a long row of weaver's cottages. The air was full of smoke from a number of furnaces that were being used to dry the cloth for which the town was famous and the smell produced by the dying process was horrendous. A number of mills spanned the stream each one emitting a constant thump, thump, thump as their huge water wheels drove large fulling hammers that crashed onto the newly woven woollen cloth to thicken the material to make it waterproof. He was glad to reach the end of the lane and enter a long lush green field flanking the river Frome. A stand of scythes propped against a wicker fence told him where Nat's unit was resting, but as he walked towards their campfires he could see no sign of his son. Sergeant Samuel White was in discussion with one of his men,

'.....I tell you sergeant they had blue hands and faces!'

'Who did?'

'They people working back there.'

'They must be dyers then,' chipped in another man, 'the colour comes from the woad that they boils up, dirty smelly work!'

'Smells like a mixture of cabbage and shit!'

White was about to comment further when he glanced up and saw John approaching. 'Damn!' he muttered under his breath. He looked away quickly but not before John had seen the look on his face.

'Where's Nat?' the old man said quietly.

'Sit down John, I've some bad news for 'e.'

'I'd rather stand thank 'e. Now tell me, where's my son?'

'As you wish.' White paused before saying as kindly as he could, 'I'm afeared that young Nat's been taken from us, I saw him fall at Philipsnorton.' Tears came to his eyes as he continued, 'he wuz shot in the head, there was nothing we could do for him John.'

The old man seemed to age before their eyes and dropped to his knees. 'Where's his body?' he asked at last.

'We were told that the local priest would see to his burial. I'm sorry.'

'So you've not seen him since he lay on the battlefield then? He could've been wounded not killed; he could still be alive!'

'Now don't get your 'opes up John, he looked dead when I did last see 'im. Philipsnorton's most likely in royal hands by now so there's no going back to check.'

John stood slowly and turned away, 'I needs to be on my own,' he said and walked towards the river.

It was Sunday and most of the soldiers had gone off in search of a religious service. Church attendances had been falling for years but in troubled times like these many found the need for the sort of comfort that only their God could provide. Whilst some went to the large parish church dedicated to St. John the Baptist, others joined gatherings of dissenters of several persuasions, Baptists, Adamites, Quakers, Muggletonians and many others. It was said that over half of the town attended these non-conformist meetings and such were the numbers involved that the authorities had been obliged to turn a blind eye to what were still technically illegal assemblies. With five thousand Protestant soldiers in town, many of them non-conformists, anyone attempting to enforce the conventicles laws would be asking for trouble on that particular Sunday.

The Constable of Broome
putting up Mr treasonable Dec...

22 HARD DECISIONS

Monday 29th June 1685

Thomas Edgecott and William Pearce found themselves on guard duty the following morning, watching the road to Warminster. The bad weather which had plagued the army since Westonzoyland had passed for the time being and the two men were pleased to have the chance of drying their clothes in the strong sunshine. They were kept busy with patrols of rebel horsemen coming and going and small groups of men appearing from the surrounding countryside to join the army. William found it hard to judge the mood of the men, for although their spirits had been lifted by the victory at Philipsnorton and by the tents that had finally been provided, they still had no idea where they would be sent next or when they would be free to return to their homes. About mid-morning a group of twenty or so horsemen appeared and Thomas called for his lieutenant even though the riders had their swords sheathed and appeared to be friendly.

'Good day gentlemen,' said the lieutenant, stepping into the road.

'Good day *my lord*, you mean,' growled their leader stressing his title. He was a small dark man with a mass of curly black hair and several days growth of beard, who would look more at home working in the fields than making small talk in the elegant drawing room of some great house.

'I beg your apology my lord. I had no way of knowing from your attire.'

'I am in my fighting clothes you fool. I am Sir John Kidd of Warminster and I would speak with the king.'

The lieutenant directed him to Cork Street, a side street off the upper marketplace where the king had taken up temporary residence in a merchant's house. Kidd said he knew the place and the horsemen rode off.

'Well it seems that the nobility are coming in at last,' said Thomas. 'About bloody time too!'

'Nobility my arse!' They turned to see an old man in a dirty white smock leading a string of donkeys laden down with bundles of wool. 'That were no lord, that were Baron Thynne's gamekeeper from his Longleat estate. Sir John indeed!'

The king had been ensconced with his senior officers and advisors since first light and was in no mood to greet Kidd, knight or not. The euphoria of the previous day's victory had evaporated with the news that Argyll's rebellion had been put down, his army scattered and the earl himself held prisoner. Any hope that the rising in Scotland would split James' limited forces had been dispelled. Despite being in trade, and therefore not a proper gentleman, Foe had proved himself remarkably resourceful on several occasions and was now on the fringes of the king's inner circle. He listened with interest to the heated discussion as Wade and others tried to persuade the king to continue with the campaign.

'How can we continue when every hand is against us! Argyll has failed and now both Churchill and Grafton have taken up arms against me. At the very least I expected some of the Guards officers to defect to my cause. In God's name, I fought beside those men, indeed I commanded many of them when I led my father's forces. How can they turn their backs on me?'

'I believe that many would have come to us if command hadn't passed to Feversham your majesty,' suggested Ferguson.

'If only Churchill had stayed in charge, the man saved my life at the siege of Maastricht in '73 and yet now he acts like the master of the hunt pursuing me at my uncle's bidding,' Monmouth raged.

'The militia has performed far better than expected and desertions from the rank and file have all but dried up after the large number that came across at Axminster,' Venner added unhelpfully.

'I am betrayed on all sides,' complained Monmouth. 'Promises of reinforcements have all proved false and there is still no news of the promised risings in Cheshire or London.'

'Maybe the time has come to abandon the rebellion sire, although it pains me to suggest it. You should consider taking a boat to the continent and regrouping. Maybe the Prince of Orange will be willing to help finance a new attempt.'

'Such a suggestion is vile Colonel Venner!' stormed Ferguson. 'Sire, your name would go down in infamy if you were to abandon your men now, men who have given so much for your cause. You would be damned in the eyes of man and God.'

The king nodded slowly. 'Then it is agreed that we will fight on.'

'With what though sire? We are desperately short of weapons and powder,' protested Venner. Foe had to suppress a smile when Venner suggested that he and Major Parsons of the Green Regiment should take the remainder of Monmouth's war chest and return to Holland to buy further armaments. Foe didn't expect to see either them or the money again and was surprised when Monmouth agreed.

'In the meantime,' the king continued, 'I shall send Nathaniel Hook, my domestic chaplain to London to urge Colonel Danvers to raise rebellion there, as he has long promised.'

When Thomas and William were relieved of their guard duty they returned to their camp on Rodden field where all the talk was of the pardon that King James had offered to any of the rebels who wished to return home. On Sunday Richard Jenkins, the vicar of St John's had read the document from his pulpit and had called on the congregation to end the unholy rebellion, Christians should not be killing fellow Christians he said. No such announcements were made at the various dissenter meetings where the majority of the preachers and their congregations longed for a return to a puritanical commonwealth ruled by parliament, it was what many of them had fought for during the late civil wars. Monmouth's officers tried to suppress the news of the pardon but hand printed notices had been produced and they circulated freely amongst the rebels. Men like Nat, Samuel White and John Carver still held a strong belief in Monmouth's cause but others were starting to take a more pragmatic view.

'What do you reckon then Thomas?' asked William. 'Be honest and be assured that this conversation will go no further.'

Thomas thought for a while before answering. 'I believed in Ferguson's assurances that the whole country would rise, commoner and gentry alike and that we would be met everywhere with ale, cider and a warm welcome. It was like that to start with wasn't it, apart from the lack of support from the nobs that is, but you can't trust those buggers can you? When we was welcomed into Taunton I thought that nothing could stop us but we was bested at Keynsham then turned away from both Bristol and Bath. All that early promise has gone and even the victory, if you can call it that, at Philipsnorton seems hollow as we was forced to slip away with our tails between our legs.'

William was listening carefully and nodding as Thomas tickled the points off on his fingers.

'I agrees with you. I too had hopes of being part of a triumphal progress through the west before turning to London, but those ambitions look to be over. You thinking of leaving for home then Thomas?'

'Who isn't?' Thomas had killed men and after initially being surprised to find that he enjoyed the experience, he now wanted more of the same, but the lure of Eliza waiting in vain for Nat to return was too strong.

'So what are you going to do about it?'

'I'm not sure to be honest. Taking the pardon would entail getting a note from a Justice of the Peace.'

Word had quickly spread about where such notes could be obtained and although the officers tried to quarantine the Justices' houses, the authorities were keen to encourage as many desertions as they could and clandestine arrangements were put in place for the rebels to present themselves away from the prying eyes of their officers and comrades.

'The other option is to sneak away in the night and look to get a pardon elsewhere. I expect I can get one at any town between here and Lyme but until I gets one I would be liable to arrest. What about you?'

'I can't bring myself to ask for a pardon. I can't leave my friends in that way, even though I too am ready to return home. I do miss my dear wife and my girls so. With me away and with no son to bring in a wage they will be living on charity and whatever work they can find and poor Ginny will have to give up her schooling with no money to pay the fees. I reckon I'll stay with the army for now and hope that our route takes us closer to Taunton, where my knowledge of the lie of the land will make it easier for me to slip away. But I wish you luck Thomas, you've done as much as any man and you can rely on me to keep quiet.'

Orders had come that the men were to be ready to march for Warminster the following morning, horsemen having already been dispatched to the Wiltshire town to arrange for suitable accommodation for the officers. The men spent the day quietly in their new tents attending to their equipment and mending worn out clothing as best they could. The training that was usually undertaken whenever the army went into camp was abandoned as the officers and sergeants were fully employed trying to stop the steady flow of deserters. John visited the field beside the River Frome again in the evening hoping against hope to hear news of his son. He was loathed to leave the army without knowing for certain where Nat was but he was encouraged by his friends to go, now that he had his discharge papers signed by his regimental colonel. The pickets posted to stop deserters were bound to question anyone leaving the town, papers or not so the sooner he got out the better they told him.

Tuesday 30th June 1685

The plan to move to Warminster, in the general direction of London was abandoned as patrols reported that the royal army was camped at nearby Westbury and that the swarms of enemy cavalry they had seen would make short work of the rebel infantry in the open countryside. Instead the rebel column struggled up Frome's steep hill to the south-west before taking the old ridgeway road towards Shepton Mallet. Thomas didn't march with them, having slipped away in the night.

The ancient road ran along the top of the Mendip hills until reaching the small hamlet of Doulting, where the land dropped away sharply towards a sizeable village in the middle distance. As they wound their way down past the parish church which stood sentinel on the very edge of the escarpment Samuel White spotted an old man struggling back up the hill towards the village, bent double under the huge bundle of firewood that he carried. Samuel pointed to the village ahead and called to the man. 'Father, what's the name of that place?'

'Shep'on Mall'it,' came the terse reply. It was obviously not the first time he had been asked the question that day.

'Shepton? Shit! We're back where we damned well started. We 're going round in bloody circles!'

The army straggled into Shepton, their welcome being noticeably less enthusiastic than when they were last there. Countryfolk weren't stupid, they knew that if an army visited a place twice then they were almost certainly retreating the second time around. If their grasp of military tactics wasn't up to drawing such conclusions, the downcast looks on the faces of the rebel soldiers was enough to tell them all they needed to know. The heavy wagons which were interspersed with the marching men overflowed with wounded, only adding to the impression of a beaten army. If King Monmouth was losing the war as it appeared, then best not to show too much support for him. Tales that there had been widespread looting in Frome had preceded the rebel's arrival making the villagers of Shepton more cautious still, even though those stories had become confused in the telling, with the royal troops having done their fair share of pillaging both before and after Monmouth's troops had descended on the town. Doors that were opened to them just a week earlier were now firmly closed, the villagers hoping that the ragtag rebels would pass through quickly.

'Have you heard the latest rumour?' Thomas Cleeve the carpenter from Stoford asked his new mate John Harries as a group of rebels searched in vain for food and shelter.

'Tis said that a Quaker minister named Thomas Pheere has arrived from the Polden Hills, wherever they are, and has promised that ten thousand clubmen are waiting to join us at Axbridge. Maybe that's why we're heading west again.'

'I'll believe that when I sees it,' moaned Harries. 'Ow many times have us 'eard of men waiting to join us who then fail to turn up. What in Heaven's name is a clubman anyways?' he asked no-one in particular.

Geoffrey Littlechild, a card maker who had joined in Bridgwater had been listening to the conversation.

'In the civil war, the men of the Poldens grouped together to protect their villages against violation from both sides,' he said. 'They didn't support the king or parliament, they just looked out for their own property.'

'Why are they called clubmen?'

'Cos they had no proper weapons to defend their homesteads, only thick wooden clubs. Primitive but deadly in the hands of a strong man.'

'Well they'll be most welcome,' said Cleeve, 'as long as they brings their own food that is!'

For the second time in two days Nat found himself waking up in a strange bed, although this one was nowhere near as luxurious as the one in Philipsnorton. From elsewhere in the building he heard the screams of men who were receiving rudimental medical treatment. An orderly passed the open doorway and noticed that he was awake.

'Awake at last!' he said as he entered the dirty room and poured water into a tankard.

'Thank you.....'

'Simon,' replied the orderly. 'You were found collapsed in the marketplace and brought here. You've been asleep for a day and a half.'

Nat drained the cooling liquid before swinging his feet to the floor and making his way unsteadily across the room. The sun was beginning to set, slanting through the thick glass of the windows that looked out onto a narrow twisting street with a small stream running in a gully down the middle. Simon told him that the stream was fed from a fountain at the top of the hill, just below the church and as Nat watched the clear water ran pink for a few seconds where someone further up the hill had emptied a bucket of blood tainted water into it.

'The leet proves useful for getting rid of all the blood. Runs out into the river near the bridge. Near every house on the street is being used to treat the wounded.'

'By God I feel weak,' Nat said, leaning on the windowsill.

'I'm not surprised. You've lost a lot of blood from that wound. Then of course the chirurgeon had to bleed you.'

'What! He drew blood even though I've lost so much?'

'Oh yes, he had to. Had to balance your humours. The potion that he administered to empty your bowels will have left you drained as well. Standard practice. Now you must rest and let your body replace the blood you've lost.'

'What do you mean, let my body replace the blood?'

'The Lord God in his infinite wisdom has made it possible for your body to make new blood to replace what it has lost.'

'Are you sure?'

'Of course. Do you think that there is only so much blood in your body and that it will simply run out at some point? What do you think happens with new-born babies? How could they fit all the blood needed by an adult into their little bodies?'

'I'd not thought about it,' admitted Nat, beginning to tire of the conversation. Before turning back towards the bed he took a final look out of the window and was surprised at how quiet the town seemed.

'Where is everyone?'

'All gone, pulled out this morning, headed towards Shepton Mallett. Now back to bed and rest!'

It was dark outside when Nat was awoken by the orderly.

'We've just heard that outriders from King James' army have been seen down at Welshmill, they could be here any minute! We'd best see about getting you out of town before they arrive.'

Nat began to dress as quickly as his emaciated body would allow but was still not ready when a voice called up the stairs, 'Simon! James' cavalry are in the marketplace!'

'With me! Now!' shouted Simon, half dragging Nat into the corridor, through the house and out into a dark alleyway. Turning first to the left then right they ascended a series of wide stone steps before passing in front of the huge wooden doors of the parish church. Simon led Nat quickly up the steep cobbled road that ran along the side of the upper churchyard, then rapped three times on the door of the first house on the right-hand side. The door was opened immediately and Nat was pushed inside. The door slammed behind him.

'We need to use the tunnels!' explained the orderly. The householder simply nodded and led the way into the kitchen where he pulled open a pantry door and began removing the floorboards to reveal a large dark hole. By the light of a flaming torch Nat was amazed to see that the hole dropped some twenty feet into an underground passageway. He could just make out the handholds that had been cut into the walls to aid descent.

'Hurry, the troopers will be scouring the town for rebels.'

Once in the subterranean passageway Nat could see that it led away in both directions and was surprised that it was high enough for him to be able to stand upright.

'This way,' said the orderly, squeezing past him and trotting away to the right.

'Where are we going? Where do these tunnels lead?

'They go all over, or should I say all under the town. No idea who built them or when but folk have been using them for years to move about unseen. Some say that they were built to spirit away priests when they were liable to arrest and persecution more than a hundred years ago, but no one knows for certain. These days they're only used by children or those looking to avoid the excisemen. We've a long way to go to get out of the town, so move as quick as you can.'

Side passageways led off at irregular intervals but the pair continued in the same general direction as far as Nat could tell by the flickering light of the torch. After thirty minutes or so they came to a junction where a much wider passage led away to the left. The passage they had been using had been cut through the living rock, but this new tunnel was far more regular and was lined with cut stone.

'This is where I must leave you. Take the torch and follow this new tunnel as far as it goes, there's no other turnings so you can't get lost. You'll come out in the village of Nunney, just above the old castle. Once out of the tunnel continue west and you'll reach Shepton Mallet. God go with you.'

Nat thanked him, grateful that once again he had been saved by the kindness of strangers. The new tunnel seemed endless and more than once Nat worried that he had missed a turning before reminding himself that Simon had said that there were no side tunnels. He walked on until the torch gutted and went out, plunging him into total darkness. He stumbled onwards with his arms straight in front of him, the last thing he needed in his weakened state was to walk straight into a stone wall, although the tunnel did seem to run more or less in a straight line. After another ten minutes or so the air started to taste sweeter and he noticed that the darkness before him was more dark grey than inky black. He staggered on given new energy by the prospect of getting out of the tunnel until without warning the tunnel turned sharply to the left and he was outside. After the darkness of the tunnels the full moon seemed unnaturally bright showing up every little detail of the countryside. The towering remains of Nunney Castle to his left blotted out the stars as he set off across the fields hoping that he would come up with the tail of the army before too long and praying that the enemy cavalry would not take up the chase until the morning.

23 REUNION AND DESERTION

Tuesday 30th June 1685

After walking all night and having lost so much blood Nat was exhausted and almost fell into the arms of the picket that was posted on the road between Frome and Shepton Mallet. It was clear from his appearance that he was no royal soldier and that in his wretched state he posed no threat to anyone but the guards were still wary. They had been living on their nerves all night after a long day which had seen the column under continual harassment by royal cavalry patrols. He was given a drink of water as one of the guards was sent to fetch an officer.

The sergeant who finally appeared looked as if he hadn't slept for days and he too was taking no chances.

Two men were summoned from the reserve picket some fifty yards further back and they escorted Nat to the tents of the Red Regiment where it was hoped that someone would vouch for him. As he was led away Nat heard the crash of musket fire as yet another royal patrol came within range of the pickets; the enemy were pressing again after the brief respite that followed the battle at Philipsnorton.

Samuel White, Henry Outwell and a couple of the other scythemen were sheltering in the same cow shed that they had used on their last visit to the town and they were delighted and shocked in equal measure when Nat walked in.

'Bloody hell Nat, you nearly gave I an 'art attack! I thought you was dead!' said Samuel. 'I saw you shot down at Philpsnorton and thought you a gonner!'

Nat told them all about the Reverend Piggott and Simon the orderly taking him through the Frome tunnels when a look of horror came over White's face.

'What is it?' said Nat.

'Your poor father! I told him that you were dead!'

Nat jumped to his feet. 'Do you know where the Greens' are camping Sam? I should go and let 'im know I'm safe.'

'I knows where they be, but John won't be there. He's headed home to Lyme Nat, took a musket ball in his shoulder.' He saw the concern on Nat's face. 'He should make a full recovery but it were clear that he'd be no further use to the king.'

White was unaware that John had decided to stick with the army when it left Frome and was at that very moment safe and well in Shepton. There was safety in numbers John reckoned and he would take his leave of the army when they got closer to home.

Nat told his friends of his adventures since they were

last together.

'And what of Thomas Edgecott, William Pearce and Sergeant Stuckley, are they all well?' he asked Samuel.

'Stuckley's dead. Had his head knocked clean off by a cannonball at Philipsnorton. I saw William this morning as the regiment was dispersed to look for shelter but I've not seen Thomas since we were in Frome. I'll ask around,' he said and stepped out into the rain.

Nat was famished, he hadn't eaten for nearly two days and he looked hungrily at the pot hanging over the small fire.

'Sorry it's not much Nat but there was nothing to be 'ad in Frome, the militia from Wiltshire took everything of value just before we got there,' Outwell apologised as he filled a small bowl with a thin broth.

As Nat sat sipping at the thin pottage Aaron Tucker ducked under the door lintel. 'Look what I've found,' he beamed. He was holding a squawking chicken upside down by its legs. 'Proper food at last!'

'You be careful Aaron,' said Outwell, 'if the provosts catch you it'll be the rope for 'e. You knows that the king 'as banned thievery.'

'Can't be thievery if there b'aint no one to thieve it off. I found this 'un wandering around in the rain and felt sorry for the poor little orphan.'

The unfortunate foul was soon killed, plucked, quartered and added to the pot. Nat's exertions were catching up with him and he began to doze, dreaming that he was sitting beside a roaring fire with Eliza at his side, a mug of cider in his hand and the remnants of a good meal on a wooden plate. A dog was licking at the plate as a small child, his son maybe, teased it with a stick. He was jerked back to reality by raised voices and looked up to see that two officers had entered the shed, no doubt alerted by the fine smell coming from the cooking pot. Tucker was pleading his innocence but his efforts were undermined by the drumstick that he was waving around as he spoke. Realising the futility of his argument he tried a different approach.

'All right. All right. So I've found a chicken, but you ain't got no right to arrest me for it. I'm a member of the clergy, so by law you 'as to 'and me over to my bishop for judgement.'

'If you're a clergyman then I'm Nell Gwynn,' sneered the provost.

'If you don't believe me then give I zummat to read and I'll prove it to 'e.'

The provost produced a small bible and opened it at a random page. 'From the top,' he instructed, raising his voice as the rain grew heavier and drummed on the roof of the shed. Tucker took the proffered bible and read the text in a clear and strong voice.

'Proverbs 30:31. The strutting rooster, the male goat also, and a king when his army is with him....' He laughed; the provost couldn't have picked a more appropriate passage if he'd tried.

'All right, that's enough. It still don't prove you're a clergyman,' interrupted the officer.

'I knows the law as well as you do. If a man can read he's to be treated as clergy and is entitled to be handed over to 'is own bishop for punishment. You can't touch I.'

The two officers looked at each other, they had one last card to play. 'Show us your thumb then,' said one grabbing Tucker's arm in a vice like grip. With difficulty Tucker twisted his hand around to show a dirty but otherwise undamaged thumb. Benefit of the Clergy could only be claimed once and the provost was hoping to see the tell-tale 'T' that would be branded on the thumb of anyone found guilty of theft by his bishop.

'So you gunna arrest I then? Take me to my bishop?' The tension in the shed was palpable and Nat was wondering which way things would go when the situation was resolved in an unexpected way as one of the other scythemen broke wind loudly.

'Sorry 'bout that!'

The others burst out laughing and the provosts knowing that the spell had been broken turned and strode away. They didn't believe for one minute that Tucker was a clergyman, but God alone knew where they would be able to find a bishop and then the man could rightly claim that he had the right to be brought before his own bishop. They had no option but to let him go, it was just too much bother to take the man into custody especially as they would have to guard and feed him. They knew full well that having got away with it this time he would use the same ruse again but their hands were tied.

Once the provosts were out of earshot the men fell into conversation about the way the campaign was going. They had stayed with the army rather than desert or take the king's pardon but they were clearly unhappy with their situation. The rain, the lack of food and the feeling of being hunted by enemy horsemen was grinding down their resolve. Just as they were settling down to digest their unexpected meal the call came to turn out for a review.

'What in this bloody weather? What the hell for?' asked Tucker to no one in particular.

'You're in the army now my son, so if the officers say we have to parade up and down in the rain, then that's what we have to do. If they say jump you answer how high?' replied White.

'Do you think the king's trying to impress some local dignitary?' asked Nat.

'I suspect it's more to do with lining us all up so he can count how many men he's got left after Philipsnorton and the desertions that followed.'

Once the review was over, the bedraggled men returned sullenly to their various billets. As Samuel White stirred their fire back into life the others sheltering in the cow shed resumed their discussion about the rebellion and in particular the lack of support from what they called the better sort.

'What I still don't understand is why none of they gentry 'as joined us yet,' queried Tucker.

'Some 'ave,' replied White, looking up from the fire, 'but not as many as I'd expected or hoped for.'

'You still got that pamphlet with 'e sergeant?' asked Tucker. 'The one that talked of the duke's visit to your old master's house at Forde Abbey.'

'*King's* visit,' corrected White.

'Whatever. So 'ave 'e got it?'

White sat back and carefully removed a folded copy of *A True Narrative* from his waistcoat pocket. 'I do, what of it?'

'Just read out to us the names of those that the ....,' he hesitated, '*the king* .... stayed with on his tour.'

By the light of the rekindled fire Samuel scanned the document, calling out the various names as he reached them.

'Esquire Thynne at Longleat, Esquire Speke at Whitelackington, Sir Sydenham at Brempton, William Stroud Esquire of Barrington, my old master Edmund Prideaux of course, Sir Walter Young at Calliton, esquire Dukes at Otterton, Sir William Courtney at Exeter and Esquire Harvey at Yeovil. Satisfied?'

'No, I b'aint!'

'Because....?'

'Because none of they buggers have shown their faces since the duke, sorry, the king landed at Lyme these three weeks since. Now why do 'e think that might be?' Before anyone could answer Tucker continued, 'because my friends, they've got better sense than to get mixed up in this mess.'

'Be fair,' said Nat, 'they've got far more to lose than the likes of you or me.'

'Really? What's more to lose than one's life? I do wonder if they've kept out of it 'cos they're starting to doubt whether our king is truly the legitimate heir to the throne.'

'Don't you go believing all that papist talk about the king being a bastard, pardon the language,' said White. 'We've 'ad this out afore, many times. King Monmouth is the right and proper heir, according to God and the Commons and that's an end to it!'

The rain hammered so loud on the shed roof that any further discussion was impossible. Nat glanced out at the falling rain and felt for those rebel troops who had been unable to find proper shelter and would now be huddled under their coats and cloaks, soaked to the skin. The weather would do nothing to improve the mood of the army he thought. Tucker wasn't the only man sowing dissent and Nat decided that he would have to keep an eye on him.

Back in Frome Thomas was also out in the rain, down at the river's edge, concealed by its high bank and the overhanging willow trees. He had hoped to rest up for a day or two to put some distance between himself and the rebel army before making his way south, but the arrival of the king's horsemen had forced a change of plan. He thought that Lyme lay to the south and west of Frome but the direct route, as he understood it, would mean him having to follow the rebels and risk being caught between his erstwhile comrades and the pursuing cavalry. He decided instead to follow the River Frome which seemed to be heading in the right general direction, although he realised that he might have to leave the waterway if it veered too far to the east for he knew from his time on sentry duty that that would place him too close to Warminster and Longleat estate. He had heard from some of the men who had ridden in with Kidd that the baron had taken himself off to London as soon as the rebellion had started and he had no doubt that James' men would have taken the opportunity to move themselves into his comfortable house.

Fortunately for him the river continued to head the right way, even though it was getting progressively narrower as it twisted through the broken countryside south of Frome. He had thrown away anything that might identify him as a rebel soldier apart from his bayonet which was hidden inside his long coat. He was thankful that they had marched off to war in their own clothes and that Monmouth had not provided proper uniforms, as being forced to discard a stout woollen uniform coat in such weather would have been a real hardship. His musings were interrupted by the sound of voices ahead, women's voices. He crept forward using the long reeds that grew beside the river as cover and spotted a group of women washing clothes in the river. There seemed to be no men about and deciding that the women posed no threat he straightened himself up and walked as casually as he could towards them.

'Good morning ladies,' he called when he was some twenty paces from them.

The women looked up from their chores in surprise and not a little alarm. The first to recover herself was a large woman of about forty, with thick arms and her hair pulled tight in a severe bun.

'You stay away,' she threatened pulling a large heavy stone from the riverbed and waving it menacingly.

Thomas held his arms out placatingly. 'No need to be afeared ladies, I mean no harm and as you can see I carry no weapon.'

'A man is still a man, weapon or no. We've 'ad enough of sol'jurs and their ways to be wary of any strangers, no matter how innocent they look.' Thomas was aware that his boyish figure and light curly hair always served to make him appear less of a threat. Little do they know he thought smiling to himself.

'All I seek is a bit of Christian charity to help me on my way, a bite of food and directions home.'

'No point asking us for victuals, the rebels came through yesterday and helped themselves to all we 'ad. When they were last in Shepton they paid for what they took, but all we saw this time was hungry men taking whatever they wanted.'

'I'm truly sorry to hear that, may God punish those who break His commandments.' Once again he was happy to invoke the Lord's name to put the women at ease even though he was personally in no doubt that there was no God. 'Is this place called Shepton then?'

'No. This 'ere's Witham Friary, Shepton's hours away over the hills there.' She turned and pointed to the low hills that stood behind the tiny hamlet.

Thomas's evident concern at their ill treatment had softened the woman's attitude somewhat and she lowered the rock that she had been holding. 'Where be it that you're headed then?'

'I lives right down on the coast, a place called Lyme, in Dorsetshire.'

'Never 'eard of it, so I can't tell 'e the way. Sorry.'

'Don't concern yourself,' Thomas smiled. 'Where will I get to if I continue to follow this stream?'

'Just carry on along the valley and you'll come to Bruton.'

The name meant nothing to Thomas. He was very hungry but a quick glance towards the sorry cluster of cottages that made up Witham Friary convinced him that there would be little chance of him being able to steal the food that he desperately needed, especially if the rebels had already stripped the place clean. If Bruton was a larger settlement as seemed likely then it held more promise. Having heard their parents talk of the civil war when soldiers of both sides had defiled the area the women knew better than to ask too many questions of strangers, they were just happy to see the back of him when he thanked them and strode away up the valley.

Rebells plundering the
Loyall Gent: houses at Wells

24 DESECRATION AND DEBAUCHERY

Wednesday 1ˢᵗ July 1685

Another early start saw the army on the road not long after the sun had dragged itself reluctantly above the horizon only to disappear into dark grey clouds that showed no sign of dispersing. As he tramped along the narrow lane leading out of Shepton with his replacement scythe over his shoulder Nat wondered what the commanders could do to raise the men's morale. At the start of the campaign he had looked about with interest at the unfamiliar landscape and the different plants or birds that they encountered, but now his world had narrowed to the sodden back of the man marching in front of him. How much longer could this go on?

A familiar voice called him and he looked up from his reverie to see Foe sat astride his fine horse. He was as immaculately turned out as always, as if he had stepped straight out of a fashionable London coffee house. Nat wondered how he was able to keep so clean.

'A miserable day Nat. How are you? I heard that you had been injured. I looked for you in Frome but without luck.'

'I'm mostly recovered thank 'e, though my head still hurts from time to time and this weather doesn't help. Have you any idea where we are headed?'

'Wells. No more than five or six miles, just as well given the rain. A fine town with one of the most handsome cathedrals in all England.'

'I'm sure we're not going there just to look at the buildings!'

'No of course not,' laughed Foe. 'Word has it that James has been foolish enough to leave several wagons belonging to Kirke's regiment there with only a small guard. The king intends to make him pay for his foolishness.'

'And we all have to go do we?'

'Best to keep the men together with so many enemy patrols about.'

'And how will we be received there do you think?'

'There's no telling to be honest with you. The people of the West Country are generally still well disposed to our cause but the canons of the cathedral are known to have sent monies to London to aid James in his war against us, so we will need to be on our guard. Right, I must away to my duties, it is good to see you well Nat.'

Samuel White had not been marching with the other scythemen and he now jogged to the front of the column to join Nat.

'Thought I'd let you now, William Pearce is further back down the line of march, fit and well but there's no sign of Thomas. I think he might have deserted.'

'Not Thomas surely.'

'It seems so. Whether it was someone dripping poison into his ear in Frome or of his own volition I know not.'

They tramped on into the teeth of a gale, a strong wind driving the rain into the faces of the men. The road from Shepton Mallet fell away into a wooded valley with a fast-flowing stream at the bottom which the locals called the River Sheppey. Nat thought this was a grand name for a watercourse that looked no more than six inches deep at most despite the recent rains and which he felt he could jump clear over with a decent run up. The road followed the river through the villages of Croscombe and Dinder before climbing slightly towards Dulcote from where the twin towers of Wells cathedral and a taller tower, presumably belonging to the parish church showed in the near distance above the treetops.

It was still early in the morning when the head of the column moved down the slope towards Wells and the Bishop's Palace with its high walls and surrounding moat.

'I'm hoping the place is free of enemy troops, I wouldn't fancy trying to take that place if it were well garrisoned,' said Samuel White.

The wagons they had come to find were quickly located behind the arched entrance to the Vicars' Close where two parallel rows of alms houses and a small chapel made up a long, enclosed courtyard. It was clear from the piles of droppings on the cobbles that the draught animals had been housed in the courtyard as well, but there were none there now nor any sign of the troopers that were meant to be guarding the wagons. They had disappeared leaving the wagons with their valuable cargo behind them. A guard was posted on the wagons and the rest of the men were told that the army would spend the rest of the day in Wells to allow time for Pheere's clubmen to come in. As usual the cavalry, being the first to arrive had claimed the best indoor cover, but as the Red Regiment headed the long column of foot soldiers they got next choice and set up camp in the Bishop's Palace grounds. Their officers were able to find reasonable accommodation in the palace itself, whilst the men pitched their tents on the large lawns that lay within the high walls of the roofless ruins of the great hall. With nothing better to do Nat decided to take a look at the cathedral which stood nearby.

Its size was impressive although Nat disapproved of the decoration, the front being adorned with hundreds of carved stone figures of kings, apostles, angels and others whose identity Nat could only guess at. It all smacked of popery and idolatry. As he turned to take in the other buildings that surrounded the large green in front of the cathedral he saw an old man with a familiar stoop walking slowly towards him.

'Father!' he called. The two men ran towards each other and embraced. They both started talking at once, anxious to check that the other was well. Nat noticed that his father winced when he held his shoulders and stepped back quickly.

'I'm sorry father, I forgot about your wound, how is it?'

'Well enough, but my fighting days are over. I intend to strike out for home soon but I'll stay with the army so long as it takes me nearer Lyme. I looked for you in Frome and feared that you were lost.'

'I nearly wuz. I were struck by a ball at Philipsnorton and was left for dead. The kindness of the vicar there and the good people of Frome kept me safe 'til I was fit enough to return to the army.' They fell silent, lost in their own thoughts.

'What say you we find something to eat and drink before the army strips the place bare?' said John. 'I think I still have a few pennies somewhere.'

As they turned away to search for a tavern a unit of horsemen trotted across the grass and entered the cathedral by a large side door.

'Stabling the horses in the cathedral. Not sure how I feels about that,' said John with a shake of his head.

They had thought to visit one of the many inns along Sadler Street which faced the cathedral green but the White Hart, the Flower de Luce and the Swan were all full to bursting with drunken soldiers spilling out onto the street. In the end they found a small alehouse called the Rainbow alongside the lock-up in High Street.

'I reckons there'll be trouble in the city later,' said John. 'Far too many men drinking heavily.'

'You're right and I can't see this lock-up being anywhere near big enough when things do turn ugly.'

The food at the Rainbow was little better than the pottage that they had been living off for the past two weeks but at least they were out of the persistent drizzle. They finished their meals and sat back enjoying the warmth of the fire until the inn keeper, keen to capitalise on the huge number of potential customers, hurried them out into the rain. The cathedral promised shelter from the elements but as they approached it they were disturbed to see a large crowd of men gathered outside and heard the sound of breaking glass and the crack of hammers against stone. The army contained a great many men of a puritanical persuasion and they had taken it upon themselves to smash as many of the ornately decorated windows and carved figures as they could reach. Others, full of ale or cider were joining in for the fun of it and father and son quickly realised that there was nothing they could do to stop it.

They slipped through the Judas gate that was set into the huge wooden doors of the western façade hoping to find some peace, only to be met with a scene of utter chaos. Horses stamped and defecated and men were running around breaking whatever they could, windows, furniture, statues. At the far end of the nave beyond the choir, a large group had gathered and as Nat and John walked slowly towards them Nat recognised the figure of Lord Grey, the man who had fled from the fight in Bridport, stood protectively in front of the altar with a drawn sword. Nat's sense of duty overcame his distaste for the ornate decoration and imagery of the place and he rushed to help Grey keep the crowd at bay. He had left his deadly scythe back in the camp in the Bishop's Palace but he still had his long dagger. Most of the men appeared to be drunk and Nat noticed that they were helping themselves from a beer barrel that had been propped on the ancient font.

'This is God's house!' cried Grey waving his sword from side to side. 'Get back you damned animals! Be gone from this place!'

The men dispersed in search of easier targets for their frustration, smashing the organ and the stained-glass windows of the Lady Chapel as they left. The pulpit was spared as the carved inscription was in English rather than Latin and therefore not thought to be popish, but the effigy of a dead bishop, Ralph of Shrewsbury did not fare so well as soldiers lined up to carve their initials into the smooth stone.

'I can understand their anger,' Grey admitted, 'they are hungry, they are far from home and they are frightened, but we cannot hope to build a better, fairer country through destruction.'

More officers had arrived to support Grey and Nat found that his help was no longer needed. He and John went back outside, pausing only to marvel at the concentric circles of the astronomical clock that had been marking the time of day and the phases of the moon for more than three hundred years. As they watched, the small sun on the inner disc reached the '15' position to mark the quarter hour and the four models of mounted knights above the clock face began to go round, two clockwise and two anticlockwise. On each rotation the knight on the left was unhorsed by his opponent's lance to cries of 'there goes the usurper James, knocked on his arse again....and again...and again.'

John was pleased to see that the clock showed the earth at the centre of the universe, where he felt it rightly belonged despite the claims of the so-called natural philosophers in London that the earth actually revolved around the sun. What rubbish! Being younger, Nat was more inclined to believe the new discoveries that were being made on an almost daily basis.

'Not sure why anyone would want to know the time anyway,' said John. 'You gets up when it's light and goes to bed when it gets dark, that seems simple enough to me.'

Outside the rain has stopped although the skies remained leaden. The lack of discipline they had witnessed inside the cathedral seemed to have spread into the wider town and screams could be heard as men used axes to break into private homes in search of food, drink, valuables or women.

'This is madness!' exclaimed John. 'What is happening to this army?'

'It's as my Lord Grey said, the men have had enough. There seems to be no direction or plan anymore, if there ever was one! We just march and march, going around in circles with the enemy horsemen snapping at our heels like dogs at a bear baiting. If the king can't bring the enemy to battle soon the whole lot of them'll go home. When I joined the army in Lyme the men were sober and God-fearing. There were no blasphemy and only moderate drinking as one would take with a meal. But now this.'

With the town in uproar no one would notice that John was not with his own unit who had commandeered the walled enclosure of the Deanery courtyard, besides he was officially no longer a part of the army so he returned with Nat to the Bishop's Palace where a guard post had been established inside the gatehouse that stood at the end of the short drawbridge over the moat.

'Can't be too careful,' said the sergeant in charge of the picket as he recognised Nat. 'Don't want no drunks coming in 'ere and pilfering from the regiment's tents.'

Nat led the way to his own tent where father and son laid down together and tried to sleep despite the devilish noise from the town that went on throughout the night, seemingly without anyone being willing or able to stop it.

'What was that Nat? John asked sleepily, 'did 'e say zummat?'

'No father, I was just saying goodnight to Eliza!'

While Nat and John were struggling to get to sleep in Wells, Thomas was making his way stealthily towards Bruton. He had followed the River Frome until it disappeared into an area of swampy ground but he soon picked up another stream that looked to be headed in the right direction. He continued along the valley floor between high wooded hills for the next hour or so until a farm track to the right of the stream offered easier going. He was happy that he was able to make better progress but after half an hour his heart sank as he saw that the track led through a dark stand of trees. The drop back down to the river had become far too precipitous to attempt in the gathering darkness and he was forced to go on. He had always had a fear of confined places since being locked in a cupboard by a drunken uncle and as the track narrowed and the banks became higher on each side he slowed his pace. The sun had set and the moon had yet to rise so that it was hard to see more than a few yards under the canopy of the trees. He was about half-way along the sunken lane when he heard the thump of hooves and the jingle of bridles. He pressed himself into the ferns that grew from the steep sides of the lane hoping that in the gloom he would be overlooked, but it was not to be as two riders reigned in and challenged him.

'You there, come out of the shadows and show yourself.' Thomas' hand moved to his hidden bayonet but he knew that he would have no chance against the two horsemen who had now drawn their pistols. He stepped into the centre of the lane.

'By God, you scared me zummut rotten. Can't a man go about 'is business on the king's road without being accosted?'

'And what business might that be on this road at night? Decided to desert the rebel army have you?'

'Don't take I for one of they traitors I beg 'e! I lives in the village back there, Witham Friary, and I'm on my way to see my sister in Bruton. Her youngest lad called to say that she'd taken ill and that I was to come quickly.' He was pleased with himself that he had remembered both place names.

'So where's the boy now?'

'Back home with my wife Eliza.' How easily the lie that he had a wife named Eliza came he thought. 'He was fair worn out running to us all the way from Bruton so Eliza made him sit and take a bite of supper. He'll stay the night now cos the roads ain't safe with so many rebels running loose in the area.'

His quickly contrived story seemed to satisfy the riders. He was lucky that the men were part of the royal army normally based near London for if they had been local men they would surely have noticed that his thick Dorset accent was far different from that of the Frome area. To them he sounded like just another country bumpkin.

'Have you seen any of the traitors?'

'I did as it 'appens. Two of them on the high ground to the right there, a mile or so back. It was hard to be sure in the darkness but I think they was wearing red coats.'

'Probably deserters from the militia. Be on your way then.' They turned their horses and cantered back in the direction of Frome and Thomas breathed a sigh of relief before hurrying on, anxious to clear the woods as soon as he could.

25 BACK TO BRIDGWATER

Thursday 2nd July 1685

By morning things in Wells had calmed down as the men slept off the effects of their drinking. There would be no early march this day. The captured wagons intended for Kirke's Lambs, a battle-hardened regiment recently returned from action in Tangiers, had contained some food and a little coin but not much in the way of shot or powder. The rebel army's stock of both was running low following the long exchange of musketry and cannon fire at Philipsnorton and Nat and John sat and watched as men clambered onto the roof of the cathedral and began stripping the lead, which could then be cast into musket balls. Whether the wagons that accompanied the army carried large enough moulds to replace the cannon balls that had been fired Nat did not know, but he had heard that some of the miners recruited from the Mendips had been set to work sculpting round shot from locally sourced granite. The gunners complained that these crudely shaped projectiles would carry far less force, as some of the explosive energy would find its way around the sides of the irregular shot, but by using hay and bits of old cloth to pack the balls in tightly they might just suffice.

Nat was reminded of all the time he spent in Lyme making up paper cartridges which had then dissolved into a soggy mess in his pockets when it rained and was glad that as a scytheman he did not have to make more. The lead for shot and the capture of the wagons were welcome plunder to an army that was having to live off the land, but Nat wondered again if it was necessary for the whole army to have come to Wells. There again he reasoned, he had no idea where they would have gone instead. He hoped that the king and his advisors knew.

Nat returned to his tent where a couple of his fellows had set a pot over a fire made from wood torn from an old fence.

'Pottage again I suppose,' he sighed.

'A mite better than that today,' smiled the man designated as cook, 'Jem here managed to bring down a brace of wood pigeons with that sling of 'is.'

'Then we'll have a proper feast as I've just found some of those fancy tea leaves that Master Foe did give I.'

The army was assembled in the early afternoon and word was that they were headed back to Bridgwater with the expectation of collecting the clubmen on the way. Bridgwater was home for many in the army and the chance to see friends and family again was welcome, besides the town was believed to have been untouched by royal troops giving the hope that the army would be able to resupply itself there.

Others did not take the news so well. Morale was low and retreating to the west meant that the prospect of a triumphal march on London which would bring the campaign to an end was receding. There was a general feeling that the king had failed to take advantage of the victory at Philipsnorton where the much-feared regulars had been put to flight.

Their route to Bridgwater would take them back across the marshy Somerset levels and the men knew that they would find little to forage there so when, on the outskirts of Wells they passed a large cider apple orchard the temptation proved too much for many. Discipline was breaking down and men who two weeks ago would never have dreamed of stealing another mans' apples were stripping the branches bare. The apples were small and tasted sour and although someone suggested that they should wait until they camped that night when the fruit could be stewed to prevent stomach cramps, the men were hungry and greedily consumed the unripe fruit. The last few hedgerows before the land levelled out contained patches of bramble which provided a few blackberries although these too were some weeks from being properly ripe. Most of the berries were still green and whilst the occasional bush was a little further on, that fruit was dark red and sour rather than black and sweet. William Pearce was lucky to spot the pale green leaves and shiny black fruit of a blackcurrant bush as he pushed into the undergrowth to relief himself. A few more weeks and there would be ample fruit he thought, but for now the pickings were very slim and whilst the handful of berries he was able to find were palatable they did little to assuage his hunger.

John had re-joined his old regiment for the march and as such found himself towards the back of the column where there would be no chance of finding anything edible still growing. He couldn't believe the amount of discarded equipment that littered the road or the number of men who had dropped out through a combination of fatigue, hunger or simple lack of resolve. He knew that the stragglers would prove easy targets for the enemy horsemen who shadowed the army but little effort was being made to help them, each man looking solely to his own salvation. Monmouth sat with his senior officers and watched the men trudge past. A few saw him and raised a half-hearted cheer but most passed without looking up.

'The king looks troubled,' Nat said to Daniel Foe who was walking his horse alongside.

'Uneasy is the head that wears a crown,' replied Foe enigmatically.

'Eh?'

'Sorry Nat, I forgot that you are still to be acquainted with William Shakespeare. Henry the fourth, part two.'

'But Monmouth doesn't wear a crown yet and seems increasing unlikely to do so.'

'The men need to rest sire,' Ferguson said as he watched the tired army tramp past, 'they are hardy souls but they are not conditioned to marching day after day. I fear they will be in no fit state to fight when the moment arrives.'

'We will rest in Bridgwater and God, with your help Master Ferguson will inspire them when the time comes.'

'I pray that you are right your majesty.'

If the men were suffering badly, the horses were much worse off. Most were accustomed to pulling ploughs or wagons and whilst that was heavy work, it was generally slow and plodding and rarely involved having a man sat on their back. Now they were being ridden long and hard day after day and many were being pushed to the limits of their endurance.

The road from Wells ran south and west between low hills before re-crossing the small River Sheppey outside a hamlet that was apparently called Coxley. Here the terrain changed abruptly and Nat and Samuel White, leading their scythemen at the front of the army suddenly found themselves on the open moors.

'Easy to see why the locals call these the levels, it be as flat as a mill pond.'

'Apart from that!' Samuel was pointing at the now familiar tor atop its hill at Glastonbury which lay directly ahead of them, but before they reached that landmark the army turned right onto a track that Nat could see would skirt around the town. After crossing another small river, the track turned again to avoid another settlement which Wilmott said was called Street. Nat was amazed how things had changed in just the few days since they had last walked this way, there was colour everywhere with yellow wild mustard and meadowsweet and purple touch-me-nots. The rains had given everything a boost, with the hogweed and burdock growing well above head height and Nat was sure that if the pikes and colours were lowered the foot soldiers would be able to pass through this landscape totally unnoticed. The tall reeds swayed in the light breeze as the men marched along the well-trodden paths that twisted between the shallow ponds and areas of marshland.

They were only on the levels for a short while before they turned and began to climb a long gentle slope towards a tree covered ridge which Wilmott with his local knowledge said was the old ridgeway that led arrow straight to Bridgwater. He was clearly relishing the journey, knowing that he would soon be back in his home town. After their last crossing of the levels a number of men had fallen ill with what the physicians travelling with the army described as a quartan ague, a shivering fever which left men unable to continue. They had been loaded onto carts where available or else left at the isolated cottages that dotted the countryside. Samuel suggested that the new higher route was being taken to avoid any more men falling ill.

'We've lost enough to desertion to risk many more going down with the ague.'

'I'd rather have stayed on the levels myself, despite the ague,' said Nat. 'At least down there we were safe from the risk of ambush and the going was easier.'

The rebels moved down the ridgeway as it ran along the top of the Polden hills. In places the track became so narrow that the big baggage wagons and the officers' carriages were forced to move in single file and the men who had been marching in two parallel groups in an attempt to shorten the length of the column had to bunch together. Each time this happened the rate of progress slowed and Monmouth's aides were obliged to force their tired mounts up and down the column urging the men to pick up the pace. On these narrow sections, deep valleys could be glimpsed through the trees that clung to the steep slopes on either side and the countryside seemed empty, but as soon as the track widened out the ubiquitous royal cavalry could be seen moving through the trees on the far side of the fields of ripening crops that edged up to the road. For now they seemed content to escort Monmouth's army into Bridgwater, no doubt waiting for further regulars to arrive from London so that they could attack the rebels with overwhelming force. Nat was certain that the king would have to turn and face his pursuers sooner rather than later before his army simply dissolved.

Although they made steady progress the army had left Wells too late in the day to cover the twenty-two miles to Bridgwater by nightfall and the decision was made to camp in the damp fields on either side of the track. The men were exhausted and slept where they fell, despite the hunger that gnawed at their bellies.

Back in the Mendip hills Thomas had reached the outskirts of Bruton in the early hours and decided it was best to go to ground and get some much-needed sleep. For now he wished to avoid the town which stood on the right bank of the stream and he was fortunate that he found a place where the water was easily fordable. The high ground to the south of the town looked promising and he eventually found shelter of sorts in an old barn behind the church. The roof had long since fallen in and only three walls remained, each one covered in a thick curtain of ivy. The remains of the fourth wall lay scattered among the long grass. A young elder tree grew from the top of the western wall, no doubt the result of seeds contained in the droppings of one of the many crows that nested on the walls' top. The barn stood on a steeply sided hill that gave him a good view of anyone approaching from any direction and he made himself as comfortable as he could in the corner formed by the western and southern walls where he was sheltered from the chill wind that blew up the slope. In the morning he would investigate the town, maybe even find a magistrate to obtain his pardon, but for now he needed to rest. He was asleep within minutes and didn't stir again until nearly mid-day.

Friday 3ʳᵈ July 1685

Nat had been woken just before dawn to take his turn on guard duty. The sky to the east was already light enough to hide the stars although they still shone brightly to the west. He had just begun his tour of the various pickets under his command when he was hailed by one of the guards watching the main road towards Bridgwater.

'Sergeant, I can hear voices and the tramp of feet coming from the trees to the right of the road. No sound of horses though.'

'Well done Jeb. Have the men stood ready and send word back to Major Wade.'

The pickets made their weapons ready as the sound of marching men grew louder. Nat couldn't understand where they could have come from. They had seen countless cavalry patrols as they made their way from Wells but had seen no formed bodies of infantry. Nerves were stretched to breaking point as the pickets stared into the gloom beneath the trees.

'There!' Nat called. A banner of sorts could be made out carried high above a solid phalanx of men. Nat could not discern any uniformity in their appearance in fact they appeared to be wearing ordinary peasant smocks.

'It's the clubmen! Welcome friends, welcome!'

The pickets gratefully lowered their weapons and parted to allow the group through. Their leader stepped to one side with his standard bearer who carried an apron nailed to a long pole, to allow his men to pass, then turned and shook hands with Nat.

'Thomas Plaice of Edington at your service.'

'God be praised.' Nat responded with glee. 'We are truly happy to see you, when we heard you approach we thought that the enemy had decided to attack us at last.'

Rank after rank of grim-faced men carrying an assortment of weapons marched past. Nat smiled as he noticed that many carried stout wooden clubs, but his smile disappeared as the stream of men ran out, a few boys and women bringing up the rear.

'Where are the rest?'

'This is it,' said Plaice. 'I expected more myself but the militia have been very active and many men have been prevented from joining us.'

'But there are what, a hundred and fifty, two hundred at most!'

'One hundred and sixty, but worth five hundred in a fight.'

'I'm sure they are but we were promised ten thousand or more.'

'What the duke, or should I now call 'im the king, don't understand is that the clubmen gather to defend their own, they ain't there to fight anyone else's battles for them and t'was a mistake for Pastor Pheere to suggest otherwise.'

Nat felt thoroughly deflated. He had hoped that the arrival of the clubmen would raise the army's morale and even a quarter of the numbers promised would more than compensate for the losses that they had suffered through battles, sickness, attrition and desertion. He wondered how the news that so few had come would be received by an army in which spirits were already so low. He told Plaice where he could find the king and he feared for the reaction that their small numbers would bring from his commander.

Foe was reporting on his latest scouting mission when Plaice was shown into the king's tent. The king was clearly shocked that so few had come, although his innate good manners meant that he greeted the captain with good grace. As always Ferguson tried to look on the bright side.

'Your majesty, I have no doubt that there will be many more awaiting us in Bridgwater, men who have made their way to the town having been unable to avoid the militia checkpoints to join us here. May I suggest that when we march to Bridgwater, the clubmen with their banner be allowed to lead the army. It will encourage others to join.'

'If I may your majesty,' interjected Foe, 'but I have lately returned from the town and I am afraid that our welcome may not be as enthusiastic as we would all hope. Indeed, I bear a request from the mayor and his corporation that the army does not enter the town at all. The town was besieged during the late wars between your grandfather and parliament and held out for only eleven days before most of it was burnt to the ground. They are frightened that the same thing will happen again sire.'

'By God Foe, who are they to decide where the King of England may or may not go! We will march on the town this very morning with the clubmen at our head as suggested and God help them if they try to deny us entry.'

26 CORNERED

Friday 3rd July 1685

For the first time in days the dawn revealed high thin clouds without any hint of the atrocious weather that had dogged the army for more than a week. The cooking fires in Bridgwater had already thrown a smoky haze over the town whilst away to the right the sun shone golden on the twists and turns of the River Parrett as it wound its way towards the sea that could be seen shimmering in the distance. It was a scene to gladden any heart and for the first time in days the men sang as they came down from the Polden Hills. With the clubmen in the vanguard the army picked up the old road to Bristol and entered Bridgwater over a wooden drawbridge which crossed the wide moat that was re-filled twice a day when the turning tide poured up the Parrett. Even when the tide was out the ditch would be a considerable obstacle, with several feet of thick mud in the bottom.

When they had first marched into the town two weeks ago the welcome had been overpowering, but not so this time around. There was no greenery hanging from the houses, no men pressing forward to enlist and the civic dignitaries were nowhere to be seen. There were some townsfolk on the streets but they were mainly the families of men who had left the town to join the rebellion, anxious to see if their loved ones had come home. Although most had returned safely there were wails of despair when wives, now widows, found out that their men had been lost at Keynsham or Philipsnorton or taken sick somewhere in between. There were no more clubmen waiting for them, King James having ordered that three companies of militia be sent from Bristol with the sole intent of keeping any potential rebel recruits from gathering in the town. The plan had worked admirably even though the militia had scuttled back to the safety of Bristol's strong walls as soon as the rebel army had been spotted.

Tents were erected in the fields adjoining the ruins of the old castle and rebels who had family in the town were allowed to go to their homes, although with morale having fallen so low Nat wondered how many would return to duty when the call came. In mid-afternoon a deputation from the town made their way through the encampment on their way to see King Monmouth who had made his headquarters in the elegant new house that had been built within the old castle walls. Samuel White nudged Nat as the dignitaries passed in their finery.

'They don't look too happy do they? A couple of the boys who joined us when we was last 'ere told I that the king is not wanted here. They'll be glad when us 'ave gone. They knows that James' men be closing on us and don't wanna get caught in the middle of a fight.'

'Can't say as I blames them!' replied Nat.

It was some hours before the party made their way back through the rebel camp and it was clear from their demeanour that they had not got their way. Nat and Samuel returned to the task of patching the many holes that had appeared in their clothing. Samuel was in mid flow complaining about the lice that inhabited every seam in his undershirt and breeches and were slowly eating him alive when Lieutenant Lillingstoke marched up to them.

'On your feet my boys, there's proper work to be done. The king has decided that he wants to fortify the town. It's no secret that we have our backs to the sea and that the royal cavalry has us hemmed in, so if we can't get out, we need to make sure that they can't get in.'

'And what then? Are we to sit here until we all die of starvation?' asked Samuel. Nat was surprised that even Samuel had succumbed to the general malaise that had settled over the army.

'That's enough of that defeatist talk! I expect my sergeants to set an example for the rest of the men. I'm sure that the king and his advisors will think of a way out. So you do the doing and leave the clever thinking to those that are used to it. Word is being sent out to gather materials to strengthen the walls and make barricades for the road across the moat. I want you two to get your men together and see that it's done.'

'What about those men what 'ave gone to their homes? Are they to be brought back?'

'Not just yet. It'll take some time for the materials to be collected, let them have a day with their families. I'm certain that there's a battle coming so let them rest while they can.'

'Shame we can't go home to our families,' grumbled Samuel as Lillingstoke strode off to give orders to the other companies.

Nat and Samuel were directed to a stretch of castle wall that looked to have collapsed some years ago and as they began organising their men another work party from the Red Regiment joined them, William Pearce amongst them.

'How are things with Major Wade's pretty boys then?' he teased. The nickname had been given to the scythemen ever since the major had decided to use them as his unofficial personal bodyguard.

'Not great to be honest with 'e. Tis hard keeping the men's spirits up when all we do is march and march with no food in our bellies and no shoes on our feet,' replied Samuel.

'Quiet Sam,' hissed Nat. 'Don't let the lieutenant hear you talk like that!'

'Or what? Take away my rank? Send me home? As if I care. All responsibility and no reward!'

'Nat's right to council caution,' said Pearce. 'Things be getting nasty. One of the men in my company, Richard Thomas, a cooper from Street was hung yesterday. He was found to have a copy of the pardon in his pocket, fell out when he was looking for zummat. It weren't signed or nothing so he hadn't been to a justice, but it was enough to get him lynched all the same.'

At the end of a long tiring day working on the defences the men retired to their tents with no prospect of a decent meal to sustain them. Nat prayed that Eliza, Daniel and young Nancy were coping better than he was.

Saturday 4th July 1685

With the army safely inside Bridgwater there was no need for the daily ritual of standing ready before dawn. Samuel White was expecting another day working on the defences so he was surprised to receive orders to have his men readied for inspection and exercise by mid-morning. He chatted to Nat as the men assembled on Castle Green.

'No idea what this is all about. Maybe the king wants to remind the mayor that we still have an army strong enough to see off the regulars.'

'Or to check how many of the men that were allowed to return to their homes last night have decided to come back.'

The Red Regiment had been raised in Lyme so had very few Bridgwater men in it, just the handful who had been allocated to fill gaps left by death or illness, but to a man they all reported back for duty. Nat glanced across to where the Blue Regiment stood in their distinctive red and purple coats and could detect no thinning of the ranks. The Blues had been formed at Taunton and supplemented with men from Bridgwater, so if any unit was going to be affected by desertions it was them. The king rode his white horse along the front of the army. He looked to be in good humour, pausing to speak and laugh with the senior officers of each regiment in turn. Nat turned to his men.

'His majesty looks to be enjoying himself. I trust that means that he has come up with a plan.'

'Be the first time 'eez 'ad any sort'a plan since 'e bloody landed,' grumbled one of the men.

'Quiet in the ranks!' came the thin high voice of young Lieutenant Ascue. The parade did not last long and Nat assumed that it had served its purpose. As the men were dismissed and started to return to their tents William Pearce, Nat and Samuel White got together.

'When me and my men were pulled away from 'elping you with the old castle wall yesterday arternoon we wuz ordered to scour the town for horses, although I'm not sure why so many horses be needed in a siege,' said William. 'My lieutenant thinks that all this talk of a siege is a ruse to make the enemy think we're staying here. He reckons the king intends to strike out north to meet up with his supporters in Cheshire.'

'We've 'erd enough about Cheshire before! I doubt there's anyone waiting for us there, wherever it is! And what about us poor bloody infantry?' mused Samuel. 'How are we s'posed to keep up with the horse? Unless the king intends for us to wait in Bridgwater 'til he gets back of course.'

'I do wonder if William might be right though,' added Nat. 'We knows that the reg'lers are moving up from Zummertun in the south and Feversham is bound to be somewhere between us and London to the east after Philipsnorton. With the sea behind us we 'ave nowhere else to go, except north. When I marched my men here this morning I couldn't help but notice that all the transport was loaded, the wagons and the officers' carriages alike, all packed and ready to go. Even the oxen that pull the guns had been brought into the artillery park.'

John had joined the small group.

'Well it looks like its back on the road then but I think my time with the army is done. I'm not able to fight anymore, I've got me discharge papers and I don't reckon I'm up to marching north again. No, my way heads south to Lyme.'

'I'm glad to hear it,' said Nat, 'though I do urge you to be careful. There be cavalry patrols everywhere and they'll be on the lookout for deserters. Your papers will only serve to confirm that you were with the king's army and that'll make things even worse for you.'

'Don't you worry son. I've got the papers well concealed and I've got my story all worked out if I'm stopped. I've spoken to Master Foe who's given I a few pointers about which way I needs to go.'

'Then God go with you. Give my love to Daniel and Nancy and tell Eliza that the last time I saw her father he was safe and well.'

John gave his son a final hug then turned quickly away before the tears came. He wondered when, or if, the two would ever meet again.

'I'm off too in a sense,' said Samuel White.

'What? Surely you're not thinking of deserting!'

'No young'un, but it looks like you and I are not going to be together at the end of this affair, no matter how it turns out. Seems I've been posted to Colonel Holmes' Green Regiment. Their senior sergeant 'as died of 'is wounds so everyone gets to move up and they need me to make up the numbers.'

'Things must be bad if you're the one in demand!' joked Nat.

The walls on the southern and eastern sides of the town, where the enemy were expected to appear at any moment were the first to be repaired and were now well guarded but little attention had so far been paid to the western defences. John made his way through the town, mingling with the townsfolk who headed for the west gate. The guards who were dozing just inside the remnants of the gate paid no attention to the stooped old man who was no doubt going to fetch firewood or tend the crops. He had no reason to sneak out but his discharge papers were carefully sewn into the seam of his coat and he didn't want to have to unpick the stitching if he could avoid it.

John was not the only man to leave the army that day. William Pearce had decided that whichever direction the army was to take in the morning it would certainly not be south, so he was now as close to his home in Taunton as he was likely to get. It was the time to leave the king to his failing rebellion. He desperately needed to see his family and while he still believed fervently in the cause he doubted that Monmouth was the right man to follow, despite his obvious talents. True, the new king was brave and had proved to be a good battlefield general, but he seemed to lack any real idea of how to pursue the campaign, to see the bigger picture. William realised that there was probably much going on that he did not understand, to explain the king's apparent indecision but he had had enough.

Although the sun had set there were still plenty of people in the streets with the Bridgwater rebels making their way to their homes for the night once their duties were finished. As he made his way towards the western walls he noticed others moving more furtively than a man heading for his own bed should, clearly he was not the only one planning to leave without permission. The ditch presented no obstacle, as years of neglect had caused large sections of the stone and earth rampart to fall into it. He crouched low and stilled his breathing as he checked that his actions had not drawn any undue attention then sprang to his feet and ran for the cover afforded by the woods that lay a short distance away.

27 HOMEWARD BOUND

Sunday 5th July 1685

Nat laid in his tent listening to the sounds of the town coming awake around him. Amid the occasional calls of the sentries and the bawled orders of the sergeants there were the ordinary domestic noises that he realised he had missed so much. The splatter of night buckets being emptied into the street, the chatter of the women as they went to draw water, milk the cows or start on the hundred and one daily jobs that needed doing. Small boys whistled as they ran on errands, the tradesmen and carters argued good-naturedly as they unloaded goods in the marketplace. He realised that he missed home, he missed the ordinary, the humdrum. John had headed for home although God alone knew if he was safe. Thomas had apparently deserted and was no doubt on his way back to Lyme as well. Nat wondered if the two would meet somewhere on the road and be able to look out for each other, one standing watch whilst the other slept maybe. Gough, Dabinett and Stuckley were all dead. Samuel White who had been with him since the very beginning had been transferred to a different regiment which left only Henry Outwell and William Pearce although as Nat now marched with the scythemen and William was with the musketeers, he saw little of him too. He wondered how he could feel so alone in the midst of so many people.

Samuel White was also thinking of home and of the friends that he had lost. Like so many in the army he was confused. The past few days had seen every man working on repairing the town's defences as if the king were preparing to withstand a siege, yet the wagons had been loaded and parties of horsemen were arriving hourly with fresh mounts. He remembered what William Pearce had said about the siege works being a ruse. Was the army staying behind the walls or moving? Were the infantry to be left in Bridgwater whilst the mounted men and the wagons went elsewhere?

Food was beginning to run short again and the men had very little to break their fast before assembling for another day of manual labour on the walls. He wondered what had happened to the ships that were meant to have been bringing supplies from Wales.

Nat was back working on the same stretch of wall as before, when Thomas Cleeve the ex-militiaman from Stoford strode over.

'Good morning Sergeant Carver,' he said with mock deference, 'don't s'pose you've seen old Sergeant Willis have you? He went back to his house in the town last night after he were relieved but hasn't been seen since. The lieutenant sent a few of us to look for him.'

'Have you tried his house?'

'First place we looked but his wife swears that she hasn't seen 'im since he left her to follow the king two weeks back.'

'That's bad. Most of my men were recruited in Lyme or Axminster, but those few from Bridgwater who went to their homes last night have all come back this morning.'

'Most of ours have too apart from Sergeant Willis of course. Saying that, I can't find William Pearce anywhere either.'

'I'm sure they'll both turn up soon,' said Nat hoping that they hadn't absconded.

The rest of the morning passed quickly as the men set to repairing the walls and clearing the ditches of years of undergrowth. What food could be found was pooled by the men who shared a meagre lunch before returning to their labours. No-one paid much attention to the lone horseman who rode into the town in mid-afternoon followed at some distance by a farm hand on an old nag, demanding to know where the king was to be found. Another gentleman scout full of his own importance thought Nat.

As Nat and the others worked to improve the town defences John was making his way slowly westwards. Once clear of Bridgwater he had found a dense copse of birch trees on a small rise and had slept for most of the morning. As far as he was aware the enemy were to the east and south of Bridgwater so by keeping the sun behind him for a few hours he should be well clear of them. At some point he would need to cut south, but for his cover story to hold he had to avoid anywhere tainted by rebellion and that meant keeping well clear of Taunton. No one paid any notice to the old man with his bandaged arm as he walked slowly from village to village. He was amazed that life appeared to be going on as normal as if nothing had changed; sheep and cattle munched on the new grass that had shot up following the rains, children played and women fetched water. The rebels had not visited this area in their wanderings although the lack of men working the fields spoke of the numbers that had left to join the rebel army in Bridgwater. If the fate of the country was about to be decided just back down the road, the few people he encountered were either blissfully unaware or too frightened to let it show.

By mid-afternoon he reckoned he had covered more than ten miles and had gone far enough west, so he took the next track that headed southwards. This area was alien to him and he had no idea if the locals supported the new king or not so he proceeded carefully. It was quite possible that the militia would be out and about to stop anyone travelling to join the rebels in Bridgwater and to round up any who like himself had decided to leave for home. Foe had given him a very rough sketch map of the area and he knew that as well as avoiding Taunton he must also give Wellington a wide berth, the Devon militia having so recently been quartered there.

As the sun began to sink behind the clouds to his right he was cheered by the sight of the high wooded ground that stretched across the horizon in front of him, the Blackdown Hills. He knew that once he crested the ridge he would be able to look down onto his beloved Dorset once again. The thought put new energy into his steps and he picked up his pace, but after another two hours the Blackdown Hills seemed no nearer and he realised that he would need to find shelter for the night before tackling those steep slopes the following morning. He chose a small wood and worked himself into a shallow hollow beside a fallen tree trunk. He ate the last of his food before settling back against the trunk, the thick carpet of moss and lichen providing a natural pillow. The stars were starting to appear in the gaps between the overhanging branches and though John was a very practical man, not the type given to wistful thoughts, it was hard not to be taken in by the beauty of his sylvan surroundings. He was struck by how quiet it was and he realised with a start that this was the first night in nearly a month that he had been alone, instead of being surrounded by the mass of humanity that was army life. He sighed contentedly, closed his eyes and was soon asleep.

Unbeknown to John, William Pearce was on an almost parallel course. He too had hidden up after clearing Bridgwater but having a much better understanding of the area he had turned south much sooner, his route laying to the east of Taunton, not the west. God willing he could be back in Lambrook by nightfall and although he was sorely tempted to carry on and be reunited with his young family, he decided that it would be safer for all concerned if he delayed his arrival until the next morning. He had no idea if the enemy had occupied Taunton after the rebels had left nor whether his family were still in the town or had returned to their cottage near the mill. He settled down to wait in the ruins of an abandoned cottage. It had no roof and only two standing walls but it would suffice, as tomorrow he would be back under his own roof with his family.

Thomas had been heading slowly south since leaving Bruton in the early hours of Friday. He had stayed longer in the town than he had originally intended but he was dog tired after his escape from Frome and his brush with the militia outside Witham Friary. No one had come near his hiding place and he had been able to sneak into the town twice to steal food, the first time taking a hot pie left carelessly on a windowsill to cool and the second time helping himself to fruit and vegetables from a trader's basket when the man was distracted whilst unloading his cart ready for the weekly market. He still needed to get his pardon signed but having picked up snatches of conversations as he crept through the back streets he decided that Bruton was still too close to rebellious Frome to be certain that enquires after a magistrate would not be met with anger. Back in North Petherton he had been dismissive of Foe's marvellous maps but had seen enough to know that Yeovil lay somewhere to the south of Bruton and he would look for a magistrate there, but until he had the papers signed he would have to be very wary of royal patrols. The countryside was swarming with militia cavalry and he had been forced to find cover several times. This was fairly easy in the broken country south of Bruton, but the open flat ground that lay between the village of Queen Camel and the town of Yeovil, high on its hill overlooking the Yeo valley presented problems. He spent hours at a time hiding in shallow ditches as the militia rode back and forth, and it took him more than two days, filled with anxiety and angst to reach the foot of the steep slopes below Yeovil.

His most difficult moment came when a lone horseman saw him running across a narrow lane between two thick hedges and gave chase. Thomas had managed to reach a dense patch of undergrowth before the horseman could catch him and he dropped into the thick reeds that bordered a stream flowing through the trees. He held his breath as the rider rode up and down the bank and just when he thought that the man was about to give up, a fish coming to the surface to take a fly splashed in the clear water behind him and the rider turned towards the sound. Thomas sprang up and grabbed the rider's arm just as he was reaching for his holstered pistol and pulled him to the ground. The couple grappled on the bank before rolling into the shallow water, the horseman catching his head on a sharp rock on the way down. Thomas seized his chance and pushed the man's head under the water, watching as his long hair flowed with the current like so much waterweed. His struggles became weaker and weaker until a string of bubbles burst from his mouth as the last of the air left his lungs. Thomas released his grip and smiled to himself as the body drifted slowly downstream, the feeling of power as he took another life leaving him light-headed and he wished that he still had his musket so that he could cut another notch in the stock.

He dragged himself back to the bank and rifled the dead man's saddlebags before hitching the horse to a tree; he couldn't risk the animal wandering off and being spotted by other militia cavalry. He removed his wet clothing, draping them over a convenient bush before wrapping himself in the thick blanket that was rolled up on the back of the saddle and fell asleep almost at once.

As John, Thomas and William slept on their separate journeys home they were blissfully unaware that in their absence the campaign was about to come to a climatic finale outside Bridgwater. They had escaped the army just in time.

28 ONE FINAL THROW OF THE DICE

Bridgwater, Sunday 5th July 1685

There was no longer any doubt that the army was preparing to move out. The wagons, artillery and draught animals were all drawn up in a long line of march that reached from one side of the town to the other, although work continued on improving the town's defence, presumably to convince the watching royalists that they intended to stay in the town. Nat was wondering when and where the army was to be sent when Daniel Foe rode up.

'Arternoon Daniel. Any idea what's going on? Where are we bound next?'

'Good afternoon Nat. It seems that one of our scouts encountered a messenger sent by a Master Sparke of

Chedzoy who reported that the royal army had arrived and gone into camp on the moors to our south. The king now has to make a choice between going north to Bristol and thence to Cheshire or east to London. Of course, there is a third option which is to attack the royal army.'

The similarity between the name of the informer and his beloved Eliza's family caught Nat off guard and it was some seconds before he replied, 'is that really a possibility?'

'It is. We still have more men than they do although they will undoubtably receive reinforcements before too long, so now may be the time to take the battle to them.' Lowering his voice he added, 'you can't have failed to notice that our army is not as numerous as it once was. Some say that men have lost their nerve, others say that they have simply recovered their senses. Either way those that remain are the stoutest and will prove to be the most reliable in a fight, but methinks the king must make a decisive move soon before too many more drift away. No doubt he will consult the Wheel of Pythagoras before coming to a decision.'

'The wheel of what?'

'Pythagoras, he was a famous Greek philosopher who died some two thousand years ago. The wheel which is named for him is a form of divination.'

'A way to tell the future?'

'So it is said.'

'And the king uses such a devilish device?' Nat was shocked.

'I believe that his majesty makes his decisions based solely on logic and prayer. I am certain that the wheel has no power but it serves to comfort him, he reads it in such a way as to always confirm the decisions that he has already made.'

'But he cannot mean to attack the enemy. They have more cannon than us and better cavalry, no insult intended my friend. Surely to attack them when they are well set would be suicidal?'

'Ah, but there's the rub as Master Shakespeare put it. The messenger has reported that the guns are all on the main road between here and Weston Zoyland, the cavalry are in billets in the village and the infantry are camped on the moor itself. None of the three arms are supporting each other. Their deployment is poor considering the experience of their officers. If we take them by surprise we might be able to destroy their infantry before they know what's happening.'

'And how do we surprise them. Surely they will have scouts and guards posted?'

'One imagines so, but Sparke's messenger, a certain Benjamin Godfrey, says he can pick a way through the marshland that will let us come upon the enemy unseen. The king sent him back to see whether the enemy infantry have dug defensive entrenchments for themselves. If they haven't then I believe we may attack tonight, using the cover of darkness.'

Nat returned to his work on the walls his mind buzzing with the possibility of attacking the royal army. Barely thirty minutes later the soldiers were told to stop their work and fall in for inspection on Castle Ground to the north of the town. They were instructed to leave their tents pitched and take only their weapons and enough food, if they could find any, for one day. Clearly a decision had been made and it looked like the battle which many yearned for as a way of ending the campaign was imminent. After they had assembled the army was addressed by Ferguson who delivered a rousing speech.

'Our moment has arrived and God Himself has presented the king with this fine chance for victory. The enemy are helplessly incapacitated by the demon drink and are totally unprepared to defend themselves. The artillery, cavalry and infantry are so poorly deployed that they cannot support each other. Their guns cannot be moved due to the soft state of the ground and in any case we have it on good authority that the civilians employed by the usurper James to manage the draught animals that pull the guns have all absconded due to lack of pay. Feversham, the Frenchman who commands the false king's army is so conceited and so dismissive of the brave men of the west country that he has not bothered to dig even the most rudimentary of defences to protect his Irish heathens. The enemy are at our mercy, although no mercy will be shown! We will move out this very night and by lunchtime tomorrow the enemy will be scattered and the road to London will be open! God go with you.'

The men cheered as Ferguson finished and the officers waved their feathered hats in the air.

By eleven o'clock that night the order of march had been agreed and as a member of Major Wade's bodyguard of scythemen Nat found himself near the front of the column as they waited patiently on the long straight road that led from Bridgwater towards Bristol. If any enemy scouts should see them, and it was hard to see how they could fail to, it would seem as if they were headed for the crossing over the River Avon at Keynsham.

The rain that had dogged them for the past week or so had finally abated and a full moon hung low in a clear sky. The sight of the moon made Nat think again of the promise he had made to Eliza and he prayed that he would survive the coming battle. The wheels of the guns and wagons had been greased and lined with straw and the horses' hooves were wrapped in old cloth to reduce noise but it still seemed inconceivable to Nat that they could achieve surprise. He was slightly reassured as he looked back down the long line of soldiers and realised that most of them were hidden from his view by the mist that had started to rise from the rivers, drainage ditches and marshes as soon as the sun had gone down. The men appeared to be ready for a fight, fired as they were by Ferguson's speech and for those so inclined, a fortifying issue of spirits. Major Wade made his way down the line pausing by each of his lieutenants to advise them of the agreed password, Soho.

'So Ho? Who or what is a so ho?' Nat asked Lieutenant Ascue.

'It's Soho Nat, one word, the place where the king has his London home.'

Wade returned to the head of the column and they set off as quietly as five thousand marching men can. As they came nearer to the damp moorland, the mist became thicker still, helping to deaden any sound.

'Ow far are we going sir?' asked Henry Outwell as he walked with one hand on the shoulder of the man in front of him so as not to stumble into him or lose his way in the poor light.

'Some three or four miles I believe,' whispered his lieutenant in response. 'Now let's have no more talking, absolute silence from now on.'

'Let's hope that the enemy are all fast asleep or drunk so we can surprise them,' Henry whispered to Nat.

'It's good to have hope,' Nat replied, 'but not if it is at the expense of a proper plan. We can't rely on hope alone!'

'Hope, a good plan and God's grace, not much to wish for surely.'

'What part of absolute silence do you not understand?' hissed the lieutenant.

They trudged on. The cavalry had been kept towards the back of the column as even in the best of hands horses are unpredictable and prone to make noises whereas men can be ordered not to. There was also a fear that if they were placed at the front they would move too fast and leave the infantry behind. The enemy had made a mistake by splitting his forces and Monmouth was determined not to do the same. As far as Henry Outwell was concerned the rebel cavalry had proved themselves worse than useless so far, how apt he thought that they might be the ones to ruin the element of surprise through a loose piece of equipment, a whinnying horse or a cursing rider. If the cavalry didn't give the game away the artillery were bound to. They were following close behind the mounted men with their long train of recalcitrant draught oxen, groaning axles and clanking trace chains.

The plan was for the rebel cavalry to move to the front of the column once they were close to the enemy lines, before sweeping through the sleeping enemy encampment from one end to the other bringing confusion and death. They would scatter the royal horses before their riders could reach them, set fire to the infantry's tents then reform ready to pursue the broken enemy. As soon as the cavalry were clear the infantry would deploy, deliver a mighty volley then charge in to finish off the demoralised enemy in hand-to-hand combat. The chances were that the enemy would break and run long before the rebel infantry made contact and the battle would be won long before the royal cavalry or guns could be brought up.

'Sounds like a good plan as far as I can tell,' Henry whispered to Nat, 'but only if we're able to achieve surprise and only if the damned cavalry don't cock things up!'

Samuel White's Green Regiment was half-way down the column of men, with the Red and Yellow Regiments in front and the Blues and Whites behind. He thought it ironic that he had spent nearly ten years fighting for parliament against King Charles the First and yet here he was marching behind that man's grandson, looking to put him on the throne. In the Red Regiment Thomas Cleeve and John Harries marched together in silence. Both longed for a return to Cromwell's commonwealth and although they had spent hours discussing Monmouth's decision to declare himself king, Harries had failed to convince his friend that Ferguson had spoken the truth when he had said that it was no more than a ruse to attract the gentry to his cause. Well that hadn't worked out too well so far Cleeve mused.

Although the men had been ordered to march in silence there was too much pent-up excitement, anxiety and nervous energy to stop their tongues wagging. Humphrey Wilmott the tanner from Bridgwater who had made the crude remarks about the shape of Glastonbury Tor was walking behind Aaron Tucker. Despite constantly teasing Tucker about his religious convictions the two had become firm friends.

'Well Aaron me old mucker. Not having doubts now that it looks like we are in for a battle?' he asked in a voice barely above a whisper.

'Not at all Humphrey. I trust in God's good grace to protect me, but if I should fall I will be able to stand tall at the gates of Heaven and tell St Peter that I did the right thing.'

The long column snaked along the Bristol road. More local men had come forward to help guide the army across the wetlands and one such was attached to each regiment to prevent them losing their way in the featureless landscape in the dark. Nat couldn't help feeling nervous. He was certain that the enemy would have posted men on the Bristol road to prevent the rebels from leaving in that direction and he voiced those concerns to Roland Barrett, the thin grey-haired man of about fifty who had been assigned to guide the Red Regiment.

'Now don't you worry yersel' young'un. The cav'ry be sitting tight in Bawdrip, a while up the road still. Uz'll be turning off this road long a'for we reach they buggers.'

A glare from Lieutenant Ascue prevented any further questions Nat may have had.

Half an hour later, just as Barrett had suggested, the front of the column turned right onto a narrow track lined with high hedges. The call was passed down the line for complete silence as there were bound to be pickets the nearer they got to the enemy camp. With the high hedges on either side and the thickening mist Nat's whole world was compressed to a few yards. He could hear men praying quietly to themselves or cursing when the calls of hunting owls cut through the silence making them jump. A sharp turn in the track took them onto another lane, and although the high hedges quickly fell away this track was even narrower, a mere droveway for moving cattle, with gullies full of dirty looking water on either side.

'Make sure you stays on the track,' hissed Barrett. 'Those ditches be deep and full o' thick shitty mud. It'll be the Devil's own job to 'ave to pull one of you out'a there.'

They marched for another hour until a number of low buildings appeared out of the mist.

'Peasy Farm,' whispered Barrett to Major Wade, 'we'll 'ave to leave the waguns here. After the farm the land'll be too soft for them to continue.'

There were no lights on in the farmhouse; clearly whoever lived there had moved out upon hearing rumours that there was to be a battle.

'I pray that it's not much further to the battle site if we have to leave our ammunition wagons here,' said Wade so quietly that Barrett had to strain to hear him. He wondered if the guns would be able to go any further.

Barrett indicated a small cluster of lights slightly behind them and to their left. 'That be Bawdrip, and Chedzoy'll be coming up shortly on t'other side of the track. Plenty of folks from both have joined the duke's army, but I can't guarantee the loyalty of either place, so best avoided.'

No one bothered to pick him up for using Monmouth's old title, rather than calling him the king. They passed a large field of standing corn and Nat could not believe that they had penetrated so far onto the moor without being spotted. The wetlands were quiet and empty, although in their heightened state of anxiety men mistook the occasional stunted hornbeam or willow that appeared out of the mist as an enemy horseman. Thank God for the guides thought Nat as the whole army disappeared into the landscape. It was a world of marsh and shadows where the small noises made by the marching men were drowned out by the booming of bitterns as they searched for a mate in the reed beds.

Still no alarm was raised even though to Nat's ears the slightest sound seemed loud enough to wake the dead on Judgement Day, let alone the enemy patrols that must be close. He could not imagine how Feversham could not be aware of their plans when everyone in Bridgwater and the surrounding villages seemed to know that an attack was planned. The moon was full and ordinarily would have given more than enough light to betray the rebel army but the thick mist that clung to the marshy ground provided the perfect cover. Suddenly a nasty thought came to him. What if Feversham *was* aware and had the royal army lying in wait, ready to pounce? He realised that he had been holding his breath, anticipating the crash of muskets, but the night remained silent but for the bitterns and the cries of hunting tawny owls. Maybe Ferguson's assurances that every man in the royal army was drunk were true and that they really would catch the enemy unprepared after all.

As they approached the village of Chedzoy the signal was given for the column to halt. It was known that there was a unit of enemy cavalry stationed in the village and the scouts who were cautiously creeping ahead of the rebel army had heard the tell-tale jingle of harnesses and the snorting of horses somewhere ahead in the dark. The word was passed down the column for the men to sit down on the track in the hope that they would merge into the landscape. This was the moment that Henry Outwell had dreaded. Fighting against an enemy that you could see was one thing, but the thought of big men on heavy horses erupting out of the night and cutting men down before they had a chance to fight back was quite another. Many of the men in his unit had drunk a quantity of cider to bolster their spirits and now one of those men started to stand up.

'Get down you fool!' Henry hissed as he grabbed at the man's coat to pull him back down.

'Got to piss!' came the reply. Henry leapt to his feet and pulled the man down, his only reward being a splash of warm liquid across his legs as the man was unable to control himself any longer. Henry strained his ears for any indication that they had been heard by enemy pickets but all he could hear was the noise of the blood pumping in his ears. After a fraught wait the signal was given to resume the march, Henry letting out a long low sigh of relief that they had not been detected.

Unbeknown to Henry the rebel army had been spotted. The royal cavalry patrols might have been negligent in their duties but the eight men of the Chedzoy village watch had seen the long line of men making their slow way across the wetlands.

'What do thee reckon Amos? Should we raise the alarm?

'Hush Jethro, think on before you start trying to be a blerry hero. Just who are you proposing we should tell?'

'Well King James' army camped outside Weston of course. I'm sure there'll be a goodly reward if us tells 'em what we've seen.'

'My brother is marching with the rebels and I won't see him betrayed, even if I don't hold with the action he's taken by siding with Monmouth. Besides if you goes running to James' men now the chances are that their pickets'll take you for a rebel and shoot you down a'for you can report what we've seen.'

'So what shall us do then?'

'Well I don't know about you but I'm going to find somewhere nice and safe to sit and watch.'

He climbed over the fence that kept the livestock out of the large cornfield, disturbing a flock of buntings as he did so and headed for the lone windmill that stood forlornly on a small rise in the middle of the growing crops.

'Should get a good view from there,' he called back softly over his shoulder. Jethro and the other members of the watch hurried to join him.

Further back down the straggling line of men, Samuel White was marching at the head of the Green Regiment. He couldn't understand why the column kept coming to a sudden stop, surely they had guides with them who knew the way. He was just about to ask his lieutenant if he had any idea what was happening when the march resumed. The lieutenant had served for a while in the wars that had raged across continental Europe and that had taught him the dangers of a night march over unfamiliar ground with poorly trained irregular troops. He was surprised that they had managed to get this far without raising the alarm or becoming hopelessly lost.

'Just making sure that we don't blunder into any cavalry patrols I expect,' he hissed. 'Now keep the men moving. We want to hit the enemy whilst it's still dark cos we'll be sitting ducks if the sun comes up and we're still on the march.'

At the front of the column where Nat led his scythemen, the track had at last run out and they were crossing unmarked fields. Their guide held up a hand as he came upon a dark, wide and deep looking ditch blocking the way. The smell of stagnant water and rotting vegetation made Nat gag.

'What is it man?' whispered Wade, 'I thought you knew the way Master Barrett.'

'Course I knows the way your honour. This 'ere be the Langmoor Rhine, which uz'll have to cross. There should be a ford hereabouts where the cows cross, I'm just looking for the stone that marks the exact place.'

After scouting up and down the steep bank for two or three minutes he called back softly.

'Over here. The Devils' Upping Stock they calls it, strange name, don't know the origins of it, but it marks the way over the ditch. Follow me your honour. Another hour and we should hit the Bussex Rhine where the enemy be said to be camped.'

Wade found it hard to countenance that the royal commander had not thought to post a guard at so vital a point. Such negligence bode well for the success of the night attack that relied so heavily on catching the enemy by surprise.

'No guards! The man must be a fool,' he murmured.

'No fool like an old fool,' replied Lieutenant Ascue.

'If that's true then bloody Monmouth must be a damned site older than he looks!' said one of the men.

'Quiet! Wade whispered. 'Wait here,' he said as he jogged across to consult with the king who was leading his horse by the reins near the front of the column. After a brief conversation Wade hurried back to his regiment.

'Right men, stand aside. The king has decided that now is the time for the cavalry to be released, they will be coming through shortly and I don't want us to be half-way across the ford when they get here.'

The men grumbled as they shuffled aside to make a passage to the place where the stone marked the ford. It seemed an age before the first of Grey's mounted men arrived at the rhine, the name that the locals gave to the drainage ditches. It was soon apparent that everyone had underestimated the amount of space that the cavalry needed. The ford and the passageway that the infantry had made were simply not wide enough and as more and more horsemen arrived the situation threatened to get out of control. The foot-soldiers were pushed further and further into the soggy fields and more than one man was knocked down by the combination of a frightened horse and a nervous rider. Voices were raised in outrage as men were pushed into the foul-smelling ditches and had to be hauled out by their comrades.

'Quiet there, damn your eyes!' hissed Wade, concerned that the noise would alert any pickets that the seemingly complacent enemy had seen fit to deploy. Slowly the pressure eased as more and more riders found their way to the other bank but just as Wade feared the commotion at the ford had been heard. A bright flash was followed instantly by the sharp report of a pistol being discharged. A warning shot to alert the enemy camp. They had been discovered at last.

The Battaile att Bridgwater

29 JUDGEMENT DAY

Sedgemoor, Monday 6th July 1685

Now that the alarm had been sounded caution gave way to the need for swift and decisive action. Monmouth came alive as he issued a string of orders.

'My Lord Grey, get the rest of your horsemen across this ditch as smartly as you can and onto the next one, the Bussex Rhine! You must be across that before the enemy camp is fully awake or else all is lost.'

Grey acknowledged the order and urged his horsemen on, while the king turned to Wade.

'The King's Own will follow as soon as the horse have cleared the ford. Remember, once you reach the Bussex Rhine march to your right and keep going until you are opposite the far end of the enemy lines. The other regiments will follow you and take station accordingly.'

It was the first time the men of the Red Regiment had heard themselves referred to as the King's Own and they voiced their approval.

'Will the guns be coming to support us your majesty?' asked Wade.

'Yes, yes. I will ride for them myself,' and with that the king mounted his horse and spurred back down the column, not trusting the task to any of his retinue who hurried to catch up with him.

Wade led his men across the ford once the last of Grey's horsemen had passed, shouting that they should make haste. There was still a chance to hit the enemy hard before they had time to shake off their drunken stupor and organise themselves, especially if the rebel horse could get among them. The Red Regiment soon reached the banks of the dark wide ditch that separated them from the enemy's camp and wheeled to their right as ordered, following the ditch towards the west. They could clearly hear the shouts of the sergeants on the opposite bank calling their men to order amid the furious banging of drums and blare of cavalry trumpets.

'Keep going!' shouted Wade. 'Keep going! My Lord Grey's cavalry will soon be sweeping through their camp and the burning tents will be our guide,' he panted as he ran. 'We stop opposite the last of the fires which will mark the furthest extent of their encampment.'

Hezekiah Sprake was riding with the main body of Grey's horsemen as they chased the frightened pickets before them. In no time they came up upon the ditch and desperately sought the ford, the so-called upper plungeon.

'Where the hell is it?' shouted Grey in frustration. 'Where is that damned guide?'

The guide was nowhere to be seen, he'd either decided that his work was done and sidled back to his home to await the outcome or else he'd simply been left behind in the confusion at the Langmoor crossing. Grey knew that time was of the essence but he could not decide whether to head to this left or his right to find the crossing. The cavalry milled about while he weighed up the options in the absence of their guide.

'My lord we must act now!' shouted one of his officers.

'I know, damn your impertinence!' he replied but still prevaricated. After several long minutes he appeared to have made up his mind.

'This way!' he cried eventually and led the horsemen to their right moving slowly along the line of the ditch hoping to find the crossing point himself. Drums could be heard from across the water as the royal army was being called to arms. Sprake, who was riding close to the ditch heard a challenge called from the far bank.

'Who goes there? Identify yourselves!'

'Devonshire militia under the Duke of Albemarle!' Sprake shouted. The ruse must have worked because no shots came out of the dark and they rode on looking for the crossing.

It was hard to think logically with the adrenaline running high and no landmarks to act as a guide but Sprake felt that there was something wrong. Suddenly it came to him. They were supposed to be riding for the crossing point which was known to lay beyond the extreme right flank of the enemy camp, but there were formed bodies of enemy troops to their left. He spotted Grey and drove his frightened mount to his side.

'Your Grace!' he shouted, 'I fear that we are going the wrong way.'

'Nonsense man, get back to your position and leave the thinking to those that are born to it.'

'But sir, if we seek the right flank of their camp, the enemy should be to our right, not to our left!' He saw a flicker of indecision and alarm flash across Grey's face, but before he could press the matter further another challenge rang out from across the ditch. Sprake wheeled his horse to repeat his claim that they were loyal militiamen under the Duke of Albemarle when a trooper nearer to the bank of the rhine replied.

'For the king!'

'Which king?'

'King Monmouth and God with us!'

'Then take this with you!'

The far bank exploded as the men of the Guards delivered a devastating volley and as Grey's frightened horsemen continued down the line of the rhine they were hit by a succession of volleys as they passed each royal regiment in turn. The mist had started to thin and the solid mass of horsemen made an easy target. Sprake found it hard to believe that the carefully laid plan had fallen apart so quickly. The loss of the guide, Grey's error and the proud boast of the unknown horseman was costing them dear. Although Sprake himself wasn't hit many others were toppled from their saddles and it all proved too much for the inexperienced riders on terrified mounts. Unused to the noise and the devastating effect of the massed muskets they turned their horses' heads away from the rhine and fled into the night.

The Red Regiment were still marching steadily west, keeping an eye out for the first of the fires on the opposite bank. The flames from the burning tents would be the only beacon they would have in the dark and the mist. They were in good spirits and ready for the fight, the men singing as they marched now that the need for stealth had gone. Nat was with his scythemen at the front of the unit near to the colours, followed by half of the musketeers, then the pikemen with their long ash poles, with the remaining musketeers bringing up the rear. When they reached their designated position on the far left of Feversham's battle line the whole regiment would take a quarter turn to their left, the pikes forming a solid block in the middle of the line, five ranks deep with the musketmen, six ranks deep on either flank. That was the way that foot soldiers had fought during the civil war and therefore the way that the experienced drill sergeants had trained Monmouth's volunteer army. The scythemen would gather around Wade and the colours behind the pikemen. Suddenly the sound of disciplined volleys crashed across the dark fields from somewhere behind them. Many of Nat's comrades flinched at the sound expecting to see bloody holes torn in their ranks, whilst others turned to search for both the source and the target. A cry of 'horsemen on the left flank!' came from the back of the regiment but before anyone had chance to react, Grey's mounted men came thundering out of the dark racing into the narrow space between the Red Regiment and the Bussex Rhine.

'What the devil are they doing here?' shouted Wade. 'They are supposed to be on the other side of the ditch!'

It was clear that nothing was going to stop the horsemen in their headlong flight and all Nat and the others could do was bunch as closely together as they could in the hope that if the riders couldn't control their mounts the horses at least would have the natural sense to avoid the solid phalanx of men. The earth shook as the riders, many clinging desperately to their terrified mounts charged past, throwing up huge clods of wet mud. Some of the infantry on the fringes of the formation were bowled over whilst others were sucked into the mass of wild horseflesh and disappeared under the thundering hooves. No sooner had they arrived than they had gone. Lieutenants and sergeants shouted orders as they tried to get their shocked men back under control. Wade called his senior officers to him.

'I think we should stop here and turn to face the enemy. God alone knows where their line ends but Grey's cavalry aren't going to be lighting any fires to aid us now, so this is as good a place as any. I would hate to march too far, beyond the end of their line and find we had no one to attack. That would mean retracing our steps and disordering the regiments that are following us. We will stop here.'

'We were told that their line extended to Weston Zoyland and I can see lights opposite us which may well be the village,' suggested Lieutenant Ascue.

'Indeed it may, it is as good an indication as we are likely to get. Get your men ready to cross the ditch on my order. One volley then everyone over and into them as quickly as possible. They won't stand once the scythemen start on their deadly harvest.'

Nat was confident that his men would do their duty. They had faced the regular troops at Philipsnorton and acquitted themselves well, but he had to remind himself that that victory was won with the benefit of walls, hedges, buildings and a barricade. This would be the real test as they faced the royal army in open terrain.

Samuel White marching with the Green Regiment had no idea what was going on. It was still dark although the sky away to the east was just starting to show a glimmer of light. It would be at least another hour before the sun showed itself above the horizon and in the mist and the dark, he could see little more than the back of the man in front of him. Sudden gunfire to his front lit the mist with a lurid glow by which he was just able to make out the bulk of the Red Regiment to his extreme right and the backs of the men of the Matthews' Yellow Regiment immediately to his front. In their hurry to catch up with the Reds, Holmes' Green Regiment had run into the back of the Yellows who had inexplicably come to a halt. Holmes knew that his regiment was meant to line up beside the Yellows on the bank of the rhine but the waterway was nowhere to be seen. There was complete chaos as the two regiments tried to disentangle themselves. The reason for the Yellows having stopped was soon apparent as their musketeers delivered a ragged volley. They had also been spooked by the flight of Grey's cavalry and seeing that the Red Regiment had stopped they too decided that they had come far enough and had dropped to their knees and opened fire.

'Too damned early! 'screamed Holmes, sending a runner to urge Matthews to move his men further along the bank.

'Tell him that the Whites and Blues will have no space to deploy when they arrive.'

The runner returned with Matthews' apologetic reply that his men could not be persuaded to move, but that he hoped that they might force their way across the rhine once the light permitted. The sky was brightening but it would be some time before the sun rose to burn off the mist which was turning a milky white in the growing light. Matthews' men were simply aiming in the direction of the musket flashes that punctuated the bank of mist to their front and Samuel preyed that they were shooting at the enemy and not at the Red Regiment in error. He wondered how anyone was supposed to fight a battle when no-one could see what was happening or who was shooting at who.

Holmes knew that they were in the wrong position but that wasn't going to change any time soon. 'Green Regiment!' he called. 'A quarter turn to the left! Fire when ready!' and with that the Greens added their firepower to the growing cacophony.

Order had been restored in the Red Regiment after their brush with their own cavalry and Wade was about to give the order to advance to the edge of the ditch to deliver what he knew would be a telling volley when the musketeers on the extreme left of his regiment became caught up in the excitement of the firing from the Yellows and the Greens and began discharging their own pieces.

'No, no!' shouted the major. 'Someone get those men back under control. We need to get across the water while the enemy is still unformed.'

Nat could see that it was already too late as more and more of the Red Regiment's musketeers were firing and having done so dropped to their knees to reload. In the dark the still waters of the ditch looked forbidding and the men knew that with the enemy now fully awake they would be easy prey if they attempted to struggle across the water and up the steep bank on the other side. Far safer to keep their feet and their powder dry and stop where they were.

'Fall on, fall on!' cried the officers but the moment had been lost, there was no chance now of persuading the frightened men to cross the ditch. Even if they could be made to cross, with the Yellows and the Greens blasting away into the dark there was every chance that they would hit the men of the Red Regiment advancing to their front without knowing it. The whole line had to cross together and that wasn't going to happen now.

It was at this juncture that the king returned to the field with three rebel guns, the fourth having been left at Peasy Farm with a broken axle. In his absence each regiment had been obliged to make their own decisions without anyone to direct the overall battle. The guns were pushed into position between the Yellow and Green Regiments and opened fire on the troops on the opposite bank.

'Where are Bovet's Blues and Foulkes' Whites?' the king demanded. He was shouting in frustration that his carefully laid plans were already falling apart. With a wry smile, Foe who was riding with the king's retinue recalled Monmouth's comments at dinner only days previously when he had said, 'in war the first casualty is always the plan.'

Foe knew full well where those two regiments with their desperately needed thousand men were, they were still on the wrong side of the Langmoor Rhine. They had been forced to stand aside as first Grey's cavalry had advanced then the artillery had been brought up from the back on the column. Then just as they were preparing to resume their march towards the sound of the guns they were further disorganised as the small cavalry detachment under Captain John Jones who had actually found the upper plungeon but been repulsed by weigh of numbers, charged back past them. Many of the infantry turned tail and followed them.

As the light increased, the situation became clearer and riders were dispatched this way and that to pass on the king's instructions as he tried to regain control. With uncommitted troops still to arrive and with his three guns in place there was still a chance for victory over the only royal force that realistically stood between him and

London. Daniel Foe was sent charging across the field to the Red Regiment. Wade's attention was fixed firmly on the enemy unit to his front when Foe reined in beside him, grabbed his arm and gestured to their right. In the gathering light Wade could just make out two unengaged regiments of royal infantry.

'Damn!' he exclaimed. 'That's where we should be, opposite those fellows. We've not come far enough! Does the king want me to move?'

Before Foe could respond the two grey masses on the opposite bank seemed to shake themselves to life having realised that they too had no target. As Nat watched, the two enemy regiments with flags flying and drums playing turned smartly to their right and started to make their way behind the royal troops who held the bank opposite the Red Regiment.

'Can you see who they are?' asked Wade.

Foe took a spyglass from his pocket and trained it on the far bank. The light had grown a little stronger so that colours could now be seen, whereas minutes earlier everything was various shades of grey.

'The first unit are in red coats with yellow turn-backs and they carry a standard showing a red cross against a yellow background, that'll be Trelawney's regiment. Those behind have green turn-backs and their standard has a green background with a flaming yellow sun. Kirke's Lambs, the Devils!' Nat wasn't sure why it mattered who they were but Wade seemed to want to know.

'And those we face?' Foe refocused his glass as lead bullets whistled overhead.

'The Foot Guards to the right and Dumbarton's with their blue and white saltire to the left.'

Wade seemed satisfied with the news and suggested that Foe should return and pass the information to the king. Foe nodded curtly and was gone. Kirke's and Trelawney's regiments were clearly going to support their right flank where Wade hoped that the Blue and White Regiments of the rebel army were already deployed. Nat stood leaning on his scythe helpless to join in the firefight although in truth he was not overly concerned that he couldn't contribute to the ongoing battle. He had no real desire to sink his deadly blade into the flesh of some unknown soldier whose only crime was to have taken the King's Shilling at the insistence of his landlord or duped into joining the army by the recruiting sergeant having placed the coin in the bottom of the poor man's beer mug. Whilst Nat stood impotently watching the battle unfold, Henry Outwell was loading his musket for the umpteenth time. His face was blackened from the gunpowder, his ears rang terribly and his mouth was parched. He bit into another home-made cartridge, holding the lead bullet in his mouth as he tipped the loose powder into the barrel, before spitting the bullet in after it. He longed for a splash of water to wash the remnants of the powder from his mouth but he had drained his water sack more than half an hour earlier.

As the rising sun began to illuminate the scene the firing on both sides became more accurate. Up to this point the inexperience rebels had been blasting away into the dark guided only by the sounds and flashes of the royalists returning their fire and as a result most of the rebel shot had gone high. The rebel cannons with their professional Dutch gun master were the first to take advantage of the increasing light and were soon doing great execution, the bright tongues of flame that accompanied each shot seeming to almost reach to the enemy on the far bank. A snatch of wind momentarily pulled back the thick curtain of gun smoke and Henry watched with awe as the cannons ripped ragged holes in the long red line of Dumbarton's Regiment, the men falling like skittles. He watched transfixed as one of Dumbarton's standard bearers was snatched away in a red mist of blood and brain, only for the soldier next to him to drop his musket and raise the blue and white flag high. Henry turned to the man next to him.

'Thank God that the enemy has no cannon,' he shouted.

The man didn't reply, he just pointed across the rhine to where a number of guns were being dragged forward having somehow been moved from their positions on the Bridgwater road. Henry offered up a silent prayer for whoever would soon be coming under their lethal fire. 'For what we are about to receive...' he whispered.

30 A DEADLY HARVEST

Sedgemoor, Monday 6th July 1685

The bodies were slowly piling up on both sides of the ditch. Samuel White was calmly loading and firing his musket from the front rank of the Green Regiment although he had no real idea of the effect his efforts were having, so thick was the smoke. Not for the first time in his military career he found it incredible that anyone could still be standing such was the weight of lead that the two sides were hurling at each other.

Men were falling about him, the soft thuds of lead hitting flesh still distinguishable amid the roar of the muskets. Long tongues of flame lit the grey bank of smoke, followed a split second later by a mighty roar and then came bloody carnage. The royal cannons were firing partridge shot, hessian bags crammed with musket balls that split apart as they left the cannons' muzzles, spraying the rebels with a deadly hail. Whole swathes of rebels went down, arms and heads being ripped from bodies as they were flung back like so many childrens' rag dolls. This was beyond the wildest imaginings of the rebels' worst nightmares. The man stood next to Samuel suddenly dropped his musket and clutched at his torn throat from which blood pumped out in thick jets and the rebel cannons fell silent as their gunners were swept away in an instant. In the face of such unimaginable slaughter the Green Regiment recoiled away from the edge of the rhine and blundered into the forward ranks of Bovet's Blue Regiment who had at last arrived on the battlefield.

'Stand your ground!' yelled the officers. 'We must hold the bank of the ditch.'

Back on the right flank things were becoming desperate for the Red Regiment. More royal guns had been brought forward and were soon playing upon the brave men of the King's Own. Despite his reluctance Nat felt that he could no longer just stand by and watch as his friends died. He dropped his scythe and snatched up a discarded musket from the ground. Its erstwhile owner lay on his back a few feet away, the top part of his head carried away by a musket ball. Nat tugged the bag of cartridges from the lifeless body and began to load the musket.

'Make way for the king!' called an officer as Monmouth and his staff rode up to the rear of the formation.

The king dismounted and ignoring the pleas of his staff snatched a half-pike from one of the sergeants guarding the regiment's colours and pushed himself to the front of the unit. If the men had been thinking of breaking, the presence of their king stiffened their resolve and both Nat and Henry found themselves shouting defiant oaths at the enemy and calling encouragement to their comrades as they loaded and fired, loaded and fired.

Henry reached into his pouch for his next cartridge but found that the bag was empty. He bent to retrieve a bag from a fallen man but that had only two charges left.

'Cartridges, cartridges!' he shouted, 'has anyone got any cartridges for me?'

The men close enough to hear over the noise of battle shook their heads, they too were running low on ammunition having been in action for more than an hour. They had used all that they had brought with them in their pouches and pockets and the wagons containing fresh supplies were still stuck back at Peasy farm. The king turned to his servant.

'Williams. Get you back to the wagons and bring them forward, take Thomas Boad my groom with you, and if the wagons cannot move then commandeer their horses and bring back what you can carry on them. Hurry man, every minute may be vital.'

Having just marched over the sodden ground between Peasy farm and the rhine, Nat could well understand why their guide Barrett had said that the wagons could go no further. He was unsure how much ammunition the two riders would be able to bring or whether they would arrive back in time, especially as the cartridges would have to be unpacked from the large chests in which they were transported then transferred into smaller containers that could be managed on horseback. Suddenly, as if a tap had been turned off, the firing from the opposite bank stopped. The men around Nat looked about in confusion, their ears still ringing.

'I think the bastards 'ave had enough lads!' someone called. They started to congratulate each other and many dropped to their knees to offer up prayers of thanks for their safe deliverance.

'A Monmouth, A Monmouth!' they cheered as the king handed the half-pike back to the sergeant and remounted his horse, but their celebrations were short lived as the ground began to shake and the reason for the cessation of firing became obvious.

'Horsemen, coming this way!' someone called.

'Thank God! Lord Grey has reformed his horse and has come back to the fight!' said another.

Nat wasn't so sure. If it was Grey returning with the rebel horse why had the enemy stopped firing? There was only one answer.

'They ain't ours!' came a horrified cry.

Despite their apparent disregard for the lives of their own men the royal commanders were not stupid enough to risk hitting their own cavalry who were now approaching the right flank of the Red Regiment.

'They must've got over the lower plungeon!'

'Right turn! Pikes and scythes to the front!' shouted Wade.

Nat dropped his newly acquired musket, snatched up his scythe and pushed his way through the shocked musketeers, ready to face the threat of the horsemen. No horse would willingly charge into a wall of sharp points, if only the pikemen and scythemen could get into position quickly enough. The men waited nervously as the enemy cavalry got closer. Some prayed, others vomited or found that they had lost control of their bladders. Nat felt the bile rising in his throat but swallowed it down.

The horsemen stopped some fifty paces from the rebel formation, they had no immediate intention of charging the disorganised rebels. These were horse grenadiers armed with a carbine and a brace of pistols in addition to their wickedly sharp swords. They moved slowly towards the waiting rebels riding boot to boot before calmly discharging their firearms into the mass of rebels. Lead whistled through the air striking men down in their scores. Next to Nat a pikeman was hit high on the right arm spinning him around. He fell at Nat's feet clutching his shattered limb and crying softly for his mother. Having fired, the front row of horse grenadiers peeled away to either flank and another rank took their place to repeat the punishment. Rank after rank of horseman, maybe a hundred and fifty riders in all, each one reloading as he reached the back of the formation only to advance and fire again in turn. The Red Regiment began to back away from the slaughter to which they had little answer, their front ranks being filled with pikes and scythes so that only a few musketeers could bring their weapons to bear, causing minimal casualties. At length the grenadiers stopped firing and drew their swords.

As Nat was preparing to fend off the cavalry that had crossed the rhine at the lower plungeon, the royal cavalry over on Samuel White's side of the battlefield were also on the move. They had swept away Jones' brave defence of the upper plungeon and were now threatening the left flank of the Greens and the newly arrived Blue Regiment. Samuel looked over his shoulder and was relieved to see the head of the White Regiment edging towards the battle. If they could come up to protect the flank there was a chance of holding the enemy back, but then with a mighty roar Kirke's and Trelawney's infantry who had completed their march across from the other end of the battlefield plunged into the ditch. If the Greens and Blues had still held the lip of the bank they could have repulsed them, but they had been forced back by the artillery fire and having half turned to face the threat posed by the cavalry there was no chance of them stopping the previously uncommitted royal infantry who were keen to get into the action. The brave but untrained men of Monmouth's army had been reluctant to cross the ditch but daylight had revealed that it was not the serious obstacle that it had appeared in the dark.

The fresh, disciplined men under Feversham waded across just as their cavalry smashed into the side of the Blue Regiment. The Blues were pushed back against the men of the Greens and both units broke and ran, taking the White Regiment with them. The game was up and Samuel found himself running for his life, discarding his heavy musket and any other piece of equipment that might slow him down. His slim chance of outrunning a man on a horse were reduced further when his flight was impeded by a crowd of frightened rebels whose own escape route was blocked by the Longmoor rhine. He glanced nervously behind him catching a brief glimpse of the flashing blade that all but removed his head from his shoulders.

The rebels were in full retreat. The left flank was a jumble of running men whilst the Yellow Regiment which had been immediately alongside the Reds had simply disappeared. Monmouth looked over the battlefield and its grisly crop of broken bodies that bled their life away into the damp soil.

'Major Wade. It seems that the enemy have the better of us. Be so good as to pull your regiment back in the best order that can be managed. The King's Own have fought as valiantly as any men that it has been my privilege to command.'

Wade gave the order and the remnants of the Red Regiment began to retrace their steps back towards the sturdy walls of Peasy Farm with its perceived promise of safety. Nat was filled with pride that they did so in such a calm manner, facing the enemy as they went. Never in his worst nightmares could Nat have imagined such carnage. Men lay in mangled heaps, many missing limbs and the ground was covered in a hellish mixture of blood, spilled guts and shit. The king was immediately surrounded by his staff and Nat was certain that he saw the king being forced to remove his feathered hat and his distinctive purple and red dress-coat and don a nondescript felt cap and brown coat. He was clearly resisting all their efforts to disguise him but his aides were most insistent, manhandling the sovereign in a way that would have been unthinkable just hours before.

The enemy cavalry were reluctant to press home their attack on the disciplined mass of the Red Regiment with their steel tipped wall of pikes and scythes, especially as there were plenty of easier targets spread across the battlefield. Leaving enough troopers to watch them, ready to pounce should the rebels lose their cohesion, the bulk of the horsemen rode off, providing Nat's regiment with some welcome respite. Nat caught up with Henry.

'I think our best bet is to stick together as a unit and try and fight our way off the field. If we break, we die.'

'Happen as you might be right Nat. The left has gone completely and God knows where my Lord Grey and his blerry cav'ry 'ave gone.'

'Just like Bridport' Nat laughed derisively.

'Just like Bridport.' Henry replied.

The Defeat of the Rebells 2000 Slayn & thear Canon taken

31 NOWHERE TO RUN, NOWHERE TO HIDE

Bridgwater, Monday 6th July 1685

The mist that had shrouded the battlefield had been burnt off by the rising sun, revealing the extent of the catastrophe that had befallen the rebels. The ordered regiments that had marched out of Bridgwater in such a confident mood had simply disintegrated. Small knots of men ran in every direction desperate to avoid the sharp bayonets and swords of the vengeful royal army. The few rebel horsemen that remained on the field had the best chance of escape and they made sure that they took it, riding down their own infantry with complete indifference in their haste to reach safety.

'What a fucking shambles!' exclaimed Henry Outwell as he surveyed the marshland. He was not normally a man given to profanities but he was completely overwhelmed by the sheer scale of the disaster. The rebels had attacked with cries of '*God with us!*' but it seemed to Nat that God had abandoned them, turning his back on King Monmouth and his loyal, brave followers. How could that be so when they were taking part in a holy crusade? The Red Regiment appeared to be the only rebel unit that had retained some semblance of order as Wade led them slowly back towards Bridgwater, turning frequently to fight off the pursuing cavalry.

As the remnants of the rebel army left one side of the battlefield the men of the Wiltshire militia were entering from the opposite side. They had been kept away from the fighting because of their dubious loyalty and the fact that most had been roaring drunk when battle was joined. They had been away from home for nearly three weeks after mustering at Salisbury and so far they had been given no opportunity for a decent bit of looting to supplement their militia pay, which in any case was still outstanding. Now they were crossing a field of battle which although littered with the enemy's dead, had already been stripped bare by the regulars.

'I wonder if they've looked in this cornfield,' said one of the men as he climbed over the flimsy wooden fence.

A search revealed several rebels who had crawled into the standing corn to die but there were slim pickings for the militia. A groan drew them to a man who was nursing a badly broken arm. Aaron Tucker had survived Bridport, Keynsham and Philipsnorton unscathed but his luck had run out at Sedgemoor, a ball spat from an exploding cannister round had smashed his musket before ploughing into his right arm.

Splinters from his shattered musket stock were still embedded in his face. The militiamen, still sore about the lack of loot were in no mood for charity and they pulled Aaron to his feet, bringing forth a cry of pain as the ends of the broken bones scrapped together. He was marched across the bloody fields and thrown into St Mary's church in Westonzoyland where some five hundred captured rebels were already crammed together in unsanitary conditions. A couple of the prisoners tried to reset their comrades' broken bones but when the pain became too much they were forced to abandon their efforts. No doctor came to tend to the wounded and neither food nor water was provided.

As Aaron lay in his own filth in Westonzoyland church, the hundred and fifty survivors of the Red Regiment had reached the relative safety of Bridgwater. Wade was infuriated to find large numbers of rebel horsemen milling about but his exhortations to return to the battlefield to screen the retreat of the fleeing infantry fell on deaf ears and it was only the pikes and scythes of his men that prevented them from being ridden down by their own horsemen.

Wade gathered his men about him.

'I fear that our cause is lost. I intend to ride for the north Devon coast where I hope to find a ship. I would welcome the company of any of you who can ride and want to join me, otherwise I wish you God's speed in making a safe return to your homes.'

Nat and Henry exchanged glances. Their homes lay to the south but that way was currently blocked by the enemy.

'Strikes I that our only way 'ome be to follow his lordship for now. Maybe we can cut back to the south once the hue and cry is over,' said Henry.

'Reckon you be right there 'enry,' replied Nat. 'Can you ride a horse?'

'Well enough. My uncle had a farm outside of Whitford, I learnt to ride there. What about you?'

'Soon find out!' Nat laughed.

It didn't take long to find enough loose horses for the thirty or so men who had decided to stick with Wade. As they trotted slowly through the town, anxious to escape but well aware of the need to keep their new mounts as fresh as possible they came upon a ghastly spectacle. A number of chirurgeons were busy at work tending to the many wounded who had streamed off the battlefield. Men screamed as mangled arms and legs were amputated and added to the piles outside the large tent. With only a mouthful of strong spirits to dull the pain, wooden spoons had to be clamped between their teeth to stop them from biting off their own tongues. Dogs licked at the pools of fresh blood and fought over the discarded limbs.

'Tis like a scene from Dante's nine levels of hell!' exclaimed Wade.

'Who's Danty?' asked Henry.

'Never mind,' replied Wade turning his attention to the tall man who seemed to be in charge of the makeshift infirmary.

'Master William Oliver is it not?'

The chirurgeon looked up as one of his orderlies applied a hot iron to the truncated arm of his latest patient to seal the severed blood vessels.

'Major Nathaniel Wade,' he replied in a strong Cornish accent. 'I am glad to see that you still live Nathaniel.'

'You too William. I would urge you to consider pulling out, the enemy cavalry are hot on our heels.'

'I've too much work to do here with these poor souls. I will trust to the enemy's good faith.'

As the two men talked the rest of those that had decided to follow Wade were busy divesting themselves of anything that could identify them with the failed rebellion. As they were about to depart Daniel Foe trotted up, nodding to Nat before addressing Wade.

'Sorry to interrupt Major but I believe the king intends to work his way south and look for a ship to the continent. Will you be joining him?'

'No. Our way lies to the north where I have business contacts who should be able to secure us a boat. Will you ride with us Master Foe?'

'My thanks but I think I will find my own way. I have travelled this area many times in my work and believe that my best chance is to travel alone as if on another business trip.'

'Let's be about it then,' called Wade.

He clicked his tongue, nudging his horse into a trot as he led his small force towards the ruined western gate. Behind them the town was in chaos. The fleeing rebels had taken it upon themselves to make off with whatever they could carry, breaking down the cottage doors that had until recently been freely open to them. Many were already drunk on stolen spirits but they and those that tarried too long in their search for booty were already being rounded up by the first of the royal horsemen.

It wasn't long before Nat started to regret his decision to ride with Wade. He had never been on a horse before and had great difficulty copying the way the more experienced riders rose and fell in the saddle. He couldn't get the rhythm right, he always seemed to be coming down as the horse was going up resulting in a series of hard bumps which soon gave him a sore backside. He was overjoyed when Wade decided that there was no immediate threat of pursuit and called a halt in a dense copse of elm trees. It was mid-afternoon and both men and horses needed a break. The horses in particular could not be pushed too hard if they were to carry the tired men across the Quantock and Brendon Hills and the vast empty expanse of Exmoor. Nat eased himself painfully out of the saddle, anxious to do no further damage to the inside of his thighs which felt as if they had been rubbed raw.

All too soon for Nat's liking Wade called for the men to mount up again.

'I believe that we are free from immediate danger but I would like to be on the other side of the Quantocks before we look for somewhere to rest for the night.'

Now that they were clear of Bridgwater some of the men decided to leave the group. They were worried that each day they rode west took them further from their homes and feared that travelling in such a large company would attract too much attention. After much discussion ten of them rode off in ones and twos leaving Wade and twenty others to continue towards the coast.

Nat pulled himself into the saddle with some reluctance and had been riding for no more than five minutes before his thighs began to burn again. The rough track they were following climbed higher and higher and eventually the thick woods gave way to open heathland. There was no hope of finding cover in such bleak surroundings and they pushed on.

'We need to find water for the horses and shelter for ourselves,' Wade called back over his shoulder.

The land before them dropped away and they found themselves looking down into a narrow valley through which a small river reflected the light of the lowering sun. They picked up a small stream that tumbled down from the Quantocks to meet this river somewhere out of sight to their right and stopped to allow the horses to drink. As his horse drank Nat looked across to the far side of the valley where church spires indicated the existence of several small communities clinging to the eastern edge of the Brendon Hills.

'We'll ride down to the valley floor and look for somewhere to camp,' decided Wade leading the small troop of rebels as they walked their mounts carefully down the steep slopes.

Despite their frequent stops the horses were clearly tiring and with the sun starting to sink below the high land before them they took shelter in a stand of ancient oak trees and settled down for the night. They decided against a fire thinking they should put at least another day between themselves and any possible pursuit before running such a risk.

While the fate of the rebellion, indeed the future of the monarchy itself was being decided on the bloody fields outside Bridgwater, William, John and Thomas had all been making their separate ways home.

William was the first to make it back. Having rested for a few hours in the abandoned cottage he woke well before dawn and crept down to the banks of the River Tone, following the river as it wound its way towards Taunton. From the cover of a thick patch of brambles he looked upon the familiar clutch of cottages that huddled around Lambrook Mill, watching for a full ten minutes before deciding that it was safe to leave cover and dash across the road to his home. He rose to his feet and had gone no more than five paces before a challenge rang out, followed by a pistol shot. The militiaman missed but it served to alert the rest of the picket who had been placed on the road from Bridgwater to intercept any rebels looking to sneak back into Taunton. The sound brought many of the villagers to their doors including Rebecca Pearce who was just in time to see her husband being manhandled into the clearing outside her cottage.

Thomas was more fortunate. He approached Yeovil with some trepidation but the rebellion had not touched the town so there were no militia guarding the roads and he was able to stroll up the hill and into the town just after breakfast time. News of the general pardon offered by King James had reached the town but as yet no word had come to tell the inhabitants that James' army had fought and won a great victory.

A few judicious enquiries led Thomas to a large town house in Middle Street where a servant showed him into a waiting room already half full of petitioners waiting to speak to the local Justice of the Peace. Thomas kept himself to himself as the other supplicants chatted about their various gripes and grievances that they expected the magistrate to resolve for them. When it was Thomas' turn he was ushered into the parlour where a large-bellied man sat behind a huge oak table covered in books and papers. He wore an old wig and the burst blood vessels in his nose and cheeks spoke of his fondness for port, a half empty decanter standing to one side of the desk. Despite the warm weather a huge fire burned in the fireplace making the room uncomfortably hot.

'Well, what do you want?' he snapped.

'I've come to take up the king's offer of a pardon your worship.'

'Have you now?' replied the magistrate, looking up from his paperwork for the first time. He laid down his quill and refilled his glass.

'And why would you want to do that?'

'I was tricked and misled into following the bastard Monmouth, excuse my language your 'onor.'

'And pray tell what is happening with regard to the rebellion? We have had no news here for some days.'

'I have no idea, truth be told your 'onor. I left the rebels' camp as soon as I could get away. I think there may have been a battle someplace north of Frome but I had no part of it. God's truth I've done nothing but walk since I left Lyme.'

'So you've not actually raised your hand against the king?'

'No sir, only marched, this way and that, just march, march, march.'

'And did you take up arms?'

'No yur 'onor. There were niver enough weapons to go round even if I wanted one. I niver carried more than a stout stave and I only did that to protect myself from the lawless rabble who followed the duke. How they expected me to face up to his majesty's brave and loyal troops with only a stick I'll niver know.'

'And now you wish to take advantage of his majesty's overly generous offer to forgive the traitors who had the temerity to take up arms against him?' It was a statement rather than a question.

'I didn't want to go off to war in the first place yur 'onor. I'm a simple country boy and had no idea what was going on. My master at the mill where I worked used to beat me zummat rotten and he forced me to join the rebellion, said he'd turn me out of my work and my home if I didn't.'

'I can't say that I fully believe you and if I had my way you'd be hanging from a gibbet before the day was done, but alas the matter is out of my hands. You are fortunate to present yourself when you do as the offer of clemency expires the day after tomorrow. Name and place of residence?'

The magistrate took a printed sheet of paper from his drawer, filled in the details that Thomas gave then signed and sealed it before handing it to Thomas who couldn't believe that it had been so simple. In the anteroom Thomas persuaded one of the clerks to read the paper to him.

'Thomas Edgecott of Lyme Regis, Dorsetshire latterly in the camp of James Scott, late Duke of Monmouth, hath laid down his arms and is returned to his obedience and craves the liberty of his Majesty's most gracious pardon.'

Thomas was free to return to Lyme without fear of arrest. Nat was dead and stupid old Hezekiah Sprake too probably. Eliza would need someone to look out for her and he knew that he was just the man to do it. For the first time in weeks he was free to walk about without having to check over his shoulder all the time.

He still had some of the silver coins taken from the trooper he had killed outside Pensford, each one stamped with the strange image of a seated woman holding a trident. He had not seen this design on any coins before but given the quality and crispness he assumed that these were newly minted. He turned one of the coins over in his hand looking at the raised edge that would make them very hard to 'clip'. Clipping the edges off coins to sell the slim slivers of precious metal to make the money go further was treated as treason and carried the threat of being hung, drawn and quartered if caught, but it was still a common enough practice in Dorset and no doubt elsewhere.

'That'll put a dent in many a poor man's earnings,' he said to himself as he strolled into the first inn that he came to and ordered food, beer and a bed for the night.

John had risen while it was still dark, eager to cross the Blackdown Hills as quickly as his old legs would permit. He stretched, scratched fiercely at the lice in the seams of his undershirt before trying to rub some warmth into his old bones. He left his improvised campsite just as the sky began to lighten over the eastern hills, the faint glow gradually extending north and south until the sun exploded over the horizon, chasing away the shadows one by one as the light spread across the land.

Two and a half hours of steady climbing up the thickly wooded slopes brought him to the summit and at last he was able to look down on the broken landscape below him. Somewhere among the hills and valleys lay the border between Somerset and Dorset and with a weird logic John knew that once he crossed that unmarked boundary he would be safe. He hurried down the far side heading for a small village where he hoped that some kind soul would take pity on a crippled old man and give him something to eat.

Crossing a fast-flowing stream he headed for the church which stood close to the ruined remains of an old castle. He thought that the church would be the best place to find alms but as he approached the churchyard he heard hoof beats behind him and turned to see two troopers of the Devonshire militia.

'Stop there old timer!' called the taller of the two, pulling his short carbine from its holster. 'State your business and be quick about it.'

Despite his fear John launched into his cover story hoping that it would be good enough to fool the two riders who had now positioned themselves on either side of him. He turned to face one then the other as he spoke.

'Please have pity on an old seaman who wants nothing but a bite of food and a quick journey back to 'is 'ome.'

'And where might home be?'

'Honiton sir.' He had deliberately chosen a town which he knew well but one that had not been visited by the rebel army.

'You're a long way from home. Not running away from the rebel army are you? Took off before they were annihilated on the moors outside Bridgwater did you?'

John hoped that the distress caused by their news of the battle did not show on his face. Nat was still with the army when he had last seen him and he prayed that the news was false.

He steadied himself before replying. 'I was working on a coastal trader, carrying Cornish tin from Penzance to Bristol when we was hit by a storm in the Channel. A spar broke and came down on my arm. We put into Minehead to effect repairs and I was paid off by the master. Bastard said I was no use to him with only one good arm. I've been walking for the best part of a week.'

The tale seemed to satisfy the militiamen and they made to ride away.

'Don't s'pose you 'as any bread I could 'ave?'

'Don't push it old man. I've given you the benefit of the doubt even though I'm not sure I believes your story. Now be on your way before I change my mind.'

John watched them trot away before turning into the lynch-gate where a notice announced the church to be St Mary's in Hemyock. He walked slowly into the cool and quiet of the church where he offered a quick prayer of thanks for his deliverance. As he struggled to rise from his knees he was approached by the vicar, a short rotund man with a bald head and large soft hands that helped John back to his feet. John repeated his cover story before asking if there was any chance of any food.

'These are hard times,' the vicar said sadly.

Looking at the man's large paunch John thought that the vicar didn't seem to be doing so badly in these 'hard times.'

'I'll be finished here in a few minutes. I'm sure my housekeeper will be able to find something to assuage your hunger.'

The parsonage was only a short walk away, standing on the opposite side of the courtyard from the huge gatehouse that was all that remained of the old castle. The kindly vicar was good for his word and told his maid to give John a hunk of day-old bread and a slab of hard cheese that he gratefully wolfed down, keeping just a small amount back for later. It was just past midday when he thanked the vicar and made to leave.

'I suppose you've heard about the battle at Bridgwater?' said the vicar conversationally.

'No. A battle 'tween who? I've been at sea for weeks, I've no notion of what's been happening ashore.'

'King James, God bless and save him has routed the rebels. The throne is secured and the traitor Monmouth is on the run. He may even have been captured by now.'

John had hoped that the trooper had told him the story in the hope of eliciting a reaction but now it seemed that the news was true.

'And what of the duke's army?' he asked. 'I only ask as I don't want to run into any of them on my way 'ome.'

'No fear of that. The rebels were completely destroyed thanks be to God.'

John forced a smile in response and took his leave. He left Hemyock on a rutted track that headed south, running alongside a small stream. After about a mile or so the track began climbing towards a farm that stood on a high promontory to his left. He didn't fancy the climb so he left the track and continued along the valley floor where the stream took him past the ruins of what looked like an old abbey. It promised a secluded shelter for the night but there was still some daylight left and he decided to press on.

The stream eventually petered out in a large mossy area at the foot of a small cliff where the heavily wooded hills pressed close on either side and John decided he could go no further that day. He ate the last of the food that the vicar had provided, drank sparingly from the stream then curled up under the boughs of a large elm tree. He was worried about Nat. He knew that his son wasn't cut out to be a soldier even though there was no doubting his bravery or his devotion to the Protestant cause and he prayed that he had been wise enough to keep himself safe. He wouldn't know if Nat had survived until he reached home so he resolved to rise early the following morning in the hope of reaching Lyme by the evening. Sleep came quickly but his dark dreams were filled with images of his son laid on a ruined battlefield, staring blankly at a blood red sky.

Severall of ye Rebells hang'd upon a Tree

32 ACROSS THE HIGH MOORS

Tuesday 7th[th] and Wednesday 8th July 1685

Aaron Tucker had been unable to sleep on the cold floor of the church due to the pain in his arm and the noise made by the other prisoners as they cried aloud for their mothers or moaned quietly as they awaited their fate. By the morning six of the men had died of their wounds and Tucker suspected that many others would not see another day. The common consensus was that they would be loaded into carts and taken to gaol either in Bridgwater or Taunton to await trial. Around mid-morning the church doors were flung open and a flamboyantly dressed man strode in.

'Sergeant, bring me five men!'

'Which ones your grace?'

'Any of the damned rascals will do,' snapped Albemarle, the commander of the Devon militia. 'Just drag any five of them outside and don't be gentle about it.'

Being a late arrival, Aaron was propped just inside the door and was seized by the sergeant causing him to scream with pain. Once outside the five men were hustled towards a large tree in the churchyard where ropes hung from a sturdy bough.

'String them up!' ordered Albemarle.

'Is that legal your grace?' questioned Thomas Perratt the vicar. 'Surely these men must be put on trial.'

'I would appreciate it if you could refrain from interfering reverend. I have received authority from the king himself. He has declared martial law, which means that as Lord Lieutenant of Devon I am empowered to dispense justice as I see fit.'

Noticing the look of disbelief on Perratt's face Albemarle reached into his coat and withdrew a folded sheet of stiff paper. 'I quote...you are to make an example for a terror to the rest...'

Perratt was about to point out that they were actually in Somersetshire not Devonshire but thought better of it. The five men were unceremoniously stripped and made to stand on a bench that had been set up below the branch. The ropes were placed around their necks and without further ado the bench was kicked away. The men died slowly, the drop being insufficient to break their necks, instead they swung back and forth as they choked to death, their bowels emptying, their eyes bulging and their blue swollen tongues sticking from their mouths.

At about the time that Tucker was meeting his end, Wade's small band of increasingly desperate men were lighting a small fire to try to warm themselves after a chilly night beside the Doniford Stream. They had no idea how wide the victorious royal forces would spread their net in their efforts to catch any rebels who had managed to escape the slaughter at Sedgemoor, but if they were to keep ahead of any such pursuit they would have to be on their way soon.

'We need to find food,' said Wade, 'but I'll be damned if I'm going to steal it. I've a small amount of money left so I'm going to ride on alone to see what I can find. I doubt there'll be much to have once we reach the high ground ahead so it's now or never. Wait for me here and stay under cover.'

'Wait!' said Henry Outwell. 'One of us should go with you.'

'You don't trust me? Do you think I might just ride off and leave you to your fate?'

'No! It's nothing like that Major, but if you finds anyone willing to sell you food you'll need someone to watch your back while you deals with them, someone to hold the horses like. Besides no gintl'mun would be out without a manservant to look arter him.'

'You're right by God! You'll come with me then sergeant.'

They rode for about twenty minutes with the hot sun on their backs before happening upon a man leading a string of pack animals. He had no food to spare but seeing the quality of Wade's clothing and horse he suggested they try the manor house in Lydiard St Lawrence.

'I knows that name from somewhere,' whispered Henry, 'but I can't place it just yet.'

'The house belongs to the Manton family,' added the man.

'I've got it!' shouted Henry after the old man had gone on his way. 'I knew I'd heard the name Lydiard St Lawrence afore. Thomas Manton used to preach at our church in Colyton. I remembers my father saying as how he was a good puritan minister, all fire and brimstone. He put the fear of God into people and it were he that persuaded my father to side with parliament in the late wars. I've no idea if he still lives in Lydiard or if he lives at all, he'd be near 70 by now but it seems like the family still lives locally and might be well disposed to our plight.'

They rode on following the directions that the man had given and soon came to an imposing house set in well-tended grounds. Wade rang the bell and the door was opened by an old footman in a slightly faded blue coat and powdered wig. Wade was shown into a comfortable sitting room whilst Henry remained outside with the horses, taking the opportunity to flirt with a comely maid servant who was returning to the kitchens after collecting eggs from a nearby coop. Wade did not have to wait for long before an elegantly dressed woman of about sixty entered the room. He rose and apologised for presenting himself so early in the day.

'Please think nothing of it. We see so few people out here that any intrusion is welcomed,' she replied graciously. 'Will you take breakfast with us? Wade nodded his assent.

'Good! I'll see that your man is looked after in the kitchen.'

It transpired that the minister Henry remembered had passed away some years previously whist preaching in London at which point the family had returned to their ancestral home in Somerset. It was soon evident that the widow and her two sons who had joined Wade for breakfast shared Manton's strong

Protestant leanings and food, drink and extra clothing was quickly forthcoming. The younger son Oliver offered to act as a guide for them.

'There's a decent road that leads through the Brendon Hills. I can take you as far as the River Avill where you should be able to find food and lodgings in the village of Cutcombe if you've a mind to.'

'Thank you. A guide would be most appreciated although I feel we should continue to avoid towns and villages for a while yet.'

'That's probably a good idea. Riders have arrived in the area with instructions to apprehend any strangers and the mayors and justices are falling over themselves to demonstrate their loyalty to King James now that the rebellion has been crushed. You've been lucky to avoid running into any militia so far.'

Once the meal had been completed Wade took his leave and the three men rode back to find the rest of the party still at their overnight campsite. The food was shared out and Wade and Henry took over sentry duties as the other men ate. Nat sat quietly on a fallen tree chewing on a chicken leg.

'You look miles away Nat,' said Aaron Smith as he eased himself down beside him with a low groan.

'Leg still troubling you I see,' said Nat sympathetically. Aaron had been hit in the leg at Bridport and the wound had still not mended properly.

'S'pect it'll niver mend proper now. So what are you daydreaming about?'

'I can't decide which way to turn Aaron. Sticking with Major Wade seemed the right thing to do at the time but every mile we go is a mile further from home.'

'I've been thinking the same. Problem is that there'll be a lot of militia between here and home. But if the major finds a boat to take 'im to Holland he'll have to sail right past Lyme on the way and he might be able to drop us off like.'

'I agree Aaron. Let's stick together for now.'

'Time to move out,' called Wade.

Oliver Manton led them along a wide track across the top of the Brendon Hills. Nat was not sure about the wisdom of riding on such an exposed road but Oliver argued that it gave them the best chance of spotting any pursuers. He said that he knew enough secluded valleys in which they could hide if the need arose. They were able to keep up a steady pace without tiring the horses and by mid-afternoon they reined in beside an old stone cross that marked the meeting of four tracks. Oliver turned his horse to face the rebels.

'The road ahead drops down to the river that lies in the valley bottom but you'll come to Cutcombe just before you reach the river. From there you can follow the river north all the way to the coast near Minehead, but if you still intend to make for Ilfracombe then you must cross the river and keep heading west over the moors. Try to keep to the track, if you lose it you could be wandering the moors for the rest of eternity. If you don't lose your way you should reach Ilfracombe by tomorrow lunchtime, depending on how often you need to stop.'

'Thank you, Oliver. I'd like to put a few more miles behind us whilst there is still light, so will we find anywhere to rest tonight if we carry on past Cutcombe?'

'You will. Exford is about five miles further on but after that there is very little until you reach the Bovey house at Simonsbath. We don't have too much to do with them given that Bovey acted as an agent for the late

King Charles II when he was in exile whilst my father was chaplain to Oliver Cromwell!'

'Hence your Christian name, Oliver?'

'Quite. As I say I cannot guarantee what sort of reception you might receive at Simonsbath. These are strange times but you were fighting for Charles' son which might stand in your favour.'

Wade shook the young man's hand and thanked him profusely. As Oliver Manton headed for home Wade led his men down into the valley, through Cutcombe, across the River Quarme and up onto the moors where the shadows of clouds chased each other across the desolate landscape pushed by a brisk westerly wind.

The road rose gently before dropping suddenly into another valley where the thatched cottages of Exford clustered either side of a narrow stone bridge. An overgrown track led to the water's edge near the bridge and Nat supposed that this was the site of the old ford from which the village derived its name. He guessed that the ford would become unusable when the snows on the high moors melted in spring and turned the infant River Exe into a raging torrent, hence the need for a bridge.

The pot-holed main street of the wretched hamlet was deserted as they rode slowly through, a band of villainous looking horsemen was best avoided in these uncertain times. As the shadows began to lengthen Wade decided that the horses needed resting and they turned off the road where a shallow stream rushed down to join the Exe. The horses were hobbled and were soon munching happily on the lush grass that grew beside the stream while the men shared out the last of the cold rations that Widow Manton had provided. They suspected that they had been seen as they passed through Exford but there was no point drawing further attention to themselves by lighting a fire.

Deep into the dark night it was Nat's turn to relieve Henry Outwell who had been standing watch for the past two hours. He climbed to the lip of the valley and starred in awe at the ocean of bright stars before looking around for Henry. He found him huddled in the lea of one of the large boulders that littered the high moors. God alone knew how these huge stones had ended up stranded on these hill tops he thought. A large moon sat low on the eastern skyline and Nat spent the next two hours watching it slowly climb the sky, dimming each of the stars in turn, his thoughts focused on Eliza and home. The silence was so complete that the snoring of the men camped below carried up to him clearly and he thought they might just as well light a signal fire to let the enemy know where they were such was the noise that the sleeping men made.

The pre-dawn light crept across the grey empty moorland as the horses were watered and saddled and they were on their way again before dawn had fully broken over the hills behind them. Moses Armitage, an old poacher who could slip unseen through almost any landscape was sent on ahead to scout the route even though they had seen no one else on the road since the previous afternoon, when the sight of a lone horseman had been enough for Oliver Manton to lead them quickly down into a narrow valley that twisted this way and that. If the horseman had seen them he must have decided that discretion was the better part of valour because he had gone when the party eventually rejoined the road.

Wade had decided to bypass Simonsbath House being uncertain of the welcome that they might receive and three hours easy riding brought them to the end of the moors where, as so often happens at the point where one type of landscape meets another a number of ancient burial mounds and hillforts adorned the edge of the escarpment. The land below the moors was more broken with steep sided valleys and large patches of woodland whilst away to their right the sea sparkled with its promise of freedom.

They rode down off the high moors and headed for a small wood that grew close to the edge of the track. Ducking under the low hanging boughs they discovered a small glade with a stream running through the middle and Nat was overjoyed when the order to dismount was given, so sore was his backside. After an all too brief stop they remounted and followed a rough track towards an isolated farm high on a bluff. As they crested the ridge, the small town of Ilfracombe came into view with its distinctive chapel dedicated to St Nicholas standing proud on the headland above the busy harbour. The farmstead turned out to be deserted and Wade thought it would make an ideal base until he could find them passage on a ship. Once they had seen to the horses Wade gathered the small group about him.

'I need to go into the town to speak to my contact there. If he can secure me a boat I intend to sail for the Low Countries, as Bristol will not be safe for a while yet. If you wish you can try to find a magistrate in the town to obtain a pardon. I will make discreet enquiries to see whether the offer of amnesty still stands now that a major battle has been fought. It is conceivable that news of the action outside Bridgwater has yet to reach this place as Master Manton made no reference to it. You may of course decide to take ship with me and I would truly welcome your company.'

'If we comes with you will we be able to stop in at Lyme on the way to 'olland?' asked Aaron Smith.

'I'm certain of it as long as the place isn't held by James' men, but even then there are coves aplenty where we can put you safely ashore.'

They all agreed to stick with Wade and settled down in the shelter of the abandoned buildings whilst the major rode into Ilfracombe in search of a suitable vessel.

33 HOMECOMING

Tuesday 7thth July 1685

Thomas rose late with the sun streaming through the dirty cloth that served as a curtain. He was certain that no one had seen him murder Nat, so with his pardon safely tucked into his coat pocket there was no great need to hurry back to Lyme apart from the growing desire to see Eliza.

Over a leisurely breakfast of eggs and bacon he got talking to a carter called Jacob Bridger and his twelve-year-old son Billy who were headed for Exeter with a large consignment of Frome broadcloth. Bridger was grossly overweight, with thinning grey hair and a florid complexion. He agreed to Thomas riding on the wagon in exchange for a promise to buy the ale and pay for accommodation for all three when they stopped in Crewkerne and again in Axminster. Bridger thought that Thomas would provide some welcome adult company on the long journey and would be available to act as a brakeman when they came to some of the steeper downhill sections.

Thomas, or Peter Smith of Honiton as he had given his name, was called into action not long after leaving Yeovil as the heavy wagon rolled down the steep hill into East Chinnock. Thomas hauled on a length of rope attached to the rear of the wagon while Jacob pulled on the brake with all his strength and Billy tried to slow the oxen. It was warm work and when they reached the bottom of the hill Thomas removed his heavy woollen topcoat, folded it and placed it on the hard wooden bench where it could act as a cushion.

They were stopped twice between Yeovil and Crewkerne by militia horsemen. Bills of lading answered for the carter and his son whilst Thomas' pardon was accepted without question, although he made certain that Jacob never got to see his real name on the paper. Thomas was tempted to boast about his exploits with Monmouth's army when the carter questioned him but decided that it was best to stick with the story that he had given to the magistrate in Yeovil.

They stopped at the Red Lion in Crewkerne in mid-afternoon where Jacob did his best to extract the maximum fare from Thomas by consuming as much ale as he could. Counting his few remaining coppers Thomas worried that a similar exhibition of drinking at their next stop would leave him penniless. The old man slept for much of the journey the following day, waking only to demand more of Thomas' dwindling supply of money for cider at a roadside inn in the middle of the afternoon. Young Billy took charge of the driving and from the way he handled the oxen it was clear that this was a common occurrence.

Jacob barely stirred when the wagon pulled to a halt in the yard behind the Spotted Horse in Axminster where they would stop for the night. With Billy seeing to the oxen and Jacob sleeping soundly Thomas decided that now would be a good time to quietly slip off, Lyme being no more than five or six miles away. As he climbed down from the front bench he accidently brushed against Jacob and heard the jingle of coins coming from the man's overcoat pocket. A few more coppers wouldn't hurt he thought as he began to search for Jacob's purse.

'Oy, what are you doing mister?' Billy had finished with the oxen and had returned to rouse his father, knowing that he would be scolded if he let him sleep too long, only to wake stiff, cold and above all sober during the night.

'You'll shut that mouth of yours if you know what's good fer 'e,' hissed Thomas.

'Dad! Dad! Wake up!'

Thomas dropped to the ground and grabbed the boy, spinning him round and clamping a firm hand across his mouth, his other hand going instinctively to the bayonet that he kept tucked in his belt. The boy struggled to get free, biting down hard on Thomas' hand and as Thomas released his grip Billy started to shout again.

'Little bastard! Bite me would 'e?' hissed Thomas and he thrust the knife into Billy's back. The boy slid to the ground and Thomas stared aghast at what he had done. Slowly though, the look of horror turned into a smirk as he wiped the wet blade on the boy's coat.

'Got what he deserved, the little shit!' he said as he checked to see if Jacob had stirred, but the old man had slept through it all, fortified as he was with the copious amounts of cider that Thomas had paid for.

Thomas found Jacob's purse before creeping away into the night and aided by a clear sky and a full moon he reached the hills above Lyme by a little after midnight. Approaching the locked town gates at such an hour could be dangerous as he had no idea whether royal troops were still there or not, besides which whoever was on guard that night was bound to be nervous and trigger happy. He decided to wait until the morning before entering the town and breaking the bad news about Nat to Eliza. He settled down in the lea of a gorse bush and fell asleep, his dreams filled with leud thoughts of the pastor's daughter.

John had slept longer than he intended. The sun had been up for several hours even though it had still to fully penetrate the deep wooded valley in which he had camped overnight. He shivered and pulled his coat tighter to himself as he went over the next stage of his journey in his mind. Now that he was near to Honiton he would need a new cover story and he struggled to come up with something plausible until the obvious hit him. Keep the same story about being put ashore injured at Minehead but change his hometown from Honiton to Seaton. Simple. He hoped that should suffice to see him safe to the south coast, although he was well aware that the closer he came to Lyme, the birthplace of the rebellion, the greater the risk of being picked up by the authorities.

The cliff face at the end of his little valley proved too difficult to scale so he was obliged to tackle the wooded slope to his left and as he reached the top the sun hit him full in the face. Far to the east wispy grey tendrils hung from the bottom of dirty clouds that showed that someone somewhere was getting a drenching, but up on the high common north of Honiton the weather looked set fair for the rest of the day. He cursed himself for sleeping so late that any hope of making it home by nightfall had already gone as he made his way south.

As he descended from the high ground where buzzards soared on the warm air currents, the morning sun picked out the meandering course of the River Otter as it wound its way towards Honiton. Having lost so much of the day already he decided to press on straight through Honiton after crossing the river, even though he knew that he would have to look for food sooner rather than later. He took the Axminster road which ran alongside the Usborne Brook, totally unaware that the hill he passed on his left was where Nat had helped to face down the Devonshire militia some three weeks earlier. A spur from Shute Hill caused the brook to turn abruptly to the south and John followed it hoping that it would soon join with the River Axe which he knew emptied into the sea near Seaton.

Some four hours after leaving Honiton he reached Colyton, another small West Country village that had seen a large number of its menfolk join the rebellion. The place seemed deserted and if the vicar of Hemyock had spoken truly the majority of those men would not be returning. The widows and orphans that were left would suffer for years to come with so few men to plant the fields or collect in the harvest. The situation was exactly the same in Colyford just a mile further south and John despaired for the future with so many villages shorn of their men. In the centre of the village he took a track that led towards the river knowing that he needed to get across the Exe before it widened to run through treacherous tidal mud flats that could suck a man to his death.

As he walked down the narrow lane between ramshackle hovels an old man looked up from the eel trap that he was mending and asked in a thin voice, 'have 'e any news friend?'

'News? What sort of news?'

''Bout the rebel'yon of course.'

John decided to stick to his cover story. 'Not sure I knows much. I've been at sea for months before I were injured.'

The old man's shoulders slumped.

'I were hoping to hear news of my son Martin who left to join the duke.'

John was surprised that the man had confided so openly to a stranger but reckoned that with no news of his son the man felt that he had nothing left to lose. He felt for the man and decided to trust to his luck.

'Sorry,' he said softly, 'I lied about being at sea but you 'as to be careful what you say to who these days. I was with the king's army right through to Bridgwater. I left there for home three days ago.'

'The king's army?' the man said in alarm.

'King Monmouth's army,' John explained. 'He 'ad himself declared king at Taunton.'

'Did he now? How did that go down with the men?'

'Not great to be 'onest with 'e.'

'And did you come across my son? Is he well? Is he alive?'

'I came across several good men from Colyford, but I'm sorry I don't recall any by the name of Martin.'

'We've had no news at all. What can you tell me?'

'We saw off the militia at Axminster and won a great victory against James' reg'lers at a place called Philipsnorton near Frome. That's where I got my injury.'

'Niver heard of it.'

'Nor 'ad I 'til we got there. Anyway, since then we've been on the march all the way back to Bridgwater where James' men had us boxed in. I left my own son Nat there and I pray to God that he and your Martin are both safe. I heard a rumour that Monmouth had been defeated in a big battle just after I left but I've no way of knowing if it be true or not.'

'Well I thank 'e for what you have told I. You look all in friend, can I get you a bite to eat?'

John accepted the offer gratefully and bolted down the bread and salted fish that he was given.

'Do you need a bed for the night?'

'No, thankee kindly, but I've a notion to see my home as soon as I can. I have another son named Daniel and he will be worried about me so I must get on. Thank 'e again for the food, I shall mention your son in my prayers.'

John made his way towards the river, glancing back to see that the old man was bent over his traps again.

Once over the river the track climbed up the far side of the wide valley till it emerged onto a high plateau from where John could see the sea. He longed for home but there was no way he could make it to Lyme before the town gates were shut for the night. He pushed on a little further until he could look down on Lyme Bay even though the town itself remained hidden nestled deep in its valley, then he settled down behind a large boulder to wait for morning unaware that Thomas had come to exactly the same decision on the opposite side of Lyme.

Wednesday 8th July

Thomas opened his eyes and for a few seconds struggled to remember where he was. It was barely light and a gentle breeze brought with it the smell of the sea. He was stiff from lying on the hard ground and a heavy dew has left his hair and clothes dripping wet.

'What the hell did I do with my coat?' he asked himself, 'I could have done with it last night.'

Never mind he thought, he could get another. He could pinch one of Nat's he thought with a smile, he wouldn't need it anymore. He sat up slowly and looked around taking in the familiar surroundings of his native Dorset. He was home.

He made his way carefully through the undergrowth until he could look down into the valley where the thatched cottages of Lyme clustered tightly about the church and the old mill. He could see men on the rudimentary walls that surrounded the town but in the poor light he could not tell if they wore a uniform or not. He would have to wait for the sun to strengthen before he could make a proper assessment.

On the other side of the town John had also woken to the tangy smell of seaweed that he had missed so much over the past month. Like Thomas he too was worried that soldiers could still be in Lyme. The rebels had received word about Churchill occupying the town when they were camped at Pensford, but that was more than two weeks ago and much could have changed in that time. It seemed likely that Churchill would have marched his men to the confrontation at Bridgwater that the vicar of Hemyock had talked about, but he was sure to have left some men in Lyme to search for rebel sympathisers. John was well known in the town and would be instantly recognised, so if the royal troops were still there or if men like Mayor Alford had returned there would be nothing but trouble. He had many friends who had decided not to march to war for one reason or another despite their strong religious beliefs and some of those had served in the town watch. If it were they who were guarding the gates into the town today he might be able to sneak back in. There was only one way to find out.

He struggled to his feet and started along the coastal path that would bring him out on the west side of the Cobb. Maybe he could pass through the Cobb Gate when the local fishermen bustled through, each one hoping to get the best prices by being the first to offer their night catch in the marketplace.

Thomas was the first of the pair to enter the town, having decided that the men on the walls were from the town watch, not soldiers or militia. He could see no horsemen in the town and from what he could tell daily life was going on much as before with people entering or leaving through the gates with no obvious checks. He strolled out onto the Charmouth road and began the long descent to the town heading for the remains of Newell's fort that had once guarded the approach to the town. Maybe the loss of his coat was not such a bad thing he considered for he was well known for wearing it even on the hottest of days, so the lack of his distinctive coat might just be enough for him to pass unrecognised. He had always struggled to grow facial hair before he left with Monmouth's army but after a month away he now had a wispy beard that would also help to disguise his appearance.

He need not have worried as no one challenged him as he passed through the open gates whistling as he went. Cutting through the back lanes he crossed the River Lim above the old mill and made his way to the Goodman's house on Silver Street where he hoped to find Eliza. Creeping around to the back of the building he peered in through the scullery window; Eliza was there! He rapped gently on the glass and Eliza looked up in surprise. For a moment she could not put a name to the dirty bearded face staring in at her and was about to call out for help when suddenly her hand went to her mouth as recognition dawned. She yanked open the door and ran out into the yard throwing her arms round his neck.

'It's you Thomas, it's really you!'

'Yes it's me. I can't tell you how good it is to be back!'

Eliza grabbed his arm and dragged him into the scullery.

'In here quick, before anyone sees you. There are still many in the town who would be happy to turn you in.'

As soon as they were inside she bombarded Thomas with questions.

'How are you? Are you injured? What's happening with the duke's army? Have you seen my father?'

Mistress Goodman appeared in the doorway, drawn by Eliza's excited questioning.

'Praise the Lord, Master Edgecott. We are so pleased to see you safe and well. Can I get you something? Are you hungry? Thirsty?...'

'I would welcome a crust of bread, maybe some cheese if you have some and a drop of water if you'd be so kind.'

As Mistress Goodman hurried off to fetch food and drink Thomas took Eliza's hands in his and held her at arms' length.

'It's so good to see you again. Now to answer your questions. I'm fine and uninjured thank the Lord.' He thought it best to invoke the Lord's name in the Goodman's house. 'As to the course of the rebellion I have no idea. I was on a foraging expedition near Wells when we wuz surprised by a troop of enemy horse. I was knocked to the ground and left for dead. When I came round the army had moved on and the countryside was swarming with royal cavalry. There was no way I could get back to the army so I decided to head home. We'd heard that the enemy were in Lyme and I wanted to see if there was anything I could do to help, to protect you.'

'Did you see my father?'

'Indeed I did, shortly before I went out foraging. He was leading a unit of horsemen and appeared to be in good health.'

'And Nat?'

Thomas dropped her hands and turned to look out of the window.

'What is it, tell me!' Eliza cried.

He turned back to face her, tears in his eyes. 'I regret that I have the most grievous of news. Nat's dead. I saw him fall in battle at Philipsnorton as he stopped to help an injured man. He had been made into a sergeant and risked himself to help one of his men.'

The colour drained from Eliza's face and she dropped to the flagstone floor.

'Please, someone, help!' shouted Thomas.

Elizabeth Goodman ran back into the scullery dropping the plate and mug that she had being carrying onto a table.

'My goodness, what's happened?'

Thomas repeated his story about Nat as Elizabeth stooped to comfort Eliza who was sat on the cold flagstone floor, the heels of her hands pressed into her eyes as she sobbed quietly.

'Are you sure of this news?'

'As God is my witness. I was running to aid him when an officer pulled me back just in time as the cavalry charged past us. They ran right over poor Nat,' he said wiping away a tear. 'I went to him as soon as I was able but he was beyond my help. He had taken a musket ball to the head and would have been dead even before the horsemen reached him. My only consolation is that he would have felt no pain, thank the Lord.'

Elizabeth had helped Eliza up onto a chair. 'This is indeed sad news Thomas. Have his poor father and brother been told?'

'I haven't seen John since before the battle as we were in different regiments but I assume he's still with the army. If you could look after Mistress Sprake I will go directly to Coombe Street and see Daniel.'

He looked sadly at Eliza slumped in the chair, her shoulders heaving as she wept, before slipping out the back door. So far so good, he thought. He was certain in his own mind that Nat was dead, but what if he had somehow survived? If that were the case then he would have to think of some way to take care of him and he was so set on taking Eliza for himself that he did not rule out any solution.

He walked the short distance to the narrow slip of land that lay between the mill leat and the Lim River where the soothing sound of running water made this his favourite spot to sit when he had things to think over. Having gone over the story again in his mind and thought through all the questions he might possibly face he jumped to his feet and hurried to the Carvers' smithy.

At about the same time that Thomas was breaking the news to Eliza, John was making his way down to the beach that stood to the west of the Cobb where Monmouth had landed so full of hope only weeks before. He had slept for longer than he intended and realised that he had missed his chance to enter the town with the fishermen. Turning up the collar of his coat and pulling his hat down as far as he could he walked slowly past the inns that backed onto the Cobb. Everything seemed calm and people appeared to be going about their normal daily tasks. A small ship had just docked and men were busy unloading the cargo and placing it on hand carts. Keeping to the shadows he watched the unloading hoping that an opportunity would present itself and he soon spotted an old friend among the dockers.

Gabriel Smith's son Peter had joined the rebellion on the first day and had gone off to fight with his father's blessing so John had no doubts about his loyalty to the cause. Several carts were being propelled along the coast towards the Cobb Gate and as Gabriel came around the corner of the Dolphin Inn with his heavily laden cart John called quietly to him. It took Gabriel a moment to recognise his old friend in his 'disguise' but when he did a broad smile split his weathered face.

'John, when did you get back you old bugger?'

'Just this minute Gabriel. It's so good to see a friendly face. Have you had any news of your Peter or my Nat?'

'No, nothing. The king's men were here for a few days but they've all gone now. They were so cock sure that they had the duke's army in a trap they couldn't wait to join the hunt as they called it. Has there been a battle yet do you know?'

'There was, at a place called Philipsnorton in Somersetshire and we got the better of it,' he said proudly. 'Nat was badly hurt but has recovered well, praise the Lord and I picked up this,' he said opening his coat to show the rough sling that supported him shoulder. 'There were nothing I could do with my shoulder like this so I slipped away when the army was camped in Bridgwater. The royal army had us surrounded there and I later heard tale that a mighty battle had been fought outside the town but I know no details. I'm afraid that I ain't seen that boy of yours since we marched for Axminster.'

'God will watch him for me but first we needs to get you safe home,' said Gabriel. 'There are those in the town that support the usurper so we must be careful. Can you use your other arm?'

John nodded. 'Good then grab a hold of one of the handles on the cart, I'll take the other one. We're both getting on a bit so no one will think it odd that it takes two of us to pull the thing.'

They set off along the path that led above the beach to the town. They passed through the Cobb Gate without drawing any undue comment from the customs men that were checking the incoming goods and once clear of the gate John was able to duck into Coombe Street and make his way the short distance to the smithy. As he approached the workshop he was surprised that there was no sound of hammering coming from the dark interior. Young Daniel should have been hard at work by this hour, God help him if he had used his father's absence to idle.

He peeped inside and noted that the coals in the forge were glowing red hot so Daniel must be about somewhere. Good lad he thought to himself. He walked to the back of the smithy where a small wooden door led through into the family's accommodation. As he lifted the latch and entered the small kitchen he saw that Daniel and their maid Nancy were sat at the rough table and that both were crying. At the sound of the latch Daniel looked up.

'Father!' he cried, 'thank the Lord you're safe.'

'I am praise Him. But pray tell what's going on here? Why the tears?'

'Thomas Edgecott was here not five minutes past. He told us that...that....that Nat had perished in battle.'

He burst into tears again. John was not surprised to hear that Thomas was in town given the general consensus was that he had deserted when the army was at Frome.

'And where did Thomas say that was my son was killed?'

Daniel couldn't understand the importance of such a question but answered anyway, 'a place called Fips Norton or some such. Does it matter where it was, he's gone!'

'It matters a great deal. I saw Nat alive and well a week *after* the battle you speak of. I even had a meal with him in Wells. Tis true he was wounded, but not dead I assures you.'

Nancy took the handkerchief from her eyes. 'Truly?'

'Yes, truly.' A sudden nasty thought hit him. 'Did Master Edgecott say whether he had been to see Mistress Sprake?'

'He did father. He said that he thought it best that she knew as soon as possible. He came here directly from the Goodman's house.'

'I bet he did!' said John through clenched teeth and he stormed back into the smithy, slamming the door behind him. His first priority was to ensure that Eliza knew the truth he thought as he took the back way to Silver Street, walking along the mill leat. He would decide what to do about Thomas bloody Edgecott later.

As he walked his mind began to clear and his anger was replaced with reason. Maybe Thomas did see Nat go down at Philipsnorton and truly believed him dead, after all he himself believed that his son was dead until he saw him in Wells and Thomas had left the army long before then. His suspicions about Thomas receded only to be replaced by another thought. When he himself had left the army in Bridgwater it was clear that a major action could not be far off, presumably the battle that the vicar at Hemyock had crowed about. Had Monmouth's army really been annihilated he wondered and if so had Nat been spared for a second time? His dark thoughts were interrupted by a call.

'John! John Carver is that you sweltering there under that hat and coat on such a hot day?'

John turned to see Thomas rising to his feet. He had been sat in the shade of a blackthorn tree beside the leat.

'Thomas! When did you get back?'

'Only this morning. I'm sorry about Nat, he was like a brother to me.'

'Nat's fine, or at least he was when I last saw him in Bridgwater.'

'When was that? Before Philipsnorton...?'

'No afterwards, not three or four days back. We marched to Bridgwater together after leaving Frome.'

Thomas tried hard to hide his surprise but couldn't be sure if the old man had seen the look of disappointment that flashed briefly across his face.

'But I saw him fall! He was hit in the head!'

'So he was, but he's got a thick skull that boy of mine. He lost a lot of blood but was right as rain when I left him. And what about you? Nobody's seen you since Frome. Why are you back here when the army's in Bridgwater?'

Thomas repeated the lie that he had given to both Eliza and Daniel.

'Well that's as maybe, we'll talk later but first I must be away to see Mistress Sprake, she must be beside herself with grief.'

'I can't let that happen I'm afraid,' said Thomas rising to his feet. Before John could react Thomas has pushed him to the ground and drawn his bayonet.

'What in God's name are you doing Thomas?'

'Eliza's mine. She's far too good for that oaf of a son of yours.'

'I thought he was a friend of yours.'

'He is, or was, but Nat stands between Eliza and me.'

He raised his blade then seemed to think better of it. John let out a sigh of relief but his deliverance was short lived. Thomas had decided that a body with stab wounds would raise awkward questions so instead he reached for a large stone that had worked its way loose from the wall of the leat. He struck John hard on the head, once, twice and again until he was sure that the old man was dead. He dropped the stone into the water.

He couldn't leave John where he was, the track beside the leat may have been little used but the body would be found sooner rather than later. Instead he rolled the corpse to the edge of the leat and pushed it in. It was soon taken up by the strong current and drawn under the overhanging wall of the mill where it caught against the sturdy metal grill that stopped branches and other debris from entering the mill and fouling the wheel. The grill was some way under the overhang so the body was hidden from view and with any luck would not be found until the following spring when the grill was routinely cleared. Thomas hurried back to his lodgings entering by a back door and quietly made his way up to his small room in the eaves. If questioned about John's disappearance he would claim that he had gone straight home after seeing the Carver family and had not seen John since Frome. Now he had to think about disposing of Nat.

Goodenough and others taken near Ilfercomb.

34 ESCAPE BY SEA

Thursday 9th[th] July 1685

Wade returned just before dark, looking pleased with himself. 'Good news. My agent has found us a ship which sails on the morning tide and I've negotiated a sale for the horses which we shall leave here for the buyer to collect. I wasn't able to get a great price as the man could tell that I was desperate to sell but it was enough to pay for our passage and leave a small amount over which I shall share out. We will stay here tonight and make our way down to the quay tomorrow in small groups so as not to attract too much attention. I suggest you all get a good night's sleep. I shall take the first watch.'

Thursday dawned clear and bright. The good weather that marked the start of the rebellion had returned although a brisk wind meant that the men were still chilly as they ate their sparse breakfast. When they had finished Wade led the first batch of five men down the track towards the sleeping town having given instructions that further groups should leave the camp at ten-minute intervals. He left his time-piece, which was to be passed to the next group in turn as each one left. The men had drawn straws to determine their order and although Nat had insisted that as sergeant he should be the last to leave he was persuaded to take his drawn place in the third of the four groups. Going down to the harbour was potentially the most dangerous part of their flight and Wade had stressed the need for each group to remain as inconspicuous as possible.

When it was Nat's turn he shook hands with those still to leave and picked up his small bundle of possessions. He kept his coat and felt hat, leaving behind anything that could arouse suspicion including the carbine and pistols that had been attached to the saddle of his borrowed horse but decided that he could conceal his bayonet well enough to risk taking it with him. As his small group reached the heights above the town the salty tang of the sea hit him and he suddenly felt very homesick. He prayed that the ship that Wade had found would deliver him quickly back to his beloved Lyme and that John, Daniel, Nancy, Thomas and above all Eliza would be there to greet him.

The small harbour was a hive of activity and people were too busy to take much notice of the small groups of men that appeared on the quayside at regular intervals. To give them a plausible reason for being on the dock a number of small barrels and packages had been left alongside the boat and each man picked one up in turn as he made his way up the gangplank.

The final group of five men was preparing to leave the campsite when one of the horses began to fidget and neigh, the noise soon being taken up by the others. Before the rebels could react a small patrol of militia horsemen appeared around a bend in the track. The two sides starred at each other unsure what to do, the rebels were heavily outnumbered whilst the militiamen could see lots of saddled horses but only five men.

'Rebels! Run them down boys, there'll be a nice bounty on their 'eads!' called one of the riders drawing his sword.

'Wait!' cried their leader. 'Five men, but what ... thirty horses? Where's the rest of 'em?'

'Gone into Ilfracombe to look for a boat I'll be bound.'

'Or foraging...or waiting in ambush...' said the leader. He turned in his saddle and addressed his two section leaders.

'Take ten men each and circle round either side to get behind them, the rest of us will wait here until you're in position.'

Seeing that they would soon be surrounded the five remaining rebels leapt onto their horses and made for the open moors before the ring of militiamen was complete.

'After them!' cried the militia leader as he dug his spurs into his horse's flank.

Down in the harbour Wade was becoming anxious. The boat would have to sail soon or miss the tide but he was still five men short.

'Can't wait no longer your 'onor. Time and tide waits for no man, even your men,' said the skipper ruefully. 'I'm afraid if they ain't here now, they ain't coming.'

Wade nodded reluctantly and gave permission for the boat to make way, the sailors casting off the mooring ropes and the small craft slipping quietly out of the harbour. Nat kept his eyes on the quayside hoping that the missing men would appear but eventually he was forced to admit that they were lost. As soon as they were clear of the harbour the strong south westerly wind hit them forcing the captain to place the vessel on a starboard tack to enable them to clear Capstone Point.

'With the wind blowing as it is from the southwest,' he shouted to Wade, 'we'll have to tack back and forth to beat our way down the channel all the way to Land's End. I hope you're not hoping for a fast passage.'

'I'll settle for safety over speed.'

The ship stayed on the starboard tack for the next hour, heading for the southern coast of Wales before a string of commands had the sailors hauling on the ropes to bring the ship onto the opposite tack. As the vessel came around, bringing the distant island of Lundy into view there was a cry from the masthead.

'Deck there! Sail ahead! Frigate by the looks of it.... and another beyond it, standing further out to sea.'

'Everyone below decks now!' Cried Wade, 'and pray God they think we are nothing but a coastal trader going about our legal business.'

For the next thirty minutes it seemed that they would indeed be ignored as the frigates made no move to intercept them but just when it appeared that the danger was past a flurry of signal flags flew up the lines of the further ship and the three masts of the nearer frigate slowly came into line as it turned directly towards them. Wade had removed his flamboyant hat and coat and stood beside the captain, hoping to pass for an ordinary seaman.

'What do we do now?' he asked nervously.

'For now, we carry on exactly as we are. With any luck they will simply sail close enough to see what we are about but make sure your men stay out of sight! Depending on how long they've been at sea they might just want to hail us for any news.'

As Wade watched the frigate, trying to judge how quickly it was closing on them a puff of dirty smoke shot through with a bright orange flame appeared at the frigate's bow followed almost immediately by a dull boom. The ball fired by the bow-chaser threw up a huge column of seawater just ahead of them.

'Well that settles it! They want us to heave-to. That was just a warning, the next one won't miss!' cried the skipper. 'We'll never outrun them with the spread of canvas they can deploy and if you're found aboard we'll all swing. All I can do is try to beach us on the sands at Woolacombe and then it'll be every man for himself.'

Shouting orders as he went the skipper ran to the wheel as seamen scurried up the ratlines to carry out his instructions. With the sails reset and the rudder responding to the weight of both the helmsman and the skipper on the wheel the ship came about and headed for the shore. Pushed by the strong wind the vessel ran onto the hard sands and tilted alarmingly as it stuck fast. Men tumbled over the side, rebels and seamen alike, dropping into the shallow waters and running for the low hills that backed the beach desperately searching for somewhere to hide.

'It's each man for himself now lads!' called Wade. 'May God guide you all home safely.'

The men scattered into the surrounding countryside with Nat and Henry heading for the same thicket of field elder. It would be some time before the royal ships could dock and report to the authorities but the fact that the last group of their party had failed to make it to the ship suggested that the alarm may have already been raised and that the hunt was on. Their suspicions were soon confirmed when a dozen horsemen appeared on the brow of the steep road that led up from the village that nestled at the north end of the long sandy beach.

'Best we lay low here until nightfall,' said Nat. 'Try to get some sleep as it looks like we'll be travelling by night from now on. I'll take first watch.'

The day passed slowly under clear skies with Nat and Henry alternating watch for two hours at a time. Every so often groups of horsemen wearing the green coats of the Devonshire militia would trot past but none dismounted to search the heavy undergrowth where they were hiding until just before dusk when four riders turned off the track and made towards the thicket. Nat woke Henry by gently touching him behind the ear. It was an old soldiers' way for waking someone instantly but quietly, a trick he had learnt from Samuel White. The militia's voices drifted across to them.

'Right lads, we'll just check 'round 'ere then get off for the night. I doubt any of they rebels be still hanging about but I saw the squire watching us a while back and he'll be none too pleased if we don't at least go through the motions of searching.'

The group dismounted and drew their swords but left their pistols in the saddle holsters. Nat and Henry had only their knives to defend themselves but hoped that the element of surprise would even the odds. They tried to wriggle deeper into the tangle of briar and elder saplings but just as it appeared that they would be discovered another man wearing militia uniform rode up.

'Come quick! Three rebels have been spotted on the Georgeham road!'

The men sprinted back to their horses anxious to chase down the fugitives and claim the bounty that the king had placed on rebel heads. Nat and Henry waited a full five minutes before creeping from their hiding place.

'Time we was moving,' said Nat.

The moon had been full only three days earlier so there would be plenty of light to show them the way as they headed inland leaving the sound of the surf behind them. Taking care not to expose themselves when they reached the crest of the hill they dropped down the other side. They knew that they needed to head to the south and east. This near to the coast the trees had been permanently bent into grotesque shapes by the prevailing westerly wind that blew off the sea and they acted like signposts pointing to the east but once Nat and Henry left the high exposed ground the trees grew tall and straight.

'When I wuz young,' said Henry, 'my old dad used to tell I that if I ever got lost to look for the moss on tree trunks as it grows thickest on the northern side. Didn't help much if you didn't know which direction home wuz, but I remembered it all the same. Might come in 'andy.'

A steep wooded valley appeared to head in the right direction as well as affording them a good deal of cover and for the next four hours they made their way slowly across country, following small streams and dried up river beds and keeping off the high ground as much as possible. There were a surprising number of tiny hamlets hidden in the folds of land and each one had to be carefully skirted for fear that a barking dog or honking goose might betray their presence.

As the dark sky to the east took on the pearly grey hue that heralded the approach of dawn thoughts turned to finding somewhere to hide up for the day, but before that they had to find food. They had been able to drink from the streams that they had stumbled across in the dark but they hadn't eaten for nearly a day. They stumbled on. Through the trees they could see where the River Taw ran into Barnstaple, the rising sun glossing the water with a shimmer of gold. Going into the busy river-port could be dangerous but with nowhere else holding out the promise of finding a meal they decided to rest in the cover of an old hill fort for a few hours before risking entering the town.

The sound of a horse neighing woke Nat. Henry was supposed to be on watch but the exertions of the past few days had taken their toll and the Colyton dyer had dropped off. Nat crawled to the edge of the ancient earthen fortification and carefully peered over the crest. On the track at the foot of the slopes on which the old fort had been built a strong force of horsemen were making their way slowly towards Barnstaple on tired horses. No doubt they had been out all night searching for rebels and were now anxious to get home. Nat slid back below the lip of the embankment and dragged himself towards Henry who lay some yards away snoring quietly. As Nat reached him Henry awoke with a start, jumping to his feet in alarm and shouting out in sleep fuddled confusion before remembering the predicament that they were in and dropping quickly to his knees. Not quickly enough.

One of the riders had heard him and glanced up the slope in time to see a head pop above the lip of the old fort and drop back down again. Calling to the other riders he turned his weary horse towards the slope and urged the poor animal up the steep incline. Nat grabbed Henry's arm and the pair began to run. Tumbling out the far side of the old fort Nat and Henry ran for their lives towards a thick wood that stood high on the slopes of a narrow river valley some two hundred yards away. It would take the enemy horsemen a little time to climb the steep sides of the fort and then cross the interior space and Nat hoped that they might make the cover of the woods before the riders started down the other side. They had almost reached the shelter of the trees when the first horseman appeared on the crest behind them. With a whoop he spurred his mount after them.

The descent was treacherous and the militiamen were forced to curb their speed allowing the two rebels to dive below the outer branches of the woods. They ran on for a few minutes before stopping in a small clearing to get their breath. Henry was full of contrition about falling asleep on watch and tried to apologise to Nat.

'Don't beat yourself up about it 'enry,' Nat panted. 'I've fallen asleep on guard duty twice since leaving Bridgwater but was lucky that there were no enemy about to take advantage of it. The horsemen will be upon us shortly although these woods are dense enough to slow them. I think it best that we separate here, giving them two trails to choose between might just buy us a little time. God's speed.'

Henry reached for the proffered hand.

'May the Lord see you safely home too Nat,' he said before turning and trotting off deeper into the trees.

The sound of breaking branches and cursing told Nat that their pursuers had entered the woods and he heard the leader of the group shout for the men to dismount and spread out. Henry had taken the obvious path through the trees, a narrow track no doubt made by some wild animal and Nat decided to follow him until a better opportunity presented itself. The woods proved to be quite narrow, no more than a thin strip of trees following the lip of the valley and there was nowhere to turn aside from the track that he was following. After two or three minutes and with the sound of pursuit growing louder Nat noticed that just ahead the land dropped away sharply to his right where a part of the ridge had collapsed towards the river far below. He jumped from the track and slid down the precipitous slope before coming to a rest in a thick patch of brambles. Struggling to catch his breath he watched as the soldiers appeared on the path above him.

'There he is!' cried one of the men.

Nat was about to throw himself further down the slope when he realised that the men had run past the spot where he had left the track. They must have spotted Henry but there was nothing he could do to help his friend. Even if he was able to climb back up to the track, a task that he thought looked all but impossible, he would be facing a dozen heavily armed militia with just his knife. Henry would have to look out for himself. He lowered himself further into the thicket, finding a thick root that he was able to brace his foot against to prevent him tumbling to the valley below.

Cramp was beginning to set in and Nat knew that he would have to move soon when he heard voices above him. The soldiers were returning.

'Well that's one traitor that won't bother the justices,' laughed one of the men. 'We still get the bounty, dead or alive!'

'Waste of time dragging his sorry arse all the way back into town when we can bring the clerk to the justice out here this afternoon. Shame the other bugger got away though.'

The men passed Nat's hiding place without a glance and once he was sure that they had gone he struggled

his way back to the path and went in search of his friend.
He found him hanging from a tree.

35 IN THE COCKMOIL

Friday 10th^th July 1685

Thomas had kept to his bed the day after killing John. He didn't want to chance meeting anyone especially Daniel Carver or that simple maid of theirs. He worried that old John's body may have been found but if it had he would surely have heard the commotion from his small room. No, his dark secret would stay hidden until the spring, so all he had to do was keep to his story and he would be safe.

By the next morning he decided that he must go out if only to get some food until he remembered that he had spent all the money he had taken from the trooper that he had killed at Pensford in that hostelry in Yeovil and the few coins that he found in John's pockets and those stolen from Bridger wouldn't last long. He needed to earn some money and with so many men having left to fight with Monmouth there was certain to be plenty of work available. Maybe he would give up making shoes and try for something a little better, something that might impress Eliza although he still wasn't sure if he just craved her body or if he wanted something more permanent. If it was to be the latter he would need to find a position that could support them both and maybe children one day. Too much like hard work he thought, start with the sex, see if she's any good then take it from there.

He slid out of bed and dipped his head in the cold water that filled the basin on the windowsill. He was ruffling his hair dry when there was a commotion in the street below. He opened his window to see the town crier dressed in his full regalia, ringing his handbell above his head as he marched down the street accompanied by the mayor. Thomas thought that it was bold of Mayor Alford to show his face in Lyme where he was so hated but as the town crier began to speak it was clear why Alford felt able to show himself so openly.

'Oyez, oyez!' Now here this! James, by the Grace of God, King of England and Scotland is pleased to inform his loyal subjects that the late rebellion against his legal and God given rule has been defeated. The former Duke of Monmouth's traitorous army has been scattered and destroyed. The cowardly and villainous Monmouth fled the battle outside Bridgwater leaving his men to their grisly fate but with God's help he will soon be brought under his majesty's justice. Any man found to have sided with the king's nephew will be hunted down and tried for treason, the period of grace given by his majesty having now expired. God save the king!'

As the crier stepped aside, the mayor called forward four constables who had been stood quietly to one side.

'You have your orders. Visit every house. I want a full list of those men who joined the rebellion or those that can show no lawful reason for having been away from their homes during the uprising.'

The constables nodded and moved off to begin their work. Thomas wasn't worried for although many people in the town knew that he had taken part in the shambolic attack on Bridport before marching to Axminster with the rebel army he had his pardon signed by the magistrate in Yeovil. He spent the morning touring the various businesses in the town weighing up his options for future employment, but when he returned to his lodgings he found two constables waiting for him.

'Thomas Edgecott?' asked the taller of the two. Thomas nodded. 'Have you been outside the town in the last month?'

'Yes, I have.'

'Can I ask for what purpose.'

'That's my own business.'

The constable looked to his colleague who was holding a large ledger. 'Absent and presumed,' he dictated. The second man began to write in the ledger.

'Absent and presumed?' asked Thomas, 'what's that mean?'

'It means my lad that you have refused to give a legitimate reason for being absent from your dwelling and the law therefore presumes you to have been involved in the dastardly rebellion.' He grabbed for his arm but Thomas shook himself free.

'Wait a moment,' he said quietly, not wanting the conversation to be overheard. 'I have a pardon from a magistrate in Yeovil.'

He searched in his waistcoat pockets for the piece of paper that was guaranteed to keep him out of prison.

'Where is the damned thing? It must be in my coat in my room, wait there.'

'Not so fast you villain, we'll come in with you if you don't mind.'

They followed Thomas to his attic room but there was no sign of his coat. With a chilling certainty Thomas remembered placing it on the bench seat of Jacob Bridger's cart to act as a cushion.

'So no pardon, as I suspected,' said the constable.

'No, honestly I did have one but I must've lost it somewhere.'

'Of course you did, and I'm the Queen of Spain's brother,' laughed the constable. 'Take him to the lockup. He'll keep in there until the next assizes.'

'Send to Yeovil, they'll have a record of my pardon!'

'What makes you think we have either the time or the interest to bother?' laughed the constable.

Thomas was marched down the street to the square where he was thrown into the cockmoil with several other men. The lockup which formed the basement of the town hall was intended for holding drunks until they sobered up enough to be allowed home or to house the odd smuggler pending his collection by officers from the county gaol in Dorchester. It was never intended to hold the large number of men who now sat on the dirty straw that covered the cold flagstones. No effort was made to supply either food or water for those incarcerated in the windowless room and the bucket that had been provided for their waste was full to the brim and the foul smell that emanated from it made Thomas gag. He tried to sleep but the cold and damp made it difficult and when he did eventually drop off his dreams were full of dark images of Nat, John and the gallows.

Mayor Alford was sat at dinner when the constables called on him to report their findings and to present him with their ledger.

'Any problems?'

'Not really. Only one man made a fuss, Thomas Edgecott of Coombe Street, claimed to have a royal pardon from a magistrate in Yeovil but couldn't produce it.'

Alford looked up with concern, a piece of meat on the end of his fork hovering before his open mouth.

'If he did have a pardon, legally given by a magistrate in the king's name then we have to be very careful. It could all be a ruse but we had best be sure. Go and ask this Master Edgecott for details of this magistrate of his in Yeovil and then send a man to speak to his clerk to confirm whether or not a pardon was given. In the meantime, make sure you keep him alive. He is certainly a traitorous rebel, but if the king has seen fit to pardon him I don't want to be the man that's responsible for killing him.'

Thomas was happy to give the name and address of the magistrate and settled back against the damp wall in the corner of the lockup. He began to wonder what to do about Nat if old John's story about him surviving the gunshot at Philipsnorton was true and he turned up safe and well in Lyme.

Slowly his worried frown turned into a wicked smile as the best possible answer came to him, one which would carry no personal risk and make him some money into the bargain. All he had to do was turn Nat in to the authorities. Once his own pardon was confirmed the mayor would surely agree to protect his anonymity in exchange for information about Nat and John, and Pastor Sprake for that matter. Betraying that God bothering old sod would further clear his path to Eliza. Turn them all in and he would no doubt pick up some form of reward or bounty. He drifted off to sleep in the happy certainty of a bit of money in his pocket, Nat and Sprake out of the way and Eliza all to himself.

36 EGGS FOR BREAKFAST

Saturday 11thth – Sunday 12th July 1685

Jacob Bridger came to slowly, his head hurt and last night's ale had left a nasty stale taste in his mouth.

'Billy, fetch me a cup of water, there's a good boy, then see to the oxen, we need to be on our way.'

When there was no response he called again.

'Billy, where are you boy, come on look lively, there's work to be done.'

It was some minutes before Jacob was able to prop himself up on one elbow and peer over the side of the wagon, to see Billy laid on his side in the dirty straw of the stable.

'Ah there you are, you lazy bugger, get up and give me a hand down, I needs a piss.'

When Billy didn't move, Jacob cursed and clambered unsteadily down from the driving bench.

'Come on now, up you get you little devil,' he growled, giving his son a gentle prod with his foot.

The first signs of concern flickered across his weather-beaten face as Billy failed to stir and made no sound. Jacob dropped to his knees and gave the boy a hard shake.

'Billy? Billy! Wake up!' He reached around behind his son's back to roll him over and his hand came away sticky.

'Not been lying in some horse shit have you boy?' he said as he brought his hand up to the poor light cast by a lantern that hung from the stable wall. He stared in puzzlement at the congealed red mess that covered his fingers. Blood!

'Billy, what's happened to you lad?' he cried as he hauled the boy into a sitting position. Billy's head rolled to one side and the awful truth hit Jacob like a hammer blow.

'Billy! Help me someone, call a physician, my boy's been hurt!'

His cries brought a stable lad from his bed in the hayloft and between them they carried the inert body into the inn. It was clear that Billy was dead, his eyes were wide open and his skin was icy cold to the touch.

'Murder, murder!' shouted Jacob. 'Fetch the constables!'

The commotion had woken half the occupants of the inn and it wasn't long before two members of the town watch arrived to see what all the fuss was about. Jacob told them what he could remember of the night before and of his mysterious passenger who seemed to have disappeared along with his purse. Being in a state of shock and nursing a heavy hangover his mind was anything but clear and the description that he gave of Thomas was vague at best. All he could remember was that he was called Peter Smith and came from Honiton in Devonshire.

As Thomas' cowardly crime was being discovered in Axminster, Nat was some fifty miles away in the woods above the River Yeo, to the north-east of Barnstaple. He had cut Henry's body down and carried it carefully to a secluded spot where he had used his knife to scrape a shallow grave in the soft earth between the exposed roots of an old elm tree. He would have liked to have made it deep enough to stop the wild animals finding it but he had neither the time nor the tools required. In the end he collected a number of large stones and piled them on the top of the impromptu grave to protect the body as best he could. He fashioned a simple cross out of twigs and mumbled a short prayer.

He knew that he must keep moving as there was a chance that Henry's killers would be back with the constable to verify their claim to the bounty that was on every rebel's head. He hoped that he had moved the body far enough from the scene of the execution to elude detection and deny the murderers of their ill-gotten gain. Satisfied that he could do no more for his friend Nat jogged away.

The countryside was full of gently rolling hills and shallow valleys and he reckoned that once he crossed the river that lay at the foot of the ridge he would be able to make his way safely eastwards towards the rising sun. He eventually found a safe way down from the woods and headed towards a small hamlet where a large mill stood astride the fast-running river. He was anxious to avoid meeting anyone but he needed to find food.

As he approached the mill he heard the distinctive sound of horses' hooves on the track behind him. He glanced round but the riders were hidden by a bend in the track. He had only seconds to look for cover but nothing looked even remotely suitable apart from the mill building itself. The wooden shutters that directed the water away from the river and into the mill leat were closed as the miller had not started work for the day and Nat lowered himself into the chill waters of the leat hoping to hide behind the tall shutters but it was soon apparent that the water in the leat was too shallow to cover him and that he would need to find a better place of concealment. Desperately he waded knee deep towards the water wheel expecting to hear the sound of discovery and pursuit any second. He dived for the cover of the wheel just as the first horseman appeared around the bend. He was safe for now, hidden by the paddles of the huge wheel but he could already feel the cold seeping into his aching bones and God alone knew what would happen if the miller decided that now was the time to start the wheel turning.

He stayed concealed until the horsemen had ridden on then pulled himself onto the bank of the leat hoping that the strengthening sun would soon dry him out. With the militia about he dared not stay in the hamlet to look for food so he took a rough track that led between two small hills and soon picked up a shallow stream that seemed to be headed in the right general direction. The whole area was criss-crossed by small lanes connecting isolated farmsteads and tiny villages and twice more during that morning he was forced to leave the track to hide as patrols raced along the narrow lanes. On the first occasion he was able to lie low in a field of standing corn but the second time, just as the sun was at its highest he was walking along an empty stretch of road when he heard the sound of horses. He cursed himself for his carelessness. There was nowhere to hide, the only feature in the otherwise bleak landscape was an old tree stump, all that remained of a large solitary elm that had at some point in the past been struck by lightning. It would have to do.

He ran to the tree as fast as his tired legs would carry him and was surprised to find that it was far bigger than it had appeared from the road, standing some eight feet high. The blackened centre of the dead tree was hollow and he was able to squeeze inside through a jagged slit that reached down to the springy turf. The tree had stood alone and forlorn in the field for decades and was so much a part of the landscape that the horsemen passed by without a second glance. Nat decided to try to get some rest but the open centre of the tree was no more than two feet across, not quite enough for him to be able to sit comfortably on the ground so he carefully lowered himself down until he was wedged in with his knees tight to his chest, his back against one side of the hollowed trunk and his toes hard pressed against the opposite side. Despite the awkward position he was asleep within minutes, hidden in plain view.

He was woken early the following morning by the cock-a-doodle-do of a cockerel. He had not seen a farm yesterday but it had to be nearby, hidden by a fold in the land. A cockerel implied eggs and Nat was starving but as he made to stand up he found that he couldn't move. His body had completely seized up in his cramped hiding space and it was some minutes before he was able to rise. He rubbed his numbed limbs until the feeling started to return, the sharp pains in his arms and legs gradually dulling to pins and needles as the blood returned to his extremities.

Dawn lit the sky above the distant hills to the east but the sun had yet to rise above the false horizon as he crept out of the tree trunk and looked cautiously around for any signs of danger before moving off towards the sound of the cockerel. The long dew-wet grass was littered with tiny mushrooms and Nat scooped up a handful and dropped them into his pocket, they would make a nice accompaniment to the eggs that he hoped to find.

After fifty yards or so the land dropped away sharply into a sheltered valley where a small farm stood on the side of a narrow stream. Smoke rose lazily from the solitary chimney but he could see no one in the yard as he crept down the valley side and leapt across the stream, heading for the hen house. Fortunately there were no guard dogs or geese to alert the farm's occupants to his presence and he was able to get into the chicken run without being discovered. He was rewarded with eight newly laid eggs. With no way of cooking them he broke two open and tipped the contents into his mouth, putting the other six into his coat pocket for later. He'd never eaten raw eggs before and found the experience mildly unpleasant but such was his hunger that he forced himself to swallow the slimy concoction.

A burst of laughter from the direction of the farm buildings made him start and he turned to see a young girl and what he assumed was her mother strolling across the yard with an empty basket, no doubt set on collecting the eggs that he had just stolen. He turned and ran hoping that the two women were so distracted by their conversation that they would not notice him. He had gone only a few yards when the older woman shouted.

'Stop, thief!' He ran on as the two women turned back towards the farmhouse to raise the alarm. He raced beside the stream with the intention of skirting the low hills to his left once the shallow valley ran out but before he reached the safety of the next valley a shot rang out. The range was long and the fowling piece that the farmer had fired was filled with old nails and scraps of metal which lacked the accuracy of a moulded bullet. Nat ran on while the farmer shouted and cursed impotently being too old to move at more than a slow waddle.

Nat had no way of knowing where the nearest town was but it would probably be some time before the theft could be reported to the constables and any search launched. Ordinarily such a minor theft would not raise much excitement but these weren't ordinary times and with the militia scouring the countryside for hungry and desperate rebels the farmer's news was bound to elicit a response from the authorities.

By mid-morning Nat was certain that he had thrown off anyone who might be looking for him so he stopped in a small copse to finish his breakfast. One of the eggs had broken to leave a sticky mess in his pocket but the other five were fine and he cracked open the first one, only to find that now he had taken the edge off his hunger he could not stomach the slimy raw interior. He flung the egg away and determined to either find a way of cooking the rest or bartering them for something more palatable. He left the woods and struck out along the narrow valley until it merged with a much wider one through which ran a fast-flowing stream. He did not know it but this was the River Bray, the headwaters of which he had crossed with Wade and his men on the way to Ilfracombe some four days earlier. He could see smoke rising from a small fire on the near bank where an old man was bent over a cooking pot suspended from a forked stick. He watched the man for five minutes from the cover of a bramble bush until he was certain that he was alone, then stood up and walked slowly towards the fire.

A snapped twig made the old man look up suddenly and he jumped to his feet and swept up a stout club that had been lying unseen in the long grass. Nat stopped and held out his arms to show that he was unarmed and posed no threat.

'Can I share your fire friend?' he called.

The man looked about his father's age and had an untidy shock of white hair that hung well below the collar of his tatty brown coat. Clearly neither his hair nor his wispy beard had been trimmed for some time. His deeply wrinkled face suggested a man who lived rough.

'Who are you? Come no closer!' he shouted holding the heavy club unsteadily.

'The name's Nat Carver. I mean you no harm. I just want to warm myself in exchange for what little food I have.'

'You say you have food but I can see no bag. What have you got?'

'I've four newly laid eggs that I would be happy to share with you master.....?'

'Zachary Ford,' the man replied warily.

Nat reached into his pocket and pulled out the remaining eggs. Zachary began to lick his scabbed lips.

'Well that seems a fair exchange, come over here then young'un but don't you try nothing, I might look old but I can handle m'self if needs be.'

Nat approached the fire making sure to give the man no cause for alarm. He was certain he could overpower him if things turned nasty but a whack from the heavy club could break bones and Nat knew that was a risk that he dare not take. The pot contained a thin mixture of leaves and roots and Nat offered to add some of the mushrooms that he had picked early that morning.

'Not those!' the old man cried striking the fungi from Nat's hands, 'unless you wants to be shitting yourself for the rest of the week.'

They shared the pottage, the old man graciously letting Nat use his battered pewter mug, while he himself sipped from a long-handled ladle.

'That was most welcome,' said Nat, wiping with mouth on the back of his hand. 'And now for my part of the bargain.'

Zachary balanced an old metal plate on the embers of the fire and once it had warmed through Nat carefully broke two of the eggs onto it. They ate one each but they tasted so good that Nat had no hesitation in frying the other two as well. Afterwards the two men sat in silent amiable companionship, each lost in his own thoughts until the sound of two swans slapping the water with their wings as they struggled into the air brought them back to the present.

'Wonder what spooked them?' said Nat jumping to his feet and scanning up and down the river.

'Horsemen!' said Zachary 'I can just make them out above the reeds on the far bank.'

Nat grabbed his coat and ran for the cover of the thick vegetation that lined the river, hoping that the watercourse was too wide and deep for the riders to cross. He dropped to the soggy ground and lay still. When the horseman were directly opposite Zachary's fire the leading horseman reigned in his mount and shouted across the water.

'Morning Zach. I hope you ain't been out a poaching again.'

'Not me. I swears it on me father's life.'

The rider laughed. 'As if you know who your father is! The law'll catch up with you one day Master Ford. Just make sure the squire's men don't catch 'e after his trout.'

'Oh I'll make sure they don't catch I,' he replied.

'Now then Zach, have you seen any strangers here abouts today?'

'Strangers? What would anyone want around here Josh?'

'The magistrate's been told to be on the lookout for rebels from the Duke of Monmouth's army though I can't see any of 'em being this far west. Still he's paying us well to look for 'em so I don't mind.'

'Well, I've seen no one for days, not since I left Chittlehampton least ways, but I'll be sure to let you know if I do see anyone.'

'We'll be on our way then and remember, leave they trout alone!'

'I can't help it if the Good Lord puts it into their simple minds to jump clear from the river of their own accord and land in my bag!'

The men in Josh's little troop laughed then turned their mounts away to continue their patrol down the far bank. Once they were out of sight Nat emerged from his hiding place and returned to the fire.

'Thanks for that Zachary.'

'Don't bother me none. I was hoping that the duke would kick that popish bastard James all the way back to Scotland where he belongs! If you do be one of they rebels then good luck to you.'

Nat decided to confide in the old man. 'I'm looking at getting back to Lyme Regis on the south coast, have you any idea of the way I should take?'

'Ah a Dorsetshire boy, I thought your accent were a bit strange. I'd head for South Molton if I were you, it be that-a-way,' he said pointing. 'When you gets there someone'll be able to put you in the direction of Tiverton.'

Nat thanked him again and took off in the direction that Zachary had indicated. Wary of meeting further patrols he made very slow progress and it was late into the afternoon before he was able to look down on a sizeable village clustered around a substantial church with a tall tower. He realised with a start that he had not eaten since his meeting with Zachary and he was tempted to sneak into what he assumed was South Molton to look for food but was realistic enough to know that blundering about in a strange place in the half-light was foolhardy. The best he could do was find somewhere soft and secluded, curl into a ball and wait for morning.

Back in Lyme the efforts of the constables in compiling their *Presentments of Rebels* had been given extra impetus by the arrival of a company of the feared Kirke's Lambs, tough soldiers who had arrived on the battlefield of Sedgemoor after years of brutal service in Tangiers. They believed that the local constables had been lackadaisical in the way they had been undertaking their task, using the exercise as a way of settling old scores with some and accepting bribes to leave others off the lists.

The soldiers had no scruples, taking whatever they wanted, be it food, property or women and Eliza was once again hidden away in the attic of the Goodman's house. Thomas was locked up in the cockmoil and Kirke's men were happy to leave the constables to determine if he had been part of the rebellion or not while they got on with terrorising the locals. Thomas for his part was glad that he was out of the reach of the

Queen Dowager's Regiment of Foot as they were properly called and was happy to sit and await his release. He well remembered the magistrate's clerk in Yeovil recording his name in his big black ledger so the constables would have no option but to let him go. With any luck they might even bring back a duplicate pardon for him. He prayed that the soldiers would have left Lyme by the time the constables returned as such was the Lambs' reputation that even a royal pardon might not stop them hanging him from the nearest tree. The longer he remained in the cockmoil the safer he would be, besides which as long as no one knew exactly when he had been put into the prison he would have the perfect alibi for the disappearance of John Carver. A commotion outside his cell door was followed by the grating sound of the key in the lock.

'Damn them for their efficiency,' he muttered as two constables entered the cell.

'Thomas Edgecott?' Thomas nodded and rose to his feet. 'Come with us!'

'I can find my own way free out of here thank you!' Thomas sneered.

'Free?' laughed the constable. 'You're not going free; you're coming with us to Dorchester gaol on a charge of common murder!'

37 'KINGS HAVE LONG ARMS'

Monday 13th and Tuesday 14th July 1685

The twenty-five-mile journey to Dorchester would take a whole day, so it was decided to leave Thomas in the cockmoil for another night and make an early start in the morning. The constables accepted an invitation to dine with Mayor Alford who was only too pleased to have the responsibility for Thomas taken out of his hands.

Thomas was woken early still wondering how John's body could have been discovered so quickly and what evidence they could have against him. He was given a beaker of cold water before his hands were bound and he was led out into the street where the other end of the rope was attached to the saddle of one of the constable's horse. The two officers mounted and started up the steep hill out of Lyme, past the church and onto the road that led through Bridport towards Dorchester with Thomas stumbling along behind them.

'Who am I s'posed to 'ave murdered then and who is it that falsely accuses me so?'

'Don't play the innocent with us, you knows who. Young Billy Bridger as you well know.'

Thomas's mind raced. He was being charged with killing the carter's boy, not John. How had they found out that he was responsible? He had been careful not to give his real name to the old man, claiming he was called Peter Smith, a soap boiler from Honiton.

'And where and when is this murder s'posed to 'ave 'appened?'

'You know where you devil, the Spotted Horse in Axminster.'

'Niver heard of the place, niver bin to the town!'

'Well the evidence says otherwise an' it'll be enough to see you dancing from a rope once it's brought before the judge at the next assizes.'

'What evidence? Bring me a bible and I'll swear on its holy pages that I've not murdered no one. Who accuses me?'

'Jacob Bridger, the boy's father,' the constable called back over his shoulder. 'You left your coat on his wagon and guess what he found when he looked in the pockets.'

'Dunno, tell me!'

'He found a pardon given in Yeovil, with your name and place of abode on it.'

'It may have been my coat but that don't mean that I killed no one.'

'No it don't, but it does prove that you were a traitorous rebel and I don't think the judge'll have much difficulty in finding you guilty of murder, the law'll get you one way or the other. You can't escape the long arm of the King's Law and you'll answer for the soul of that poor child on the end of a rope, if you're lucky.'

'If I'm lucky?'

'If you're lucky you'll be hanged for murder, but if the judge decides that because of your crime he can ignore the pardon it'll be a charge of treason which means being hung, drawn and quartered!' he laughed.

On the hills above South Molton Nat woke and eased his cramped muscles as he crawled from his crude bed. He had tried to make himself comfortable by lining a slight depression in the ground with ferns but whichever way he had turned in the night something always seemed to be sticking into him. He tried to work out how long he had been on the run and realised with a start that today was the thirteenth of July, his birthday! People always told him that the thirteenth was unlucky because there had been thirteen at the table for the Lord's last supper on a day that just happened to be the thirteenth day of Nisan in the old Hebrew calendar.

He wondered if today would prove to be lucky for him or not. He descended into the shallow valley that separated his resting place from the village and drank at the trickling stream that flowed along the valley bottom. He needed to eat and he needed to get directions for the next stage of his journey. In desperation he decided to risk calling at a small farm that lay on the outskirts of the village. The old couple who lived there were only too glad to give him a meal in exchange for a day's labour in their fields, their two sons having left some weeks ago. Nat guessed that the boys might have joined the rebellion but the couple didn't elaborate further and Nat decided it best not to ask.

At the end of a tiring day Nat gratefully accepted the offer of one of the boy's beds for the night and enjoyed his best night's sleep for a month. Not a bad birthday after all he decided.

The following morning the old couple implored him to stay for a few more days but understood his desire to be on his way when he explained that he had an aged father who would need help with the family business, and a girl that he intended to marry. They wished him God's speed, gave him sufficient food to last for two days and pointed him in the direction of the road to Tiverton. After all the violence and hatred that he had experienced since leaving Lyme in June the kindness he had again been shown restored his faith in the goodness of people and he smiled to himself and whistled a tune as he took the track that skirted the village, picking up the Tiverton road on the far side. He had been walking for about two hours following the course of the River Yeo when the waterway split into several small streams that made their separate ways up tiny valleys into the high ground on his left. He was concerned that he may have taken the wrong road as the sun had been directly ahead of him the whole time, meaning he had been walking due east and he resolved to turn south as soon as he cleared the woods that he was currently negotiating.

His thoughts were interrupted by the sound of voices ahead of him. He couldn't see who was making the noise due to a sharp curve in the track but he couldn't afford to take any chances and dived off the track into the thin undergrowth before crawling quietly towards a fallen tree. Where the tree had come down its roots had torn a large circular hole in the ground and Nat was able to slip into this depression just as a company of red coated militia came into view. A large burrow had been dug into the soft earth behind the wall of roots, a strong musky odour telling Nat that a fox had made its den there.

'I'll share your home for a few short minutes Master Reynard if you don't mind,' he said to himself, the irony of having been hunted like a fox for so long making him smile. He knew that he would be safe as long as the soldiers didn't leave the road but just when he thought the threat had passed a voice called out behind him.

'On your feet! Bloody poacher!'

Nat spun round to see an aged gamekeeper with an even older fowling piece. He had to get away before the gamekeeper's shouts brought the militia from the road but as he stood to run the old man raised the gun to his shoulder and fired. Nat felt the air quiver as the shot narrowly missed his head but his relief was short lived as the militia, alerted by the shot broke ranks and dashed into the woods. Nat had no chance of evading so many pursuers and was soon being pressed roughly to the damp soil.

'A runaway rebel if I'm not mistaken,' crowed the sergeant in charge of the detachment. 'On your feet you traitor.'

Nat tried to protest his innocence but the man was having none of it. His hands were bound and he was marched off. His birthday luck had run out, the law had caught up with him at last.

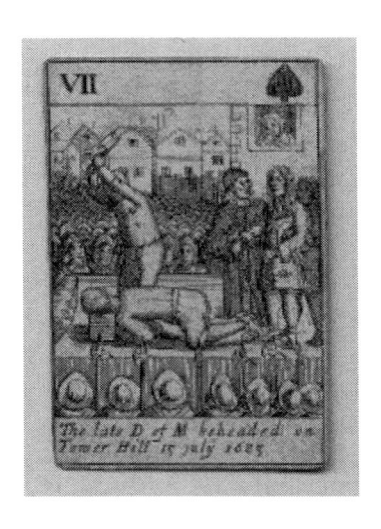

The late D. of M. beheaded on Tower Hill 15 july 1685

38 AWAITING THE KING'S PLEASURE

Taunton Gaol.
July – September 1685

The militiamen told Nat that he had strayed into Somersetshire and would therefore be taken to Taunton prison to await trial. Although he dreaded the prospect of incarceration, the alternative of summary execution as suffered by Henry was far less palatable.

The distance to Taunton was only thirty miles or so but took four days to complete with numerous stops to allow other patrols to come in, each with their own contingent of captured rebels. As he was led through the gates of the old castle that served as the prison Nat reflected that it was on this very spot that he had been brought before Major Wade to report on the skirmish at

Lambrook. So much had happened since that meeting barely a month ago. The promise of a glorious campaign, ending with a triumphal march to London to place Monmouth on the throne had ended in bloody ruin on the wet fields of Sedgemoor and so many of his friends had been sacrificed to that dream. Joshua Stuckley decapitated at Philipsnorton, Henry Outwell left hanging from a tree like a common criminal, Amos Gough and Stephen Dabinett both killed on the dirty streets of Keynsham. He had no idea what had become of Samuel White or Aaron Tucker (both dead) nor Daniel Foe or Eliza's father Hezekiah. He suspected that William Pearce and Thomas Edgecott had both deserted. So many other names and faces flashed through his mind. He wondered if Aaron Smith and Moses Armitage who had been on the boat with him when they had beached at Woolacombe had escaped capture. Above all he prayed that his own father had made it back to Lyme and that Eliza and Daniel were safe.

Nat was delivered to the gaoler who recorded his name, place of birth and occupation in the gaol delivery book.

'What's this man charged with?'

'Levying war against the king,' the militia sergeant replied.

Once the whole group of thirty prisoners had been recorded they were taken down a worn flight of stones steps and made to wait while the gaoler selected a large key from the bunch that hung from his belt. The key grated in the lock of a thick wooden door studded with iron bolts and the door swung back on its hinges with a groan. Nat could see nothing inside the room but the smell that came out of the darkness made him choke. He was thrust inside and landed on the hard stone floor, the thin layer of rotting straw doing nothing to soften the blow. His left hand had landed in something soft and when he raised it to his face he realised that it was human excrement.

The smell was even worse when the heavy door was pulled shut and it was some while before his eyes became adjusted to the weak light that filtered in through a high barred window. He stood up unsteadily and made his way carefully across the crowded cell sweeping the fetid straw to one side with his foot before sliding to the floor against one of the damp walls. He was desperate for news of his father, brother and fiancée and wondered if any of his fellow inmates had any heard anything.

'Is there anyone here from Lyme?' he called out.

'I'm from Chideock,' came a quiet voice from the other side of the room. Nat rose and made his way towards the voice, wincing every time his foot slipped on another pile of human waste.

'Don't they ever clean this place out?' He asked as he sat down next to the man who had answered him.

'Every couple of days they come in and drag out those who have died. When that happens we're allowed out for a few minutes fresh air and the straw is taken out and burnt.'

Nat thought that he recognised the voice. 'Is that you Amos Thorne?'

'Aye, I'm Amos, but I don't recognise you.'

'Carver, Nat Carver. I last saw you after Bridport. Thomas Edgecott and I carried you back to your cottage after you were hit in the shoulder.'

'Then I should thank you, I suppose, but as you can imagine I'm not in the best of humours.'

'How did you end up here?'

'As soon as the duke's army left Lyme my neighbours felt bold enough to come looking for me, knowing there was a bounty of one pound on the head of any who had aided the rebellion. You remember I told you they was mostly bloody Catholics where I lived. I tried to make a run for it but I didn't get far what with my injury. They caught up with me just outside Whitchurch and handed me over to the constables.'

His story was interrupted by a bout of coughing that wracked his thin frame.

'I should've gone to Dorchester prison being as I were taken in Dorsetshire, but that was said to be too overcrowded.'

'How it can be any worse there than here I can't imagine.' Thorne coughed again, the effort draining all his energy. He fell silent and Nat feared the worst but when he leant closer he could just make out the small rise and fall of the old man's chest.

'Nat, over here!' came another voice in the darkness. 'It's William Pearce.'

'William, I niver thought to see you again. Are you well?'

'Well? I'm stuck in this place and facing the rope but otherwise I'm fine,' he laughed. He told Nat how he came to be taken after leaving the army at Bridgwater.

'It was the hardest decision of my life to leave you boys but I couldn't take it anymore. I kept thinking of my Rebecca and the four little ones, wondering how they were faring in Taunton. I'm sorry.'

'There's no need to apologise William. A man must put his family before anything else. If you'd stayed with the army and fallen at Sedgemoor where would your family be?'

'In the same fucking mess as they are now!'

At that moment the cell door creaked open and two women brought in a tray of bread and two buckets of water.

'Shall we dine?' William asked with a wry smile. By the light that flooded into the cell before the door was closed again Nat could see that several of the men were nursing serious injuries.

'Does no one tend to their injuries?'

'No. We did hear that there's a Doctor Winter who visits the sick in Ilchester gaol but tis said that he is only permitted to do so to keep the prisoners alive so that they can be put on trial. Wouldn't want rebels dying before the law 'as a chance to kill them.'

'So you do get news in here then?' asked Nat hopefully.

'Not much. My dear wife has been twice but she's only allowed to speak to me through the bars and only then by bribing the guards. I daren't ask her what she 'as to give the guards to let us speak.'

Two weeks after Nat's imprisonment word was received that the Duke of Monmouth had been executed at the Tower of London. The men were pulled from their cells into the harsh sunlight where the governor of the gaol, a short fat man who moped his sweaty brow constantly was happy to pass on the news.

It was said that the duke had been arrested in the New Forest and taken before his uncle the king who had listened to his pleas for mercy before confirming the death sentence. With obvious pleasure the governor added that the duke had died badly, the executioner making a mess of the job which the duke had apparently paid him handsomely to undertake well and quickly. Many of the prisoners had hoped that the duke would have been able to come to an accommodation with the king which would have led to the rebel captives being released but that hope was now gone and the men resigned themselves to their fate.

At the end of August, the prisoners were advised that King James had seen fit to dispatch the Lord Chief Justice, Baron George Jeffreys of Wem to the West Country to ensure that the king's justice was done and that the Taunton assizes would start as soon as the judge had dealt with the hundreds of rebels that awaited his arrival at Dorchester gaol. Jeffreys had a reputation for harshness, condemning more than twenty Jesuits to death when a plot to assassinate the late king, Charles II was uncovered. The assizes would be heard by a bench consisting of Jeffreys and four other judges and it was hoped that the other four would temper his penchant for passing harsh sentences.

Severall Rebells tryed in the West.

39 DORCHESTER ASSIZES

5th – 10th September 1685

Conditions in Dorchester prison where Thomas had been held for six weeks were no better than at Taunton. Here too men died of their wounds or from any one of a number of diseases that spread like wildfire through the crowded unsanitary accommodation. Food and water supplies were fitful at best. The gaolers delighted in beating the prisoners at every opportunity and the bodies of those who died in the miserable conditions could sometimes lay in the crowded cells for days before being dragged outside. The lice that they had endured on campaign now seemed trivial by comparison.

The day before the assizes were due to start the county clerk toured the cells promising that any man who pleaded guilty to the charge of treason would 'be given all the kindness that they could.' Thomas couldn't understand why such an offer would be made.

'That's simple,' said Jonah Gubbins, one of the men who shared his crowded cell. 'It's to save time. If everyone pleads not guilty the judges will be here until Christmas, but if a large number plead guilty their trials will pass straight to sentencing and judgement can be passed on the whole group at once.'

A number of men decided that they would accept the promise of leniency and their confessions were recorded by the clerk and his deputies.

On the morning on the opening day of the assizes the first batch of thirty rebels who had decided to plead not guilty were taken up into the Oak room at the Antelope Inn where the trials were to be held. The gaolers returned a short time later to advise those awaiting their turn that of the thirty tried, twenty-nine had been found guilty by the jury. Many wondered aloud how so many men could have been fairly tried within such a short time when the prosecution was required to produce two witnesses against each man accused, each of whom was permitted by law to produce witnesses of his own. With some relish the gaoler read out the judgement handed down to each of the twenty-nine.

'You shall be hanged up by the neck, but cut down alive, your entrails and privy members cut off your body, and burnt in your sight, your head to be severed from your body, and your body divided into four parts, and disposed at the King's pleasure.'

No wonder effigies of Judge Jeffreys had been burnt on the streets of London thought Thomas, grateful for the fact that he was charged with a felony rather than treason.

The sentences were met with stunned silence. No one had expected such wholesale executions and many of those who had held back from admitting their guilt to the clerk rushed to change their pleas to guilty. As the clerk was busy recording their confessions the next filthy batch of thirty-four men were taken up. These men had all entered guilty pleas on the promise of leniency but they too were all sentenced to death, although this was commuted to transportation in many cases. Gubbins turned to Thomas.

'So that's the way of it,' he whispered. 'Plead not guilty and die or admit to your guilt and take a chance on being transported to the colonies instead. That in itself might be a death sentence but it's still a chance of life.'

The trials took five days to complete, Thomas having to wait while all of the treason charges were dealt with before the court could turn to the felony cases that would normally have made up the bulk of the assizes' workload.

He was ushered into the temporary court room with the last five rebels who despite everything had decided to plead not guilty to the charge of treason. Jeffreys sat in the middle of the five judges laughing and joking with them and sipping from a small wine glass as the prisoners were led in. Thomas thought him quite a handsome man, probably in his early forties.

The jollity stopped as the first defendant stepped into the box and it quickly became apparent to Thomas that the trials were a sham. Whenever anyone spoke for the defendants Jeffreys threatened to fine them if they persisted with their lies, he frequently interrupted proceedings and over-ruled the jury when they had the temerity to find one of the men not guilty. If any of the other four judges tried to speak he shouted them down. The last of the rebels, John Spraggs from Colyton, was asked why he had decided to challenge the court and plead not guilty. Unlike the majority of those on trial who had stood with shoulders stooped, heads bowed, twisting their hats in their hands, Spraggs stood tall in the dock, looked Jeffreys full in the face and answered.

'No Christian ought to resist a lawful power, but this case being between popery and Protestantism altered the matter.'

'Guilty by his own admission!' declared Jeffreys without bothering to question the witnesses or consult the jury. He was the Lord Chief Justice and the west was under martial law, Jeffrey's law.

Then it was Thomas' turn to face the bench. He was the first of the felony cases to be heard and he hoped that Jeffrey's blood lust had been sated by the number of death sentences that he had already handed down. He was certain that he had not been seen committing the boy's murder and wondered who the prosecution would produce to stand witness against him, although from what he had seen so far that did not appear to be an issue in this court. The details of the charge were read out and the first witness was called.

Jacob the carter told the court how he had picked Thomas up in Yeovil even though he 'had the look of a villain about him.' He admitted that he had been asleep when the crime had taken place but put his state down to exhaustion from 'good honest labour' rather than alcohol. Thomas smiled to himself. If this was the best witness against him then there would be no case to answer, but he had not reckoned on Jacob's desire to see his son avenged. The next witness was called, a feckless stable boy who swore that he had seen Thomas stab the child. Next to speak against him was a maid from the inn who said she had seen the deed done as she was emptying a chamber pot in the yard. Both claimed that they had been threatened by Thomas to keep quiet and that 'he appeared to be so filled with the devil's evil' that neither dared raise the alarm until later. The stories were so similar that it was clear that they had been paid for their evidence.

'I've heard enough!' said Jeffreys. 'My damned kidney stone is playing up again, let's be done here so I can retire to my rooms.'

'My lord,' stammered Thomas, 'these witnesses have clearly been bought!'

'Quiet!' shouted Jeffreys. 'How dare you suggest that I cannot tell whether a witness is lying or telling the truth. Is it a fact that you were traced by a pardon found in your coat pocket at the scene of the murder?'

'Yes my lord.'

'Then you deserve to hang twice, once as a murderer and again as a traitorous rebel, it makes no difference to me which charge sends you to your maker. Take him away!'

Major Holmes and a other Rebells Hanged in Chaines

40 ON TRIAL FOR THEIR LIVES

Taunton 18th September 1685

Nat was aware from his chat with William that the gaolers at Taunton were keen to make what they could by allowing the prisoners to have visitors even if that was limited to conversing through the bars of their cells. He had managed to get word to Lyme that he was alive and begged Eliza to visit him before his trial, fearful that he might never see her again. He had asked that his father provide a generous purse to ensure that Eliza did not have to demean herself to the gaolers in any way. He was not to know that John was missing and that in his absence Daniel had found sufficient coin to protect Eliza's honour.

She arrived late on the day before the Taunton assizes were due to start. Although she was clearly relieved to see him alive and as well as could be expected, Nat detected that there was something that she wished to say but dare not.

'What is it, dearest thing?' he asked softly. 'What troubles you so?'

'It's my father,' she sobbed. 'He was captured near Salisbury, riding to take shelter with a friend who has a living near there. He was tried at the Salisbury assizes.' She took a deep breath before continuing. 'He was found guilty of treason and sentenced to death.'

'There's hope yet,' said Nat kindly. 'Many of those convicted are having their sentences reviewed and are being deported to the colonies instead. Your father has a strong constitution and will surely survive life on the plantations and return to you in good time.'

'No he won't!' cried Eliza. 'He was hung on the beach at Lyme last week.'

'I am so sorry,' said Nat tenderly. He longed to comfort her but the best he could manage was to entwine his fingers with hers through the bars. 'But take heart my love, he is in the loving care of our Lord now, he can feel no more pain.'

'That's not all of it,' she added quietly.

'My father!' cried Nat in horror.

'No one has seen your father since he spoke to Daniel and young Nancy at the smithy. He told them that he was on his way to see me, to tell me that you were safe after Thomas had earlier said that he saw you fall in battle, but he never arrived at the Goodman's house.'

Nat's earlier suspicions about Thomas were resurrected. 'What news of Thomas?'

'A list was posted on the market cross in Lyme of those tried at Dorchester and Thomas's name was on it, he was hung on a charge of murder!'

Nat was badly shaken, his joy at seeing Eliza quickly turning to despair at so much bad news. Like many of the men he had been hoping for compassion and leniency from the courts but rumours of the harsh sentences being handed down at the other assizes had filtered through to them and now Eliza was able to confirm that the stories were true.

Nat was brought before the bench on the Friday morning following Eliza's visit. As he was taken from the cells he noticed a distinct chill in the air which reminded him that he had spent more than half of the summer languishing in prison.

He had thought long and hard whether to plead guilty or not guilty. He knew that by taking up arms against King James he was guilty of treason but if James had really murdered his brother to take the crown as Monmouth's proclamation had said then was he truly the rightful king? He thought about Monmouth's decision to have himself declared king in Taunton and wondered at Ferguson's explanation that the move was intended to give legal protection to his followers. He asked another prisoner for his views as they shuffled towards the temporary courtroom.

'Don't make no diff'rence, old Jeffreys'll hang us all, whatever the law says,' came the dour reply.

It seemed that very few men had been acquitted and that those who argued their innocence but had still been found guilty were invariably sentenced to death. The authorities were happy for such stories to circulate among the prisoners in the hope that the majority of the five hundred or so rebels due to be tried in Taunton would plead guilty thus saving hours of court time.

The one thing that Nat had decided was that he would not refuse to enter a plea at all, on that issue the law was very clear. Anyone refusing to answer either guilty or not guilty would be pressed, that is to say covered with heavy stones and given minimal food and water until they died. That was no way to die. He had no remorse about joining the rebellion and pleading guilty would at least leave open the possibility of transportation rather than execution but if he did plead guilty he would have to answer to his conscience for whatever was left of his life.

'Not Guilty!' he replied when the clerk asked for his plea. The clerk instructed his scribe to write '*Po. Se, non cul.*' next to his name.

'What does that mean? Nat asked.

'It's Latin,' replied the clerk, pleased to show off his knowledge. 'It's short for Ponit se, non culpabilis, meaning that you plead not guilty.'

The prisoners were put into two groups depending on how they had pleaded and those that had decided to throw themselves on the mercy of the court were taken up first in an effort to clear as many cases as possible before lunch. Nat and the other 'non culpabilis' prisoners were made to sit and wait until their lordships had finished their luncheon.

'All stand for the Lord Chief Justice George, Baron Jeffreys of Wem, Sir Cresswell Levins, Sir Francis Wythens, Sir Robert Wright and his lordship William Montagu.'

One of Nat's fellow prisoners, a lawyer from Dunster had explained the court system to him but it was immediately apparent that these hearings would bear little resemblance to the way that law was usually administered. The judges had dispensed with the normal formality of calling a grand jury to decide if there was a case to answer and had already selected the twelve men from the twenty-four 'possibles' who would make up the jury that would hear the actual trial. The law stated that the defendants could object to any of the twelve but Jeffreys was having none of it.

'To save us time, I have picked these twelve good men and that should be good enough for you scoundrels,' Jeffreys said in reply to the defendants' complaints.

The first to be tried was Thomas Speke, gentleman of Whitelackington, charged with 'aiding and assisting' the rebellion in that he was seen to kiss Monmouth's gloved hand when the duke had ridden through Ilchester.

'It seems a clear-cut case to me,' said Jeffreys to his four compatriots. 'Why do you think to challenge it man?'

'Who here speaks against me? The law says there should be two witnesses, but none have been produced.'

'The word of the arresting constable is good enough for me. Have you anything else to add before I pass sentence?'

Nat was shocked that the judge appeared to have made up his mind without consulting either the other members of the bench or the jury, most of whom looked totally disinterested in proceedings. At least four of them appeared to be drunk and two were fast asleep.

'My Lord, I took no part in the rebellion, I was not even in the county when the late duke visited my father's estate, t'was my brother William who greeted him.'

Jeffreys turned to the constable. 'Where is this brother of his?'

'He could not be found your worship.'

'In that case the family owes us a life and yours is as good as any other. You are found guilty sir and sentenced to death. Next!'

The four other men on the bench and the twelve men of the jury watched on in mute acceptance of Jeffreys' decision. The next man to be sentenced to death was Thomas Lawrence who Nat recognised as the bailiff of a farm just outside Lyme. He was guilty of nothing more than having had three of his horses stolen by Monmouth's men but that was enough for Jeffreys to convict him of having 'joined in the rebellion.'

Nat realised that whatever defence he hoped to offer was going to be pointless, it was clearly a case of being guilty until proved innocent but without any opportunity to prove that innocence. On the rare occasions when the jury were asked for their verdict Jeffreys made it clear that if they found the defendant to be innocent they themselves would be charged with treason. Despite the serious nature of the charges the judge seemed to be in good humour. Upon hearing that one defendant was a pauper, supported by the parish poor relief Jeffreys quipped, 'then I will ease the parish of the burden' and sentenced him to death.

Nat's trial was as brief as the others although he did take the opportunity to explain why he had joined the rebellion stating in a clear voice, 'it's better to incur the wrath of an earthly king, than an Almighty God.'

Jeffreys was unmoved and pronounced him guilty, the clerk writing '*Tr. Et ss.*' against his name meaning he was to be hung, drawn and quartered. He was led back to the cells to await punishment but there was one final thing that could save him. It was rumoured that the government was looking at ways to recover the huge cost of suppressing the rebellion and had appointed pardonmongers to issue pardons upon payment of a fine of fifty pounds. This amounted to about fifteen years wages for a servant but was not perhaps outside the means of a man whose family had a successful business and Nat arranged for a message to be sent to Lyme so that his father, if he still lived, could consult the local pardonmonger. He hoped that his father could raise such a sum before the sentence was carried out. It was a slim hope but it was all he had.

No date had been set for the executions and the men were left in the cells to contemplate their fate. William Pearce and Amos Thorne had also been found guilty. Three days after the guilty verdicts the gaoler opened the cell and called Nat's name.

'I've some good news for you Carver, you're not to hang after all.' Nat's heart jumped; his father must have come up with the fine.

'I've been pardoned?'

'No bloody chance Carver. You're going on a little trip instead; your sentence has been commuted to transportation. His majesty needs strong young men to help in the colonies. You leave for Bristol in the morning.'

'What about Amos and William?'

'None of your bloody business!'

41 DEPORTATION

September 1685

Officially Nat's sentence had been commuted to 'transportation to his majesties southern plantations.' In practice he had been sold by the government to a favoured plantation owner for fifteen pounds. He was forced to sign a document, similar to an apprenticeship, confirming that he would work as an indentured servant to Lt Col Richard Vinter in Barbados for ten years.

'There you go, better than being hung,' said the clerk. 'By the terms of this indenture you'll be paid a wage and given accommodation and if you survive the hard work and the fever you'll be free to return home when your ten years are up. Put your mark on the bottom.'

'I can read and write and sign my own name thank you!' snapped Nat as he snatched the piece of paper from the officious clerk. He had learnt his letters with the help of Hezekiah Sprake and the bible which King James I, the usurper king's grandfather had made widely available in English for the first time. He quickly read through the long document ignoring the various legal terms that he didn't understand.

When he reached the end he looked up and said, 'I can't see anything that says who will pay for my passage home.'

'You'll be a free man when you've served your time so obviously it will be up to you to pay. Work hard, don't waste your wages on women and booze and you should be alright,' the clerk sneered.

Despite the warning that they were to leave for Bristol immediately there was a delay of several days. Unbeknown to Nat and the others awaiting transportation pressure had been put on Jeffreys to commute more of the death sentences as there was easy money to be made by selling the men rather than killing them.

Nat was relieved that they were to sail from Bristol rather than Weymouth thus avoiding the agony of any chance meeting with friends or family as they passed through Dorset, so it came as a blow when it was announced that the *John* had already sailed and that they would now board the *Happy Return* which was due to leave from Weymouth on the twenty-fifth. Following the signing of a replacement indenture they were now the property of Sir William Booth a Barbados merchant who was certain to sell them on to a plantation owner as soon as they arrived in the colonies. The men were manacled in pairs with long chains attached to each pair to form a column two men wide and fifty yards long. Nat introduced himself to his partner, Elias King a drover from Hinton St George.

As they shuffled along the rough roads towards Weymouth they passed through a number of towns and villages each of which was adorned with the quarters of those already executed and butchered, the grisly body parts that hung from churches and gibbets being coated in tar to preserve them. In other places the limp bodies of rebels given a summary execution remained hanging from the branches of elms and oaks, their eyes taken by greedy crows. Awful though the sight was it served to remind the prisoners that they had escaped lightly even though ten years in the colonies could well prove to be a death sentence in its own way.

After a hard day's marching the column reached the outskirts of Crewkerne and the prisoners were bundled into an old barn for the night. Once the militiamen had checked the manacles they withdrew to a local inn leaving two men to guard the doors. Nat had spent a lot of time examining the poorly made lock on the manacles which had been quickly produced in large numbers to meet the sudden unexpected demand. If these had been made in the smithy in Lyme his father would have rejected the lot of them he thought. By the pallid light of the moon that made its way into the barn through one of the many holes in the roof Nat began to work on the lock with a rusty nail that he had found lying in the soiled straw. It proved far easier than he had expected and within twenty minutes he was able to prise the restraints from his wrists.

He had hoped that King would not be woken by his actions but as he eased his manacles off the other man whispered, 'mine too friend, unless you want me to call out.'

Nat had no option and went to work immediately. Once they were both free Nat turned his attention to the problem of getting out of the old barn.

'I can't see any way out of here except through the big double doors at the front and I can't see the guards who are posted outside letting us do that,' he said quietly.

'I've already worked that one out,' replied King. 'Call it my contribution to our partnership. There's a loose panel in the wall just behind us, I felt it give when I leaned back against it. We should be able to prise it away easily enough. Now all we need is a distraction.'

Without further ado he stood up and called out, 'wake up everyone! This man has unlocked our manacles!'

There was pandemonium as every man in the barn demanded to have his hands freed, the commotion soon bringing the two guards into the building. As the sentries set about the mob with their musket butts Nat and King attacked the loose boards. The rotten wood gave way easily and the two men slipped out into the cool night air.

'Thank you my friend,' called King as he ran for the cover of the dark farmhouse on the other side of the yard.

Nat went in the opposite direction heading for the high stone wall that surrounded the yard. He jumped up onto the bed of an old cart and hauled himself onto the top of the wall before dropping to the ground on the other side. He could hear the sound of fighting from the barn and as he crouched in the long, wet grass he could see other militiamen running to the open gates that led into the yard, but none were headed his way. He knew that once the guards had subdued the prisoners they would find the discarded manacles and come looking for him and King. He crawled to a shallow ditch that led away from the farm. Once he was well clear of the buildings he hauled himself out of the foul-smelling gully and broke into a stooping run anxious to put as much distance as he could between himself and the militia. He didn't stop running until he reached a low rise where a dense patch of holly bushes gave him the chance to catch his breath. He was on the run again.

Using the light of the moon Nat was able to put several miles between himself and any pursuers although he was fairly sure that the militia guards wouldn't come looking for him with so many other prisoners to escort to Weymouth, especially as time was of the essence with the ship due to sail any day. He was equally certain that the escorts would have raised the alarm and no doubt mounted patrols would be setting off at first light. He had seen plenty of bounty hunters on the march down from Taunton, a curious mixture of militia, sporting landowners out for the rare chance to hunt human prey and ordinary farmers anxious to claim the bounty on an escaped rebel.

He found a good hiding place as soon as it started to get light and prayed that those looking for him did not have dogs that could follow his scent. He had taken the precaution of walking in the cold water of a small stream for several hundred yards knowing that the dogs and their handlers would have to check both banks in both directions in the hope of picking up his trail. He should be safe for a couple of hours at least but he still had a considerable distance to cover before he got home.

As the long hot day slowly passed, questions crowded his thoughts. What would he do when he got home? Would it even be safe to return to Lyme? Was Eliza aware that he was still alive? Would she have discovered that his death sentence had been commuted to deportation and if so would she have the strength to wait ten years for him to return or would she look elsewhere for a husband, thinking him lost? One thing he did decide is that he couldn't spend the rest of his life in hiding. If he acted like a fugitive he would most likely be treated as one.

The closer he got to Lyme the less his strong Dorset accent would make him stand out and if he could wash the smell of prison from his soiled clothes there was nothing particular about his appearance that could connect him with the rebellion. He resolved that he would walk openly in the countryside as if he had every right to be there, find out the situation in Lyme and take things from there. Now that autumn had arrived there was plenty to eat in the hedgerows, so different from when the hungry army had passed through this part of Somerset all those weeks before. He fed himself with berries and apples and slaked his thirst from a sweet tasting stream before setting out down the hill towards the main road that snaked its way through rich farmland.

He had been walking for an hour when he heard the thump of hooves. He was tired of hiding and decided to brazen it out.

'You there! Stop and state your business.'

Nat turned to see a single horseman. He was elegantly turned out with tall, well-polished riding boots and a fine green coat covered by a black riding cape. He wore a patterned cravat above a richly embroidered waistcoat and his black felt hat was adorned with two bright feathers, clearly a man of some means. He held a riding crop in one hand, the other resting on the ornately decorated stock of a pistol which was carried in a holster on his saddle.

'William Smythe as it pleases your 'onor,' Nat replied bowing low and touching his forelock. 'I'm a blacksmith. I've just delivered a new pair of stable door hinges and now I'm on my way home.'

'Just who did you deliver them to and where? And where exactly is home?' Nat's mind raced as he tried to think up a name and a place to embellish his cover story, but the rider saw the look of indecision on his face.

'I thought so! A blasted runaway rebel I'm bound!'

He struck out at Nat with his crop as he tried to pull the pistol from its holster but Nat reacted quicker, grabbing the rider's arm and pulling him physically from the saddle. The man fell heavily and the pistol flew from his grip as he hit the ground. He was momentarily stunned giving Nat the chance to grab the weapon. By the time the rider had recovered his wits and began to sit himself up he saw that Nat was stood over him with the pistol aimed at his head.

'Go on then you scoundrel, shoot damn you! You're bound for hell anyway for your traitorous behaviour, another sin won't make any difference.'

Nat cocked the piece but found that he could not pull the trigger. He had seen so much blood spilt over the past few months but not, thank God, enough to have become desensitised. Instead he reversed the pistol and knocked the man out with the heavy handle before dragging the inert body into the cover of some trees. He sat the unconscious man down with his back to a tree, pulled his arms around behind the trunk and used the cravat to tie his hands. Although he could not bring himself to kill the man he had no compunction about relieving him of his purse, after all he had to eat and buy a new set of clothing. His victim's outer clothes were much too fine for an ordinary man but his undershirt would do very well and the hat, once the feathers had been removed and the brim bent about a bit would suffice. He considered taking the horse which would clearly speed his progress towards home but realised how odd it would look for someone in his tattered clothing to be riding a fine thoroughbred. Looping the reins around a nearby branch Nat slipped away wondering just how close he had really come to killing the man in cold blood.

As the sun touched the crest of the distant hills and the colour drained away from the landscape he found shelter in an abandoned forge that stood a little way off the road. The blackened rafters that supported the few remaining roof tiles told of a fire but there was no smell of smoke and the ashes were cold to the touch. He wondered if the cost of repairing the place was too high or whether the farrier had died in the blaze leaving no family to restore the place. Either way it gave him a place to rest and he was grateful for it.

In the morning he searched through the debris and discovered some rusty tools in a ramshackle outbuilding that had somehow escaped the fire. He spent several hours cleaning the worst of the dirt and rust from the tools before stuffing them into a large serge bag that he found hanging on the back of the door. 'God must be smiling on me today,' he said to himself. Despite the long months of incarceration he had retained the characteristic bulky muscles of a blacksmith and carrying these tools would help to convince anyone that he met that he was nothing more threatening than a journeyman blacksmith. True, journeymen were more often carpenters or stonemasons, travelling from one job to another but wandering blacksmiths were not unknown and it gave him a good reason to be walking the lanes of Somerset.

He spent the rest of the morning on the wide muddy road that twisted and turned between low hillocks and ancient stands of trees. He had no idea where he was and although the rising sun had told him which way was south, he didn't have any real inkling of where he was starting from, such was his hasty retreat from Crewkerne that he could have run off in any direction. The shape of the landscape was starting to take on a more familiar look and he hoped that he would soon spot something that would let him know where he was and set him on the road to Lyme.

Around midday he saw smoke rising from behind a low ridge. He turned off the road which skirted the ridge and made his way to the summit from where he was able to look down onto a small hamlet. There were perhaps two dozen dwellings spread out on either side of a small river. He could see no church, but more importantly he could see no sign of any soldiers and he decided that the risk was acceptable given that we was growing hungry again.

He didn't want to startle anyone by suddenly appearing out of the fields so he retraced his steps and re-joined the road before it emerged from the lea of the ridge. There were precious few people about when he reached the centre of the hamlet and as he looked around for somewhere that might offer the chance of a meal he heard swearing and cursing coming from a workshop that fronted the main thoroughfare. It was, by chance, a smithy and an old man wearing a grubby apron was struggling to control a frisky horse that clearly did not want the new shoe that the smith was trying to fit. Nat dropped his bag and ran to help, the noise of the metal tools hitting the cobbles causing the old man to look up.

'Do you need a hand there friend?' Nat asked as he ducked into the smithy, immediately feeling at home in the warm smoky workshop.

'Thank 'e kindly,' said the smith. 'This filly 'as been coming here for new shoes for years and she's always a handful but I'm not getting any younger.'

'You take her bridle and hold her tight,' Nat suggested, 'and let me see to the fitting of the shoe.'

Before the smith had a chance to object Nat had picked up the shoe and the hammer but seeing that the shoe had cooled he grabbed it with a pair of tongs and thrust it back into the fire.

'Seems that you know what you are about young'un. You've done this sort a thing before then?'

Nat was anxious not to give too much away until he had had the chance to gauge the man better so he simply nodded and replied, 'once or twice.'

Once the new shoe was up to the right temperature he took it from the fire and pressed it against the underside of the hoof before removing it to examine the scorch marks to see what the fit was like.

'I've done that already,' the smith said with some irritation, 'but I s'pose it don't hurt to check.'

The fit was good so Nat cooled the shoe in a bucket of water before nailing it on. Without waiting to be asked he grabbed a file from a nearby rack and proceeded to blunt the end of each nail where it protruded from the wall of the hoof before bending each one over to make a clench.

'Nicely done,' admitted the smith as he relaxed his grip on the mare's bridle and gentled rubbed her muzzle.

'Tis my pleasure,' grinned Nat. 'It's good to be back in a smithy again.'

'Well it were kindly done and I thank 'e again. Can I offer you a bite of lunch to thank you proper like? You looks like you could do with zummat, and then you can tell me how you knows your way around horses and the workings of a smithy.'

Nat followed the old man into the small cottage that adjoined the smithy and sat while the smith bent to take

427

two battered goblets and a stone flagon from a low cupboard. A slab of hard cheese and half a loaf of newly baked bread followed the ale onto the large table that dominated the room.

'First things first then young 'un. My name's Ebenezer Collins. What's yours?'

Nat was about to use the William Smythe alias that he had invented the previous day before thinking better of it. If the man he had robbed remembered the name it could spell no end of trouble so he trusted to his luck and replied, 'Nathaniel Carver sir, but folk calls me Nat.'

'Well Master Carver, I've not seen you about the village before so where are you from and what brings you here?'

As he spoke he poured strong smelling ale into the two goblets and handed one to Nat. Nat was starting to feel uncomfortable under the questioning but the old man seemed to be asking out of genuine interest. Even so he decided that a little lie would be necessary, 'I'm a blacksmith from Charmouth on the coast, do you know it?'

'Heard of it, niver been there.'

Nat was encouraged by the answer, it meant that he may be closer to home than he had dared hope.

'Do you know how far off it be, from .....wherever this place is?' he asked spreading his arms to emphasis the question.

'This 'ere be Mosterton in Devonshire. I reckons that I could reach the sea in less than half a day.'

'That close!' smiled Nat.

Collins cut a thick chunk of bread and placed it onto an old pewter plate together with a slice of cheese. It was clear that the old man was about to ask another question and Nat decided to divert the conversation by asking one of his own.

'Do you run this place by yourself Master Collins? I ain't trying to be disrespectful but it's a lot of work for a man of your age.'

He could see Collins bristling at the suggestion that he was getting past it and added quickly, 'my father works with me in the smithy in Charmouth and he struggles at times and he must be a good ten years younger than you.'

'No offence taken young man. I do find it hard at times as you yourself witnessed this morning. My boy Zak normally helps I, but he's been gone for six months now and I'm not sure if or when he'll return.'

'Gone six months? Do you know where he went, if you don't mind me asking?'

'I don't mind admitting, he went to fight for the duke and I've heard nothing of him since.'

Nat was surprised to hear Collins confess so openly about his boy joining the rebellion but he knew the biblical saying about the sins of the father not being passed to his sons and assumed that it worked both ways. Just because Zak had joined the rebels didn't condemn his father.

He decided he needed to know how the old man stood on the matter and asked gently, 'how did you feel about your son rebelling against the king?'

'I were glad he went. Oh, I know that I shouldn't say so to one I hardly knows but I'm old and they can do with I as they like. Now we'll have to tolerate the papist king until he passes on and pray that his Italian bitch of a wife doesn't produce an heir in the meantime.'

Encouraged by the old man's candour Nat confessed that he was actually from Lyme Regis and told him how he had fought in the rebel army.'

'Did you ever meet my boy?' Collins asked eagerly, 'do you know if he yet lives?'

'I'm sorry but I don't know. There were thousands in the army and I knew only a fraction of them but it's not a name I came across.'

'Ah well, time will tell. So what now for you? Home to Lyme?'

'I'm not sure how the situation is there. I think I might find somewhere safe to stop and try to get word to my family to see how the land lies.'

'Well you're welcome to stay here in the meanwhile. You can work for your board and lodgings by helping me in the smithy.'

'I'd be honoured to,' replied Nat shaking the old man's hand.

42 A NEW BEGINNING

Autumn 1685 – Spring 1686

Nat worked hard in the smithy alongside Ebenezer and wasted no time in ascertaining from him who in the village might be entrusted to deliver a message to Eliza. His enquiries bore fruit after just a week when he was told that Mark Bond, a carpenter in Mosterton and a lifelong friend of Ebenezer's had secured work in Uplyme and would be happy to take a letter to Nat's family in Lyme. Nat addressed the letter to his father John, trusting that the old man had resurfaced from wherever he'd been, and after enquiring about his health and the wellbeing of Daniel and Nancy asked whether the family was still in contact with Eliza.

He was on tenterhooks for the next week keeping a sharp look out for Bond each day, praying that his family and friends were safe and well and that Eliza had honoured her pledge to wait for him. Then one fine Autumn morning Mark Bond strolled back into the village whistling tunelessly, his bag of tools hanging from his shoulder and headed straight for the smithy. Nat washed the grime from his hands and dried them on the back of his leggings before rushing to meet him.

'Did you see them Master Bond? Did you see my father and my dear brother? Are they well?'

'Calm yourself Nat,' said Bond. 'I saw your young brother Daniel and gave him the letter as you asked.'

'Was my father not there then?'

'Just read the reply,' said Bond as he walked away. Nat thanked him profusely then tore open the letter which was written in Daniel's spidery writing. When he had finished reading he slumped down on a stool and Ebenezer came to stand behind him placing a fatherly hand on his shoulder.

'Good news or bad Nat?'

'Both really. My father got home safely as I already knew but he hasn't been seen since that day. No one knows what's become of him but everyone fears the worst. My brother Daniel has taken over the running of the smithy and has asked our maid Nancy to become his wife. She's a sweet girl and it seems that they found comfort in each other's company when father and I were away. I pray that I shall be able to attend their wedding.'

'You mentioned a girl to me, Eliza was it?'

'She is well, thank the Lord although she misses her father terribly. He was all she had in the world; her mother having died in childbirth.'

'She still has you.'

'She does. She wants to arrange to meet me but tells that it is still not possible for me to return to Lyme and I fear for her safety, travelling the roads alone.'

'Then I shall go to Lyme and collect her,' offered Ebenezer.

Eliza arrived in Mosterton on a chill late autumnal day when the beech leaves lay thick on the wet ground following two days of strong winds. Nat knew and trusted most of the villagers by this time but he still felt the need for caution, waiting impatiently in the shadows of the smithy while Eliza was helped down from Ebenezer's cart. Nat longed to hold her but as she entered the warm workshop he could tell that she had been crying.

'What is it my love? Surely this is time for rejoicing!'

'It is Nat, but I bring the saddest news with me.'

'My father?'

'Yes,' she sobbed.

Nat sat on an upturned barrel and steeled himself for whatever news Eliza brought. 'Tell me dearest.'

'They found your poor father's body yesterday morning.' Ebenezer had clearly heard the sorry tale from Eliza as they travelled from Lyme and came to put a comforting arm around Nat's broad shoulders.

Between tears Eliza continued. 'They were clearing the debris from the grill that protects the mill wheel. They normally do that in the spring but the miller had noticed that it had built up more than normal and arranged for it to be cleaned. That's where they found John's body.'

'How did he die? Did he fall in or was he attacked?'

'It's impossible to tell, he had been in the water for some time. He had terrible wounds to his head but how they were caused only God will know. I'm so sorry Nat.'

'To survive the trials and tribulations of the rebellion only to die in his hometown, it don't seem right.'

Ebenezer could sense that the two of them needed to be left alone with their grief and went to sort out the horse and cart.

Eliza stayed for two days during which time the couple swapped stories and memories. Daniel and Nancy's wedding had been set for Christmas Day and Eliza suggested that they should make it a double celebration by marrying on the same day. The service would be conducted at the Goodman's meeting house with carefully selected guests meaning that Nat would be safe from detection and arrest. Nat was delighted with the suggestion. He would loved to have had Daniel Foe as his best man but he had heard nothing of him since Bridgwater and he had no address for him in London. He could hardly ask his brother who was himself to be a groom that day, his father was dead as was his boyhood friend Thomas.

'Ebenezer, would you do me the honour of being my Best Man?'

'The honour would be all mine Nat. Since you first came here you have been like a second son to me. Of course I'll do it!'

Ebenezer was unable to attend Nat as he intended. Returning from delivering new animal traps to a nearby farm he lost control of his old cart which overturned on a steep hill throwing him from the driving bench before crushing his right arm and leg beneath a wheel. Nat blamed himself for the accident even though he was working in the smithy at the time.

'Not your fault Nat,' Ebenezer said from his sickbed.

'But I should've taken the cart, you're not as young as you once were.'

'My business, my responsibility! Of course this means that I'll be relying on you more than ever 'til I gets back on my feet, or until my son returns as I prays for daily.'

Nat doubted that the old man would ever fully recover from such injuries and when news arrived from a reliable source that his son Zak had been killed on the bloody fields of Sedgemoor and buried in an unmarked grave all the life seemed to drain out of the old man. Nat carried on working in the smithy as Ebenezer grew weaker by the day. The wedding soon came around and Nat went to see Ebenezer before leaving for Lyme.

'I'm sorry that I can't attend the wedding Nat.'

'Don't you worry about that; you just concentrate on getting better.'

'Well I wish you and Eliza all the best. Now, I have a wedding present for you.'

'You really don't need to....'

'I'm giving you the smithy.'

'I can't accept the smithy!' exclaimed Nat.

'I've no one else to leave it to with Zak dead. It would have shut down months ago if you hadn't come along so make an old man happy and be grateful! I've already had the papers drawn up and witnessed.'

Nat could think of nothing to say other than, 'thank you Ebenezer.'

The double wedding was a joyous affair. Nat's concerns about Alford and his cronies coming to arrest him proved unfounded with daily life in Lyme seemingly back to normal. Nat was still a fugitive from the law and whilst he saw others that he knew had been with the duke's army moving freely about the town, they might not have been tried and convicted as he had.

The question of where they were to live had been easily resolved. He had considered selling the business in Mosterton but could not do so in all conscience whilst Ebenezer lived, besides he had no intention of getting under the feet of young Daniel who was making such a success of running the blacksmiths in Coombe Street. There was nothing left in Lyme for Eliza and she readily agreed that they should return to Mosterton where she intended to set up a small school in the back room of the cottage that adjoined the smithy.

'I had hoped that father, God rest his soul, would have tried to secure my pardon when I was in Taunton prison,' Nat said to Daniel as he prepared to leave Lyme.

'Oh we did try Nat. Eliza and I went to see the pardonmonger. We had the money to do it but when we got there the bastard said the price had gone up and demanded three hundred pounds. We could niver raise that sum.'

'Did he by God! I think that I should pay him a visit before I leave!'

'Can't do that Nat, he was found washed up on west beach some months back, seems he tried to swindle one person too many.'

'So much blood has been spilt. Now is the time for forgiveness not retribution,' added Eliza.

'Spoken like a pastor's daughter,' smiled Nat.

'There was plenty of people looking to make money from the rebellion,' continued Daniel. 'When the constables were collecting the names of those who had joined the duke we heard that they were willing to omit names from the list for a suitable payment but we weren't sure if it were just a ruse to winkle out those who were withholding information.'

'Tis true Nat,' added Eliza, 'and when Kirke's men were here they were said to be offering to sell pardons. We thought to get one for you and your father but the authorities got to hear of it and the practice was soon stopped.'

'Couldn't have ordinary soldiers making money at the expense of the king,' said Daniel with a sad smile.

The ordinary families of Dorset and Somerset had a hard time of it that winter with insufficient men available to collect in all of the harvest and even though the women and children helped, as they did every year, valuable life-giving corn remaining rotting in the fields uncollected. Nat and Eliza returned to Mosterton where they spent most evenings sat at Ebenezer's bedside. It was clear that he didn't have long to live.

'So the rebellion is done with,' he croaked. 'Such a waste, such a waste.'

'What will happen now?' asked Eliza.

'Nothing,' replied Nat. 'Nothing to do now but wait for the king to die, he must be nearly sixty. Then his crown will pass to his eldest daughter Mary. Thank God that she's been brought up in the Protestant tradition despite the efforts of her father and stepmother.'

'Unless the king manages to sire a son before he passes,' Eliza added cautiously.

'Oh I can't see that happening, not at his age and not with his wife's history of failed pregnancies,' replied the old man.

'I can't help but feel sorry for her in a way, poor woman,' said Eliza tenderly.

'You are too kind-hearted my love. If James had renounced the throne in favour of Monmouth as he should have done both our fathers would still be alive, not to mention Thomas and all the others.'

Ebenezer died at the end of February just before word came through that King James had granted a general amnesty to any rebels still at large. It wasn't clear whether the pardon would extend to those who had been convicted but escaped, but Nat reasoned that as he had been tried in Taunton he should be safe going to his own local assizes in Dorchester for his pardon. His luck held as the authorities hadn't thought it necessary to share conviction records across county borders and he was given his official pardon. He was a free man at last. As he was leaving the courthouse he was delighted to see Thomas Cleeve.

'Thomas! I've heard nothing of you since before we marched from Bridgwater. I'm glad to see that you survived that terrible day. How have you been, did you evade capture?'

'It's a long tale Nat, I suggest we repair to an inn and talk over a celebratory pint.'

Nat quickly told the story of his escape and subsequent adventures. Cleeve was thrilled to hear of the wedding. 'I'm glad that Eliza waited for you.'

'And what of you Thomas?'

'I too was captured and sentenced to death but it was commuted to transportation same as you. I was put aboard a ship with William Pearce bound for Jamaica.'

'William Pearce is alive?'

'I'm afraid not Nat. He took ill with the plague that swept through the ship. Our dear Lord decided to save me for some reason. Poor William's body was tipped over the side of the boat like so much excess baggage, only for the sharks to tear his remains apart. I'd niver seen a shark afore and hope not to see another!'

'I will pray for his soul,' said Nat quietly.

'As do I.'

'But if you were sent to Jamaica how do you come to be here now?'

'A group of us escaped not long after landing, stole a boat and made it safely to the Americas. But that's a story for another day. I have a pardon to collect.'

The two friends shook hands and went their separate ways after exchanging addresses and promising to stay in touch.

When Nat reached Mosterton he was anxious to tell Eliza all about his meeting with Cleeve but Eliza put a delicate finger to his lips and said, 'my news first.....'

The West Country would take many years to recover from the rebellion and its bloody aftermath but maybe the small life growing inside Eliza would be the first tentative step along the way.

HISTORICAL NOTES

Although this book is a work of fiction, the ill-fated campaign of James, Duke of Monmouth played out very much as described although some events have been moved by a day or so to help the flow of the story and some minor incidents, which were not significant enough to appear in contemporary sources have come entirely from my own imagination.

Many of the characters in these pages such as Monmouth, James II and Nathaniel Wade were of course real people. Their actions during the rebellion are generally in line with the narrative of the book although their conversations, private thoughts and motivations are my own invention. Where I have created characters, such as Nat and his family and friends, I have used the assizes records from 1685 to identify common names and occupations from the Lyme Regis and Bridport area. Pastor Sprake is based on the real-life Pastor Sampson Larke, who being deprived of his 'living' under the 1662 Act of Uniformity had continued to preach in secret, until joining Monmouth as a captain of Horse. He was later arrested, tried and hung on the beach at Lyme Regis on 12th September 1685 alongside 'Sir' John Kidd of Longleat fame and Abraham Holmes, the commander of the Green Regiment. The hosiery salesman Daniel Foe who features heavily in the book is the birth name of Daniel Defoe who fought with the rebels throughout the campaign. After Sedgemoor he fled abroad to avoid arrest, changed his name and later fulfilled his wish to write, producing many classics including *Robinson Crusoe*. Monmouth's appeals to

Churchill and Albemarle are historical facts although using Defoe as the messenger is my own device.

I have generally used modern spellings for place names with the exception of Norton St Philip and Lyme Regis, which appear as Philipsnorton and Lyme respectively in the vast majority of contemporary accounts. There is evidence that Philipsnorton was also referred to simply as Norton or Norton Town both before and after the battle and there is no consensus over when the current name of Norton St Philip was adopted. The title 'Regis' was granted to Lyme by Edward I as far back as 1284 but seems to have been little used at the time of the rebellion. Chapter two is properly headed 'The United Provinces of the Netherlands', but Wade called it Holland in his confession and I have done the same throughout the novel.

Monmouth's Rebellion is often referred to as *The Pitchfork Rebellion*, even the tourist signs outside Norton St Philip use the name but this is something of a misnomer. Whilst there were undoubtably many agricultural labourers armed with farm implements in Monmouth's army, the majority of his men were artisans and tradesmen, weavers, clothiers and the like, and many were as well armed as the militia. There has been much debate about the effectiveness of the militia during the rebellion and research undertaken by Dr. Christopher Scott has demonstrated that they were nowhere near as bad as they are often portrayed in both contemporary and modern accounts, including this novel! That said they were more akin to county police forces than military units, good for breaking up conventicles and manning roadblocks but generally unsuited to standing in line of battle. Most of Monmouth's troops of course fell into the same category.

The Old George where Monmouth stayed in Lyme was destroyed by fire in 1844 and the landing beach has since been lost to erosion. John and Elizabeth Goodman's house in Silver Street was indeed used for Baptist meetings, proving more convenient than the old Loughwood meeting house at Dalwood. Baptist meetings started in Lyme Regis in about 1653 and John Goodman was still alive in 1689 when the Tolerance Act was passed, making non-conformist meetings legal.

Judge Jeffreys is a name still remembered in the West Country as a symbol of cruelty and oppression even though the Monmouth Rebellion itself may have been largely forgotten. Jeffreys was arrested in 1689 and held 'for his own safety' in the Tower of London where he died of kidney disease a short time later. Ironically he was initially buried in the Church of Saint Peter ad Vincula, the final resting place of the Duke of Monmouth. In 1692 Jeffreys' body was moved to St Mary Aldermanbury where it remained until the Second World War, when all traces of body and tomb were destroyed by a German bomb.

The brunt of the reprisals fell on the common soldier and whilst precise numbers are uncertain due to incomplete records, it is known that over three hundred rebels were put to death after the bloody assizes with a further nine hundred transported to the colonies. Over a thousand more were thought to have been killed at Sedgemoor, either in the battle or during the rout that followed. Likewise, the number who survived the battles and the court cases to return to normal life is uncertain. Whilst the constables drew up their 'presentments', only those rebels that were captured could be put on trial. In Frome for example, only twelve of the fifty-three named were eventually tried, with nine being transported and three either pardoned or bound over. It can only be assumed that the other forty-one had either been killed in the fighting or were in hiding, probably deep within the surrounding Selwood Forest. These lists were not overly accurate and the potential for names to be added to settle personal scores or deliberately omitted in exchange for financial or other inducements cannot be ignored.

Several notable rebel leaders were able to avoid prosecution by turning kings' evidence including William Williams (Monmouth's steward), Wade and Lord Grey. Wade went on to become Town Clerk of Bristol and Grey became a Privy Councillor and later Lord Privy Seal. Samuel White's old master, Edmund Prideaux was arrested and sent to the Tower of London in July 1685 before being 'given' to Judge Jeffrey. He bought his freedom for the astronomical sum of fifteen thousand pounds (well over two million pounds at the time of writing). Many of Monmouth's officers who escaped to the continent returned with William and Mary in 1688 including Ferguson, Lt Cols Foulkes and Matthews, Lieutenant Fox and surgeon William Oliver. Venner also reappeared to join William III's army in 1691. Others of course were not so fortunate. William Plumley, lord of the manor of Locking survived Sedgemoor and made it home only for his hiding place to be unwittingly exposed by his pet dog. He was hung at Wells. Samuel Robbins, the man who sold his catch to the rebels when they first landed in Lyme was caught, tried and hanged at Wareham. Whilst the vast majority of those tried and executed were men, women were not exempt from Jeffreys' harsh justice. Dame Alice Lisle of Moyles Court in Hampshire was found guilty of sheltering a rebel, one John Hicks. Men found guilty of treason in 1685 were generally hung, but the legal punishment for women was burning at the stake. Pleas for clemency were made to King James who allowed her to be beheaded instead! The dispensing of justice seems to have been a somewhat arbitrary affair. At Wells over five hundred and fifty men were sentenced to death or deportation before the court ran out of time, with one hundred and forty others still to be tried. They were all bound over to appear at the next assizes in the sum of one hundred pounds each, although one imagines that the majority were unable to raise such a sum and thus remained in prison. Many of them would have died there.

The general pardon of March 1686 should not be seen as a sign of leniency on the part of James II, rather an economic necessity. A large number of rebels had fled to Holland and under the leadership of Joseph Tiley, the man who had read Monmouth's proclamations at Lyme and Taunton, had set themselves up to manufacture English Cloth in Leeuwarden. Such was the threat to British trade that the pardon was conceived to persuade the renegades to return, which the majority did.

All the men transported to the colonies were freed by an order signed by King William III in January 1690 and whilst some paid their own passage back to England, most could not afford the fare and stayed on in the West Indies where many of their descendants live to this day. Needless to say the plantation owners were richly compensated by the government for the loss of their 'property.'

James' accession to the throne was initially well received and Monmouth was tricked into believing that the country was ready to rise in rebellion by stronger willed men, pursuing their own personal and political agendas.

James was unable to sire a male heir and most people seemed content to wait for him to die at which point Mary, his eldest daughter by his first marriage and a staunch Protestant would become queen. Those hopes were thwarted when James' wife Mary of Modena gave birth to a healthy son in 1688. This was highly surprising because in the fifteen years of her marriage to James she had suffered at least two miscarriages, three stillbirths and had five other children, none of whom reached their fifth birthday. Rumours persist to this day that the queen had suffered another stillbirth and that a baby, born to a servant had been smuggled into the bedchamber inside a warming pan. That child grew up to become James Stuart, also known as The Old Pretender. In the aftermath of the rebellion James' reputation had plummeted due to the brutality of the bloody assizes, his suspension of parliament, expansion of the standing army and the granting of high positions to Catholics in contravention of the law. The birth of a male Catholic heir was the final straw and parliament offered the crown jointly to James' daughter Mary and her Dutch husband William of Orange. William and Mary landed at Brixham in November 1688 with a force of fourteen thousand men and, crucially, the backing of the gentry. After a short campaign, the so-called Glorious Revolution, James fled to France and William and Mary were crowned in the following April.

SUGGESTED FURTHER READING

Bevan, Bryan, *James Duke of Monmouth* (London: Robert Hale, 1973).

Chandler, David, *Sedgemoor 1685: An Account and Anthology* (London: Anthony Mott, 1985).

Clarke, Nigel, J., *Monmouth's West Country Rebellion of 1685* (Lyme Regis: Nigel Clarke, 1985).

D'Oyley, Elizabeth, *James, Duke of Monmouth* (London: Geoffrey Bles, 1938).

Dunning, Robert, *The Monmouth Rebellion* (Wimborne: The Dovecote Press, 1984).

Earle, Peter, *Monmouth's Rebels: The road to Sedgemoor 1685* (London: Weldenfeld & Nicolson, 1977).

Mitchard, Ralph, *The Days of King Monmouth* (Radstock: Radstock Books, 2005).

Mortimer, Ian, *The Time Traveller's Guide to Restoration Britain* (London: Vintage, 2018).

Sawers, Geoff, *The Monmouth Rebellion and the Bloody Assizes* (Reading: Two Rivers Press, 1999).

Scott, Chris, *The Armies and Uniforms of the Monmouth Rebellion* (Nottingham: Partizan Press, 2018).

Tincey, John, *Armies of the Sedgemoor Campaign* (Leigh-on-Sea: Partizan Press, 1998).

Trench, Charles, Chenevix, *The Western Rising: An account of Monmouth's Rebellion* (London: Longmans, 1969).

Wigfield, W., MacDonald, *The Monmouth Rebels 1685* (Gloucester: Alan Sutton Publishing, 1985).

Wyndham, Violet, *The Protestant King: A life of Monmouth* (London: Weidenfeld & Nicolson, 1976).

ABOUT THE AUTHOR

Gary Kearley was born in Oxford in 1957. Taking early retirement in 2016 he enrolled on an undergraduate *History, Heritage and Archaeology* programme at Strode College in association with Plymouth University. The Monmouth Rebellion was the subject of his dissertation and he was awarded a first-class honours degree. This novel is the result of his frustration that there was so much more that he wanted to say than could be squeezed into a 10,000-word essay. He lives in Frome, Somerset, with his wife Susan, just eight miles from Norton St Philip, the site of the penultimate battle fought on English soil.

Printed in Great Britain
by Amazon

16589271R00260